Sputnik's CHILDREN

Sputnik's
CHILDREN

Terri Favro

Published by ECW Press
665 Gerrard Street East, Toronto,
Ontario, Canada M4M 1Y2
416-694-3348 / info@ecwpress.com

This is a work of fiction. Names, characters, places, and incidents either are the product of the author's imagination or are used fictitiously, and any resemblance to actual persons, living or dead, business establishments, events, or locales is entirely coincidental.

LIBRARY AND ARCHIVES CANADA
CATALOGUING IN PUBLICATION

Favro, Terri, author
Sputnik's children : a novel / Terri Favro.

Issued in print and electronic formats.
ISBN 978-1-77041-341-2 (paperback)
ISBN 978-1-77305-006-5 (pdf)
ISBN 978-1-77305-005-8 (epub)

I. Title.

PS8611.A93S68 2017   C813'.6   C2016-906360-7
C2016-906361-5

Editor: Jennifer Hale
Cover design: David A. Gee
Type: Rachel Ironstone
Author photo: Ayelet Tsabari

The publication of *Sputnik's Children* has been generously supported by the Canada Council for the Arts, which last year invested $153 million to bring the arts to Canadians throughout the country, and by the Government of Canada through the Canada Book Fund. *Nous remercions le Conseil des arts du Canada de son soutien. L'an dernier, le Conseil a investi 153 millions de dollars pour mettre de l'art dans la vie des Canadiennes et des Canadiens de tout le pays. Ce livre est financé en partie par le gouvernement du Canada.* We also acknowledge the support of the Ontario Arts Council (OAC), an agency of the Government of Ontario, which last year funded 1,737 individual artists and 1,095 organizations in 223 communities across Ontario for a total of $52.1 million, and the contribution of the Government of Ontario through the Ontario Book Publishing Tax Credit and the Ontario Media Development Corporation.

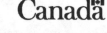

Canada Council for the Arts
Conseil des Arts du Canada

Canada

Ontario
Ontario Media Development Corporation

ONTARIO ARTS COUNCIL
CONSEIL DES ARTS DE L'ONTARIO
an Ontario government agency
un organisme du gouvernement de l'Ontario

FSC
www.fsc.org
MIX
Paper from responsible sources
FSC® C016245

Printed and bound in Canada by Friesens   5   4   3   2   1

For Ron, Jacob and Joey

and in memory of Rosa Scrocchi, "Nonna Gigi"

"Did I save a universe — or have I awakened
as from a dream? Can a future that was, be
forever erased? Is the cosmos itself but a
flickering ember of imagination — only to be
snuffed out at will? When all's said and done,
who is the dreamer and which is the dream?"

The Silver Surfer (Stan Lee)
"Worlds Without End"
1969

"Suppose you came across a woman lying on the street with an elephant sitting on her chest. You notice she is short of breath. Shortness of breath can be a symptom of heart problems. In her case the much more likely cause is the elephant on her chest."

Sally Ride, *first American woman in space*

A thin line of mutants, villains and superheroes stretches from the entrance to Conference Room B all the way to the slot machines. Yawning into their Red Bulls, gently farting and burping as they slump against windows and walls, most of them look like they partied all night on the American side, crossing the Rainbow Bridge at dawn for the free all-you-can-eat breakfast at ComicFanFest Expo.

No one makes eye contact with me. When a representative of Grey Wizard Comics hands me my contractually obligated low-fat chai latte before escorting me to the book-signing suite, a buzz ripples through the crowd. It's starting to dawn on them that I'm the one they're here to see.

It's a better turnout than I expected, mostly teens and twenty-somethings with a smattering of stuck-in-the-past baby boomers costumed as characters who sprang out of my head twenty-five years ago. True believers, every one of them desperate for my comics to lift them out of their disappointing lives and turn them into ass-kicking saviours of the planet.

Sputnik Chick fans of all colours, shapes, sizes and genders — better known as Spunkies — form a queue, many of them wearing the trademark black tights, thunderbolt cleavage and lopsided haircut of the Girl With No Past herself. Mingled in the crowd are versions of Marco, his handsome Latin features

1

unapologetically queer in MAC makeup, chatting up fans dressed as Johnny the K, the tall black love interest, with his wet-look anti-radiation suit and thermonuclearmagnetic boogie board. A lone Blond Barracuda towers over the others, all-white Andy Warhol hair and black synthetic armour covering his overdeveloped muscles like a spray tan.

A handful of Spunkies have shown up as Exceptionals, post-nuclear mutants who live short, tragic lives in the form of gooey baked goods with a single functioning lung under their pulsating carapaces. Mutations are as likely to be bacteria, spores or yeast as flesh and blood, I've tweeted, but I only started describing the Exceptionals as glutinous geopods after Bum Bum gave me the idea by baking a batch of hash-laced sourdough muffins and forgetting to fold in the baking soda.

A girl — I think — stands before me in a garment that's been coated with podge to give it a gelatinous sheen. She looks like a giant wet amoeba. In my head, I dub the fan Gooey. Her fingertips protrude just far enough to drop a *Sputnik Chick* comic book in front of me to sign.

"You're a freaking legend," says Gooey, her muffled voice coming out of what can only be described as a blowhole.

"Now, now, don't go calling me a 'legend,'" I say, using a thick black Sharpie to sign my name on the front cover of her copy of Volume 25, Issue 9. "Makes me feel old."

"Why have you never written an origin story?" her friend wants to know. Mouldy bread-crusts dangle from fishing line stitched to coveralls smeared with something that looks like it was cultured in a petri dish. I nickname her Crusty. "Sputnik Chick just shows up out of nowhere in New York City in 1979. Where did she *come* from? Even if her past was obliterated, she still *has* one, right?"

Gooey nods her head vigorously. Through her blowhole,

I can smell tobacco and salt-and-vinegar chips. "Isn't she ever going to get it on with Johnny the K? Why the hell does she always have to be so alone?"

Crusty chimes in again. "And you never even say what her real name is. She must *have* one — I mean, did her parents call her Sputnik Chick?"

"Of course not. Her real name is Debbie," I say, flatlining my voice to control the quiver that afflicts me whenever the topic of Sputnik Chick's provenance comes up.

Gooey shakes her head. "You named Sputnik Chick after yourself?"

I grip my Sharpie with both hands to disguise the fact that I've got the shakes. Gooey and Crusty are starting to get on my nerves. Why do so many young Spunkies become obsessed with knowing all these little details?

"Seems to me I can call Sputnik Chick whatever the hell I want," I say. This time, it's impossible to disguise the quiver in my voice.

The two of them look at one another through their eye slits.

"It's just sort of weird," says Gooey slowly.

I push the autographed comic across the table, hoping they don't notice how shaky my signature is. "As for how Sputnik Chick got to New York City from another time and place — let's just say I'm working on her origin story right now."

Gooey and Crusty squeal and hop up and down, their Exceptional costumes billowing around them like rising bread dough.

"Cool!" exclaims Gooey.

"Anything you're willing to, like, talk about?" asks Crusty.

"Not. Quite. Yet," I answer slowly, trying not to stare at the nasty blue spores on an ancient slab of rye dangling from

Crusty's costume. "You know how it is — you talk about what's in your head, you can't get it down on paper."

After oozing their thanks, Gooey and Crusty move on. Next in queue is a six-foot cross-dressing Spunky costumed as Sputnik Chick, gripping a vintage, not reprint, copy of Volume 5, Issue 2, "Love Hurts," an all-time fan favourite. I handle the comic with care. A collector's item these days, it could have cost this fan a month's pay. It's the issue where Sputnik Chick finally breaks up with Johnny the K after she tangled with the evil Barracuda. The Dark Lord of the Seas, as he calls himself, might be a sadistic psychopath, but Sputnik Chick finds herself irresistibly drawn to him.

The Spunky takes my hand and tells me she understands the complex interplay of emotions leading to Sputnik Chick's inexplicable betrayal of Johnny the K. "Who *wouldn't* want to fuck Barracuda?" she says breathily. "I *totally* get it." She asks me to autograph the centre spread with the infamous fight/ love scene, where Sputnik Chick brings Barracuda to his knees with a well-executed kick to the chin and a Pussy Galore–style over-the-shoulder judo toss. Barracuda responds by seizing her ankle and pulling her off her feet. Sex ensues. Six pulsating pages of it, the Barracuda's submarine-shaped penis quivering in front of Sputnik Chick's then-futuristic shaved pussy, a decade before every suburban mom got Brazilianed. I think it might have been the naked pudendum, rather than the penis, that got "Love Hurts" stopped at the border by the censor board in 1989, simultaneously transforming *The Girl With No Past* from an underground cult comic into a commercial hit and making me enough money to quit my day job art-directing *Psychics of Fortune* magazine out of an industrial park in Fort Lee, New Jersey.

Over the entwined bodies of Sputnik Chick and her arch-enemy sharing a post-coital cigarette, I sign the page with a flourish.

Next up is a South-Asian Johnny the K wearing what looks like a custom-tailored anti-radiation suit, silver and green. I can tell that he's got a beef with me from the way he brandishes his rolled-up comic.

"Your fight scenes suck," he says, shaking the comic at me like a club. "Your characters throw punches like ballerinas."

I keep my eyes on the comic I'm signing for him. Don't engage, I tell myself.

"Thanks for the tip," I say, pushing him the comic. "That's an awesome anti-radiation suit, by the way."

Unexpectedly, he smiles at me. "Thanks. My mom made it."

A few dozen more mutants and supervillains and I'm done. A respectable crowd, but not even close to the numbers I saw ten years ago. Cold War paranoia doesn't sell like it used to. Even a Sputnik Chick movie has been back-burnered until I come up with an origin story exciting enough to reignite the fire in the bellies of the Spunkies who have drifted off to the respectable world of graphic novels, most of which bore the hell out of me. What's wrong with superhero comics? They meet our collective need for gods and monsters, heroes and villains, demons and mystics, and other mythical forces that keep our universe glued together. Not that Sputnik Chick is a myth.

In the ladies' room, releasing a morning's worth of low-fat chai latte into the toilet bowl, I hear the sound of feet shuffling into the bathroom.

"She is so cool," says a familiar voice: Gooey.

"Older than I expected, though," says her friend Crusty. "She looks like a Normal."

I sit frozen on the toilet. What did Crusty expect — that I'd look like Sputnik Chick? All wet-look, skin-tight black vinyl, fast-twitch muscle fibre and fetish boots?

"I just hope that the origin story doesn't, like, suck. You get the feeling she's tired of the whole thing?" continues Crusty.

"Roger that," says Gooey.

I take a vial from my backpack and slip a white tab of lorazepam under my tongue. When the shaking doesn't stop, I pop another — these days I need more and more milligrams to help me escape under a numbing blanket of calm.

Once I'm sure that Gooey and Crusty have moved on, I exit the bathroom and head for the casino. The stickman at a craps table smiles at me, her blonde hair in a French twist. The badge on her vest reads *Emily Andolini*. When I ask if she's the daughter of Rocco Andolini, she says, "Granddaughter. You from around here?"

"Not far away. I grew up in Shipman's Corners but now I'm from a lot of places. I'm always on the move."

The stickman laughs. "Awesome. It must be exciting to spend your life travelling."

"It gets old after a while," I say.

I glance around the casino. A few bleary gamblers at the craps table look at me incuriously. One guy sways on his stool. Another nods and blinks, fighting to stay awake. The two of them have probably been here all night. Emily the stickman offers me the dice. I'm to be the shooter.

"Boxcars," I say, shaking the dice in my fist.

Two sixes: I win. I may be losing fans, but at least I still have my predictive powers. I roll the bones a few more times, then head to the bar with my winnings to fortify myself before going back to my hotel room to work on my origin story.

I sip my vodka martini (wet, dirty, Stoli, olives, rocks) and nibble peanuts from a tray of complimentary snacks on the bar. As usual, I'm starving. I catch myself calculating how long I'll have to spend on the hotel treadmill to burn off the calories. In order not to create an imbalance in the time-space continuum, I have to maintain the same volume and mass as Sputnik Chick on the day she hopped from one time continuum to another — a trim one-twenty-five, give or take a few ounces. Otherwise, I could wake up without a limb or vital organ as time compensates for the extra space I take up. I discovered this fact when I woke up missing the little toe on my right foot after a week of all-you-can-eat breakfast buffets at a New Jersey Ramada Inn in the 1980s. I make a mental note to weigh myself later.

The bored barman channel surfs on the TV over the bar. A rocket appears, nose to the sky, the white fog of exhaust indicating that it's about to launch. Across the bottom of the screen, a news crawl reads IT'S A BEAUTIFUL DAY AT THE CAPE. I slip the barman a twenty from my winnings to unmute the sound.

An American voice as smooth as Skippy peanut butter reports that all systems are go for the final flight of the space shuttle *Endeavour*. After this mission, *Endeavour* will be retired to some space museum on the west coast.

"You know what this means?" I ask the barman.

He shakes his head. I take a slug of my martini, preparing to enlighten him.

"They're scrapping the shuttle program. From now on, NASA astronauts will have to hitch rides with the Russians on Soyuz. Whose side won the Cold War, anyway?"

The barman stares at me.

"Ours?" he says uncertainly.

"Unbefuckinglievable," I murmur to myself.

I watch *Endeavour* rise magnificently off the launch pad, the roar of thrusters shivering the racks of gimlet glasses suspended over the bar. Is Bum Bum watching this? Is my sister, Linda, out on Crazy Lady Island? Once upon a time, she and I sprawled in front of the Westinghouse for every liftoff, the long countdown wiping out everything else in the programming day — even the mighty daytime soaps bowed down before *Apollo*. Along with the rest of the Free World, we watched crewcutted cowboys rocket to heaven, their spent engines circumcising themselves on the knife edge of Earth's atmosphere. Now I glimpse launches in passing between celebrity news and stock-market reports.

In a few minutes, *Endeavour* will enter the region of maximum dynamic pressure, 13,000 kilometres above the Earth. If she passes through safely, she'll escape the fate of her doomed sister, *Challenger*. Bum Bum and I witnessed that disaster together at a twenty-four-hour greasy spoon on Bleecker near Broadway, hungover from a night at the clubs. I can almost smell the fug of cigarette smoke, bacon grease and Poison, a perfume as subtle as a kick to the groin — my signature scent, in those days. On a TV over the grill, white smoke split into devil's horns mid-air as the shaky voice of Mission Control said: *Obviously a major malfunction*. Sealed inside the plummeting crew cabin, seven astronauts were alive and likely conscious when they crashed into the Atlantic at three hundred miles an hour. Watching the disaster unfold, Bum Bum laced his tangerine-tipped fingers through my magenta ones and breathed out a single horrified *Fuuuuck*.

After *Challenger* fell out of the sky, I sketched the very first *Sputnik Chick: Girl With No Past*. That's why she looks so much like I had on that chilly day in 1986: asymmetrical haircut, purple lipstick, untamed eyebrows, linebacker shoulder pads, a black river of tears running down her cheeks. A lonely she-wolf who prowled the streets of a city that would never see the horror of a mutant dawn, thanks to trading her past for an alternative reality that didn't include the planet being nuked to shit in 1979. And not just her past, but her identity. Hell, she didn't even have a real name anymore.

On the final panel of Volume 1, Issue 1 — "Disaster!" — her thought bubble reads: *Challenger was no accident! It rushed in to fill a void in the time-space continuum — and it's my freakin' fault!*

Fast forward twenty-five years and Sputnik Chick is still an angry, horny, nameless twenty-nine-year-old, roaming the streets of New York City by night to kill mutants and, sometimes, have sex with them. She hasn't aged. Unlike her creator.

* * *

With *Endeavour* safely in the mesosphere, I'm about to pay my tab and head upstairs when John Kendal's chocolate eyes and cut-glass cheekbones swim onto the TV screen over the bar. The news crawl identifies him as "DAVID JOHN KENDAL JR.: 'CANADA'S OBAMA.'" The sight of his face triggers an old familiar ache, like a migraine before a thunderstorm.

Kendal, my one and only love. He wouldn't recognize me if I passed him on the street. I've thought about stalking him but Bum Bum says that would be pointlessly self-destructive, even by my standards. Seeing Kendal in the media — and he's *always* in the media — feels like a having cigarette snuffed out on my heart. To prolong the pain, I ask the barman to stay on CNN for a few more minutes. Obligingly, he crosses his arms to watch with me.

"They say this Kendal dude could be running the country one day," the barman tells me, a note of pride in his voice. "Local boy."

I keep my eyes on the screen, wincing inwardly at the barman's use of the word "boy."

The host is in the middle of asking a question that implies Kendal has first-hand knowledge of the immigrant experience. Kendal scratches his nose, a sign of annoyance. Far from being a newcomer, Kendal is descended from a family that escaped slavery to live in Shipman's Corners half a century before my grandparents even got off the boat.

As Kendal's beautiful face fades to a commercial for erectile dysfunction medication, I sip my martini and ponder the key question of *Sputnik Chick: Girl With No Past*. The one that makes me sketch and discard and accidentally ruin her origin story, again and again and again. As Gooey said, how the hell did Sputnik Chick end up so *alone*?

"Okay if I change the channel, miss?"

The barman's question drags me back to reality. "Go right ahead."

As he switches to Ultimate Fighting, I ask if he has anything I can draw on. Lately, I come up with my best ideas on barstools. After rummaging under the bar, he hands me a thick stack of cocktail napkins. One side is printed with the purple and gold logo of Soaring Starling Estate Wines, its name a distant echo of Sparkling Sparrow, the sweet plonk of my youth. The other side of the napkin is as empty as a sketchbook.

I take out my Sharpie and start to storyboard, filling square after square with sketches. At first, I'm doing the usual stick ninjas, battling tiny Sputnik Chick figures — crash, bam, pow! I could draw her fight scenes in my sleep.

The tinkle of the slots and groans of the craps players fade away. Even that piped-in soft rock isn't reaching me anymore. I'm doodling generic planets and stars — Saturn with its iconic rings, a lumpy cheese of a moon — until I find myself sketching a man-made celestial object, a cross between a star and a hedgehog, about the size of a basketball, floating in a black void. A dead satellite. Sputnik, Vanguard, Telstar — they're all still out in deep space. On the next napkin, I sketch the triangular shape of a solar sail, the power source for the first generation of space stations Skylab I and II, way back in the early 1970s.

That's where my story really begins. Not in an unknown world, as most origin stories do. Not on Krypton, or in the hidden Amazonian realm of Wonder Woman, or an earthquake-prone cartoon lab full of radioactive spiders able to endow superpowers with a single bite.

It wasn't an unknown place that made Sputnik Chick who she was, true believer, but an unknown time. Before Sputnik Chick was Sputnik Chick. When she was still just Debbie.

The Untold Origin Story of
THE GIRL WITH NO PAST

Volume 1
ESCAPE FROM THE Z-LANDS!

featuring
THE TRESPASSER

one
A Tale of Two Timelines

Sputnik Chick was a child of Atomic Mean Time, different from the past you think you know. (FYI, you're living in Earth Standard Time, which you snobbishly regard as "Real Time.")

Up until the middle of the twentieth century, time was simply time: a single arrow flying through upheavals, bloodbaths, renaissances, revolutions and all the boring bits in between.

Then, in 1945, that self-described destroyer of worlds, Robert Oppenheimer, split the atom. Pow, crash, bam! Subatomic cracks and fissures appeared, shattering time's arrow into a quiver of alternate realities. Atomic Mean Time was calved during the Trinity nuclear test in New Mexico — the first parallel world, but far from the last. Every detonation since then has created a new timeline, peeling away from the one before it like a stock car burning rubber at the start line.

In this vast spectrum of histories, Atomic Mean Time and Earth Standard Time existed side by side — *weakly coupled worlds*, the pipe-smoking quantum physicists like to call them — separated by the thinnest imaginable membrane of dark matter.

(How do I know this? Patience, true believer. All will be revealed in due course.)

Despite quirky differences from Earth Standard Time — rogue viruses you've never caught, odd hem lengths, the sour-apple taste of Neutron Coke — if you were dropped into Atomic Mean Time, you would not feel totally out of place. You might even find it pleasantly nostalgic. All of the cultural touchstones of the pristine, pre-atomic age carried on undisturbed into Atomic Mean Time — Superman, Buster Keaton, Blondie & Dagwood, jazz, *Casablanca*, Mickey Mouse, the novels of Virginia Woolf, *The Wizard of Oz* and the Great American Songbook. Even after the split, many of the same cultural milestones popped up in both timelines: *The Silver Surfer* comics. Fins on cars. Disco. *Beetle Bailey*. Those smiley-face buttons that told you to *Have a nice day!* Sean Connery as James Bond, until he was imprisoned for attempting to overthrow the Scottish Parliament.

Everyone on Earth — correction, *almost* everyone — existed in both worlds. Some lived very different lives, while others unconsciously thrummed to the same sympathetic harmonies as their alt-time doppelgängers. In moments of distress or ecstasy, a few sensitive souls, like my friend Bum Bum, could sense the actions of their alt-time selves, naively chalking up the eerie sensation to déjà vu. A select few, however, were keenly aware of their existence in parallel worlds, David Bowie being an obvious example. But of course, Bowie was an Exceptional. (Not the kind of degraded Exceptional portrayed by Crusty and Gooey, known as Twisties, but a shape-shifting mutant gifted with the ability to explore a full spectrum of diverse possibilities. How else could he be both the Thin White Duke *and* Ziggy Stardust?)

Suffice it to say that in Atomic Mean Time, we had many of the same hit TV shows, movies and comic books you knew and loved and most of the postwar world events that you slept through in history class, with one important exception: in Atomic Mean Time, the second great war of the twentieth century never ended, even after the surrenders had been signed. GIs segued from battlefields to factories. Their mission: the ceaseless manufacturing of nuclear weapons. As if the Cold War of Earth Standard Time was a flash-frozen fish stick that took thirty-odd years to thaw.

Atomic Mean Time saw no peace movement in its 1960s, except for a furtive, floundering one that wormed its way deep underground and stayed there. The few young radicals who attempted to organize a Ban the Bomb protest march in Washington, D.C., in 1965, were arrested as anarchists and swiftly exiled. Nothing would be permitted to get in the way of our world's highly profitable march toward self-destruction.

Fortunately, in the event that the superpowers blew up Earth, we were prepared to colonize the moon. By 1969, unmanned rockets were sending geodesic domes and lunar life-support systems to the Sea of Tranquility, ready for the first batch of refugees from Earth.

I liked the idea of moving to the moon, even if it did mean my home planet had to be nuked first. I longed to be shaken out of the monotony of a childhood where the biggest challenge was deciding which flavour of Pop-Tart to warm up in the toaster oven. Whether on a flying saucer or an intergalactic surfboard, I was determined to escape from Shipman's Corners. Population: 126,000. Economic activities: cross-border smuggling, the cultivation of local grapes into a sweet, bubbly wine known as plonk and the manufacturing of atomic bombs. Occasionally, rusty drums of radioactive leftovers heaved their way up out of vacant lots and construction sites where they had been dumped without much thought — until someone noticed things were a little off in those parts of town. Like kids being born with three ears and an extra set of teeth.

It was my father's job to make sure nobody decided to build

a school or playground or subdivision on the hot spots before the drums could be quietly whisked away to the deep, distant waters of Hudson's Bay. Problem was, you couldn't stop kids from playing hide-and-seek on contaminated land. Dad had barbed wire fences put up, but as he pointed out, there was only so much you could do.

Every year at back-to-school time, he took Linda and me on his sweep of a decontaminated landfill known as the Z-Lands, just before the annual Labour Day company picnic. Dad's boss encouraged him to bring us along. Good public relations for the company's community cleanup program, he said. People were comforted knowing that Dad wasn't afraid to take his own kids to a former nuclear dumpsite.

The cleanup of the Z-Lands was one of Dad's big successes. A year earlier, he had been promoted to Senior Decontamination Supervisor, a really important job. The local newspaper took a picture of him with Linda and me, smiling over bouquets of mutated wildflowers. The story's headline read: "Z-Lands soon safe enough for underprivileged children to play in, ShipCo Decon Chief promises." Dad told us later that he'd promised no such thing, but the company framed the story and stuck it in the foyer outside Dad's office. His boss said that maybe now everyone would relax and stop writing letters to the big shots in Queen's Park, who really couldn't do anything about the dumpsites, anyway. We were answerable to a higher authority: the ShipCo Corporation, managing body of the North American federal jurisdiction officially known as the Industrial Nation of Canusa, a fertile peninsula that hung like a ragged tooth between two Great Lakes with the world's most potent waterfall leaking out of its tip. Canusa was a murky grey zone where territorial and commercial interests merged. Canadian laws were observed, as long as ShipCo didn't mind.

When a new warfront opened up in Korea, quickly followed by Vietnam, Thailand, Cambodia, New Guinea and New Zealand — a series of linked conflicts known as the Domino Wars — American draft dodgers were as welcome in Canusa as they were in Canada. ShipCo considered them useful. If they wouldn't fight, they could still build bombs.

*   *   *

In the summer of 1969 (A.M.T.), I was a couple of months shy of my thirteenth birthday. Linda was sixteen. We arrived in the Z-Lands at sun-up, the daisies already turning their monstrous heads toward the sticky, honey-coloured sky. Dad's plaid clip-on tie dangled like a noose as he ran his Geiger counter over the hard-packed dirt. Linda hovered beside him in her skort and Keds, her volleyball-hardened arms crossed. Waiting for the verdict.

While Dad and Linda watched for the jump of the red needle, I wandered through Queen Anne's lace and black-eyed Susans the size of trees, to an iron ship's bollard squatting pointlessly beside the abandoned canal. I didn't need the bollard to warn me of the thirty-foot drop ahead. The stench of industrial chemicals floated up from the bottom of the canal, where wrecked cars sat half-submerged in a frothy sulfate soup the colour of day-old dishwater.

Despite a fence topped with barbed wire and a DANGER: NO TRESPASSING sign, a couple of new wrecks had been pushed over the edge since our last visit: a banana yellow school bus and a pickup with the truck bed ripped off.

Something else I hadn't seen down there before: a trespasser, crouched on top of the bus in the glare of the rising sun. At first I thought I was having a vision, like those kids at

Lourdes. The figure slowly came into focus like a television picture tube warming up. An old man, with white hair to his shoulders. He was stooped over, his hands on his knees. He straightened himself up slowly and, it seemed to me, painfully. He couldn't catch his breath. As if he had been running a long, long way.

In the distance, Dad's Geiger counter started to click, no doubt picking up background radiation.

The Trespasser looked up at me, chest heaving. He was tall and as skinny as a twig, his face pink and peeling with something like a bad sunburn. He was dressed in a silver shirt and tight trousers that belled at the hems like a flamenco dancer's.

"Debbie?" As if he knew me.

"I'm not supposed to talk to strangers," I told him.

"I'm not a stranger. We know one another very well."

Weirdly, I believed him, even though I'd never met anyone who wasn't from Shipman's Corners. Weirder still, I noticed that parts of his body were starting to shimmer and run like watercolours. Pink globs of flesh fell from the end of one arm into the frothy scum at the bottom of the canal.

"You're melting," I told him.

He looked down at himself, his mouth falling open at the sight of his liquefaction. Lifting his remaining hand, he pointed at me.

"You're it, Debbie. Never forget that."

I didn't know what to say so I stuck out my tongue. He responded by holding up two dripping fingers in the shape of a V — a lopsided one, because his middle finger ended at the knuckle.

Sunlight bounced off the roof of the banana bus, blinding me for a moment. When I could see again, the Trespasser had vanished. Mingled with the stench of the chemical soup, I caught a whiff of something pleasantly spicy. As if, in liquefying, the Trespasser had turned into cinnamon.

Before I could decide whether he was what Dad called "a Fig Newton of my imagination," the Geiger counter went nuts, chattering away like a set of wind-up teeth. Dad's voice came loud and sharp and even a little scared sounding, telling us it was time to get a move on.

"But Daddy, we just got . . ." I heard Linda say.

Dad was already striding toward the gate, windmilling his arms to hurry us up. Linda moved toward me through the field of flowers. No time to tell her about the Trespasser. The two of us sprinted after Dad, Linda dragging me by the hand.

At the gate, a tendril of barbed wire, draped over the fence like a forgotten scarf, snagged my ponytail. The barbs clawed at my scalp as I struggled to free myself. My yelp of pain brought Dad rushing back.

"Hold still, Debbie, you'll only make it worse," he said, tossing my sister the car keys. "Linda, start the engine."

I could feel him breathing hard behind me, his fingers fumbling with my hair. He grunted a quiet swear as the barbs pricked his fingers. "You're hooked like a fish. I'm going to have to cut you free."

He gripped my scalp with one hand while he sawed at my hair with the jackknife he always carried in his trouser pocket. My ponytail, still in its elastic band, bobbed from the barbed wire like a foxtail. Warm air licked the back of my neck as Dad and I ran for the car.

In the driver's seat of the Country Squire, Linda was singing along with the radio. Dad shoved her over into the passenger seat as I jumped in back.

"But you said I could drive home!" she protested.

"Not this time." He threw the car into a fast reverse.

As we tore along the dirt track, kicking up a fog of probably radioactive dust, Linda said, "Mom's going to kill you, Dad. You made Debbie look like a boy!"

"It'll grow back." The station wagon hit a rut, bouncing me to the car floor. "There's no margin of safety for the levels I was getting. They've been going down steady as she goes, year after year. Now it's higher than it's been since '55."

"That doesn't make sense," said Linda.

"No, it sure as hell doesn't — pardon my French," said Dad.

I got up from the floor and draped my arms over the front seat, my chin on top of Linda's elbow, while Dad tore out of the Z-Lands. I'd never seen him drive so fast. In the rear-view, I imitated the V sign that the Trespasser had made.

"Don't do that," said Linda, slapping my hand. "It's rude."

I stared at her through my fingers. "What's it mean?"

"It's how anarchists say hello to one another."

I frowned. "Anarchists? Like spiders?"

"You're thinking of arachnids," said Linda. "No. Like Yammers."

A drop of blood rolled off the tip of my nose and lazily hit the beige upholstery. Linda pulled out a crumpled tissue and spit in it. She dabbed at the bloodstain, then pressed it to my forehead. The tissue came away all bloody.

We were well away from the gate, bouncing along the dirt road at high speed, when we hit a pothole. A big one. The car listed to one side, engine revving and back wheel spinning.

Dad made a swear again — twice in one day! — then got out, slamming the door so hard it made my teeth rattle. He stomped around to the back of the car and groaned. When he stuck his head in the window, his face looked as saggy and white as a dead trout.

"Blew the tire right down to the rim. You'll have to get home on your own. Debbie, tell Mom to draw you a decon bath right away. Linda, you scrub down over at Nonno's. Use those emergency kits in the basement I bought at Canadian Tire during the last missile crisis."

Linda groaned. "I hate that stinky old shower in Nonno's cellar. And I just set my hair, Daddy."

"Do as I say, for once, Linda. And make sure your clothes go in the incineration bags."

"But Daddy, how are we supposed to get home? It's five miles, at least. Debbie'll never keep up."

"Carry her piggyback if you have to. Now go!"

We got out of the car and started running, first on dirt, then on gravel. By the time we reached the second gate with its PRIVATE PROPERTY: NO TRESPASSING BY ORDER OF SHIPCO CORPORATION sign, we had slowed to a walk; Linda had a stitch in her side and I had a stone in my sneaker. Standing on one foot to shake it out, I looked back down the roadway. I could see the car but could barely make out Dad. I'd never seen him look so small before.

We started walking toward a hydro pole at the end of the gravel road, marking the beginning of Zurich Street — civilization, sort of. The pole reminded me of the lamppost at the entrance to Narnia. Maybe Mister Tumnus from *The Lion, the Witch and the Wardrobe* would be leaning against it, enjoying a cigarette and waiting for the floating craps game to start.

I rubbed the barbed-wire cuts on my head with my grubby fingers, trying to send germs into my skin to do battle. Linda slapped my hand away.

"Stop that. You'll get infected."

"I'm invulnerable, like Superman," I told her.

"Says who?"

"Says the doctor, after he gave me the Universal Vaccine. 'This little lady's generation might just live forever, if the Ruskies don't drop the Bomb on us.' That's what he told Mom."

Linda snorted. "He was making a joke, Debbie. The Universal Vaccine is just a polio shot with some immunizations for other stuff. That does not mean you're invulnerable."

"You're just jealous 'cause you're too old for the U-shot."

"Change the subject," she said. "Better yet, don't talk at all. We should be saving our breath to find help for Dad."

For the first time, it dawned on me that Linda was worried about him. That we actually should be finding someone to rescue him. That he was in trouble and so were we. It hadn't occurred to me to be afraid for him, or Linda, or even myself. Nothing bad had ever happened to us before.

We had reached the cracked pavement of Zurich Street — or Z Street, as we liked to call it. End of the alphabet, end of the line. Wedged between the railway tracks and the canal, it was a neighbourhood of cottage-sized houses crammed haphazardly between grease-pit garages, butchers with skinned raccoon carcasses hanging in the windows and sad-looking groceterias with half-empty shelves. No trees, gardens or front yards. The houses squatted hard against the sidewalk, so that anyone passing by could look inside if the curtains weren't shut.

Dad told me once that the tiny homes had been thrown up on swampy ground as temporary shelters for troops of ShipCo workers during the '50s. After they moved on to bigger houses in the suburbs, poorer families moved in, insulating the walls with cardboard and sawdust and, if they had the cash, covering the wood frame exteriors with cheap aluminum siding.

Nothing was built to code on Z Street. If the city ever bothered to send in a fire inspector, most of the neighbourhood's houses would be condemned. Luckily for the Z Streeters, the city couldn't be bothered. There were even rumours that some of ShipCo's waste was buried deep under the basements of certain houses.

Linda and I held our noses to block the stench of urine as we walked past leftovers from the night before: broken beer bottles, cigarette butts, a discarded bra, a few wrinkled plastic sleeves that looked like transparent leeches. It was just past sunrise.

In the distance, the dignified whitewashed facade of an old church marked the part of Z Street where Shipman's Corners' oldest families lived: the Sandersons, Kendals, Smiths and Bells, all of them descended from escaped slaves who'd come from the U.S. on the Underground Railroad, guided by Harriet Tubman herself. Shipman's Corners prided itself on kindly taking in these refugees from the slave-owning Americans, then immediately pushing them to the edges of town.

Here, at last, we saw signs of intelligent life: a boy, sitting on the front stoop of a green-doored cottage, built in the narrow space between the big white church and a tiny wreck of a house, the front steps caved in as if karate-chopped by a giant.

The boy was reading a book, his head in one hand. As we clomped along the pavement, he looked up. That's when I recognized him: Bea Kendal's son, John. He came along with her when she visited our house once a week to sell Mom cleaning products and chicken soup base. Mrs. Kendal was a tall thin black woman who wore a plain grey dress with a little badge pinned to one shoulder and a matching hat that looked like a man's fedora. She always arrived with a hefty sample case lugged around by fourteen-year-old John. I had the feeling that John Kendal noticed everything, although when Mrs. Kendal was taking Mom's order over a cup of tea, he sat quietly at the kitchen table reading books that looked suspiciously like the Sunday colour comics.

"You girls are up early," he said.

Linda paused in front of the stoop to push her damp hair off her forehead. Now that the sun had fully risen, the day was getting steamy.

"Could your mom give us a lift, Kendal? Dad got a flat on a back road."

Kendal shook his head. "She left at five this morning to pick up her orders. Want me to ride out on my bike to help your dad? I've had lots of practice changing flats on my mom's car."

I could see Linda struggling with how much to say. She didn't want to admit to what we had been doing or where. One of Dad's rules was that nothing he did on the job was discussed with anyone but family.

"That's very sweet, but Dad can handle the tire himself — he just wants Debbie and me to get home safely. Would you mind if I use your phone to call our mom?"

John Kendal shrugged. "Suit yourself."

As he showed Linda into the house, I picked up the book he'd been reading: *Tintin and the Shooting Star*. I flipped pages full of flat, bright primary colours. Red, yellow, green. On one page a boy in short pants and his white dog were dancing around, singing, "Hooray! Hooray! The end of the world has been postponed!"

For someone born and brought up in Shipman's Corners, John Kendal was unusual in a number of ways. First of all, he was black. And unlike most boys, he liked to read. Third, most people called him by his last name — Kendal, not John. And maybe most important of all, his father was dead. I only knew that last fact because Dad was summoned to the plant the night that Mr. Kendal fell asleep on the job and was pulled into a press by his shirtsleeve. He bled to death before they were able to get him out of the machine.

Dad talked about it afterwards at the dinner table, shaking his head and saying what a shame it was that safety mechanisms would slow down production. He pointed out that guys like Mr. Kendal, who were willing to work double shifts, often got sleepy and sloppy, and the next thing you knew, boom. They were minus an arm or hand. He said Mr. Kendal was a smart guy — maybe too smart for his own good, rabble-rousing among the other men, talking about banding together to start a union. He should have known better. Ever since then, Mrs. Kendal came around to our house once a week to sell bleaches and detergent and a powder made from chickens that had had all the water sucked out of their bodies.

While Linda called Mom, Kendal and I sat together on the stoop.

"Where were you with your dad at the crack of dawn, anyway?" he asked.

I was a notoriously bad keeper of secrets. "The Z-Lands," I said, flipping through the *Tintin* book. "Ever been there?"

"Sure. I go there all the time," said Kendal. "It's one of the few places around here with enough space for football. Last week Bum Bum went for a pass and almost fell in the canal."

"You trespass?"

He shrugged. "It's not hard. The ground around there is like sand. We tunnelled under the fence."

"I saw a trespasser in the canal, standing on a bus. Just before Dad's Geiger counter went off," I told him. "He must've gone in through your hole."

Kendal frowned. "The Geiger counter went off? You mean, it's still radioactive out there? I thought it'd been cleaned up."

Violating Dad's rule again, I nodded. "Yeah, Dad was surprised, too. That's why we left in a hurry. He was driving so fast, he blew a tire."

"I'll bet the Trespasser had something to do with it," suggested Kendal. "In comic books, it's always visitors from some other dimension that cause gamma rays and solar flares and mutations and stuff. Maybe he ripped a hole in the time-space continuum and let in a blast of radioactive dust. Did he say anything?"

"He told me I'm 'it.' Like in a game of tag."

Kendal thought this over. "Maybe you've been picked for something. Like he has a mission for you. I wonder if you'll meet again."

I shook my head. "Negatory. He's dead. Melted away before my very eyes like the Wicked Witch of the West."

"So you think," said Kendal.

I put my head in my hands. "I shouldn't have told you about the Geiger counter. I'm not supposed to talk about Dad's job."

Kendal leaned close to me. "It's okay. You're a kid. You shouldn't be trusted with grown-up secrets."

Linda was back, shaking her head. "No answer. Maybe Mom's already gone to Plutonium Park to help set up for the company picnic."

I looked at Kendal. "You going?"

"Natch. The ShipCo brass invite me and Mom every year. We get free hot dogs and everything."

"That's nice, Kendal," said Linda. "I mean, after what happened to your dad."

Kendal's smile faded. "I wish they'd shove their hot dogs up their fat asses and give me back my dad."

Linda's face turned pink. Kendal picked up his book, pretending not to notice her embarrassment.

"Look, how about I ride the two of you home on my bike?"

Linda and I nodded, relieved we'd both worn skorts that morning. Kendal told us to wait out front while he grabbed some water to carry with us. Before he went inside, he squinted at me. "Want something for those cuts on your head, Debbie? Iodine, maybe?"

I shook my head. "I just got the U-shot. I'm invulnerable."

"Delusional, more like it," said Linda.

"Watch out for Red Kryptonite," said Kendal. "It won't kill you, but it'll sure confuse you."

"I think she's already been exposed," said Linda, circling her finger next to her ear.

Kendal grabbed a rusty CCM bike from the alley between his house and the church. With Linda in the saddle, me on the handlebars and Kendal standing up on the pedals, we started to wobble toward home just as a boy came out onto the smashed-up stoop next door to Kendal's. I recognized him as one of the no-hopers who were bussed to my school out of a sense of Catholic duty: Pasquale Pesce, the bookie's son, better known as Bum Bum because when he was a little kid, his mom dragged him from house to house, trying to use his skinny little body and pathetic starving-baby face to help her bum cash and food off the neighbours. Still deceptively baby-faced at fourteen, he had the sketchy reputation of a kid who spent a lot of time on the street and the lingering body odour of someone living in a house without a bathtub, Mr. Pesce having gambled away everything except the four walls around them. Bum Bum had come barefoot onto the stoop that morning with what I guessed was his breakfast: a slice of bread, a can of Neutron Coke and the end of a cigarette.

Bum Bum scratched under one armpit, squinting at us as we wobbled past. "Want I should take one of them girls on my bike?"

"We're okay, BB. I just got us balanced," said Kendal.

"Maybe I should ride shotgun?"

"Roger that," agreed Kendal.

I swivelled my head to see Bum Bum toss his cigarette butt into the gutter and run to grab a child-sized one-speed from behind an overflowing garbage can beside what could generously be called his house. He quickly caught up with us, his knees pumping crazily on the too-small bike. He hadn't bothered with a shirt and was wearing a pair of hot pink capris with a side zipper. Probably his mom's.

The rest of Z Street was waking up, too. Curtains twitched aside. Blank faces stared at us from windows and stoops. An empty bottle flew over our heads, smashing on the road ahead of us.

"Watch out, someone's trying to hit you, Kendal," said Linda.

"Not Kendal they're aiming for," pointed out Bum Bum, who stood up on his pedals and shouted a string of swear words in our wake. A few more bottles exploded around us like grenades. I put one arm over my head, almost losing my balance. Kendal pulled my hand firmly back down onto the handlebar.

"Sons of bitches don't know when to give up on a grudge," he muttered.

"Probably just the fuckin' special forces retirees carpet-bombing to scare the chicks," said Bum Bum, glancing backwards. "Or one of them Twistie assholes. Don't know friend from foe anymore."

"Watch your language, gentlemen, please," suggested Linda primly. "Can you go any faster, Kendal?"

With a grunt, Kendal pedalled harder, picking up enough speed to edge past Bum Bum.

"Eat my dust!" shouted Bum Bum, overtaking Kendal. The ride began to feel like a race.

At the end of Zurich Street, we sped around a corner onto Tesla Road, passing a graffiti-spattered billboard with the shadow of an ad for a cereal that hadn't existed since the '50s, the words SHIPCO KILLS a ghostly scrawl under a thin coat of whitewash.

We rode past an orchard where a woman and a man stood on ladders, filling quart baskets with plums. The couple looked as weathered and twisted as the branches around them. Grey faces, grey hair, grey clothing. They could have been man and wife, brother and sister, even mother and son. The woman said something to the man in a language I didn't understand. The man nodded and spat on the ground. Their way of letting us know Linda and I didn't belong there, tear-assing down their road with a couple of Z Streeters.

Shipman's Corners was an old U.E.L. town — U.E.L. standing for United Empire Loyalists, New England settlers who stayed loyal to Mad King George and made their way to British North America after the American Revolution. We were in what was known as the ethnic quarter: *giusta-comes*, wops, Polacks, Lithuanians, Yugoslavians, Ukrainians, Displaced Persons (sneeringly known as DPs), what have you. Whoever washed up in Shipman's Corners after the war, looking for work, ended up living in this end of town.

People tended to live with others who came from the same place. Italians, like my grandparents, settled on Fermi Road. The Ukrainians, Poles and other Eastern Europeans ended up on Tesla. Z Street took whoever didn't fit in anywhere else.

Only one thing united the neighbourhoods: we were all outsiders, isolated on the far side of the shipping canal from downtown Shipman's Corners. ShipCo believed in a certain order to its company towns. We were living examples of how their experiment was panning out.

Just beyond the plum orchard, we rode toward a dirty beige stucco bungalow with a scrap of a front yard covered by the roots of a giant peach tree. In the shadow of the branches, at a card table spread with bottles of various colours and sizes, a man with black slicked-back hair and a wide strong face sat in a white undershirt sipping clear liquid from a water glass — Mr. Holub, referred to as Mr. Capitalismo for his get-rich-quick schemes, the latest being a portable bomb shelter that looked suspiciously like an old-fashioned deep-sea diving suit with a Geiger counter stuck to it. Dad knew him from ShipCo. Nice enough guy, but a bit of a kook, he said.

As we braked to a stop, Mr. Holub ambled into the street, carrying his glass. I could smell something funny on his breath. Like onions mixed with rubbing alcohol.

"What you girls doin' way out here this early in the morning?" His voice sounded mushy.

Linda slid off the back of Kendal's bike and told our story in a rush — at least the part about Dad's flat tire out in the Z-Lands. She skipped around what we were doing exactly, no mention of the Geiger counter or why our sudden need to leave.

I stood next to Kendal, who was holding his bike uncertainly while Bum Bum popped wheelies on the road, killing time while we sorted things out. With Mr. Holub taking charge, I was worried that Kendal would feel forgotten, until I realized that he was staring at the Holubs' front door. A girl holding a broom was looking out at us through the screen, her long thick rope of black hair covered by a kerchief. I knew her from school: Sandy Holub, Mr. Capitalismo's only child. Even though she was a year older than me, she was sent to our class because of her accent. Her real name was Oleksandra, but she changed it to Sandy because someone joked that her name sounded like a cat horking up a hairball.

Sandy and I got to know each other crouching side by side in the hallway during a surprise air-raid drill. As I faced the wall with my arms around my head, I sniffed a sudden bathroom smell and realized that she had peed herself.

"Don't worry, it's not for real," I whispered, trying to reassure her.

When she turned to look at me, the fear in her pale blue eyes nicked me like a knife. As suddenly as it had started, the siren stopped, leaving a ghostly echo. "All clear," our teacher called out, followed by rustling and laughter as kids readjusted to being among the living again.

"See?" I said.

We were officially friends after that. Not the kind who go to each other's houses, but ones who stick together at recess and pick each other as partners for double dutch.

*　*　*

As Kendal stared up at Sandy, and Sandy stared back at him, I realized it wasn't Kendal who had been forgotten. It was me.

Mr. Holub broke the spell by offering Kendal his hand to shake. "Thanks for the help, boy, I take the girls from here." I could see Kendal wince at that word. *Boy.*

"See you around at the picnic, I guess," he said to me, then glanced up at Sandy one more time before signalling to Bum Bum that it was time to pedal back to Z Street. I watched the two of them bike past the grey orchard, a dog in pursuit, while Mr. Holub backed his car out of his parking spot behind the house. He said he would drop us off at home, then drive back to the Z-Lands to help Dad. I could tell Linda was relieved to have everything in grown-up hands again, but I was disappointed not to be riding home on Kendal's handlebars.

Sandy Holub stayed half-hidden behind the screen door. As the car pulled away from the curb, she lifted her hand to me in a wave, then turned away, vanishing into the darkness of the house with her broom.

two
Glow-in-the-Dark
Pat Boone Lie Detector Test

I stood naked in the bathroom, my clothes already sealed for incineration and the tub filling with hot water and a capful of Doc Von Braun's Ultraviolet Bubble Bath for Kids™ while Mom tugged at the jagged ends of my hair where the ponytail had been ripped away.

"I sure hope Claudia can do something with this mess," she said, sighing.

"I like it this way."

"When the other kids start making fun of the way you look, you won't like it at all, *cara*."

I climbed into the deep purple bath, held my breath and sank below the surface, letting the bubbles mop up all those nasty alpha and beta particles with "a zesty candy fruit scent kids love," according to the label. I soaked for a full fifteen minutes, until my skin stopped tingling, just like it said on the bottle, then dried off with a ShipKids® Exfoliation Towel. Mom dusted me down with AntiRad Atomic Girl Talcum Powder, just to be on the safe side.

After I'd dressed in my ShipCo Kids Club uniform (yellow skirt, spangled blue shirt, red ankle socks), Mom sent me next door to have my hair styled by Mrs. Donato. She and Mom had come to Canada at the same time, two little girls crossing the ocean to New York City, where Mom's mom had lived for a time, aboard the good ship *L'America*. Their friendship, if you can call it that, was formed as the two of them hung over the railing to vomit into the waves. It was later cemented by the trauma of being herded with their mothers into the Great Hall at Ellis Island. Under a giant American flag, they were told that they couldn't stay because America had enough Italians, thank you very much, but there was a cold country to the north, run by the Queen, who might just agree to take them in. After all that drama, Mom and Claudia Donato had little choice but to become lifelong friends.

Whatever Mom did, Mrs. Donato did it, too. Babywise, Mom got a head start with Linda, but when she got pregnant again with me, Mrs. Donato caught up by having twins. When Mom named me after her favourite movie star, Debbie Reynolds, Mrs. Donato one-upped her by christening her daughters Judy-Garland and Jayne-Mansfield.

Over endless lines of laundry (diapers, housedresses, aprons, girdles, their husbands' oily workpants and dusty overalls), Mrs. Donato told Mom that her girls were going to be majorettes. Mom responded that Linda would be a classically trained musician and I, a tap dancer, like my namesake. Sure enough, Linda ended up studying violin, and Judy-Garland and Jayne-Mansfield became the top two baton twirlers in Shipman's Corners (junior drum majorette division), winning the Queen of the Majorettes competition two years in a row. I, on the other hand, turned out to be as musically gifted as a fence post, flunking out of tap at age six.

*　*　*

When I got to the Donato house, Judy-Garland and Jayne-Mansfield were sprawled in front of the RCA colour console watching *Doc Von Braun's Amazing World of Tomorrow*, one of the children's shows pumped over the border like oil. Standing at her ironing board in a black slip and high heels, Mrs. Donato squinted at the screen through eyes reddened by contact lenses and cigarette smoke. In his stiff Prussian accent, a famous scientist was explaining how we'd get to the moon after Earth blew up: "Und now Goofy and Pluto vill enter zee Mercury rocket . . . but look, zey are veightless!"

"Boring old Kraut, he's a pushier snake oil salesman than the Fuller Brush Man," Mrs. Donato muttered around her du Maurier. "Okay, honey, let's see if we can turn this mess into a pixie cut. We'll give you the French girl artist look. Very sophisticated. How'd it get hacked off, anyway?"

I told her about being in the Z-Lands, on the job with Dad, and getting caught in the fence. I felt her fingers quickly lift from my scalp.

"*Cara*, you decontaminated at home, right?"

"Sure," I said. "Fifteen minutes, just like the bottle says."

Mrs. Donato grunted her approval, pushing my chin to my chest to trim the stump of my amputated ponytail. Once that was done, she backcombed the crown of my head, teasing my hair into a poofy dome not unlike her own. She emptied half a can of Final Net over it to turn it into a helmet.

"It ain't great, but it'll do for the picnic," said Mrs. Donato, taking a drag on her cigarette. "Tell your daddy to leave the haircuts to me next time."

I glanced up at her through a cloud of smoke. We both knew that Dad's job involved doing a lot worse things than cutting off a ponytail.

Afterwards, Mrs. Donato shooed me home while she backcombed the twins' hair into towering beehives.

Crossing the yard to home, past the vines where my

grandfather, Nonno Zinio, was setting up a scarecrow to keep birds off the ripening grapes, I noticed right away that something was wrong: Mr. Holub was there, talking to Mom and Linda in the driveway. His car was parked out front. I didn't see Dad anywhere. Worry radiated off Mom like heat waves.

"No Carlo, no car," I heard Mr. Holub say as I walked up. "We get to the roadway, it blocked by gate. Shut and locked up tight."

"I'd better call the plant," said Mom.

Despite it being a Saturday morning and a long weekend, Dad's boss answered her call right away. He said: Don't panic. They would find Dad. No need to get all het up. In the meantime, it was very important that Linda, Mom and I go to the company picnic. Act like nothing unusual was going on. Because nothing unusual *was* going on. Dad was lost or maybe confused, that was all. To be expected. Stress of the job. Sometimes a guy just needs time alone to think things through. They'd call the company medic, just in case Dad needed a little something to help him relax when he finally showed up. Maybe he should take up golf. Or book a few comfort meetings with one of the ShipCo Snugglegirls, if Mrs. Biondi had no objections. Most wives of managers at the senior command-level were more than happy to delegate their husbands' tension relief to skilled professionals, leaving the wives with more energy for their bridge clubs and volunteer work.

Just before hanging up, he asked Mom a question: was there any reason for her husband to desert his family *on purpose*? Mom was left speechless by that one.

After she hung up the phone, Mom stood staring out the kitchen window for a long time, then washed a sinkload of dishes she'd already washed. Linda and I sat at the table, doing one another's nails, keeping an eye on Mom while we waited for her to snap out of it. Eventually, she made coffee for the three of us, sat down at the table and told Linda and me, word for word, what Dad's boss had said.

"But Mom, we can't just go off to the picnic without Dad," said Linda, wiping tears. "People will ask questions."

Mom held up her hands wearily. "I know, *cara*, but if Dad's commanding manager says go, we go. You drive us in the Morris. I'm too upset to be behind the wheel. And not a word to Nonna Peppy or Nonno Zin."

At Plutonium Park, the picnic was in full swing. Mom went off to the tent where the women were dropping off their cakes and casseroles and Jell-O salads. Linda and I bought a string of tickets for carousel rides at a card table set up in front of the cenotaph, a huge black granite bomb with Cadillac fins hung in mid-plummet on almost-invisible steel wires. Behind it stood an older stone statue of a soldier fainting into the arms of an angel. TO OUR GLORIOUS DEAD read the faded inscription beneath the soldier's boots, followed by a list of Shipman's Corners men who had laid down their lives in two world wars. The angel and the soldier were overshadowed by the big stone bomb. Its plaque read:

> TO OUR RADIANT DEAD
> In honour of the gallant machine operators
> of ShipCo (Canusa division, Shipman's
> Corners unit)
> who answered the call of industry
> to build nuclear arms for peace.
> May the Almighty Manager grant them
> eternal rest.

*   *   *

At the carousel, a bulky-shouldered boy was tearing tickets and boosting kids up onto painted horses frozen in mid-gallop. He was wearing a ShipCo Schooners baseball cap over his crewcut and a shirt buttoned to his neck, despite the heat. When Linda and I tried to hand him our tickets, he shook his head.

"No charge for you, gorgeous. Little sister rides free, too."

His eyes kept walking up and down Linda, catching on her like fish hooks, his smile a lure. With blond, blond hair and dark, dark eyes, he was what my sister and her friends called "a hunk," except for one thing: his left ear ended in a chunk of ugly scar tissue. Amputations weren't unusual in an industrial town like ours, but most people lost limbs, not parts of their head. I couldn't stop staring at the pink worm of flesh coiled below his ear canal.

Linda made a little noise in her throat like a hum. "Giving us special treatment hardly seems fair to the other customers."

The blond boy shrugged. "Life isn't fair, is it? You're not like the rest of them. You two are exceptional. No charge."

I could feel Linda hesitating, until the boy boosted me into the saddle of a horse with flared nostrils. "There you go, little sister. Best seat on the merry-go-round."

Linda let the boy put his arms around her waist and sit her sidesaddle on the black charger beside me.

"He's crazy about you," I whispered to Linda.

"He's just a carnie," she said.

"Did you see his earlobe?"

"Maybe a dog bit it off," said Linda.

Impaled on poles, the carousel horses slowly began to drop and rise to the sound of a tinny pipe organ:

Daisy, Daisy, give me your answer true.
I'm half crazy all for the love of you.

I rode a white horse with a gold bridle; Linda rode a black

horse with a silver bridle, plunging ahead and falling back in an endless race. Like the good and bad sisters in a fairy tale. The younger sister is always the good and beautiful one, the one who gets to marry the prince and live in the castle, leaving the jealous older sister with the wicked stepmother. I liked to remind Linda of this story. I said it could be about us, because we were sort of like princesses, since our father was the Decontamination Supervisor of Shipman's Corners.

When a siren sounded the end of the ride, the blond boy came back to lift me down.

"Another ride?"

Linda shrugged. "Maybe later."

"My name's Billy. I'm off in an hour. Buy you a soda?"

Linda shrugged again. "We'll see."

"See you later, gorgeous," said Billy, and he flashed us a two-fingered V. The anarchist's salute.

"Your boyfriend's a Yammer," I whispered to Linda.

"Shut up," she responded.

We walked away from the carousel, past a pink gazebo reserved for a troop of Snugglegirls costumed as cheerleaders, French maids and Shetland ponies. Employed by ShipCo, the girls were always on duty during family picnics, in case any managing executives required tension relief. Mom had repeatedly warned us not to stare at the Snugglegirls, but I glanced in anyway. They were lounging around a table, smoking and playing cards. In a tent not far away, Mom and the other mothers were setting out platters of hot dogs in buns like rows of babies swaddled in puffy white blankets. By some unspoken agreement, the ShipCo Snugglegirls ignored the ShipCo wives, and vice versa, even though they were always stationed side by side at the company picnics.

Linda stopped outside the mothers' tent and glanced

casually back at the carousel, where the carnie was still lifting kids onto horses.

"Why don't you run along and find your friends?" she suggested.

"So you and Romeo McAnarchy can be alone?" I teased her.

"You are such a brat," she said, letting go of my hand.

I watched my sister disappear into the crowd. It felt good to be on my own. Now I not only looked like a boy, I felt free to act like one, too. I pressed on the top of my head, trying to flatten the poofy helmet of hair as I walked to the playground where the Donato twins were playing Fallout Shelter under the high slide. Judy-Garland waved an aluminum pistol in the air.

"Let's pretend to shoot people who try to get into our shelter," she suggested.

"Why not just let them in?" I asked.

Judy-Garland snorted. "You dummy, you'd run out of food. You have to look out for number one."

These words sounded straight out of the mouth of the twins' father, Al Donato. I'd heard him say pretty much the same thing at a barbecue a week earlier. Dad had argued with him: "You want to stay alive when everyone else dies? What kind of a world would that be?"

"You kiddin'? Someone has to re-people the world," Mr. Donato said, grinning and grabbing Mrs. Donato's bottom while she was handing him a beer. She smacked his hand, but she was smiling.

Dad had looked away, embarrassed.

I was arguing with the twins over whose turn it was to have the gun in our game of Shoot the Neighbours when a policeman and a nurse walked up. I couldn't tell you what they looked like. All I saw were two uniforms.

"Miss Debbie Biondi?" asked the nurse, with a bright smile.

She was wearing a white dress, white stockings, white Oxford shoes and a stiff white hat with little meringue wings.

I raised my hand. "That's me."

"Come with us, miss, please," said a tall skinny body in a blue uniform that smelled sharply of solvents, as if it had just been dry-cleaned. The policeman wore a silver badge reading OFFICER SMITH, #ABC123. He took my right hand. The nurse took my left.

I had a wild idea that I should twist out of the grown-ups' hands and start running, just as Dad had said to do when we left the Z-Lands. I shook that idea out of my head. I was a good girl with a boy's haircut and a missing father, heading off with two unknown authority figures. What could possibly happen?

"Did they find my dad?" I asked as we walked away from the playground.

"Still looking," said the policeman in a monotone.

"What's your favourite ice cream?" asked the nurse, a smile in her voice.

I looked up at her. "Butterscotch."

"Well, honey, you're in luck. Where we're going, there's a whole tub full of Scutterbotch with your name on it."

"Underlying conditions," muttered the policeman in his dead-sounding voice.

"Oh, yes, of course," said the nurse. "Honey, you look like a healthy young girl. You don't have any, oh, let's call them 'troubles'?"

My slick-soled shoes slipped on the grass as the two of them hurried me along. Off in the distance, I could hear the tinny sound of "Daisy, Daisy" again. I suddenly wished I were sitting on a horse in full gallop. "What kind of troubles?"

"Oh, I don't know. Maybe you need to take needles for sugar? Or you get sick when you have your friend?"

The policeman grunted impatiently. "Get to the point. Is she bleeding? Affects blood pressure, sweat glands, all that."

"There's no need to be crude," the nurse told him, the smile gone from her voice.

I shook my head. "I'm invulnerable."

The nurse gave a funny little laugh, as if she was worried about something. The policeman grunted. "What's that supposed to mean?"

"I got the U-shot. Nothing can hurt me now," I told them.

"Isn't that nice," said the nurse vaguely. The policeman tightened his grip on my hand.

We reached the brick building that housed the park's snack bar, shut tight for the season. As the policeman unlocked the door, I stared at the giant cardboard strawberry ice cream cone stuck to the outside. We went into a room with lumpy white walls, then through it into another room with a grey metal door and no windows. Rakes and shovels hung from hooks along the wall. Once the door to the second room was closed, I couldn't hear anything from outside anymore, not even the music from the carousel. The lights in the room were twilight-dim.

The nurse sat me down in a straight-backed wooden armchair, the kind you're sent to when you're in the principal's office, next to a table with a box on it, wires hanging down. The box was bright pink with blue polka dots and glowed palely in the gloom. The top of the box was full of knobs and dials, like a shortwave radio or the cockpit of a jet. I'd seen pictures of both in magazines with names like *MEN* and *Action!* that Dad left stacked in the bathroom.

"What's that thing?" I wasn't scared yet, but it was starting to dawn on me that maybe I should be.

"Have you ever heard of a polygraph, honey?" asked the nurse.

I shook my head.

"A lie detector," said the policeman. "This here's a special one, just for kids. So we know which of you are naughty and which are nice."

He laughed at his own joke. The nurse glared at him.

"It's a machine that shows us if you're telling the truth," explained the nurse.

"How's it do that?" I eyed the machine with growing fear. The electrical wires reminded me of the barbed-wire fence.

"It picks up signals from your body. It shows us if you're getting all tensed up and scared, the way people do when they're lying," said the nurse. "See that graph there? It jumps when you get scared. That's when it knows you're lying."

"Don't tell her how to beat it," growled the policeman.

"I'm not; I'm simply explaining to the child," said the nurse. I could tell by her tone of voice that she didn't like him.

They slid my arm into a sleeve, like the one at the doctor's office, right up to my armpit. The nurse pumped a little rubber ball attached to it and the sleeve went tight. She stuck wires on the tips of two of my fingers, then pulled a strap tight around my chest. The nurse said that Pat Boone had a lie detector just like this one in his own home to keep his kids honest. Every time they did something bad and he thought they were lying, he hooked them right up to the machine to sort things out.

"Who's Pat Boone?" I asked.

"He's a world-famous operatic tenor! Kids these days," the nurse said, sighing, as if only a juvenile delinquent wouldn't know who Pat Boone was. For a crazy moment, I thought he might be the Trespasser's secret identity. Stall for time, I told myself. That's what captive girls always did in comic books while waiting for a superhero to show up.

I said, "The strap around my chest is too tight. It hurts."

The nurse laughed her phony laugh again. "Don't worry. You'll get used to it."

The policeman sat down at the table across from me, loosened his tie and switched on a metal gooseneck lamp, illuminating a gauge that looked a lot like the one on Dad's Geiger counter. I tried not to stare at him. I'd seen police only on TV shows. We didn't have any cops in Shipman's Corners. ShipCo looked after all the troublemakers.

"Let's get a base line," said the policeman. "What's your name, girl?"

"Debbie," I said.

"State your full name," he said, louder than before. I figured this meant the test was starting for real now.

"Debbie Reynolds Biondi."

The nurse clapped her hands. She was watching the needle on the gauge move. "Very good! You're telling the truth! See how easy it is?"

"Who was with you in the Z-Lands?" asked the policeman.

"Linda. Dad," I said. Then I remembered the Trespasser. Did he even count?

The nurse shook a finger at me. "Somebody's fibbing."

"I'll repeat the question," said the policeman.

I didn't wait for him. "There was a guy in the canal. A trespasser," I said. "But I don't know who he was."

Silence. "That doesn't sound like a true memory," said the nurse.

"The polygraph says it is," said the policeman. "What happened next?"

"The Geiger counter made a lot of clicks and Dad said to leave. I got stuck on the barbed wire so he cut off my hair. Then we drove away real fast and got a flat. He said for me and Linda to run home while he fixed it."

"What did your dad tell you about the clicks?"

"That he was surprised 'cause it hadn't been that high since '55."

"What did he mean by 'high'?"

I thought about this. "I don't know. The, like, counts. The radioactive stuff, I guess."

"Did you or your sister, or the two of you together, hurt your dad?"

"No!"

"No? No *what*?"

I sat for a moment in confusion, hearing his question as *know what?*

The nurse said, "Where are your manners, honey? When you speak to Officer Smith, you call him 'sir.'"

The policeman leaned in close. His face smelled like wood chips and salt. Officer Smith used the same aftershave as Dad.

He asked, "Are you or your sister a member of the Youth Anarchy Movement, also known as 'Yammers'?"

"No, *sir*."

The nurse clucked her tongue. "Watch your tone, missy."

"Did you tell anyone else about this?" asked the policeman.

I wasn't prepared for this question. I remembered Kendal and me on the stoop. How he said kids shouldn't be expected to keep grown-up secrets.

"No, sir," I repeated.

"You're lying, Debbie," said the policeman.

"No, I'm not."

"You just lied again, Debbie. Twice in under thirty seconds. Not nice. If you want to go home — ever — you'd better start telling the truth. Otherwise, I could find you a nice little hole in the ground where you can sit in the dark until you're an old woman. I know the perfect one. We'll feed you, keep you alive and give you plenty of company. You like slugs and worms?"

I started to cry. I had a particular fear of worms and slugs.

"Now, now," said the nurse, handing me a box of tissues.

"I told a boy," I sobbed.

"What's his name? Where does he live?"

Feeling sick to my stomach, I told them about John Kendal. Meanwhile, the policeman pulled a shiny black-and-white picture out of a manila envelope. He put it on the table in front of me.

"Now, let's get back to the intruder you saw in the Z-Lands. Is this the individual?"

I stared at the photograph of a good-looking young man in an industrial army uniform. A Corporal Pipefitter, judging by the crossed wrench insignia on his collar. His fair hair was buzzed into a crewcut. He wasn't the Trespasser, but he sure looked familiar.

"No," I said.

"You know him?"

I stared at the picture. The young man's head angled to one side, but I could still make out a lumpy knot of tissue dangling from one ear. He was Linda's carnie, Billy. If I told the truth, would they punish her along with him?

"Maybe," I said slowly.

"From where?"

"I'm not sure."

"What a fibber," clucked the nurse.

Before the policeman had a chance to ask another question, Dad's boss walked into the room. He was wearing a plaid tie, just like the one Dad had on that morning, with the little red tie bar that told everyone he was a senior officer. He smiled at me unconvincingly.

"How's it going?" he asked the policeman.

The policeman told Dad's boss about Kendal. "We should get that kid in here, pronto."

"Let's not be hasty," said Dad's boss, smoothing his tie. "There are better ways. Got a widowed mother to support. We can use that." He gave me his el-fake-o smile again. "Your dad's fine, dear. He'll be home to tuck you into bed tonight. You believe me, right, kiddo?"

"Yes, sir," I said in a small voice.

The polygraph needle jumped. I might as well have called Dad's boss a liar to his face, but he patted me on the shoulder.

"That's all right, you're a good girl. Off you go now. Have fun at the picnic."

"Not finished, sir," said the policeman. "The girl saw an intruder. Might be a known anarchist. We should get her to dig into that memory. Dotty here could give her a light injection of truth serum to move things along. And we're still trying to track down the kid's sister for interrogation."

"Check the manual. She's a minor. There are limits," said Dad's boss. "As for the sister, forget it. We've got what we need."

The policeman shrugged. "Your funeral," he said to Dad's boss, then turned to me. "Don't tell anyone about this. We don't want to have to bring you back in or put you in that place I told you about before."

The nurse nodded. "That certainly would be a shame."

And just like that, the nurse unhooked me from the machine and bustled me out the door. My knees felt all jangly, like a broken walking doll. In the outer room, the nurse told me to wait. She opened a cupboard door. Inside, there was a little freezer. I watched her lean into it and dig around. Over her shoulder, she said, "You're an exceptional girl, Debbie; you cried only once. So I'm giving you *two* scoops."

I could hear the carousel. *Daisy, Daisy, give me your answer true . . .*

"Scutterbotch. Double scoop. As promised," said the nurse, handing me an ice cream cone. "All better now?" She opened the door and pushed me outside, slamming it behind me.

I felt queasy, my jaw stiff, as if I might throw up. I walked jerkily to a garbage bin and tossed in the ice cream cone. Then I started running. I'm not sure where I thought I was going. I wanted to tell someone what had happened to me, but who? If I told Linda, they'd put her in a hole for the rest of her life. Mom, too. Maybe all three of us. The only person I knew I could tell — *had* to tell — was Kendal. To warn him. Because they knew that he knew what happened in the Z-Lands. If they stuck him in a hole in the ground, it would be all my fault.

It was starting to get dark. A crowd was gathered at the bandstand just ahead of me, but somehow they seemed far, far away. Shivering despite the warm evening, I made myself walk toward them, past the carousel and the hot dog tent and the playground where I'd been playing Shoot the Neighbours with the twins just a little while ago.

I could see Mom now with Claudia Donato, both of them standing with their arms crossed, looking up at the bandstand. A troop of managing officers in ShipCo. dress uniforms — sports jackets, hard hats, plaid ties — were standing at attention behind the managing commander, Dad's boss, who was at the microphone holding a big white envelope.

I tried calling — *Mom, Mom* — but nothing came out of my mouth. When she finally saw me, she threw her arms around me in a hug. I wanted to hug her back but my arms hurt when I tried to lift them.

"Oh, Debbie, *cara*, they found Daddy. He took the car to the plant to clean it and the door locked behind him in the decontamination bay. Someone heard him yelling, finally, and got him out. He's on his way here right now. Isn't that great?"

I nodded my head. Up on the bandstand, John Kendal was walking up to Dad's boss, shaking his hand and taking the big white envelope. The other managing officers on the bandstand saluted Kendal. A photographer took their picture.

"What are they doing with John Kendal?" I whispered.

"ShipCo is giving him a scholarship," said Mom.

Oh no. Not a scholarship.

"Where to?" I asked weakly.

"The Industrial School for Boys out in Bramborough."

This was even worse news. Bramborough was farm country, a good hour from Shipman's Corners. No one who went to Bramborough on scholarship was ever seen alive again. "Being awarded a scholarship" was another way to say that a kid was a goner.

"At least his poor mother will be looked after. I'm sure it's for the best," Mom said, sighing. "Such a nice boy, though."

Mrs. Kendal was sitting on the stage, her hands clamped over her mouth. Kendal's head was down as he took the paper from Dad's boss. I couldn't see the expression on his face.

"If it's for the best, why's Mrs. Kendal crying?" I asked.

Mrs. Donato lit a du Maurier off the butt of the old one. "Tears of joy," she mumbled.

Mom was scanning the crowd: "Now, where on earth did your sister get to?"

That's when I saw a picture in my mind. Linda with Billy inside a kaleidoscope — no, that couldn't be right; they were inside the drum-shaped space in the middle of the carousel with its tiny reflecting mirrors and organ pipes. He was kissing Linda so hard that her back pressed against the lever that started the carousel going.

Daisy, Daisy — the tune played in the distance, even though no one was riding the painted horses at that time of the evening. The world began to move up and down around me: the crowd, the bandstand, the puzzled face of Mrs. Donato, Mom mouthing words I didn't understand, round and round, up and down. I felt myself falling backwards. Grass prickled the back of my neck.

A man's voice said, "Give her air."

I opened my eyes. A face was looming over me. Heavy, black horn-rimmed glasses, a ginger-coloured crewcut and the worst sunburn I'd ever seen. The man wore a plaid tie and a stethoscope around his neck. His fingers pressed the inside of my wrist.

"She's coming around now," he said. He grinned down at me and made a V shape in front of my eyes. His middle finger ended at the knuckle, just like the Trespasser.

"How many fingers?" he asked.

"One and a half."

"Good. No concussion."

"Who are you?" I whispered.

He smiled. "Dr. Duffy, but my friends call me Duff. Company medic. Biogeneticist, really, but I have basic medical training. Subbing for the regular ShipCo doc. Dr. Welby twisted his ankle on manoeuvres, so they sent me up to fill in tonight. Didn't think I'd earn my keep, 'til you fainted. Low blood sugar, I'll bet. When was the last time you ate, young lady?"

Mom was stooped over looking at me. "Oh, *cara*, with everything going on, you didn't have lunch."

"Case closed," he said. "Mom, this girl needs an ice cream cone. Two scoops. Doctor's orders. What's your favourite flavour?"

"Banana. Like that bus I saw you standing on," I whispered.

He frowned as he slipped a penlight out of his pocket. A point of light shone in one of my eyes, then the other.

"I thought you said no concussion, doctor?" said Mom, hovering beside us.

"Give me a moment, ma'am," he murmured in a brisk who's-the-doctor-here voice.

Taking the hint, Mom moved off toward the trees, arms crossed, to talk with Claudia. Once he was sure she was out of earshot, Dr. Duffy bent low to my face.

"What bus?"

"In the Z-Lands," I whispered back. "Except you were old and you had long hair, like a girl. You were melting."

"Melting?"

"Your hands fell off."

I heard him take a sharp breath. "Did I say anything?"

I nodded. "You said, 'you're it, Debbie.'"

Dr. Duffy swayed back on his heels. "'It.' As in 'I.T.' I said *you* were the Ion Tagger? Not your sister?"

I shook my head. "I dunno, you just said 'it.'" I hesitated. "A policeman was asking me questions about you. He's probably looking for you."

Dr. Duffy nodded and pulled a cotton swab out of his shirt pocket. "Open wide." The tip of the swab scraped hard at the inside of my cheek as he explained in a low, rapid voice: "Listen closely. I'm from the future, helping my partner identify the Ion Tagger. Sounds as if an older version of me thinks that's you. Which means you're going to have to collapse time and migrate the entire population of Earth into a parallel world that's weakly coupled to ours. Otherwise, humanity is doomed. Understand?"

Tears leaked from my eyes again. After the day I'd had, the last thing I wanted to hear was that I was responsible for saving the world.

"How can you expect me to do all that? I'm only twelve years old!"

"Age is irrelevant. It's your DNA that matters," he muttered, half to himself, half to me, as he slid the swab into a plastic tube and slipped it into his shirt pocket. "If your epithelia check out, I'll be back."

"Wait! What'm I supposed to do? And what's gonna happen to Kendal?"

He looked down at me. "Save John Kendal or the world is doomed."

I watched him walk off into the darkness beyond the park lights.

I love hotels. The pocket rockets of whisky in the minibars. The thumb-sized bottles of rosemary mint shampoo. The treadmills of sales reps sweating off their complimentary breakfast buffet. The well-groomed gentlemen lounging in the lobby reading *The Economist* with their shoes off. Most of all, the anonymity.

In the lobby bar, a red-vested barman with ruthlessly land-scaped face-scruff smiles at me. Pretty sure he remembers me from the night before: I'm sitting on the same stool at the dark oak bar, sketching tiny black figures executing judo chops and flying dropkicks on the cocktail napkins. The solvents in my Sharpie mix with the civet cat musk in my perfume, making me feel slightly buzzed.

"Madame?" he asks, eyebrows raised — his polite way of suggesting: *Martini?*

"*Bien sûr.* The usual," I answer. Testing him.

The barman's dimples are so deep, you could spelunk down them. "Double vodka martini. Stoli. Very wet, very dirty. Olives. Rocks. Right?"

"You have an astonishing memory."

"You were here last night, drawing. I would not forget you so fast."

He slips away and comes back with a highball glass full of ice, a little tray of bar snacks and a stainless steel art deco cocktail shaker that sweats seductively.

He shakes my drink, and I give an involuntary groan at the comforting sound of ice on steel. No one makes martinis like they do in the Queen Elizabeth Hotel Lobby Bar of Earth Standard Time.

"Hard day at the office?" he asks, pouring.

"Chained to my desk," I answer.

He leaves the shaker on the bar in front of me as I story-board on a napkin. Sputnik Chick is wearing her trademark thunderbolt bustier and coming on to a guy sipping a cocktail:

> SPUTNIK CHICK (folded up like a jackknife
> on a high bar stool): What are you, anyway —
> a Normal, a Twistie or what?
> GUY (lifting his highball glass): Stockbroker.
> That's about as normal as you get, eh?
> SPUTNIK CHICK (pulls out a shotgun, blasts
> him off the stool): That's for screwing my
> pension fund, you fucker.

Money is much on my mind. Although I should be econ-omizing, I booked a suite on the twenty-eighth floor — the Gold Status level. I tell myself it's a business expense.

At the front desk, no one reacts when I hand over the stag-gering room rate in stacks of hundreds, although a kid going down to the pool, towel around his neck, stares at me.

"You a gangster, lady?" he asks in a voice that's all New Jersey and no tact.

I shake my head solemnly. "Comic book artist."

"Wow," says the kid. "You don't look like Stan Lee."

"I'm a shape-shifter," I tell him over my shoulder as I follow the valet carrying my suitcase and portfolio to the private elevator.

Up on twenty-eight, the rooms have a rarefied air. If you're sleeping in one of them, you must be hot shit. This is the hotel where the world came to interview John and Yoko in bed. Where Eurotrash royals hung out in the swinging '60s. Buzz Aldrin slept here after he walked on the moon.

Being able to make outrageous demands is one of the perks — that and the split of Veuve Clicquot chilling beside the king-size bed. I just wish I had someone to share it with. My mind slides back to the handsome barman, but it's best not to take that relationship beyond flirtation. I don't want to ruin his generous pour.

When I booked the suite, I requested an elliptical machine, a digital scale for my twice-daily weigh-ins and a drafting table. The table is already waiting for me, facing a window overlooking Mary, Queen of the World Cathedral on Rue Mansfield. Perched on a stool, I can look down on the top of St. Anthony of Padua's tonsured and guano-spackled stone head.

I know how you feel, buddy. You think you're on top of the world, but something unpleasant always threatens to rain down on you from above. If it isn't the Bomb, it's bird shit.

I circle my hand on the paper, warming up to draw.

Spunkies debate Sputnik Chick's origins on fan sites. Most of them think she's an orphan, a feral child from the future. A survivor, living on irradiated (and therefore unspoiled) garbage in atomic waste dumpsites and biohazard compost piles.

Nothing could be further from the truth.

So far, my pencil has revealed that she came from a close, loving family of Normals who preserved their pristine DNA during the conflagration by hiding out in a hardened shelter inside a hollowed-out mountain, cultivating hydroponic tomatoes, grapes, zucchini, peppers and other fresh produce.

Her dad worked for NORAD. Not as a physicist or anything glamorous like that — he was an electrician who kept the Cold War hideout warm and comfortable for the scientists and generals. Even super-secret installations in the Colorado Rockies need someone who knows how to keep the lights on and the life-support systems working. It's amazing how those handy guys with the skills to turn piles of junk into working water processors are the ones who quickly climb the food chain once civilization goes to hell.

It's the start of an origin story, but it's all I've got so far. Many questions remain unanswered. If Sputnik Chick's dad was so shit-hot at protecting himself and his family after the apocalypse, why did she separate herself from them? Was she kidnapped? Was the rest of her family murdered? Why didn't they time hop with her? Or did she do something her family couldn't forgive, even by the standards of a post-apocalyptic world?

That's the problem with creating stories out of imagination and bullshit. You never know what's supposed to happen next. Much easier to simply write the truth, but also more painful.

I wrote *Sputnik Chick* from memory in the early years, working out what happened to me starting in July 1979, Atomic Mean Time. Therapy by comic book, you might say.

When *Sputnik Chick* became a hit, I pumped out an issue a month. Pretty soon, I ran out of first-hand experiences and had to start making things up. I couldn't bring myself to describe events that were part of my deeper past, pre-A.O.A.M.T. (Apocalypse of Atomic Mean Time), before all matter collapsed into a subatomic, deep space wormhole, hurling me into Earth Standard Time like a space station in free fall.

I rest my head in my arms and let my Sharpie roll off the drafting table. Even with a belly full of vodka and lorazepam, I don't have the stomach to go exploring in that deep dark pit of truth anymore.

* * *

On my third idea-dry, martini-wet day in Montreal, I visit the cathedral next door to the hotel. I've been a lapsed Catholic for thirty years, but I'm at the point where I'll try anything. I drop a dollar into the donation box, light a candle and ask Mary, Queen of the World to provide inspiration for my foul-mouthed, hard-drinking, sex-obsessed, ass-kicking heroine. After all, Mary, Queen of the World and Sputnik Chick both found themselves in the position of having to change the course of history without anyone checking with them first.

Back at my desk, it's no surprise when nothing comes to me. So, I decide to call Crazy Lady Island. I'm not sure if it's loneliness or an attempt to prime the pump of my rusty imagination, or a desire to talk to one of the two people who remember my prehistory, but I want to speak with my sister, Linda.

She's surprised to hear my voice. At first, we talk about nothing special: The garden she's trying to coax out of the salty Gabriola earth. The concerts she plays here and there on Vancouver Island — sad, that she's so excited about performing at a bar in Nanaimo when she used to draw a decent crowd in Greenwich Village.

"How's Dad doing?"

The pause goes on too long. Linda might be taking a sip of tea. Or she might be struggling with annoyance. Most likely both.

"Good days and bad. I dropped by the care home yesterday, and he thought I was Mom. This morning, I was there to help out with breakfast, and he's all, 'Linda, where have you been, I haven't seen you in weeks.'"

"At least he remembers you," I say, surprised by the tightness in my throat. I thought I was past the rage and sorrow of my father's memory banks being wiped clean of me. As if I never existed at all.

Again, a pause. "Maybe he'd recognize you if you visited once in a while."

"We both know that wouldn't matter," I say. "Dementia or not, he's forgotten me the same way everybody else has."

A long windy sigh travels down the line all the way from the Straits of Georgia. "Debbie, get a grip. I'm starting to think you can't tell the difference between your fantasy world and reality anymore."

"That's unfair," I say, rummaging in my purse for a vial of lorazepam.

"You've been like this ever since you were a kid," she continues. "You get bored, so you invent stuff to keep things interesting. Fun when you were a five-year-old, but now it's just weird."

"Why are you being so mean to me, Linda?"

"I'm not being mean. You need to hear this, little sister. You. Are. Not. Sputnik Chick."

The rest of the conversation sounds like the voice of the teacher in the old Charlie Brown TV specials. Wah wah wah. Eventually, I tell Linda I'm on deadline and have to cut it short. I'm relieved to hit END CALL.

I don't know why I feel so defensive. Guilt, probably. Linda is the one looking after Dad. Even if someone has a eureka moment and finds a way to cure Alzheimer's disease, too many of Dad's brain cells have already died. As one doctor told me, once they're gone, they're gone.

I pick up my pencil. Set it down again. I need to take a break, but it's too early for a drink.

Then I decide it's not.

* * *

The bar is almost empty. Too early for my favourite barman's shift, there's an older gentleman who solemnly shakes a martini for me. I open my sketchbook. The blank page looks up at me accusingly.

On a stool at the far end of the bar, a man reads a book while drinking a pint of what looks like frothy maple syrup. Guinness, I assume.

I glance over at him as I suck the brine off an olive. My fellow inebriant is a good ten years younger than me, dressed all in black with a silver patch twinkling on one pectoral muscle. He looks a bit like the Blond Barracuda. Incongruously, he has large dark eyes and wheat-blond hair. Doesn't look like a dye job but you never know.

He catches one of my glances. Smiles at me. Lifts his glass in greeting.

"You're not sketching me, I hope," he says.

"I'm working on a comic book."

He grins wider. "Really? Which one?"

"*Sputnik Chick: Girl With No Past.*"

He sets down his Guinness and lifts his book off the bar to show me the cover.

It's the bound graphic novel version of *Sputnik Chick*, Issues 7 through 12.

"Holy shit," I say.

"Holy shit, indeed," he agrees. "Just bought it this morning. Quite a coincidence."

"There are no coincidences," I say, quoting one of Sputnik Chick's favourite lines.

He picks up his beer and moves to the stool beside me.

"Darren Scofield," he says, offering his hand.

"Debbie Biondi," I respond, shaking it.

We clink glasses. At St. Dismas the Good Thief Collegiate and Technical Institute, we had a two-word descriptor for guys like this — "pretty decent." By which we did not mean honest or honourable, but someone whose decency might be called into question.

He pushes the graphic novel toward me as he takes a pen out of his shirt pocket.

"Would you mind?"

As I autograph the book — *To Darren: Stay Normal. Debbie Biondi, Girl With No Past* — he says, "I've been following your work for years. I've always thought your style owed more to Hergé's *Tintin* than to manga or the American alt-comic aesthetic. Did you study in Europe?"

I'm probably staring at his face too intently. He's one of the hottest Spunkies I've ever met. Those dark, dark eyes, that blond, blond hair. A grin some long-ago girlfriend probably once called cute. I think about the bottle of champagne up in my room. The vast, empty expanse of the luxury king-size bed.

"Correspondence courses," I tell him. "Norman Rockwell's Famous Artists School. Remember those ads in the backs of comics?"

"'We're looking for people who like to draw,'" he quotes and laughs. He thinks I'm kidding.

"Is that a symbol of your people?" I ask, nodding at the silver insignia on his pocket.

He looks down at himself, as if he's forgotten what he's wearing, and fingers the stitching. "That's a Maytag logo."

"You're the Maytag Man?"

He grimaces. "Not *the* Maytag Man, per se. I repair all brands."

Spock-like, I raise an eyebrow at that "per se." Probably not cool to talk about kitchen appliances when you're a cult comic book creator. Bad for my once-edgy brand.

"One thing I've often wondered," says Maytag Man. "I know Sputnik Chick changed history and has some kind of hate-on for mutants from the future. But I'm curious to know what she was like *before* the apocalypse in her own time. Even the Girl With No Past had to have a childhood."

"When she jumps out of Atomic Mean Time, she loses all trace of her past," I explain. "Remember, she never existed in Earth Standard Time. No doppelgänger in both continuums, unlike everybody else." .

Maytag Man picks up his beer. "But she must have had a family. A real name. Something."

"In other words, you want an origin story," I murmur.

"Yeah."

I close my notebook. "Okay, yeah. Sputnik Chick had a family. Parents, grandparents, a sister. Funny thing about family love, though: It can be cozy or it can smother you to death. Or both at once."

Darren says nothing. Looks at the TV over the bar.

Sensing that I've already gone too far, I feel stupidly compelled to go further.

"Can I tell you a secret?" I ask him in a low voice.

He looks surprised, but is politely agreeable. "Sure."

I lean toward him conspiratorially. "I'm Sputnik Chick. Or rather, I used to be. Okay, she's still twenty-nine and I'm now somewhat older than that. I mean, yeah, some of the stories are made up, but broadly speaking, it's my life story."

He takes a slow sip of his beer and looks at me. "You actually swung Schrödinger's cat?"

I nod. "Yes. I hopped out of Atomic Mean Time into your time."

He raises a brow. "Soooo . . . you must have issues dealing with the real world. I mean, with no past and all. It must be tough not to know who the hell you really are."

I nod, relieved to finally find someone who understands. "That's right. I have no identity to speak of, not officially. No fixed address. No credit history. No kids. I can't even set up a Facebook account. I live my life on a cash-only basis. Or I use cryptocurrency. I just wish more bars accepted Bitcoin."

He sips his beer and looks at me with the type of expression he probably gives an unruly fan belt.

"With no fixed address, where do you live?"

I wave my hand at our surroundings. "Hotels, mostly. When I'm in Toronto, I crash at a childhood friend's place."

"You did have a childhood, then?" he clarifies, trying to punch a hole in my story.

"Of course."

"How does this friend remember you, if you didn't grow up in Real Time?"

I signal the bartender for another martini. I've been fasting all day so I can accept the extra one hundred twenty calories.

"My friend is exceptional," I explain.

He turns his attention to the baseball game on the TV over the bar. I can see what he's thinking.

She's nuts.

I turn back to my sketchpad, my visions of champagne-fuelled hotel sex vanishing. This guy is a Normal. Not someone who wants to bed a crazy lady. As the astronauts say, I have well and truly screwed the pooch.

He drains his beer and sets the empty glass on the bar with finality, then pulls a business card out of his shirt pocket and drops it on the bar in front of me. It reads: Scofield Appliance Repair.

"All makes and models. Gas and electric. Just in case you or your friend in T-Dot ever need something fixed," he says with a smile, then gets off his stool and strolls out of the bar, swinging the bound version of my life story, Issues 7 through 12, in his hand.

The Untold Origin Story of
THE GIRL WITH NO PAST

Volume 2
SCHRÖDINGER SWINGS
LIKE A PENDULUM DO

featuring
ASTROGIRL

one
Superpowers, Secrets and a
Side Order of Salami and Cheese
October 1969, A.M.T.

My toes curled over the edge of the eavestrough as I spread my arms like a gymnast, wrists locked and fingers pointed, trying to get up enough nerve to swan dive off the roof. Thirty feet below, Mom's naked rose bushes smiled up at me expectantly, no doubt wondering whether I was about to pull a Rapunzel and give them something to talk about all winter. I was wearing my red, white and blue JCPenney Wonder Teens™ bathing suit and nothing else, even though it was October. Every hair on my body stood at attention in the breeze.

I was trying to suss out whether the radiation in the Z-Lands had turned me from an earthbound mortal into a gravity-defying mutant. Because to have any hope of rescuing Kendal from the ShipCo Industrial School for Boys, I had to find out if I could fly.

On our first day back at St. Dismas the Good Thief Middle School, Bum Bum and I had started working on a plan to rescue Kendal. I had slipped away from my friends — the discussions of lip gloss and cologne, the slap, slap, slap of the younger girls' jump ropes — to a ditch running along the boundary of school property, where the Twisties — the awful name we used for the slow learners in Exceptional Class — gathered to smoke and insult one another. They watched me approach Bum Bum, who was sitting in the grass in a bright blue jumpsuit that his mother probably got from the clothes-by-the-pound shop.

"Can I talk to you for a minute?" I asked Bum Bum.

One of the other boys laughed. "Looks like Bum Boy's developed an unexpected taste for chicks."

Bum Bum stood up and casually grabbed the boy who made the comment, driving his arm up his back until he extracted an apology. Then the two of us wandered off to where we couldn't be overheard.

"You know about Kendal?" I asked.

He nodded. "Saw the ISB van come pick him up yesterday morning. His mom was, like, a basket case."

I gathered my nerve. To gain Bum Bum's trust, I had to be honest with him. "What happened to Kendal was my fault. Think there's a way to get him out?"

Bum Bum said there was always a way, so long as you had a getaway car. He explained that, although he was still too young to get his learner's permit, he was a fast, fearless driver — no cop had ever caught him. He also knew how to hotwire any make and model of vehicle. Bum Bum was a specialist in crimes of opportunity. "When we find the right car, at the right time, we make our move," he said.

I looked around to make sure that none of the other Twisties were eavesdropping. "Keep your voice down. You don't want ShipCo to give you a scholarship, too."

Bum Bum laughed. "Never gonna happen. I'm a Twistie. We're too dumb to do anything but dig ditches. ShipCo's only interested in sending smart guys like Kendal to the ISB. They haul 'em in, teach them how to fly, maybe some quantum physics, then send 'em down to Florida."

I shook my head. "What's in Florida?"

"The New Sydney M.U.E.C.F.," said Bum Bum. "Mandatory Underprivileged Enrichment Containment Facility. It's where they send you if you're smart and poor. Know those unmanned test rockets they shoot up every month or so? They ain't unmanned. The scholarship boys have to be in good enough shape to survive the launch and smart enough to learn how to handle a rocket, least until it burns up on re-entry. All the Z Streeters know about New Sydney. Some guys even volunteer to go."

"But why would they do that, if they're just gonna die?" I asked.

"Cause they're surplus kids from underprivileged families like Kendal's. Their moms and dads are all widows and Twisties and whatnot. Once their kid's got a scholarship, they're set for life."

Bum Bum explained that, to get Kendal out, we would need to find a way over a very high, well-defended fence.

"I'll look after getting us there and back, if you look after figuring out how to get us inside," said Bum Bum. "Know how to fly?"

Normally, that question would have ended our plan. But nothing that had happened to me since Labour Day weekend could be described as normal.

"I'll see what I can do," I answered.

*   *   *

I did my research at Cresswell's Collectibles, a second-hand comic book store and pawn shop that hung off the end of the main street of Shipman's Corners like a dirty afterthought. The wood-frame building had once housed a china shop, with the words ENGLISH BONE CHINA spelled out in faded coloured tiles in the sidewalk at the entrance. There still might have been some old English teacups floating around among the concertinas, broken radios, Depression-era toasters, hip-reducing vibration machines and K-Tel patty stackers. It was a receiving hall of old and semi-worthless possessions that families couldn't quite bring themselves to throw in the garbage. Instead, they took them to Cresswell's and got a few bucks for everything in the trunk of their car — or maybe not; I think some of the junk on the shelves was so worthless, Cressie probably just agreed to stash it there until someone shoplifted it. But his main stock in trade was used comic books.

When I biked over to the store and Cressie saw the huge stack of little-kid comics I had in my basket — my lifetime collection of *Moneybags McGurk*s and *Little Henry*s — his eyebrows went up behind thick glasses held together by a wad of masking tape over the bridge of his nose. Cressie had once bought a 1939 *Superman* comic from a nine-year-old for five bucks, which seemed like a fortune until word got around that he recognized the comic as a collector's item and sold it in the States for a thousand dollars. Cressie knew that kids were the easiest customers to rip off, so he paid attention to our old issues of *Lemurman* and *Betty & Velma*, sorting them rapid-fire on the counter by genre (superheroes, little kids, romance, classic stories and everything else). Cressie wasn't neat — the store looked as if it hadn't been dusted in a decade, and he himself carried the faint stench of mouldy laundry — but he was well organized and a freak for categorization and comic book trivia.

"Two bucks for the lot," he grunted.

"I want to trade them all for superhero comics," I said. "Stuff with mutants who fly."

Cressie pushed his glasses up his nose. "Can you be more specific? Guy heroes or chicks? League or lone wolf? Mainstream or underground? Flying under their own power or with help from magic objects?"

I lost track of my choices, so I said, "Flying girls would be the coolest, but I'll take anything you think worthy, Cressie. You're the expert."

Cressie liked to be sucked up to. Clearing his throat, he lifted the hinged counter in front of the cash register and wheezed his way down a narrow aisle of boxes stuffed with comics, all magic-markered with the word SUPER/FLY/ALL GENRES, tugging out issues at random.

"*Wonder Woman, The Blaze, Falcon Man, Notorious Nine, The Silver Surfer* — and *Agents of V.E.N.G.E.A.N.C.E.* has a kickass chick crime fighter, the Contessina. Should we bother with Superman?"

I shook my head. "Nah, I'm up on him. What about Webcrawler? He has radioactive blood, right?"

"The guy doesn't *fly*, though," Cressie reminded me. "He crawls up buildings on titanium cobwebs. Big difference."

I picked up one of the old *Wonder Woman* issues. The cover showed her hanging in mid-air while bullets bounced off her bracelets.

"She didn't fly until 1960," explained Cressie. "They keep screwing around with her origin story, giving her powers, taking them away again, making her an Amazon, then a Greek goddess — no one can make up their mind who Wonder Woman really is. Interesting story: some headshrinker invented her back in the war years, based on a chick he was screwing on the side who — get this — was *also* screwing his wife. A threesome, with Wonder Woman in the middle. Wild, huh? And here's a fun fact, baby doll: the headshrinker was the inventor of guess what machine?"

I shrugged. I wasn't even going to attempt a guess or I would've been standing there with Cressie all day. Once he started in with comic book trivia, there was no end to it.

"The polygraph," said Cressie triumphantly.

"What?"

"You know — the lie detector. Same guy who came up with Wonder Woman invented it."

I stared at Cressie. Unbelievable. The coincidence was too massive to ignore.

"I'll take one *Falcon Man*, one *Agents of V.E.N.G.E.A.N.C.E.*, one *Silver Surfer* and as many *Wonder Woman*s as I can get on trade," I said.

* * *

I biked home with my stash and read them under my bed. I saw Cressie's point about Wonder Woman: her origin story kept restarting, over and over again. Comic book time wasn't so much fluid as rubbery, bouncing back and forth, up and down, like a superball. Do-overs were common: you could literally start a superhero's life again in a different time, place or dimension. Costumes were reinvented as often as backstories.

I waited until Mom went out on an errand, put on a pair of gardening gloves and my bathing suit for the full superhero effect and scaled the rose trellis on the front of the house, skinning my knees on the rough shingles as I pulled myself up onto the roof. I had no natural fear of heights, a genetic gift from my father who was born in an alpine village so steep that vertigo had been bred out of the population. From the roof, I watched my grandfather, Nonno Zinio, slowly tying vines to wires and wires to posts in the grape rows behind our house.

I wondered: Would he see me transform into a comet and burn through the atmosphere like the Blaze? Grow a giant set of angel's wings like Falcon Man? Or would the Trespasser arrive in the form of an angel and catch me in his arms? From my grandmother, I'd heard the legend of Beautiful Alda, who jumped off a tower to escape a besotted Roman soldier, only to be scooped up in mid-air by St. Michael the Archangel. Sadly, Beautiful Alda abused this divine favour by going all Evel Knievel and making a second jump to impress villagers willing to pay hard cash to see the spectacle. She plummeted to her death.

I was still considering these possibilities when the tip of an extension ladder clanged against the eavestrough and the mouse-coloured topknot of my grandmother, Nonna Peppy, popped over the edge.

"What the hell wrong witch you? You tryin' to kill you'self, for Chrissake?" she shouted.

Being a good and dutiful granddaughter, I considered telling Nonna the truth: that I was experimenting with powers and abilities far beyond those of mortal men. But I knew what she would say: *You too old to be playing with your imagination.* I couldn't tell Nonna about what Bum Bum and I were planning or she would have locked me in the root cellar. So I said, "I just want to be by myself."

"Inna bathing suit, this time-a-year? Onna *roof?* Get the hell down, now," she ordered in an accent that was pure New York Lower East Side, even after all these years in Shipman's Corners.

Following Nonna Peppy down the ladder, I could hear the unbloodied rose bushes grumbling their disappointment: why hadn't I jumped? Roses are bloodthirsty plants, especially in fall when the leaves drop off, leaving nothing but thorns and creepers. I let Nonna wrap her shawl around my shoulders and propel me into her house, on the opposite side of our house from the Donatos.

In the kitchen, Pepé the Seventh, stretched out on the scrubbed linoleum floor, greeted me with a thumping tail and a yeasty stench. Nonna Peppy was nicknamed for her dog — or rather, generations of dogs — all named Pepé, for a Cuban bandleader whom she'd heard once in a dance club in New York, where she had lived for ten years before returning to Italy to marry Nonno Zinio. As soon as one Pepé died, Nonna would grieve for a day or two, go straight to the pound and pick out another. "Life's short and you gotta get right back on the horse" was her philosophy. Pepés One through Six were small, irritable mixed-breeds that barked a lot and were too stupid to be housetrained. Pepé the Seventh was the best of the bunch, an amiable retriever with an ear infection that made him stink like rancid fish.

Nonna sat me at the table and stuck her head in the refrigerator. "I got some beautiful Calabrian crusty bread, lovely cheese, Genoa salami, maybe some anisette cookies?"

"I'm not hungry," I said, but she was already filling the table in front of me. I made a capicollo and cheese sandwich while she spooned Nescafé into mugs and put the kettle on. While we waited for the water to boil, she leaned back against the counter with her arms crossed, frowning at me.

"What the hell's wrong witch you, *cara*?" she wanted to know. "You're not yourself."

I shrugged and scratched the ears of Pepé the Seventh, his smelly head in my lap.

"C'mon, *dimmi*. Talk to me. What's make you so sad?"

"Bunch of things," I mumbled around a mouthful of food.

"Okay, big deal, you got troubles. How many? Count for me."

"Three," I answered.

Nonna snorted. "Three's *nothing*. Three's what I got on a *good* day. Your Nonno Zin, he got about three an *hour*, thanks to the damn arthritis and the cancer. What's the first one?"

"Dad."

Nonna Peppy nodded and rubbed my arm. She already knew about Dad.

Ever since the Z-Lands, he seemed as deflated as the back tire on the Country Squire. He stuck with the same story Mom had told us — that he'd managed to change the tire and drive to the plant, where he'd become trapped in a decontamination stall for about six hours. But his story didn't pass the sniff test, not even for a twelve-year-old tap dancing–school dropout. Why hadn't we seen him driving past us? Why hadn't someone at ShipCo found him sooner? But most of all, when Mom was grocery shopping and Linda at a volleyball-team tryout, why had a ShipCo employee rung our doorbell and asked for Dad, then waited at attention while Dad piled his ShipCo manager's cap and plaid tie and dress uniform in the employee's arms? Ever since then, Dad had gone to work wearing the solid blue burst-away bow tie of a mid-level officer.

"Okay, so you worryin' about Dad. Me too. Your mom, too, you don't think she's worried?" said Nonna Peppy. "Second trouble is what?"

"Linda," I said.

Nonna Peppy sighed and fiddled with one of the anisette cookies, breaking it into a little heart-shaped mound of crumbs. Linda, too, had changed after the Z-Lands, turning distant and surly and a little disgusting, accidentally-on-purpose leaving soiled industrial-sized sanitary napkins on the bathroom floor, like ketchup-splattered serviettes from the A&W.

Nonna didn't ask me about my third trouble. I wouldn't have told her anyway. I'd learned that sharing secrets could be dangerous, and I wasn't about to explain Kendal's situation. Anyway, we never got past Linda, which wasn't a surprise.

One night, when a show Linda and I were watching was interrupted by an emergency broadcast from the White House, with President Robert Kennedy telling us we were going to DEFCON 2 because of yet another missile crisis — the third in as many years — Linda stood up suddenly and stomped to our room, with me following.

I sat on my bed and watched her push open our bedroom window, then start to work at the edge of the screen with a metal nail file, as if she were trying to break out of prison. She jabbed at the screen in a sort of desperate panic that infected me, too.

"Linda, what-are-you-doing-what-are-you-doing-what-are-you-doing?" I whimpered like a frightened cat.

"You know what DEFCON two means?"

I shook my head.

She took a long breath. "It means . . . nothing. Nothing left. Some people just disintegrate and their shadows are left behind. Some people live and think they're okay, but then their skin starts peeling off. Like scalding the skin off a tomato. Understand?"

Linda stuck her hand down the front of her blouse and pulled out her scapular medal of Our Lady of Lourdes. She unclipped it and poured the thin gold chain into my palm, closing my fingers around it.

"Keep this for me. If I don't come back, it's yours."

She eased the screen out of the window and slipped it under her bed, then grabbed a comforter and stuffed it under her sheets, patting and shaping it like playdough.

Getting down on her tummy on the window ledge, she pivoted her body like a gymnast on a balance beam. It was a short drop to the narrow strip of grass; I heard the soft plop of her body hitting the ground.

The window looked obscenely naked without its screen. I went to the ledge and looked down at my stranger-sister, my stomach flipping like a pancake. Linda's eyes, as large and dark as mine, looked up at me.

"You aren't going to tattle, are you? This could be my last chance."

"Last chance for what?"

But she was already gone. I could hear the sound of her body pushing through a gap in the bushes.

I pulled down the window, not quite closing it, leaving a Peter Pan–sized space so that Linda could Tinkerbell her way back into the room. Eventually, I went to bed and dropped off into a dream about Ethel Mertz and Lucy Ricardo from *I Love Lucy* working at a long conveyor belt covered in bullet-shaped bombs. They held mallets and tapped each one on the nose. When one finally exploded, blood spurted everywhere, like the juice from an overripe tomato.

WAHHHHHH! wailed Lucy. An unseen audience was laughing, just like on TV.

The next morning, I opened my eyes to see Linda curled tightly in her quilt, her tennis shoes tossed telltale beneath the window. She smelled like cats after a rainstorm. I pulled myself over the side of the bed, found slippers and scuffed into the kitchen. Dad, making coffee, was listening to Bobby Kennedy on the radio, talking about how we had prevailed once again. Dad was late leaving for work that morning, lingering over his coffee while he smoked a cigarette, something he'd stopped doing when I was a little kid but had recently taken up again. I poured a bowl of Frosted Flakes and drowned it in milk, the radio gone to music.

When I got back to our room, Linda had disappeared. I had a moment of worry until I heard water running in the bathroom. I went to the door and lay on the floor, pressing my eye against the gap. I could just make out Linda's bare toes. She must have been sitting on the toilet.

"Linda!"

A heavy sigh from inside the bathroom. "What is it?"

"President Kennedy says we're not gonna die."

There was a long pause before Linda's voice floated out to me from under the door: "Not today, but soon, Billy says." Followed by the sound of the toilet flushing.

two
There Be Dragons

Bum Bum and I huddled together behind the half-built wall of a house out of view of the schoolyard. Lunch break was the best time to discuss our breakout plans, but I'd noticed the teachers watching us. Probably wondering what a nice girl like Debbie was doing with a loser from Z Street who occasionally showed up for class in his mother's clothes. Exceptionals and Normals didn't mix at St. Dismas Middle School.

That day, Bum Bum was in a pair of turquoise capris. We were sharing a cigarette — my first.

I coughed. I felt lightheaded in a not unpleasant way. "Bad news. I haven't found a way to fly over the wall," I told him.

Bum Bum plucked the Export A out of my fingers and took a long drag.

"Who said anything about flying?"

"You did."

"Jesus, I was just kidding. I meant climbing. We could probably manage it with a thirty-foot extension ladder."

I remembered Nonna Peppy popping over the edge of the roof. "We've got one. But I'm not sure how easy it'll be to get it on the car."

"Leave that to me."

"But won't the guards see us going over the fence?"

Bum Bum blew smoke in the air, thoughtfully aiming the stream away from my face. "It's starting to get dark early. We'll do it under cover of night."

"But BB —"

He hugged my shoulder. "Relax. Sometimes you just got to make stuff up as you go along. What's that word?"

"Improvise," I said.

"Yeah, like that. Just be ready and I'll find you when the time comes."

We left the construction site and took separate routes back to the schoolyard.

* * *

I was so distracted, waiting for a sign from Bum Bum, that I let my thirteenth birthday pass in early October without much fuss, except for a store-bought white cake and watered down wine at Nonna Peppy and Nonno Zin's house. Even Halloween snuck up on me like a wolverine following an unsuspecting hunter in a Disney live-action short. The Donatos, Sandy and I decided that we weren't too old for one last trick-or-treat. Afterwards, we could drop into a party at the candy store at the boundary of Tesla and Fermi, thrown by the junior volleyball team at St. Dismas Collegiate, where Linda was a star blocker.

I hadn't bothered to think about what to wear. Dad drove me to the five-and-dime at the plaza to browse the picked-over plastic costumes. The Donato twins had snapped up the last of the fairy princesses, of course; the boys on the street got all the soldiers, hobos, pirates and gangsters, their scars and five o'clock shadows applied with burnt cork and eyebrow pencil, as if disguised as their future selves. I had to settle for being a circus clown in the flimsy plastic mask of a white-faced, red-nosed, orange-haired man and a suit printed on a slipcover big enough to pull over a winter coat. Linda planned to dress as a witch — appropriate, given the vile mood she'd been in.

One night as I lay on my bed, Linda sat at her desk, chewing the end of a pencil and mulling over math questions. She was hiding something; I was sure of it.

Exhibit A: while I pretended to sleep, she had popped open the window screen two more times, dropping over the sill like Alice falling down the rabbit hole. When Dad finally got around to putting up the storm windows, the midnight adventures ended and her mood darkened even further.

Exhibit B: the strange things hidden under the white panties and navy knee socks in her underwear drawer. With plenty of time to snoop while she was at school, I examined astonishing black lace brassieres with the price tags still attached, bottles of dime-store perfume and bikini panties printed with cartoon devils spelling the days of the week with flaming pitchforks.

Exhibit C: a stapled booklet printed on cheap paper called the *Manifesto of the Youth Anarchist Movement (Canusa Cell)*. In it, I learned that the older generation (and in particular the military industrial complex, which you can pretty much bet was another way of saying ShipCo) was using what they called "surplus youth" for experimentation and the advancement of the space program. After the last war, people had too many babies for the country to support, and this was a way for ShipCo to put some of the poorer ones to practical use. Referring to the dog the Soviets sent up in Sputnik 2, the booklet read, *We are a generation of human* Laikas, *bred to test the space technology of the twentieth century.* It made me quietly glad to be a girl, unfit for space flight, according to the YAM Manifesto. My only role in the World of Tomorrow, it said, was as a breeder for future Laikas.

* * *

On Halloween night, the temperature plunged. Freezing rain battered Shipman's Corners, coating our windows with a thin scrim of ice.

I put on my clown mask, pulled on my winter coat and toque and squeezed on the plastic Bozo slipcase. I looked like an orange-and-white sausage bursting its skin.

Linda, sleek in a tight black turtleneck and slacks, stuck a cone-shaped bristol board witch's hat on her head and waited at the door, her black-lined eyes scanning the street as she gnawed her thumb. At the sound of a honk, she yelled "That's Tricia" and skittered down the slick front walk to a green and white Corvair. Standing at the door in my Bozo mask, I watched the car swallow her up.

The Donato twins came to pick me up in their pink princess dresses, plastic tiaras and majorette boots; Mrs. Donato had run up fluffy white jackets to wear over top so that the effect wouldn't be ruined by winter coats. Sandy arrived in her folkloric dance outfit: a full red and white skirt, red boots over heavy wool leggings and a crown of flowers stitched to a toque.

"What are *you* supposed to be?" demanded Judy-Garland.

"A Ukrainian," answered Sandy.

The four of us lumbered from house to house, Sandy and I huddled under my mother's umbrella, the Donatos wrestling pink ruffled parasols that were quickly shredded by the wind. Pumpkins grinned lopsidedly from every third or fourth house; long stretches of the block were in darkness, their shell-shocked occupants reluctant to answer the door to knocks in the night. The rain was coming down harder now. We hurried toward the candy store, its windows glowing like a last outpost of civilization. A firetrap of a wooden shack, the store sold frost-encrusted popsicles from a malfunctioning freezer, dirty magazines from a detergent box hidden under the front counter and a dog-eared selection of old *Superman* and *Artie* comics. Never much of a business, it had evolved into a teen hangout at the edge of the known world, the point where the streetlights and pavement of Fermi Road ended.

Lugging soggy pillowcases full of cheap candy, we banged our way up the steps of the store's sagging front stoop. Jayne-Mansfield slipped on the ice and fell with a cry. The three of us lifted her as best we could, our arms stiff beneath layers of winter clothing and plastic costumes. Disguised as cartoon versions of grown-ups, we peered into the vast and terrifying darkness beyond the store. *There be dragons.*

When we pushed open the door, we were welcomed by a wall of warm air and junior volleyball players, the girls dressed as cats and witches, the boys pretending to be gunslingers in their younger brothers' cowboy hats and toy holsters. One girl wore a beauty pageant sash reading "Miss Atomic Bomb," her body wrapped in chicken wire and black felt.

Piotr, the candy store owner's son, was an astronaut in a cardboard box covered in silver foil. A cluster of hair-dryer hoses bounced out of his chest like decapitated hagfish. We perched on stools next to him while he changed records on the hi-fi, watching one of the gunslingers do the Watusi with Miss Atomic Bomb.

Beside Piotr, a skinny young man with shaggy black hair riffled through a stack of 45s. He was dressed like a soldier — fatigues, combat boots, dog tags — but with buttons missing from his tunic and a T-shirt stained with something nasty, like old blood. A stethoscope hung around his neck.

When he noticed me beside him, he smiled. "Hey there, kid, what are you supposed to be?"

"Bozo the clown," I mumbled through a mouthful of caramel apple. "How about you?"

"Hawkeye Pierce," he said.

I frowned. "Who?"

"TV show character. He's kind of a clown, too."

"Never heard of him," I said.

He shrugged. "His show doesn't air in this time zone. I've only seen it because I'm an exchange student."

His voice sounded familiar. "I feel like I know you from someplace."

He shrugged. "Maybe it's déjà vu," he said, pulling out a 45. At first I thought he was reading from the record label — I'd never heard the word before.

"What's dayjawvoo?"

"It's French for 'already seen.' That sense some people have that they've lived through something before. Ever feel that way, Bozo?"

I nodded. I finally had a word to describe a feeling I knew well, although I never knew when the dayjawvoo would appear. It bubbled up as randomly as pancake batter on a hot griddle.

Hawkeye Pierce pulled a 45 from its sleeve. He was missing half of the middle finger of his right hand.

"I know who you are now. You're the guy from the future."

One of his eyebrows lifted in surprise. "And just how do you know that?"

"We've crossed paths twice. Once in the Z-Lands last spring. You were trespassing on private property, so I called you 'the Trespasser' in my head."

Hawkeye grinned. "'The Trespasser.' That's an apt name for me. And the second time?"

"You scraped my cheek cells at the ShipCo company picnic. You told me you were Dr. Duffy from the future."

Hawkeye frowned. "You're right about my name, so I guess I can look forward to harvesting your epithelia sometime soon."

"No, you already did that in the past," I said.

"Depends on your point of view," he answered.

Before I could remind him about my having to save humanity, the door banged open and Linda and Billy walked in, holding hands. Billy was wearing the blue denim shirt and pants of a farmhand and a threadbare corduroy sports jacket. His blond hair had grown long and flopped over his eyes, covering the coil of scar tissue dangling from his ear. A fake mustache drooped under his nose. It didn't seem like much of a Halloween costume.

Billy nodded at the Trespasser. "If it isn't Hawkeye."

"Meathead, I presume?" said the Trespasser. "It appears you're taking the low bandwidth transmissions of Earth Standard Time a little too seriously."

Billy frowned. "The impact of subversive entertainment is clearly observable within the youth mores of Earth Standard Time. Why not here?"

The Trespasser waved his hands dismissively. "There is no empirical evidence that televised entertainment in a parallel world is indicative of a possible shift of youth culture in our own continuum."

"It's intuitively obvious," insisted Billy.

"Are you a scientist or a sociologist?" asked the Trespasser. "And just for the record, Meathead was a buffoon, an object of satire."

Billy stiffened. "He was a freedom fighter. A teller of truth to power."

"You call his fat father-in-law powerful? A careful analysis would show that Archie Bunker was a man more to be pitied than feared."

The partygoers had stopped dancing to give their attention to the argument between Billy and the Trespasser.

"Who *are* you weirdos?" demanded Gunslinger Number One.

Billy didn't answer, just plucked the 45 out of the Trespasser's hands and read the title: "'Telstar' by The Tornadoes. Pop glamorization of spy satellite technology. You actually like this crap?"

"It's catchy," said the Trespasser.

"Give the propaganda a rest, Billy, this is supposed to be a party," said Piotr, putting "Telstar" on the hi-fi.

Miss Atomic Bomb giggled. "Don't you ever have fun, Billy?"

Billy pointed his finger at Miss Atomic Bomb as if pulling a gun on her. "They're exploding a thermonuclear device in the magnetosphere as we speak. That sound like fun to you?"

The Trespasser put his hand on Billy's shoulder as if to lead him away. Billy shrugged him off and stepped into the middle of the room.

"Listen up, everybody. If we told the ShipCo bosses to ban the Bomb, they'd have to listen to us. There's a lot more of us than there are of them."

The partygoers gasped. For the youth of Atomic Mean Time, this was wildly dangerous crazy talk.

"What the hell do you expect us to do for a living when we grow up?" demanded Gunslinger Number One. "Shipman's Corners is a bomb town, asshole."

"And if we don't do something about that, it'll soon be a smouldering radioactive crater," Billy shot back.

"You sound like a Yammer," said Miss Atomic Bomb nervously. "Better shut up or they'll send us all to New Sydney just for listening to you."

Linda stepped in front of Miss Atomic Bomb. "You're such a child," she said.

"I've seen TV broadcasts from an alternate world where youth are marching in protest," said Billy. "They're occupying buildings and calling for change. And it's working. They've even managed to limit their Domino Wars to Korea and Vietnam."

Gunslinger Two snorted. "TV from another dimension. How'd you manage that trick?"

Billy and the Trespasser traded looks.

"I'm a scientist," Billy said.

"Right, and I'm a monkey's uncle," said Gunslinger One.

"Judging by your unevolved state, I'd say that's highly likely," said Billy.

The Trespasser inserted himself between Billy and Gunslinger Number One, who was clenching and unclenching his fists. Some of the kids looked mad. Others, scared. Gunslinger Number Two had starting slowly punching the palm of his hand.

"Time to back off," said the Trespasser softly to Billy.

"It's always time to back off, according to you. You're as big a problem as the rest of them, you anti-mutant snob. Go back to the lab and let me do my job. Let's split, baby," Billy said, grabbing Linda's hand and giving a parting shot to the crowd: "Sure hope you like the taste of Strontium 90 in your chocolate milk, kids. A couple of miles from here, there's enough radium in the ground to make you all glow in the dark."

Oh no. Linda had told Billy about the Z-Lands.

Piotr jerked his thumb at the Trespasser. "You better go with your friends. Last thing I want is for this party to turn into a brawl."

Linda, Billy and the Trespasser pushed through the front door, just as a cowboy brushed in past them, dripping wet: Bum Bum. His hands were lost in the sleeves of what must have been his father's lumberjack shirt. He didn't even have a hat, just a grubby red bandanna around his neck and tin can lids stuck to the back of his shoes to hint at a costume.

Gunslinger Number Two made an ugly face. "First we got Yammers wrecking the party, now someone invited a Twistie from Z Street."

"Store's open to everybody who doesn't talk politics," Piotr said, handing a caramel apple to Bum Bum, who sank his front teeth into its shiny brown skin and chewed it as if he hadn't eaten in a week.

He tossed the apple core into the garbage, nodding in my direction, and then jerked his head at the door. His meaning was clear: *meet me outside*. He must have found a car. Time to steal my father's extension ladder and make our move.

"This party sucks. Let's get out of here," I said to my friends.

Fortified by candy and hot cider, Sandy, Judy-Garland, Jayne-Mansfield and I hoisted our pillowcases and trundled back into the rain. No lights lit the street past the candy store. I scanned the darkness for the Trespasser and caught a match flaring briefly in a car parked just outside the pool of yellow streetlight that marked the edge of Fermi Road.

"Wait up," I said to the others, handing Sandy my mother's big umbrella. Freezing raindrops pinged off my plastic clown mask like BB pellets as I squooshed to the car. My shoes were overflowing.

The Corvair's windows were sleeted over. I pulled my fist inside my coat sleeve and circled my arm against the glass, scratching a porthole. Surfer rock blasted from the car radio.

I put an eye to the porthole. I expected to see Bum Bum

smoking behind the wheel, but instead I saw Linda in one of her lacy bras, her long hair messy all over the seat. Billy's blond head was bent over her, his lips pressed to her chest as if he were trying to suck out poison from a snakebite. I'd seen this move in Westerns. I stepped away from the car and lumbered back to Sandy and the twins.

"Is it your sister and her Yammer boyfriend?" asked Judy-Garland.

"Let's find out," suggested Jayne-Mansfield, heading for the car.

I grabbed the back of her fluffy coat, sending her into a puddle of slush. The last remaining ribs of her parasol snapped. Judy-Garland reached down and hauled her weeping twin to her feet.

"We're telling!" she yelled, and the two of them stomped away, hand in hand.

"I'm going home," said Sandy miserably. She slung her pillowcase over her shoulder and headed off toward Tesla Avenue.

I was utterly alone.

Hoisting my drooping pillowcase, I crossed to the other side of the street, wondering what had happened to Bum Bum. On the sidewalk outside of a darkened house, I hit an icy patch and my feet flew out from under me like a Looney Tune character slipping on a banana peel. The back of my head smacked something hard, leaving me dazed. I found myself staring up into the dark sky with ice pellets hitting my face.

I put my hands over my eyes to protect them from the freezing rain, which is why I didn't immediately know who was speaking when someone above me said, "Plan's off."

I took my hands away from my eyes to see a soggy cowboy staring down at me. Bum Bum. He grabbed my hand and hauled me to my feet.

"Plan's *off*? Why?"

"I got a message. Kendal says someone aimed a blowtorch at him. One of his hands is fucked up."

"What? How did he get a message to you?"

"A Twistie on my street picks up garbage at ISB. He's been helping us pass messages written in lemon juice on the insides of potato peels," said Bum Bum.

"But I—"

Bum Bum shook his head, cutting me off. "Kendal can't climb down a ladder one-handed. He said they might let him go anyway 'cause he's not whole anymore. Test pilots can't be damaged goods. Go home, Debbie."

Rubbing sleet off my face, I watched Bum Bum walk off into the darkness. I hoped he would turn around and tell me that he was just testing my courage and that we were still going to rescue Kendal. But when the jingle of his tin can spurs vanished into the night, I knew he wasn't coming back. Sniffling back tears, I trudged toward home.

By the time I got there, the block was in darkness, the Donatos having already tossed their jack-o-lantern into the shrubs and killed the porch light. The princess twins were no doubt already in their pink flannel PJs, gorging themselves on candy in front of *Suburban Cavemen*.

Inside my house, I stood on the mat, letting the rain sluice off me for a few minutes, then squished my way to my room, past the statue of Our Lady Queen of the World standing in a nook near our telephone. Snakes writhed beneath her bare feet. Her modestly downcast eyes followed me down the hallway. She sent me a telepathic message: *Don't you dare rat out your sister.*

I climbed into a hot bath while Dad dumped out my pillowcase on the table and examined each piece of candy, dissecting a taffy apple in a search for pin pricks. He had heard on the news that weirdos were poisoning Halloween candy, like the evil witch in *Snow White and the Seven Dwarfs*.

Sleepless under my comforter, I listened to the clatter of sleet on the roof. I tried not to think about Kendal and blow-torches, or Billy the anarchist, or the Trespasser, who kept turning up disguised as a different doctor. Life didn't make much sense anymore.

Eventually, the front door creaked open and banged shut, followed by the accusing sound of my mother's voice. ". . . past curfew," she said, but the rest was blown away by the wind rattling the window frame. I couldn't make out Linda's answer, but it ended with ". . . for god's sake, it's Halloween night."

Linda was home now and I could sleep. At least one person I cared about was safe. I closed my eyes, trying to ignore an unpleasant soreness, as if Hot Stuff the cartoon devil was pricking his tiny pitchfork into the back of my throat.

Something was sitting on my chest. Soft, heavy, feathered, rancid-breathed. I opened my eyes to a dizzy, overheated world, my throat filled with jagged glass.

I couldn't speak but Linda sensed my distress and went to my parents' bedroom to rouse Mom, who shuffled into the room, yawning and shaking a thermometer. When she read my temperature, her eyes widened.

"One hundred and four point five."

I stared up at her. I was going to die on the day after Halloween, the Day of the Dead, despite the U-shot. This made no sense. The cover of a *LIFE* magazine on our coffee table showed a close-up of a hypodermic needle angling into the tender skin of a kid's shoulder, with block letters asking: "THE END OF DEATH?" The story was about how the Universal Vaccine had turned sickness into a Technicolor cartoon witch, all jagged bones and black-and-purple robes. If you ate her poisoned apple, a handsome prince with a stethoscope would wake you with an antibody kiss.

The doctor came that morning and immediately diagnosed tonsillitis. He said I'd need an operation and a short hospital stay.

"Dying of a viral infection is a virtual impossibility. The U-shot's pretty well eradicated polio and all strains of influenza," he assured Mom, patting her shoulder. "Her tonsils were probably inflamed before she got her shot."

Dreamy and hot, propped on pillows and rolled into a blanket, I lay across the back seat of our station wagon with my *Wonder Woman* comics. I was brought to the Children's Ward and rolled into a room full of girls in beds that looked like giant cribs.

One girl marched over to peer at me through the bars of my crib, as if I were a zoo animal. With her blonde pageboy and chenille pink bathrobe, she looked like a dwarf version of Doris Day.

"I'm Cindy. Who the hell are you?" she demanded.

I shook my head; it hurt too much to talk.

Cindy sighed theatrically. "Gosh, another deaf-mute. Who'da thunk it?"

I whispered, "Tonsils."

"Oooo, big hairy deal, daddy-o. You know how many kids have come through here to get their tonsils out? Millions. Don't be a sucky baby. This time tomorrow, you'll be sitting like a fairy princess with a big bowl of ice cream, lucky you. Now get out of the crib, we're playing Deaf-Mute Teacher movie."

You're not the boss of me, I said inside my head, but when Cindy lowered the bars of my crib, I got out, my bare feet cramping on the icy floor.

One of my roommates really was deaf and blind — Suzy, an eight-year-old with long blonde hair and huge blue eyes like a baby doll. We were three Annie Sullivans to her Helen Keller, leading her around the room, forcing her to touch things so she'd learn their names. Cindy kept mashing Suzy's fingers against her lips as she spoke.

"Let's play fallout shelter," said Cindy, pushing Suzy under my crib. Even though the other girl, Yvonne, and I, were too old for "let's pretend," we followed Cindy, Suzy's stuffed animals standing in as the household pets we'd eventually be forced to eat. Cindy made grown-up conversation while we were down there, waiting for the all-clear. "Everything's going to hell in a handbasket. The Jews and the Catholics are ruining this country."

"If you're not Catholic, why are you at Sacred Wounds?" asked Yvonne.

Cindy sneaked a look from side to side, as if about to reveal a secret, then said in a low voice, "The government put me here. It's all part of a secret plan to stop the Communists from getting hold of the best female specimens to breed with Russian men after they take over. I'm actually one hundred percent normal, not like the rest of you sicko Twistie kids." She poked Yvonne. "Show us what's under your hair."

Yvonne shook her head and moved away from Cindy, who grabbed a hank of her hair and twisted it up to reveal a seashell of lumpy pink flesh below her ear. It looked slightly obscene, as if Cindy had pulled down Yvonne's pants to expose her private parts.

"See that? It's her third ear. They're going to *fix* it," crowed Cindy, as if the word meant something dirty, like fixing a cat. Yvonne yanked down the flap of hair, mumbling something in French that sounded nasty.

"And she's not the only Twistie. There's a whole bunch of girls with cockie doodles who they've stuck in the boys' ward," said Cindy. "Hermaphrodites. Like worms. Yech. There are even a couple of monsters down the hall."

I shook my head and managed one word. "Liar."

Cindy put her fists on her hips. "Am not! Come with me and I'll show you."

"Better not," said Yvonne. "Sister will skin you alive if she catches you again."

"I don't care. I'll take the new kid with me after lights-out, if she isn't too scared," said Cindy.

Later, after the nurse turned off the lights and the sound of her steps had disappeared, I heard my crib bars sliding down. Close to me, Cindy whispered, "We've got to move fast while Sister's on rounds."

We went to the door and peered around the corner. At the far end of the hallway, nurses' white caps bobbed like sails. We could hear their crepe-soled shoes sucking against the waxy linoleum. When the coast was clear, Cindy said, "They're in the boys' ward now. Let's go."

She took my hand and hurried me down the hall to a door with a large black-lettered sign: NEGATIVE PRESSURE VENTILATOR. Cindy pushed open the door.

The room was dark except for a pool of light at the far end. I could make out two bomb-shaped objects, side by side, giving off a rhythmic whooshing and sucking sound, like the inhale and exhale of a giant. As my eyes adjusted to the dim light, I saw that the two objects had human heads sticking out of them. Girl on one side, boy on the other.

Cindy whispered, "They've been in there for years. They knew each other when they were little kids, so they stuck them together for company. Now they've gone through puberty. The boy must be getting all the urges boys get, but he can't touch the girl. They're paralyzed."

"Who's there?" The boy's voice was thin and high. "Come over here where we can see you."

"It's me and a friend," called Cindy in a sweet voice. "Sister said to come check and see if you two were still breathing."

Cindy grabbed my hand, dragging me closer to the monsters. A pink bow was pinned to the soft-looking brown hair of the girl's head, which rested on a pillow.

"Don't touch us," the girl said. She sounded as afraid of us as I was of them.

I managed to twist my hand free of Cindy's and was backing away when I bumped into something warm and soft. A hand gripped my shoulder hard.

"*Mon Dieu*. Not again, Cynthia," said a woman.

I turned to see a nun dressed head to foot in white, like a ghost: white veil, white robe, white beads around her waist, white wimple under her jutting chin.

"The new kid made me do it," whined Cindy. "She said she'd let me read her comic books if I took her to see the monsters."

Sister tsk-tsked as she gripped my shoulder and guided me out, Cindy following.

Back in our room, Cindy climbed snuffling into her crib while Sister tucked a thin coverlet around me and locked the bars in place. "If you get out of bed once more, God will give you polio, vaccine or no, and you'll wake up in an iron lung, just like Mathieu and Anne-Marie. *Comprends?*"

I lay under the thin cover, shivering with cold, my throat a furnace, my stomach empty, staring into darkness. I was afraid to sleep for fear that if I closed my eyes, I would wake up without a body, imprisoned for all time in a bomb-shaped metal coffin, my head protruding into a world I could see but couldn't touch.

First thing in the morning, while the others got their breakfast trays, a nurse in a cap as stiff and white as a restaurant napkin came to our room. For an awful moment, I thought she was the Pat Boone nurse. But this one's hair was darker, her body, thicker. "There'll be ice cream afterwards," she promised as she slid a needle into my arm.

Cindy, nibbling on toast and strawberry jam from space-age plastic packets, said in her know-it-all voice, "See? Told you so. Let me read your comic books while you're gone."

Before I could say yes or no, the nurse grabbed my comics and dumped them into Cindy's crib. Then she wheeled me into a large bright room with blue-tiled walls that looked like the girls' washroom at school. Eyes smiled at me over white masks.

"See you soon, sweetheart," said a doctor, just before another needle pushed me down through the bottom of the world and out the other side.

I hadn't been dropped into the afterlife, or what you think of as sleep, but a drugged half-life where the body surrenders itself to a surgeon who can slice and dice without his patient making a fuss. They even breathe for you. That's why they call it "going under," as if you're falling into water. For most people, it's a short plunge to nowhere from which they quickly surface.

I'm not most people.

*   *   *

The first clue that something was wrong came when I didn't wake up. As I drifted on a dreamy ocean of painkillers, flutter-kicking in and out of wakefulness, the sounds of the recovery room washed over me — the chalkboard squeak of bed wheels on linoleum, the whooshing of the breathing machine, the cries of little kids coming to from their own surgeries, all of them wanting their mothers.

A woman's voice, comforting as honey on toast, said: "Why doesn't she open her eyes?"

A man's voice answered: "If I knew that, I wouldn't be emptying bedpans."

The woman sighed. "She'll probably sleep through World War Three."

The man said, "'Scuse me, Nurse, I got a mess to clean up. One of the little darlings just woke up puking."

I opened my eyes. Instead of the recovery room, I was in the wide empty street of a black and white city. Not Shipman's Corners, but a cartoon metropolis, a Little Nemo nightmare-land where skyscrapers swayed like noodles and searchlights swept the sky. In the distance, a speck ran closer and closer. Me. The only one left alive. Overhead, the sky seethed with iron sharks, metal jaws clanking as they swooped to the attack. I tried to lift my hand to swat them away but I couldn't move. I was awake but paralyzed, like Cindy's monsters. As Sister had warned, God was punishing me with polio, and now I was locked away in an iron lung for eternity. For one despairing moment, I wanted to die.

A male voice lowered itself into my dream: *You aren't dying. You can't die now.*

You are on a quest to save the world.

Time to wake up.

I sniffed something spicy. Cinnamon toast. My eyes fluttered open on a blurry face. A woman — no, a man, with peeling pink skin, wearing a nurse's cap. The Trespasser. Or Dr. Duffy. Or both of them.

"Hey there, Sleeping Beauty."

He sat down in a chair next to the bed and leaned close to the bars.

"I have an update for you. Your friend Bum Bum took the liberty of improvising after he left you on Halloween. He stumbled over an unlocked car on his way home and tried to rescue Kendal on his own. Things didn't go well. Cops caught him with the stolen car and someone's extension ladder. But don't worry, no scholarship for him, just a stint on a reform-school farm."

Tears came to my eyes. The Trespasser patted my hand. "Hey, hey, don't get that way. Probably the best thing that ever happened to Bum Bum. Fresh air, sunshine, new friends. A second chance."

He stood up and busied himself with a tube leading from a metal IV stand into my arm before stepping out of view. I tried to turn my head to catch sight of him again but the world beyond my bed was a blur.

I don't remember being taken off the breathing machine. I do remember throwing up all over my pillow, the pain in my throat unbearable, the promised ice cream never materializing.

"It's either pseudocholinesterase deficiency or malignant hyperthermia. Both very rare," the surgeon told my parents at the side of my crib. "She'll need to be tested before she ever goes under again. Be sure to warn her dentist, too."

I spent two groggy days in my crib while Cindy read my *Wonder Woman* comics aloud; she never gave them back despite my weak protests to Sister, who told me that Cindy was here long before I came and would be here long after I left, so I should be generous and Christian and let her keep my comics. "Even the Cynthias of the world serve a higher purpose," she said.

"Your turn," Sandy said, her chin on her fist. She was getting tired of losing to me over and over again.

I popped the plastic bubble in the middle of the board, already knowing I'd roll a five. Exactly what I needed to win my tenth game in a row. As I jumped my peg around the board to another victory, Sandy shook her head.

"You cheating or something? How come you always win?"

"Just lucky," I said with a shrug.

Ever since I'd been released from Sacred Wounds Hospital, every game of Trouble I played felt like one I'd played before. Déjà vu, Dr. Duffy had called it. Not as exciting a power as flying, but handy.

I was spending two dull weeks recuperating at home. The hours moved sluggishly, the silence of the house broken only by Mom's voice on the phone and the drone of the local radio station. Sandy brought my deskwork home at lunch so I wouldn't fall behind. After she went back to school in the afternoon, I put a lid on Trouble and turned to my new hobby: drawing.

It had started when Mom sent Dad to the stationery store to find wholesome, educational activities to fill my time. Hidden in the jumble of dusty decoupage sets, pipe cleaners and greasy oil pastels, he found an art instruction book: Walter Foster's *How to Draw Horses*. No talent required, Dad reassured me.

Walter Foster had worked out a system that turned illustration into a party trick: if you could draw rectangles, triangles and circles, voila, you had a horse, as easy as one, two, three.

I filled stacks of beige manila sheets with mustangs and Appaloosas. With some minor physiological changes, I could turn the basic building blocks of the Walter Foster horse into just about any type of generic four-legged creature, including ones with monstrous dinosaur heads and the legs of a Baba Yaga chicken house.

Finally, the pain in my throat eased and I was judged healthy enough to return to school. The night before my first day back, I sat on my bed watching Linda fold sweaters and underwear into a suitcase. Her face had gone puffy, a bumpy pink rash mottling one cheek. In fact, her whole body was puffy, as if she had been inflated with a bike pump. I sat beside the suitcase, my washed-out quilt soft against my legs.

"Where you going?"

She rubbed the heel of her hand under her nose. "Toronto. A special school for girls."

"How come?"

"Mom and Dad don't want me here for a while."

"'Cause why?"

It took her a while to answer.

"I'm in trouble."

"What kind?"

"The kind boys get you into."

"Billy?" I asked.

She nodded.

"Why doesn't he, like, run away with you, or marry you, or something?"

Linda carried on packing without looking at me. "Billy got a scholarship to the same place they sent Kendal. From there, they'll send him to New Sydney, and then from there —" She didn't finish her thought, but I knew where Billy was headed: on a one-way trip to the moon.

Another lost boy. It seemed almost pointless to cry about it. Mrs. Kendal was so upset about John that she'd stopped coming to our house to sell cleansers. I suspected that, somehow, she'd discovered I was responsible for Kendal's fate.

"What's gonna happen to your baby?" I asked.

"What difference does it make what happens to it, with the world the way it is?"

I twisted my hand into the top of my ankle sock, scratching nervously at a hidden scab. "Are you afraid?"

Linda shook her head. "Mom's coming with me for a couple of weeks."

This was news. Mom never went anywhere. Linda looked at me with her big wet eyes and rashy face and said, "Debbie, can I tell you a secret?"

"What?" I asked cautiously. I was learning that my family already had too many secrets.

Linda plopped down beside me, the edge of the mattress sagging as if a boulder had been dropped on it.

"You're never going to have a chance to grow up. You won't get to fall in love, or graduate from school, or anything. It's so sad."

A chill settled over me. "How come?"

"'Cause you're going to die when they drop the Bomb, along with three-fourths of the world's population." She raised her cupped hands into the air, miming a mushroom cloud. "Poof. All gone. Remember? We'll be the first to go. Billy said that's what's going to happen, for sure. Mutual Assured Destruction. That's why you can't be a suck-up kid and do everything Mom and Dad say. The grown-ups are the ones who got us into this mess in the first place, Debbie, with their stupid Atomic War of Deterrence. Billy was trying to get all us kids to help him stop it. Now I'll never ever see him again." She sighed, picked up a pink angora sweater and rubbed it against her cheek. "At least I got to fall in love."

"What's falling in love like?" I asked.

She thought this one over.

"Like being eaten alive by wild animals, but not minding."

Linda slammed the suitcase shut and wiped her eyes with the pink sweater. Then she put her arms around me in the kind of hug that made me think one of us was going to the electric chair.

*   *   *

Dad and I drove Linda and Mom to the train station in our Country Squire station wagon, their suitcases jammed into the third row of seats, me in the second row, Linda up front with my father. I stared at the back of her head. Her black hair was scraped so tightly into an elastic band that the skin of her neck had gone pink from the tension of her ponytail. Mom sat next to me, her face like a stretched white tablecloth. When the car pulled into the train station, she said one thing to me: "Be good."

The train pulled in, making a hissing sound like the air going out of a balloon. Mom and Linda stepped up onto the train. Linda turned and gave Dad and me a sad little wave, like a beauty queen being sent into exile. Then the train pulled away and they were gone. Dad and I lingered on the platform, not saying a word. Finally, we walked slowly back to the car.

On the drive home, we saw the superstructure of a ship rising in the distance. When we got to the bridge, Dad turned off the engine and we got out of the car to sit on a bollard and watch the ship glide past, slowly, slowly — for a few seconds, the *John Foster Dulles* seemed to stand still while the ground around us moved.

The ship passed directly in front of us, a great wall of rusting steel and bolts floating into the lift lock. It was like being next to an airport where the planes flew so slowly, you could talk to the passengers as they passed over.

Where do you come from? Where are you going? Can I go too?

The two of us watched the ship go past in the chilly November air; the *John Foster Dulles* might well be the last ship of the season. We'd have to wait until spring of the new decade, 1970, to see another.

Dad lit a cigarette. I felt the way I did while playing Trouble. As if I had already lived through this day with him. I knew he was about to say something major, after which nothing would ever be the same again.

He cleared his throat. "Debbie, there's something I have to tell you before you hear about it from somebody else. I'm not at ShipCo anymore."

I said nothing. I wasn't even sure I wanted to hear the rest.

He took a deep breath and carried on. "That day in the Z-Lands, I went back to the plant and checked the Geiger counter. I thought it was malfunctioning. Turned out it wasn't, but the others I'd used in the past had been. They'd been tampered with. They weren't picking up any readings, even when radioactivity was present. Which means the Z-Lands are still dangerously contaminated."

I shook my head. "Why would anybody tamper with Geiger counters?"

Dad tossed his cigarette into the canal. "Because the company doesn't want to sink more money into trying to fix the problem."

"Is that why so many Twisties live on Z Street?" I asked quietly.

Dad rubbed his face with both hands. "I guess."

I looked up at him. "So what happens now?"

Dad shrugged. "Get another job. Start my own business. We'll see." He paused for a moment. "For now, let's keep this between you and me, Debbie."

"What's Mom think?" I asked.

"I haven't told her. She's got enough to worry about with your sister."

The two of us watched the *John Foster Dulles* float away to more interesting places than Shipman's Corners. Then we all drove home: me, Dad and the secrets we were keeping.

That night, with Dad in the living room watching TV, I lay beside the great flat expanse of Linda's deserted bed, the last of my comic books spread around me. Strange, to be all alone at night. The last thing I heard before falling asleep was the deep, concerned voice of an announcer on the Buffalo evening news: *It's eleven o'clock. Do you know where your children are?*

Torture Chamber of the Lizard King

School days lumbered by like an overloaded bulk freighter. After my two-week absence, I floundered in deskwork that our teacher Mrs. Di Pietro ran off on the Gestetner machine in the office. You could hear it kuh-thunking away every morning, the drum inking thirty copies of tedious arithmetic questions.

Not long after Linda and Mom's retreat to Toronto, I was sitting at my desk when I noticed Judy-Garland pass a note to Kathy F., who passed it to Lucy P., who passed it to Wendy D. Finally, nudged by Jayne-Mansfield, Wendy tried to toss it onto my desk with a snort of suppressed laughter. It fell short, landing on Sandy's desk. She unfolded the paper. I craned my neck to look over her shoulder but all I could see was the skin on the back of her neck reddening. With an eye on Mrs. Di Pietro, who was absent-mindedly walking the aisles while we did deskwork, Wendy snatched back the sheet from Sandy, crumpled it and lobbed it onto my desk.

The tightly folded paper sat before me like a ticking time bomb. Something told me it would explode if I opened it, but I had to know what was inside. I unfolded the sheet, creased in a million places from making the rounds of the room.

It was an ink drawing of a naked woman with breasts like balloons and bullet-shaped nipples that had been crayoned a lurid pink. Her legs were high in the air, splayed wide open with a big black inkblot scribbled over her crotch. She had the eyes of a cat but her nose and mouth were missing.

At the bottom of the drawing, in capital letters, was the word "HOOR."

I gripped the paper in disbelief, sickened by the raw hatred in it. This was a poison kids gobbled up with their breakfast cereal, or carried to school in bagged lunches, or absorbed from overheard telephone conversations between mothers: *Did you hear about the older Biondi girl leaving school in the middle of the year and the mother going away, why it's plain as the nose on your face what's going on, who would've believed she turned out to be such a . . .*

Whore. The power of the word made me queasy. I wanted Superman to spin time backwards by flying against the rotation of the Earth, so that when the wad of paper hit my desk, I would have a second chance to take it to the girls' room and flush it down the toilet without looking at it. Too late now to squeeze the naked whore out of my head: she would be stuck there, forever.

A shadow fell across my desk, accompanied by the sweet plastic odours of breath mints and drugstore cologne. Sharp pink fingernails tugged the paper out of my hands. Mrs. Di Pietro made a *tsk–tsk* sound. She didn't yell, or call the principal's office, or threaten to keep us all in at recess if we didn't tell her who had done it. She didn't even put the paper in her desk drawer, which she did with other contraband like yo-yos, comic books and gum. She just crumpled it and threw it into the wastepaper basket, where the janitor might find it at the end of the day.

When we lined up for dismissal, I stooped to tie my shoelace, grabbing the crumpled drawing out of the wastepaper basket. I slipped the wad of paper into my knee sock.

Outdoors, I walked past the group of whispering kids, past the slap, slap, slap of the skipping rope against the cracked concrete of the playground and the chants that helped the girls keep time:

Doctor, Doctor!
Call the doctor!
Someone's gonna have a brand-new baby!
Wrap it up in tissue paper!
Send it down the elevator!
Next girl come and jump with me!

* * *

Dad was waiting for me in the Country Squire to take me to have my teeth checked. With Mom gone, the duty fell to him. When I got in the car, he looked at me carefully.

"Everything okay?"

"Yup," I answered.

We drove downtown to the dentist's office in silence. He pulled up to the curb, idling the engine.

"Want me to go in and wait with you?"

I climbed out. "I'm thirteen. I'm not a little kid anymore, Dad."

"See you later," he said as I slammed the car door behind me.

From a young age, I recognized that dentistry was a type of sanctioned torture. Fortunately, because of my anaesthesia problem, they decided to play it safe by gassing me instead of sticking a needle in my mouth, which meant I forgot everything that happened while I was in the chair. Dr. Franken kept a stock of century-old comics in his waiting room to distract kids from the terrifying whir of the drill and the strangled cries of children with his hairy hands halfway down their throats.

Trying to keep my mind off of what was to come, I found myself paging through the same comics I'd read at every checkup for years. That day, I actually found one I hadn't read before. It looked like it had been drawn when dinosaurs roamed the earth: *Amazing Space Adventures Featuring ASTROGIRL!* The characters were dressed as lords and ladies from the olden days, even though they were zooming around in rocket ships and zapping one another with ray guns.

In one panel, Astrogirl, her hair in a perm that even my mother would have been ashamed of, was comforting a slave girl who looked surprisingly like Linda. Long black hair, strong chin and big breasts trapped in bra cups shaped like pointy bullets.

"Please help me, Astrogirl! I'm in trouble!" sobbed the slave girl. She even cried like Linda. Tears the size of jellybeans squeezed out of her blue-black eyes.

"What kind of trouble?" Astrogirl wanted to know, fists on her hips to show she meant business.

"I was captured by an alien race called the Muluxions on the eve of my wedding to a member of the Andorrean royal family," the slave girl said. "I'm actually a princess, not a slave! And now the Muluxions are forcing me to marry the son of their leader, but he's . . . but he's . . . not humanoid."

Astrogirl gasped. "That's unspeakable!"

She wasn't kidding. A few pages later and the slave girl was in a wedding dress, standing beside a giant iguana in a Prince Braveheart outfit.

"Soon you will be mine, my dear!" he said, his red tongue pointing at her from between green jaws.

The slave girl put a fist to her mouth in the classic comic book gesture of horror. Before I saw how it all turned out, the dentist's nurse came out and called my name.

"You're the girl with the novocaine problem. Let's get you started on the gas."

I sat in the high leather chair. From the next room, I could hear the dentist's asthmatic wheeze. Dr. Franken lumbered in, smelling of peppermints with an undertone of something sharp and boozy, and picked up one of his shiny implements of torture from the metal tray that he kept at eye level so that we could anticipate what he was about to inflict on us in the name of oral hygiene.

The nurse stuck a mask on my face and the room began to ripple like the surface of the canal on a windy day. From the venetian blinds on the big window in front of the chair, the Andorrean slave girl hung by her wrists, writhing in terror. The lizard king, in his feathered cap and a white dentist's coat, rubbed his tiny green paws in perverse glee. Groggily, I wondered what, exactly, a lizard would do with a girl. A minute later, I had my answer: the lizard yanked the girl down from the venetian blinds, unhinged his huge jaws and stuffed her into his mouth, head first. I could hear her groans of horror from inside the lizard king's gurgling digestive system. Soon all that was visible of the girl were the ghostly imprints of her hands pressed against the lizard's insides and her slippered feet protruding from his gaping mouth.

"Sssssixxx cavities! Sssssomeonesss been eating a lot of candy!" a voice accused.

Sleepily, I forced open my eyes. A long forked tongue rolled obscenely out of Dr. Franken's jaws and lolled at me for a moment before rolling back up.

That was the last thing I remember before feeling a distant stab of pain like Fred Flintstone bonking Wilma over the head with his caveman club. As the gas dragged me off to dreamland, I imagined the horror of being eaten alive by a boy. I wasn't sure I'd like it much, once there was nothing left but my screams.

"Debbie," said a voice.

Mmmm.

"Debbie. Snap out of it."

I forced open my eyes. The Trespasser was standing in front of me, wearing a white lab coat and holding a whirring drill.

"Dr. Franken had a bit of a fainting spell. Good thing I was available to take over."

Don't hurt me, I tried to say but my mouth was full of tools and cotton batten.

"Must feel like everything's going off the rails," said the Trespasser, shaking his head.

I tried to nod. Bum Bum and I had failed to rescue Kendal. Dad had lost his job and Mom still didn't know. Kendal had been hurt. Billy was going to die in a rocket. Linda was having an anarchist's baby. Everyone was calling her a hoor and getting ready to turn me into an outcast.

All my fault, I tried to say. But the Trespasser shook his head firmly.

"Open a little wider, please. Everything that's happened the last month was caused by an algorithm glitch. My not-so-esteemed asshole grad student didn't bother to double-check his data, which is what happens when you work with an Exceptional. I mean, I don't want to sound geneto-misanthropic, but Billy's SAT scores were so low, only an affirmative action PhD program like ours would accept him."

I stared at him. "*Linahsbilly?*" I managed to mumble around the cotton.

He nodded. "Yep. Linda's Billy. My grad student at MIT. Or will be, in about fifty years. As part of his thesis, he was doing research back here in the past to find a way to fix problems your generation left behind that could mean the end of humanity as we know it. But he was too convinced that he could adapt strategies he saw on low-bandwidth television from a timeline weakly coupled to ours. Earth Standard Time. That's why he thought he could change history by creating a peaceful protest movement among youth. 'Yammers.' 'Ban the Bomb.' Idiotic. Not to mention, he identified the wrong sister. Linda's not the Ion Tagger. You are, Debbie." The Trespasser paused. "You need to rinse and spit?"

I shook my head. The Trespasser picked up a suction hose and stuck it over the edge of my lip. His breath smelled of cinnamon mouthwash.

"What's done is done. Billy ended up on a one-way trip to the moon, so it's up to me to sort out this mess. We've got no time to lose. You're gonna have to swing Schrödinger's cat."

I watched him lift a syringe, clinking the glass with the stump of his amputated middle finger to check for air bubbles. "*Wha . . . Schro?*" I tried to protest as he angled the needle into my arm.

"Schrödinger's cat. A cat, in a box, with radioactive material. It's alive in one world, dead in another. A thought experiment by a buddy of Einstein's — look it up. The point is, I can't wait around for you to grow up or I'll start losing more fingers and toes, and bits I'd miss even more, to timesickness. With this little enzyme cocktail in your bloodstream, you'll hop forward in time exactly nine years to the day, November fifteenth, 1978, so you can get down to business saving-the-world-wise. Looking on the bright side, you'll get through puberty in a big hurry."

The dentist's office was starting to swim like a flashback on TV. Only the Trespasser stayed in focus, watching me closely, the empty hypo still in his hand.

"How'm I s'posed to save the world?" I managed to mumble.

The Trespasser cleared his throat. "You're going to stop the momentum of time, collapse the continuum where we're living into a black hole of non-existence and hop into a safe alternate world, sucking everyone along with you through the vacuum of space. Basic physics. Still, it's tricky. In fact, it's never been tried before. But my research suggests it's all quite doable. I'll explain further after we hop into 1978. Once we're there, we'll have about six months to figure out our next steps before they drop the big one in '79. Just don't look too surprised when the nitrous oxide gas wears off. You'll exist in two places at once, for a nanosecond or two. Don't worry, I'll be right behind you."

I open my eyes. Painfully. My head feels like a bulldozer has just ploughed through toxic waste pooled inside my cerebral cortex.

Someone is snoring.

I turn my head. A man is stretched out beside me, facing the other direction. Wispy wheat-blond hair with flecks of white. A hunched pink shoulder dotted with birthmarks and moles.

Oh Jesus God. It's all coming back to me now. I'm in bed with the Maytag Man.

I rise shakily to my feet. I am naked. And I am sticky. This alarms me until I notice two torn condom wrappers on the night table.

The anonymous, sterile environment of the room screams "hotel chain on the edge of the suburbs in a large North American metropolis." Yanking open the floor-to-ceiling beige drapes, I see twelve lanes of high-speed traffic sound- lessly flowing past a sprawling power centre anchored by a Loblaws, a Canadian Tire and a Mark's Work Wearhouse. A grey-orange sky hangs low over the soulless landscape.

Oh, thank God. Thank God. I'm still in Toronto.

Meditating on this view of a smoggy morning in the sub- urbs helps me knit my scattered scraps of memory together.

It started with the malfunctioning dishwasher in Bum Bum's condo. Pretty handy myself, I had patched together a few quick fixes with the help of YouFixIt.com and a great little shop in Scarborough, in Toronto's eastern suburbs, where you can buy spare parts for home appliances, every make and model. But the Maytag's faulty latch was defeating me. Small as it might seem compared to the pump or the rotating washer arm — both of which I'd already replaced — I saw no way to stop the latch from slipping open, spilling water all over the hardwood kitchen floor and potentially leaking into one of the pricy condo units below. I dug through my purse and found the card for Scofield Appliance Repair. Two hours later, he showed up at the door, wearing the same all-black getup he had on in Montreal.

Examining the faulty latch, he shook his head: "You used to be able to keep a Maytag dishwasher, what, fifteen, twenty years? Today it breaks in five so you're forced to buy another."

"Or have it fixed," I pointed out. "That must be good for your business."

"You'd think so, but you'd be surprised how many people junk an appliance when they hear it'll cost a couple of hundred bucks to repair it." He shook his head. "Sometimes I feel like Decker in *Do Androids Dream of Electric Sheep?*, retiring dishwashers when their predetermined lifespan is reached."

"Sounds like you're a Philip K. Dick fan," I said.

"*Blade Runner* is one of my all-time favourite films. But I read the book years before I saw the movie."

"Since you're here," I said slowly. "There's also a small problem with the washer-dryer. If you've got time, maybe you could check that out, too?"

He smiled up at me from where he was unpacking his tools on the kitchen floor. "Gladly."

I led him into the laundry room where he gently pried open the Miele washer-dryer combo. There was something almost tender about the way he removed the drum.

"I like this brand. Well engineered," he murmured.

Watching Darren's sensual handling of machinery made me oddly self-conscious. I scooped up the sweaty T-shirts and socks I'd left on the laundry room floor.

"There must be a ring of hell for people who leave dirty laundry lying around," I said, stuffing my running gear into the hamper.

Darren looked up at me. "Laundry rings — in hell? Not in Dante's time. They were less fastidious than I suspect you are."

Turns out that Darren has a master's in English lit, specializing in works in translation from the Italian Renaissance. He wrote his thesis on the *Decameron*. A repair guy who can translate Boccaccio.

"There were no jobs in academia when I finished grad school, so I started my own business. I've always been good with my hands," he explained.

How did we get from Bum Bum's condo to a Holiday Inn Express on Toronto's outer rim? He needed a piece for the Miele, which, of course, he hadn't come prepared to fix. I mentioned the great little parts shop in Scarborough. He expressed surprise — and arrogant doubt — at its existence; if it was so great, how come *he* didn't know about it? Long story short, we got in his pickup and I guided him there. Once we had the part, we both agreed that it was getting late and we should grab a bite to eat. And, he said, I know this fantastic place not far from here.

Pretty soon, we were eating samosas and drinking Kingfishers. I ordered another beer. So did he. Soon, neither of us was fit to drive. Darren pointed out the Holiday Inn

Express sign on the horizon and said there was probably a taxi stand. We walked there, hand in hand, in the rain and found the stand empty. Which is when he kissed me. I remember tasting the hot samosa spices on his tongue and lips before falling into an amber-tinged pool of forgetfulness.

On a desk littered with the detritus of a large nachos platter and empty minibar bottles of vodka and Kahlúa (was someone making White Russians last night? Did we use milk or cream? How many calories did I consume?) sits a coffee maker, dumbed down to the point that all I have to do is drop a plastic disc of Columbian Rainforest Blend into a Canadarm-like extrusion and add water.

As the coffee steams its way into a mug, I gather up my pantyhose, blouse and bra, scattered around the room. Skirt? Missing in action. Ever so gently I tug the sheet from around Darren. Nope, he's not wearing it. Eventually, I find it lying in the closet.

Darren's left hand is resting on the bedcovers in plain view. No ring. No telltale marks, like a tan line, either. Not that that means much. My grandfather and father didn't wear wedding rings: people who work with machines often don't. A ring, a tie, a watch, a scarf, earrings, a ponytail — all easily hooked by moving parts or superheated by motors and wires. The lack of jewellery might simply mean that he's cautious about taking chances in his professional life. Maybe in his personal life, too.

I sit in a chair and watch his face in sleep. A straight nose, high forehead, pale eyebrows, prominent cheekbones — Nordic. A sensitive-looking face. The outdoorsy Lutheran minister look, all dry rectitude and simmering sexuality fighting to keep itself in check.

Darren mumbles. I put down my cup. His eyes open, dark brown irises under fair lashes. An odd combination.

He smiles. "Hey there."

"Hello," I say back.

He sits up. "You feeling okay?"

I rub my head. "A little hungover. You?"

He rubs his head in sympathy, but without the conviction of the truly hungover. "Not feeling too bad, but. Well. Anyway. Wow. I guess we got a little carried away last night, eh?"

"Guess so. In fact," I pause, trying to decide whether to say this out loud, because it sounds so awful, "I'm having a hard time even *remembering* last night, after the lobby."

He nods and turns to plant his feet on the floor. Pulls the sheet modestly over himself.

"Do you remember getting into an argument about Chekov?"

I shake my head. "The writer?"

"No, the helmsman. From *Star Trek*. Original series."

"Oh, yeah," I say, and I do. Something about how amazed we both were by the retirement of the space shuttle. How wrong it seemed for future NASA astronauts to be taking off from Russia, and yet how appropriate, in that it proved that *Star Trek* got it right. That the Federation could bring together people of all nations to explore space.

"Oh, and we discussed your origin story at length," adds Darren.

For a moment, I'm so surprised, I can't take a breath.

"*My* origin story? I think you mean Sputnik Chick's."

Darren grins and shrugs. "They're really the same thing, aren't they? Just like you told me in Montreal, you're mining your own life in your work — childhood, growing up, immigrant family, et cetera. But as I said last night, I wonder whether you should go beyond personal trauma and explore more archetypal themes."

I stare at him, astonished. I never talk about my writing to anyone. *Never*. I don't discuss ideas or share work in progress. I never solicit opinions or seek out collaborators. Hell, I hardly ever listen to my editor at Grey Wizard. I'm a lone wolf, just like Sputnik Chick.

"You sound as if you're trying to fix my origin story," I say carefully.

"Sorry. I overstepped," he says. "Frustrated writer myself, I guess. It's just, despite the offbeat humour and cartoony violence, I've always felt that *The Girl With No Past* was a revenge tragedy at heart. There's a darkness at its core. That's what makes it so interesting."

I step into my skirt. "Vengeance implies some type of betrayal. Who betrayed whom, in your opinion?"

He shrugs. "You're the writer."

We say our goodbyes at the taxi stand. Sliding into a cab, I'm already chalking him up as yet another one-night stand with a Spunky, when he says, "Can I get back to you tomorrow, around noon? I have to catch up on the appointments I missed yesterday. Otherwise, I'd look after you today."

I stare at him, not comprehending. "Look after me?"

"I meant, the Miele. But I wouldn't mind looking after you again, too," he says. "If you're interested."

Either he just asked me on a date or he needs the business.

As the cab heads west, I smell something burning. Sniffing the air, I peer at the driver in the rear-view. His eyes catch my frown.

"Something wrong, miss?"

"I thought I smelled cigarette smoke. Must have been one of your previous passengers."

He shakes his head firmly and taps the NO SMOKING sign bolted to the dashboard.

An olfactory hallucination, then. It takes me a few seconds to place it: not cigarette smoke, but burnt toast, sprinkled with sugar and cinnamon. The smell of tragedy and grief, vengeance's older sisters. I dig around in my purse for the vial of lorazepam.

Just to take the edge off.

The Untold Origin Story of
THE GIRL WITH NO PAST

Volume 3
"WE'RE LOOKING FOR PEOPLE WHO LIKE TO DRAW"

featuring
THE CONTESSINA

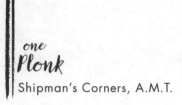

one
Plonk
Shipman's Corners, A.M.T.

When the laughing gas wore off, I understood why the Trespasser had warned me not to act surprised. Instead of waking up in the dentist's chair, I was in the open air, facing Dad, his boots sunk up to the ankles in yellow horse manure, spraying grapevines from a tank painted with the letters "DDT" strapped to his back. I saw myself standing next to him. And by "myself" I don't mean "me," but rather the future me. Taller and heavier, bookish-looking in wireframe glasses, my shoulder-length hair covered by a red bandanna, knotted at the nape of my neck. Like Dad, I was dressed in knee-high rubber boots and (surprise of surprises) a pair of blue jeans. I watched myself reach up to gently tug on a bunch of immature grapes hanging from a vine, testing their firmness.

Even with the midday sun beating down on my bare skin, I was shivering as if I'd been standing naked in a deep freeze. In a way, I had been. When you swing Schrödinger's cat (I would later learn), you are frozen in time until you re-enter the continuum where your future self already exists. Until you integrate your two selves, one of you is on the outside looking in.

I waved my hand up and down in front of Debbie-of-the-Future's face. No reaction. I was invisible to her and Dad.

For one freaky, gut-twisting moment, I felt myself moving toward me/her. The acceleration felt like the final drop on a roller coaster, when you're sure you've left a few of your internal organs behind. Next thing I knew, I was fondling the grapes and thinking about how urgently I needed to empty my bladder. I had integrated with my future self, but the body I was standing in did not feel like my own.

Dad had aged — his hair greyer, for sure — but he was skinnier and healthier-looking, with the tan of someone who spent a lot of time outdoors. I'd never seen him dressed in jeans and a denim shirt before. He was almost handsome, even with a tank of pesticide strapped to his back.

His face registered concern. I must have looked as disoriented as I felt.

"You okay, there, Debbie? Heat getting to you?"

I improvised. "I am feeling a little woozy. And I need to pee."

"Time to call it a day," said Dad. "Why don't you use the Johnny-on-the-Spot? Too gross for you?"

"I can handle it." I walked awkwardly toward a green plastic outhouse at the edge of the field. I felt so top-heavy that I kept thinking I was going to fall forward onto my face.

I tried to figure out exactly where we were: this was a much bigger vineyard than the one in our backyard, the grapevines rolling in long straight lines toward a far blue horizon that suggested we were close to a large body of water. The vines looked like the twisted bodies of burnt men, crucified on posts. Judging by the firmness of the grapes, harvest time was still months away. Strange, considering that the Trespasser had said he was sending me forward in time nine years to the day. I'd been sitting in the dentist's chair in mid-November, but the weather felt more like early summer.

Opening the door of the outhouse, I half-expected to see the Trespasser inside, waiting for me. All I found was a foul-smelling pit covered by a rudimentary toilet. As I hovered over the seat, I looked down at myself. I was wearing a bright yellow T-shirt printed with a big happy face, under which protruded a pair of breasts the size of cake mixing bowls. I was horrified to see how womanly I'd become. The Trespasser said I was supposed to save the world, but how could I do anything heroic in a body that made me feel as if I were swimming through wet cement?

I didn't see the Country Squire among the few vehicles in the gravel parking area behind a grey windowless bunker of a building, so I slowed my pace to see which one Dad would unlock. To my surprise, he threw his equipment into the truck bed of a canary yellow Ford half-ton pickup, painted with the catchphrase of Shipman's Corners' favourite brand of plonk: *Sparkling Sparrow Wine & Juice. Have A Grape Day!* A lemon-scented cardboard deodorizer in the shape of a happy face hung from the rear-view.

Sitting high in the passenger seat, I followed Dad's lead and clipped myself into a device I'd never used before — a seat belt — before we peeled out of the parking lot. I could see now that the front of the grey bunker, facing the road, was painted a cheerful yellow and purple, with a huge sign reading: *Sparkling Sparrow Wines and Juices, A Division of ShipCo Pharmaceuticals (Canusa) Limited: Your World Looks Better Though Grape-Filled Glasses.* In the near distance, a saltie cut through the canal. I had my bearings now: we were in a township on the outskirts of Shipman's Corners, on a stretch of Lakeshore Road.

*   *   *

Dad turned on the radio. The music that flowed out sounded immediately fresh and new and exciting.

"I don't know what the hell it is with the music these days," complained Dad, fiddling with the station. "Just want to hear the damn news."

I drowsed to the drone of Prime Minister Stanfield's monotone — the old fart was still in power with that perennial loser, Pierre Trudeau, still the Leader of the Opposition. Surprising that the government hadn't changed in nine years.

At the end of the newscast, the announcer said: *This has been the Canusa Broadcasting Corporation's five o'clock news for June thirtieth, 1971.*

I sat up straight in my seat. Had I heard the announcer correctly?

"What day is it today?" The voice in my ears did not sound entirely my own.

"Saturday."

"I mean, the date."

"June thirtieth," answered Dad.

"What year?"

Dad frowned. "1971. Sure you're okay?"

"Yeah, yeah, just — lost track of time."

The dizziness of disorientation was turning into heart-pounding panic. Instead of the jump of nine years to the day that the Trespasser had promised, I had landed short by seven years and six months, give or take a week. The glitch might explain the Trespasser's absence. He might not show up for years.

Dad reached over and pressed his hand to my forehead. "You've got heat stroke, honey."

I laid my head back against the seat and closed my eyes. If only my problem was as simple as a few overheated brain cells. I had been stuffed inside a strange body and thrown into summer in Shipman's Corners with no clue about what I'd been up to since 1969. If I'd changed so dramatically in a year and a half, it was scary to think about how much more I would have changed over nine. Now I had to figure out my next steps for myself, saving-the-world-wise.

No Place Like Home

I woke up with a start as Dad pulled into the driveway.

"Home again, home again, jiggity-jig," he said brightly. Yawning, I climbed out of the truck and entered the house behind him, fearing the worst.

I was surprised we had a house at all, considering Dad had lost his job at ShipCo. The fact that he and I were working as field hands — the dirtiest, lowest-paying way to make a living in Shipman's Corners — hinted at a certain financial desperation. Yet our kitchen had gained a fresh coat of harvest gold paint and a new set of avocado green appliances. The effect was cheery and sickening at the same time. I was shocked to see Mom loading up a dishwasher, an extravagance we'd never had in my time. Maytag, of course.

Mom's tight coarse black curls had turned steel grey, and her face looked thinner, as if her flesh were being slowly honed away. Like Dad, she was in Levi's and the same yellow smiley-face T-shirt I was wearing — when did dressing like a farmhand on mood-altering drugs become acceptable for matrons in their forties? I wondered. What happened to Mom's cinched-waist housedresses and demure sweater sets?

"Linda phoned. She just got to the bus station," she said.

"What? She should have been here hours ago," said Dad.

Mom shook her head. "Some idiot left their identity papers in Toronto, so there was a holdup when they crossed the Hamilton checkpoint. I told her to jump in a taxi," she told us as she put water on to boil for pasta. Except for the bottles of Sparkling Sparrow Purple People Eater Grape Drink in the middle of the table, our meals didn't seem to have changed. But what was Linda doing in Toronto — was she still forbidden from living at home after all this time? And since when did anyone in my penny-pinching family "jump in a taxi"? Everyone was acting like the Moneybags McGurk family in the comics. I stood watching Mom for a while as she hummed in front of the stove, oddly happy as she simmered a pot of tomato sauce. Something was definitely off.

I went to my room. Yellow chenille bedspreads were pulled tight on both beds. A stuffed bear wearing a T-shirt with the Sparkling Sparrow happy face was plopped on my pillow. A bowl of cinnamon-apple potpourri made the air smell like New England in autumn, a good way to cover the smoggy fug of a summer day in Shipman's Corners. A silver and black telescope stood on a tripod in one corner, the lens angled toward the window. A little engraved plaque announced that its owner, Debbie Biondi, had taken first place in the 1971 Canusa Regional School Board Science Fair. On my desk, my sketchpads, pencils and Walter Foster art instruction books were neatly lined up. I picked up the one on top — *How to Draw Flowers*. Below that, *How to Draw Cars*. The next one — *How to Draw the Human Body*. I flipped through that one. It was full of naked women with backcombed up-dos, posed in fur stoles and high-heeled slippers. Their nude bodies were tastefully rendered, revealing only the crack of a bum or the slope of a breast. No bullet-shaped nipples.

I caught sight of myself in the mirror. What did my body look like under this stupid shirt? I pulled it over my head, revealing a beige nylon bra with a tiny pink bow where the cups met. I unclipped the bra and checked the size: 36B. I was shocked — two years earlier I'd been a 32A. The reflection of my cow-like body astonished me. The dark brown orbs of my undrawable nipples. The little pout of fat around my middle. The slouch of my shoulders. If I was on a mission to save the world, why didn't I look more superheroic? I put the bra and T-shirt back on.

Everything in the bedroom seemed calm and peaceful, like something out of an air-freshener commercial. I, on the other hand, had grown into the "before" picture in a Shake Yourself Thin ad, the kind for which they cut out a fat woman's head and stuck it on the body of a skinnier woman for the "after" shot.

I went into the living room, feeling like an explorer in my own home. The Canusa six o'clock radio news drifted in from the kitchen. Something about President Nixon leading a rally against Soviet aggression. How did Nixon jump from vice-president to president? And what had happened to Bobby Kennedy, newly re-elected to the presidency just two years earlier? It would be a few days before I could sneak off to the library to scan back issues of the *Shipman Corner's Examiner*, where the scandal was covered in salacious detail: a young woman drowning in the White House pool, her nude body discovered after she'd taken late night "dictation" in the Oval Office. No wonder Kennedy had escaped to Ireland.

I slipped my hand inside the waistband of my jeans. I wasn't used to wearing pants; these ones were uncomfortable, stiff and tight around the middle. I stared at myself in a mirror Mom had put up in the living room, also new. How had I got so *big*?

As I tried to figure out how to not look like a large blue sausage, Linda breezed through the door, carrying the same suitcase she'd been packing the last time I saw her.

"Debbie, you look fantastic! Have you lost weight?" Linda lied, throwing her arms around me. I hugged her bony frame cautiously, trying not to snap her in two.

My sister was the one who looked fantastic, if strangely dressed: fashion had evolved more rapidly in two years than it had in the previous decade. Like everyone else in the house — possibly in the Free World — Linda was wearing blue jeans, paired with thick-soled, bubble-toed shoes and a polyester blouse ruched up like the folds of a bloodhound. Her thick black hair had been permed into a dandelion of frizzy curls, as if her head had been pumped full of static electricity. When I'd last seen Linda, she had looked wan and bloated, like a teabag left too long to steep in lukewarm water. Now she was back in wholesome star-volleyball-player shape. Like Mom, she seemed almost too happy.

"Sit down, Linda. Nonna Peppy is coming for dinner," fussed Mom as she set the table. "I want to have a little family conference before she gets here."

"Isn't Nonno Zin coming with her?" I asked.

All three of them looked at me with obvious surprise.

"Debbie, you've definitely had too much sun," said Dad.

From the conversation that followed, I learned that Nonno Zinio had passed away. Over time, I would eventually piece together the rest of the story as my family rehashed the tragedy for dinner guests: not long after Linda and Mom had retreated to Toronto, Dad found Nonno Zinio in the wine cellar, so eaten up by cancer that his body looked like a puddle of clothes on the floor. Nonna Peppy had been living alone next door ever since. She insisted on setting a place for Nonno Zin at every meal, even ladling food onto his plate. Sometimes, she was overheard having conversations with him. Except for old Pepé the Seventh, she had little company. Something had to be done.

Dad pointed out that the wine cellar in Nonna's house no longer served a useful purpose, so why not empty the barrels and turn it into a basement apartment? Nonna would appreciate a little bit of extra income, and the boarder would provide protection and companionship. A university student, perhaps? I sat with my head bowed and listened to this plan, a little lump of grief growing inside me for poor Nonno Zin.

We waited and waited for Nonna Peppy, but she didn't show. Mom finally threw up her hands and slammed the bowl of pasta down on the table.

"See? She knew we were going to try to talk her into something. She's probably over there now, having imaginary conversations with Pop."

They were still arguing over Nonna when a knock rattled the front screen door. Thinking that the Trespasser was about to announce himself, I hurried away from the table to answer the door. It was not the Trespasser standing on the front porch, but a sixteen-year-old John Kendal, looking like a lean, muscular David poised to crush an unseen Goliath lurking in my mother's rose bushes. He had a huge canvas sack full of *Shipman's Corners Examiners* thrown over one shoulder, one hand gripping the canvas strap. The other hand hung beside him, a maimed claw, three fingered, covered in lumpy scar tissue, startling pink in colour. I was almost dizzy with relief: just as Bum Bum had told me it would, Kendal's gruesome wound must have been his get-out-of-jail-free card from the scholarship school.

He smiled at me. "Hi, Deb. Collecting."

I couldn't believe it. Kendal was our paperboy now.

"Hold on," I said and rushed to the kitchen to get the money, relieved that my parents still left it on the windowsill. As Kendal pocketed the change, he leaned closer to me and said in a low voice, "It's finally over with Angie."

"Really?" I said. "Wow!"

I crossed my arms over my embarrassment of breasts, wondering what I was supposed to say next. The only Angie I knew was Angie Petrone, a Z Street girl who was older than Linda and had dropped out of St. Dismas in grade nine. I used to see her in her rubber apron and headscarf, smoking a cigarette while she waited at the bus stop to go to work at the canning factory.

Kendal was frowning. "I thought you'd be happy, Debbie."

Finally! A clue. Happiness! Over a breakup with Angie Petrone! (What had been going on between Kendal, Angie and me for the last year and a half, I wondered.)

I gave an unconvincing little laugh. "I'm super-happy for you, Kendal! Why wouldn't I be? Angie was all wrong for you."

Kendal fiddled awkwardly with his canvas bag. "Since I'm a free man now, want to meet up with me at Cresswell's?"

I nodded, a bit stunned at this unexpected turn of events.

"Great. Tomorrow around three. Bring any comics you want to sell, and we'll see how much we can wring out of the old dickhead," said Kendal, handing me a little ticket stamped with PAID IN FULL WEEK OF JUNE 30, 1971.

I watched Kendal head down the walk, then turn and give me a wave and a grin. I smiled and waved back. That's when it struck me: Kendal actually *liked* me. As in *like*, liked. Like *girl-boy* like. Even in this gross, stupid body with breasts sticking out all over the place.

When I went back into the kitchen, my family was still chewing over Nonna Peppy's future while Mom put the salad on the table. I sat down, feeling that, despite the Trespasser's claims, I was destined to live the simple life of a precocious small-town teenager who had been pitched through time like a speeding softball.

"It's settled then. We'll advertise for a boarder," said Dad, tucking a napkin into the neck of his denim shirt.

"Cresswell's is a good place to advertise for a renter," suggested Linda. "Debbie, you're always going there for comics. Why don't you stick up a sign tomorrow?"

"Happy to," I said. As Sputnik Chick would tell the world: there are no coincidences.

Mom reached over and refilled my glass with Sparkling Sparrow Grape Drink.

"Drink up, *cara*, it's good for you," she urged.

I'd already finished one glass but quickly downed another. It tasted super-good. And even though the grape drink was non-alcoholic, I was suddenly more relaxed and happier than I could remember feeling in a long, long time.

three
Jesus Weirdo Superstar

I might have changed over two years, but Cresswell's hadn't. Same crappy junk on the shelves. Same dandruff on Cressie's ratty cardigan. Same wad of masking tape holding his glasses together over the bridge of his nose. Same teetering walls of boxes full of comic books.

I handed Cressie my BASEMENT APARTMENT FOR RENT sign and Kendal plunked down our combined collection of comics. I'd found a stash in my room, under the bed, including a humiliating number of *Artie* and *Betty & Velma* comics, a few tattered copies of *Classics Illustrated* — Prince Braveheart and the like — and two years' worth of *Wonder Woman* issues. Sadly, they'd reinvented her origin story yet again by taking away all her powers and sticking her in a mod clothing boutique to solve crimes, true-detective style. Even her distinctive costume was gone. She was just a brunette in go-go boots now. It made me sad to see how she'd been diminished.

"Okay if we hang around and browse, Cressie?" asked Kendal as he counted our earnings.

"Knock yourself out, but if I catch you stealing anything, I'll cut off your nuts," muttered Cressie to Kendal, dumping my *Wonder Woman* and *Betty & Velma* comics into a box marked ALL GENRES/TITS & ASS. "Hey, man, anyone ever tell you how much you look like that guy on *Cool, Black and Dangerous?* Must be why all the white chicks are hot for you."

As if to prove Cressie's point, I felt a rush of embarrassed heat creeping up my face to my scalp.

"Fuck off, douchebag," muttered Kendal, just loud enough for me to hear, as he took my hand and walked me away from the counter.

We made our way through an aisle piled so high with junk that we had to walk sideways, past a shelf crammed with noisy jewellery music boxes; it looked like a ballerina insane asylum with little mechanical dancers twirling and leaping to tinny versions of the *Blue Danube* and *Swan Lake*, all playing at the same time. Beside them, a jumble of walking dolls lay on top of one another, their vinyl arms outstretched, glassy eyes wide, stiff plastic legs stuck in the air. I tried not to look at their little pink mouths, permanently pursed in the shape of an O.

Kendal and I settled down on the dusty linoleum in an aisle marked WEIRD STUFF. The comics in this part of the store weren't just second-hand *Lemurman* comics but obscure titles, a lot of them going back to the '50s, some run off on Gestetners and stapled together by hand. There were hot-rod comics, horror, monster, even religious comics. If you looked hard enough, you might find some sexy, subversive stuff, too, like the ones Cressie imported (or, more likely, smuggled) up from California, like *Zapruder!* and *Mr. Naturally* and *Kurt the Cat.*

Mixed up with WEIRD STUFF, I found a year-old copy of the tabloid *National Eavesdropper*, either misfiled or mistaken for a comic book. On the front cover, Elizabeth Taylor and Debbie Reynolds were shown together — in a clearly doctored photograph, since the two of them wouldn't have been caught dead posing for a picture at the same time. Liz Taylor was in a red sequined dress, her breasts like two missiles. Debbie Reynolds was wearing a gingham middy blouse, knotted hillbilly-style over her bare torso. The headline said: "DEBBIE AND LIZ REVEAL ALL! Including beauty and weight-loss tips."

While Kendal poked around in the boxes of comics, I scanned the weight-loss tips. Debbie Reynolds swore by fresh air, exercise and a can-do attitude. Liz Taylor preferred purging. I read her method with interest. She relied on the supervision of a noted Viennese physician, but her basic methodology sounded easy enough. Eat, toss your cookies, repeat.

"Debbie, check this out!" Kendal had yanked out a box marked PROPAGANDA and pulled out a comic called COMMUNIST MENACE IN PLEASANT VALLEY USA! On the cover, families ran out of burning houses, the aproned mothers screaming, the fathers shot dead by dark silhouettes of figures in army helmets. The story was about a typical middle-American town taken over by Communists. At first, the small-town population foolishly tried to make the best of it, believing that everything would be fine under their Soviet rulers, as long as they didn't talk about politics. "Better red than dead," said the town's mayor. He was wrong, of course: the Commies turned churches into henhouses and pigsties and burned down office buildings and banks. The capitalist factory owners were strung up in the town square as an example. Before you knew it, the mothers were being worked to death in tractor factories, their children brainwashed to squeal to the secret police if anyone in the family showed signs of counter-revolutionary activity. But the darkest fate was reserved for the fathers, who all disappeared overnight. Families were told that the men were sent to work on farms that would provide food for the people in the cities. Turned out the men had been taken to planned family centres where they were forced to impregnate American women who looked like versions of Elke Sommer — blonde, tall and beautiful.

Kendal shook his head when we got to that part. "Those guys get a comfortable bed and three squares a day, just for making out with a bunch of blondes? If that's Communism, I'd be interested in joining the Party."

"I doubt the girls like it," I pointed out. "Looks like they have to pop out one baby after another 'til they drop. Doesn't sound like much of a life."

"It's a lot like some families in Shipman's Corners," Kendal said.

We went back to reading.

I was right: the girls' only job was to remain pregnant in order to produce more workers. Every baby was fathered by a different man and raised communally in order to break down capitalist family structures and promote Free Love.

One page showed a barracks of beautiful young women with big tummies, sitting around knitting, smoking and reading *Das Kapital*. One girl had fallen in love with a widowed father, and he with her, and she begged the boss of the barracks, a mannish-looking woman named Klebb, to let her run away with him. Instead, they took the pregnant girl to a prison and kept her locked up. They didn't show the birth, of course, but the girl's cries of "AHHHH! Someone, please help me!" were drawn in ghostly letters, drifting through the bars of her solitary confinement cell. Outside, a female prison guard peered through the tiny cell window, a lone tear rolling down her cheek. When Klebb finally came to the prison to get the girl, she was curled up in a corner of the cell, weeping over a pathetic little bundle in her arms. "Are you quite recovered?" demanded Klebb coldly, and the girl whimpered, "My baby is dead." And the evil Klebb said, "Good! You were too attached to the infant.

I'll take you back to the production centre immediately — you'll soon be ready to give us more workers. A new man is waiting to produce with you now." And the girl said: "No . . . no . . . NO!" On the last page, there was a close-up drawing of the girl's eyes looking crazy, and the words — "THE END?"

I stared and stared at that page and wondered if that's what it had been like for Linda, waiting to give birth to Billy's baby, a story that seemed oddly similar to the one in *The Communist Menace*.

Kendal and I were interrupted in our reading by Cressie's voice at the cash. "Sorry, son. You boys are coming through here all the time, but I got no work. I haven't been able to afford help since 1952."

I peered down the long tunnel of the cluttered aisle and saw the back of the man Cressie was talking to. He wore a dashiki, tattered jeans and brown wavy hair down to his shoulders, like Jesus.

"I'm not here seeking gainful employment, man. I have a business deal to propose. You're a pawnbroker, I assume."

"Some call me that," said Cressie slowly, scratching the bald patch on the back of his head. "What you got for me, son?"

"A mechanism for safekeeping. I'll be back for it."

"Heard that one before," snorted Cressie.

I watched Jesus rummage in a little hobo pack, but he didn't pull anything out right away. "You a vet, Cresswell?" he asked.

The expression on Cressie's face changed to one of suspicion. "I got drafted all right, but before I could report, boom, they dropped the A-bomb and the show was over. Biggest disappointment of my life."

"Korea? New Zealand? Or one of the other Domino wars?" asked Jesus softly.

Cressie shook his head. "No draft in Canusa since Doubleyou

Doubleyou Two, 'cept for building bombs at ShipCo. What's this about?"

Jesus looked back and forth theatrically, like an actor on stage. "You just seem like the kind of guy who might have seen action. Anyone else in the shop?"

"Nah. Well, yeah, couple of kids in the back looking at comic books. No one to speak of."

I was lying flat on my stomach beside Kendal, *The Communist Menace* spread on the floor in front of us. We looked at each other. Kendal put a finger to his lips.

Jesus pulled something out of his bag and handed it to Cressie: a twisted pigtail of shiny metal, the size of a loaf of rye bread, coppery in colour. It looked like a giant Slinky that had been pulled apart and welded so that the springy bits wouldn't go back together.

"What the hell is this?" enquired Cressie, turning the copper pigtail over and over.

"It's a solenoid, obviously. Don't dick me around," answered Jesus.

"Oh, yeah," said Cressie, who didn't like anyone to have one over on him. "Just haven't had one in the shop for a while. What the hell does it do, again?"

Jesus put his hands on his hips and bent backwards slightly, shimmying back and forth, as if trying to work out a kink in his back. "It's an electromagnetic transducer."

"Right," said Cressie, nodding.

"I'd suggest keeping it behind the counter instead of out on the shelf. Wouldn't want it to fall into the wrong hands."

Cressie continued examining it. "What you want for it?"

"A hundred."

Cressie snorted. "You think this is the fucking Crown Jewels or something? I'll give you ten."

"Fifty," said Jesus. "You and I both know it's worth a shit-load more than that, so any more crap out of you and I'll take my business elsewhere, man."

"Forty. Final offer."

"Outstanding."

The two shook hands. Cressie opened the cash drawer and counted out the bills.

"You drive a hard bargain, Cresswell," said Jesus, gathering his money.

Cressie wrote out a pawn chit and Jesus slipped it carefully into a wallet that he took from his jeans pocket. I was surprised by that wallet, made of clean black leather as if it was brand new. It didn't seem like the type of thing Jesus would carry.

"I can't guarantee it'll be here when you come back for it," said Cressie, packing up the electronic pigtail in a battered Florsheim shoebox. "I get people in here looking for all sorts of shit."

Cressie was slipping the box onto the highest shelf beyond the cash when the sudden rising-falling WAHHHH of the town's air-raid siren hit the shop like a tidal wave.

When Jesus spun around, I got a clear view of his face. His eyes were covered by a pair of black sunglasses, the kind test pilots wear, but his face showed signs of sun damage: pink peeling burns with patches of tender-looking new skin. He looked like a very young version of the Trespasser, who, I knew, could show up at any age.

Had he made the jump, after all? Or was this just another version of him, dropping in from the future? Would he even know who I was? I figured the best course action was to watch and wait.

"What the hell's going on?" he shouted at Cressie.

Cressie waved his hands reassuringly. "Simmer down, it's just a malfunction. Happens all the time." Before he had finished his explanation, the siren trailed off with a groan like a dying hippo. The school caretaker must have gone up on the roof and pulled the plug. Hand on chest, the Trespasser swayed and slumped against Cressie's counter.

"You look like you seen a ghost," said Cressie, grabbing the Trespasser's arm — I couldn't tell whether he was trying to prop him up or push him out. "You gonna have a heart attack, go have it somewhere else."

The Trespasser snapped his head from side to side, as if trying to get water out of his ears, and shrugged off Cressie's hand. "Fucking siren, I thought it was World War Three starting ahead of schedule." He straightened himself and slung his backpack over one shoulder. The bell over the door chinkled as he walked out.

Kendal and I got up off the floor and brushed the grit from our legs. Through the big front window of Cressie's store, we could see the Trespasser climbing into a blue Cutlass that looked as if it had been through a war. The paint was scratched and burned away, exposing patches of rust-coloured metal. Ragged holes gaped where the passenger-side door handles had been torn off. He adjusted his rear-view, then peeled away from the curb with a squeal of his tires.

"Know what an electromagnetic transducer is?" asked Kendal.

I shook my head. "I'd love to find out."

"Let's give him a tail," said Kendal.

* * *

We left Cressie's without saying goodbye and pedalled our bikes along the main street. When we turned a corner and coasted up behind a battered blue Cutlass with Massachusetts plates, *Led Zeppelin II* throbbing out of the windows, Kendal looked back at me over his shoulder as if to say, *bingo*.

A sleek, black Mustang with a spoiler on the hood and New York plates pulled up behind the Cutlass. A woman wearing a white winged nurse's cap was behind the wheel.

The light turned green. Despite its beaten-up body, the Cutlass accelerated like a souped-up hot rod, as if the Trespasser knew someone was tailing him. Kendal stood up on his pedals and pumped his legs so fast, I fell farther and farther behind. As the Cutlass approached an amber light, its engine revved and it peeled through the intersection, tires squealing.

Kendal sailed through the red light — I shouted "Watch out!" as a driver swerved to miss him, giving Kendal the finger and a long blast on the horn. Kendal was still trying to gain on the Cutlass when the black Mustang sped past, veering into the curb lane and cutting him off. Kendal slammed into the Mustang's back bumper, his bike collapsing beneath him like a losing move in KerPlunk. The Mustang paused for a second, engine idling, then tore off, leaving Kendal lying in the street on top of the junk pile that had been his bike. I stood straddling my crossbar, hands over my mouth. The last glimpse I had of the hit-and-runner was a license plate ending in XXX. Kendal was draped over his broken bike like a rag.

"Debbie!" called a voice. I turned to see Sandy standing outside the Royal Bank of Canusa in a miniskirt, high heels and a shiny polyester blouse, her dark hair frosted with blonde streaks and her face made up like a fashion model. She would have been sixteen but looked about twenty, as gorgeous as the breeding-stock girls in *The Communist Menace*. Beside her, her father, Mr. Holub, aka Mr. Capitalismo, was clutching a sheaf of papers and staring at the scene of the accident.

"We help?" he asked.

The three of us ran down the street to where Kendal was starting to pick himself out of a pretzel of steel, aluminum and rubber.

four
Collateral Damage

"Mom's going to kill me," Kendal said, a cold can of pop pressed to the bridge of his bloody nose.

"You lucky boy. *Very* lucky." Mr. Holub pounded the steering wheel with his fist for emphasis. "This country, they drive like crazy men. Woman drivers even worse, like this one who try run you over."

Sandy, her slim arm draped elegantly across the seat, turned to look at Kendal. "When your mom hears what happened, she'll just be happy you're not seriously hurt."

"She'll be happy, right up until she kills me. No bike, no paper route, no money."

"Strawberry harvest starts in a week," Sandy said.

Kendal groaned. "That's not a job. That's slavery."

He was not wrong. Fruit picking was scraping the bottom of the barrel, but girls in Shipman's Corners couldn't find anything better. Most boys got better-paying summer jobs on a construction crew or on an assembly line at ShipCo, but they had to have family connections. Without a father, and with one weak hand, Kendal was left with the same poorly paid jobs as the girls.

I started to reach for Kendal's good hand, but drew back when I realized that under the pop can, his gaze was on Sandy.

"Why are you so dressed up, Sandy?" I asked her, trying not to let an edge of jealousy creep into my voice.

"I was helping Dad talk to the bank about a business loan. Translating, between him and the bank manager."

"Never heard of a bank open on a Saturday," said Kendal.

Sandy flipped her long hair in a maddeningly fetching manner. "A friend of my mom's works as a teller. She talked the manager into seeing Dad on the weekend 'cause he's working nights. Not that it did him any good. They wanted him to have something called 'collateral.'"

"What's that?" I asked.

"Money. Also known as 'capital,'" supplied Kendal. "As in, *Das Kapital.*"

"They want you to have money *before* they'll lend you money?" I said. "That's nuts."

Now Sandy turned to look at me. "How did your dad get the capital for the winery, Debbie?"

Kendal snorted from under the pop can. "Read the label, Sandy. Sparkling Sparrow Estates Wines is a division of ShipCo. They're the ones who bankrolled Mr. Biondi."

That's when I finally understood that Dad wasn't a field hand for Sparkling Sparrow Estate Wines. He *ran* it. No wonder we could afford a Maytag dishwasher. Pretty much everyone in town drank Sparkling Sparrow's sweet plonk; it was cheap and, because of its high sugar content, staggeringly potent. Even the non-alcoholic grape drink was intoxicating. From what I'd seen so far, plonk in all its forms had grown in popularity over the past year and a half.

"Sorry, Sandy, I don't know anything about Dad's business," I said, thinking how ironic it was that Mr. Capitalismo couldn't get capital.

"Sandy, your dad must be doing okay, selling his anti-radiation suits," Kendal said. "The way the SALT talks are going, looks like we might need them soon."

Sandy shook her head. "He sold the rights to them a long time ago for a lot less than they're worth. Now he has a new idea: a Ukrainian fast food restaurant. Like McDonald's, but with perogies and borscht."

Mr. Holub drove us all the way to Z Street. Kendal's house was still in better shape than most of the other places in the neighbourhood. The shack next door looked abandoned, its broken windows boarded over. It was clear that Bum Bum didn't live there anymore.

As Kendal unlocked his front door, I remembered the last time I'd been there, that morning Dad's tire blew and the Trespasser had appeared in the Z-Lands. I'd never gone farther than the front stoop. I wondered if I'd been here since then.

I stepped into a room with pale grey walls and a carpet of many colours. A Persian rug — I'd only ever seen one in the movies. The walls were covered with art: real oil paintings, the brushstrokes thick and angry-looking. Except for a school trip to a museum in Toronto, I'd never seen so many paintings in one room before. A few were boring old flower arrangements and bowls of fruit, but there was one of a horse standing under a tree, scrotum dangling, that beat anything in the Walter Foster *How to Draw* books. Another was a rusty old saltie tied up at a bollard. The biggest, and best, were two portraits: one of Dr. Martin Luther King in the prison uniform he was wearing when he was assassinated in his jail cell, waving his *Words, Not War* manifesto over his head. The other was the face of a boy — Kendal, as a kid. His large, serious eyes stared at me in a way I found unsettling, especially with Kendal himself standing right beside me.

Along with all the paintings, a handmade abstract crucifix hung on the wall. Instead of an emaciated half-naked body, Christ was suggested by a twisted chunk of dark wood. It was the only crucifix in Kendal's house — unlike mine, where Christ, writhing in agony and crowned in thorns, was nailed up in every room.

On a coffee table stood a cluster of framed black-and-white photographs — in one, a smiling man in a ShipCo enlistee cap. I thought it was Kendal, until I realized it had to be his dead father, Dave Kendal.

"Have a seat. Want something to drink? Pop? Juice?" asked Kendal.

"Got any Sparkling Sparrow Grape Drink?" I asked.

Kendal grinned at me. "No offence, but we still don't buy any of your dad's stuff. Mom wants me to keep a clear head."

"Okay, then. Whatever you've got."

I dropped into the soft blue corduroy couch and watched Kendal disappear into the kitchen. I liked this peaceful little house. Everything was out in the open. I couldn't imagine anyone keeping secrets here.

"What do you think of the new one?" called Kendal from the kitchen.

I looked around me: new *what?* It had to be one of the paintings. If so, which one? Was I supposed to love it or hate it? Since they all looked pretty good to me, I yelled back. "I love it."

"Me too — I told Mom it's one of her best."

That answered one question: the artist was Mrs. Kendal. Trying to pretend I knew what was going on all the time was like trying to fit together a 1,000-piece jigsaw puzzle with half the pieces missing.

We sat side by side on the sofa. Kendal popped open the Fanta with his damaged hand. His thumb and index finger were intact; the stumps of his other fingers gripped the can like a claw. I wanted to touch the thick scar tissue over his knuckles. I wondered if Debbie-of-1971 had ever done that.

"Why do you keep staring at my paw?" he asked.

That's what he called it — his paw. I shrugged and lifted a Bugle to my mouth, the cheese flavouring staining my fingers orange.

"I was just thinking how well you use that hand," I said.

"Angie said I use 'em both pretty well," said Kendal, pouring the soda.

Angie again. I tried to think of a way to find out what had happened with her.

"Must have been hard, breaking up with her," I hinted.

Kendal shrugged indifferently. "Yeah, I guess. Not that it was really my decision." He slumped back into the sofa cushions, not meeting my eyes. "Some big shot at ShipCo made her an offer. Senior Snugglegirl. I said no way was I sharing her. I said it's ShipCo or me. She picked ShipCo. Now she's the number one fuckpuppy for the top ShipCo brass. No one lower than the lieutenant-management level. Plus, the trips, clothes, parties, good drugs. And all the plonk she can guzzle."

I laid my hand on top of Kendal's bad one. "I'm sorry."

"No, you're not. Neither am I. Angie and I should've been finished with each other a long time ago. We want different things. With her, it's always about money."

"What about you?" I asked. "What do you want?"

Kendal lifted his hands as if trying to pull an answer out of the air.

"It'll sound stupid."

"Try me."

Kendal stood and turned on the TV. He gave me a look — as if he was about to share a secret — then changed the channel to a football game, turning up the volume so high that the house shook. Dropping back onto the couch beside me, he put his elbows on his knees and looked into my face. I practically had to read his lips to tell what he was saying over the roar of the crowd.

"I want to finish what my father was trying to start when he died," he said. "Changing things for folks in the Z-Lands. Everyone in this neighbourhood is sick, or poor, or a plonkhead. The surplus girls think their only way out is to fuck an executive. The surplus boys get sent on a one-way trip to the moon. The surplus Twisties get rounded up for drug trials — ShipCo Pharma pays them a few bucks to let them try out new heart meds before the managers take them. And they're always telling us the world is going to blow up, without even trying to make peace with the enemy. It's as if they *like* being at constant war. Someone has to change all that, or the planet won't survive. I feel like I could be the guy. Somebody's got to wake people up."

Kendal lowered the TV to its normal volume. We sat silently, side by side, watching the Green Bay quarterback get sacked. It struck me how much Kendal sounded like Billy.

"Kendal, are you telling me that you were mixed up with the Yammers?"

He looked up at me in alarm and shook his head, pointing to what I'd thought was a transistor radio on the side table — a SHIPCO GUARDIAN ANGEL, according to the brand name on its face, along with the words, *What have you got to hide?* The Guardian Angel was a reverse radio.

Someone was eavesdropping on us. I had the same sick, scared feeling I had when I was strapped into the Glow-in-the-Dark Pat Boone Lie Detector.

"The Yammers are a myth," Kendal said loudly. "Everyone knows that."

As he said this, he took a scratch pad and pencil from under the ShipCo Guardian Angel and wrote:

I'LL SWITCH THE SUBJECT TO COMICS.

DRIVES THEM CRAZY!

He draped his arm on the seat behind me. "I have something special to show you. A banned comic that Cressie misfiled. It was too hot for the Comics Code so they had to stop the print run, but a few got through."

I laughed. "Cressie misfiled something? That doesn't sound like him."

"Yeah, well, it's pretty sexy stuff, and anything to do with real chicks makes Cressie uncomfortable," said Kendal, looking at the floor. I was starting to think real chicks made Kendal a little uncomfortable, too. "Let me get it — the girl in it kind of reminds me of you."

He pushed open a folding door, leading to his bedroom. Despite what I thought about the lack of secrets in Kendal's house, he had done a great job of hiding the September 1967 issue of *Agents of V.E.N.G.E.A.N.C.E.*, featuring Captain Kyle Crusher and the luscious European bombshell, Contessina Doloria di Largo: it was stashed under a floorboard inside his closet. Kendal brought the comic into the living room and sat beside me on the couch, turning the pages on our knees.

The Contessina was a raven-haired, blue-eyed aristocrat-turned-crime fighter, dressed in something that looked like a cross between a ballet leotard and a bikini. The outfit was so form-fitting, it was as if she'd been drawn naked, with splashes of colour strategically added to suggest clothing. Under the clingy material, the high, proud fishbowls of her braless breasts defied gravity, her nipples protruding like gun muzzles. Her waist tapered to the slender stem of a wineglass, flaring into rounded hips and athletic thighs. I wondered how she managed to keep such a tiny waist while the rest of her body looked so pumped up. Strong. The kind of body you had to have to save the world.

"I look like her?" I said in amazement.

"Yeah," said Kendal. "Her face, anyway."

Her face, yeah, of course, I thought sadly. I could never have a body like hers. In one panel, the Contessina executed a breathtaking kick to one bad guy's groin with a stiletto-heeled boot and a right cross to another's jaw. A few pages later, she was alone with Kyle Crusher in his secret-agent bachelor pad.

Panel 1: a close-up of Crusher taking the phone off the hook — the universal sign of Do Not Disturb — while in the deep background, the Contessina teeters on a barstool, unzipping a boot.

Panel 2: the Contessina's naked back, shown from behind. She is kneeling in front of Crusher, who towers over her, fists clenched. Crusher's thought bubble: *My God she's beautiful . . . not sure I can control myself.*

"This is where it starts getting dirty," warned Kendal.

Impatient wings fluttered inside my stomach. But before he had a chance to turn the page, the front door opened. Mrs. Kendal stood before us in the entranceway, her arms full of A&P bags. Her mouth opened slightly when she saw me, but I couldn't see the look in her eyes because she was wearing sunglasses.

"Mom," said Kendal flatly, as if stating a fact.

"Hello there, Mrs. Kendal," I said, trying to sound innocent, but she wasn't falling for it. She took off her sunglasses and fixed me with a *What are you doing to my son?* look.

"Debbie Biondi. What are you doing here?" When she caught sight of Kendal's face, she almost dropped her grocery bags. "John, what happened to you? Have you been in a fight?"

"Fell off my bike. It's not as bad as it looks," he muttered, taking the bags out of her arms.

Kendal glanced at me, then his mother, as he carried the groceries into the kitchen, leaving the two of us to stare at one another. I tried to smile, but the muscles in my face kept jumping around. I had never seen Mrs. Kendal in anything but the grey suit and hat she worked in or a church dress. That day she was wearing a pair of trousers — jeans, actually — a crisp white shirt and a pair of leather sandals. She looked a million years younger than my mom, although they were probably the same age.

"I like your new painting, Mrs. Kendal," I said.

"Thank you." Still no smile.

My face flushed and I dropped my eyes, pretending to examine my shoelaces. What did Mrs. Kendal think we'd been doing? Rolling all over her pretty blue couch, feeling each other up? Not that I would have minded. Catching her get-the-hell-out-now vibe, I mumbled my goodbyes.

Out in the alleyway, Kendal rolled my bike from behind the garbage cans. I straddled the crossbar and held out the comic book.

He shook his head. "Keep it."

"I'm sorry your mom doesn't like me," I said.

"She just worries that I'm going to get into trouble again," he said. "It was the same thing with Angie."

Leaning over my handlebars, in the gloom of the passage-way, with his disapproving mom on one side of the thin wall, and the towering home church of Harriet Tubman, heroine of the Underground Railroad, on the other, Kendal kissed me. His mouth tasted enticingly of artificial orange flavouring and Bugles. Kyle Crusher and the Contessina fell out of my hands.

I touched Kendal's face. He picked up the comic and

placed it in my bike carrier. Resting his forehead against mine, he said, "How about I borrow a bike and drop by your house tomorrow? Would your folks be okay with that?"

I shrugged. "I don't care if they are or they aren't. Just come."

We stood together, our tongues exploring the sprinklings of artificial cheese in each other's mouth. Eventually, we untangled ourselves from one another and I headed home.

I passed the billboard at the corner of Z Street and Fermi Road that used to be graffitied with the words SHIPCO KILLS but was now papered over with an ad for Sparkling Sparrow Rosé Wine: *Pink, Plonk, Party Time!*

As I cycled past the giant face of a girl in pink sunglasses puckering up for a kiss, I imagined the unspeakable things the Contessina and Kyle Crusher were doing to one another in my bike carrier. Thinking about their entwined crime fighter bodies distracted me so much that I didn't notice the hum of a well-tuned car engine. As the car sped up to pass me, I recognized the Mustang that had hit Kendal. Black paint job, spoiler, New York plates. In the dashboard glow, I caught a glimpse of the driver's blonde hair under a white nurse's cap. She didn't even turn her head.

I almost steered into the drainage ditch as the car accelerated. In the distance, the Mustang's taillights signalled a turn, just before it vanished into the night.

five
Breakfast on Planet of the Mothers

Late the next morning in my sunny bedroom, I awoke to the faraway sound of a ringing phone and Mom's distant *Hello?*

I tried to rub the blur out of my eyes, then remembered: I wore glasses now. My wire frames were staring at me from the night table. I put them on and the room was thrown into crisp focus.

Something had changed overnight. The air in my bedroom seemed fresher. The traffic noises drifting in through my window, quieter. Instead of the revving of engines, I heard birdsong. I lay back on my pillow and stretched my arms luxuriously.

I hoped the Trespasser would never, ever turn up. It was summertime. My family was rich. And I was in love.

Maybe my time hop really was temporary amnesia caused by heat stroke. Maybe everything I thought I remembered — the Trespasser at the dentist's office, the sudden jump from childhood to womanhood — were mirages, like Bugs Bunny seeing an oasis in the desert when he took a wrong turn at Albuquerque.

Even if I really had been thrown forward in time, why did I have to be the one to save the world? Who said it even needed saving?

I rolled on my side to look at Linda's bed. Empty. I wrapped myself in my pink robe and padded barefoot down the hall, past the wall nook where the plaster Virgin stood sentinel in front of the telephone table, her hands spreading open her blue robe as if to say, *Behold! Nothing to hide here, kid, how about you?*

When the phone rang, Mary's lowered eyes caught mine.

Go on, what are you waiting for — pick it up!

I hesitated. What if it was the Trespasser, calling to coax me out of this pleasant state of inertia to do who-knew-what? Cautiously, I lifted the receiver.

"Hello?"

"Tell me everything — and don't leave anything out!"

"Hi, Sandy," I said, yawning and scratching under my breasts. I was finding my 36Bs annoyingly itchy.

"I am so jealous. Kendal's so gorgeous and sweet and smart. Not that my folks would ever let me go out with a coloured guy."

I felt a glug of queasiness at the word *coloured*.

"Are you guys in love?" she asked.

"I guess so," I answered, glancing at the kitchen door where I suspected my mother hovered.

"Someone's listening?"

"You could say that."

"Call me back on an extension. I've got something important to ask you."

With a glance at the Virgin's placid face, I hung up and headed down the basement stairs to where Dad had installed an extension phone in his workshop in 1969. It was still there. I dialled Sandy's number.

"Me again," I said when she answered. "Not much to tell about Kendal, except he's coming over."

"Your parents are going to freak," said Sandy.

"I don't care if they do," I answered.

"I knew he'd dump that slut Angie for you," Sandy said. "We can talk more when you come with us to Niagara Falls.

My dad set up a meeting with a loan shark for next Saturday at Table Rock House. We want you to come along."

"What's a loan shark?" I asked.

"Like a bank, except it's just one guy. Larry Kowalchuck. He told Dad to bring some cute girls to the meeting. Can you come?"

I said yes, not thinking too hard about why Larry the Loan Shark would want girls around while he was doing business.

"Hey, Sandy — how long have I been wearing glasses?"

I heard a puzzled silence on the line, followed by laughter. "You don't remember how long you've worn glasses? Man, oh, man, that boy really does have you going in circles."

"So, tell me," I insisted.

"I dunno. Six months, maybe? Which reminds me: when you come to the Falls, wear your contact lenses, okay?"

"I wear contact lenses?"

Sandy laughed again. "You've got it bad, girl. Catch you later."

I hung up the phone and was about to go back upstairs when I noticed a dull green metal door with a recessed latch set into the wall where a weathered wood door used to open into the cold cellar. I pulled at the latch, expecting it to be locked. The door slid to the side on a well-oiled track.

Inside: darkness. I was scrabbling on the interior wall, feeling for a light switch, when a fluorescent tube buzzed to life, illuminating five bodies sitting erect on white laminated stools, hands on their knees. A family of metal and plastic people, relaxing in the darkness as if waiting for a movie to start.

My heart pounding, I stepped in to look at them.

They weren't bodies, but full body suits — a lot like space suits, complete with face visors, helmets, gauntlets and boots. One black suit, two grey, one pink, one violet, each one with a small copper plate on its chest, inscribed with a name: DAD. MOM. NONNA. LINDA. DEBBIE.

The violet suit was mine. It seemed way too big until I remembered: in the blink of an eye, I had grown a whole new body.

Anti-radiation suits, one for every family member. The next inevitable step in personal survival in the event of a nuclear attack. Forget about bomb shelters: in an anti-rad suit, you were free to move around in an irradiated world for weeks, until fallout levels dropped enough to breathe the air. At least, that was the way Mr. Capitalismo had always described them as he tinkered with the idea of turning diving suits into radiation shelters. No one had taken him seriously in 1969, but Dad apparently did now. Five family members, five suits: he must have changed his mind about the pointlessness of survival of the fittest after a nuclear war.

I noticed that the bum of each suit was connected to a thick white hose that led into a metal box marked WASTE. Behind the suits, floor-to-ceiling shelves held boxes of freeze-dried food labelled by type, along with row after row of Sparkling Sparrow bottles. Red and white plonk, sparkling rosé and mock champagne. This wasn't a bomb shelter, but a nutrition and elimination room. As well as a place to get shitfaced drunk, if all else failed. I slid the door closed and shuffled upstairs to the kitchen.

Mom stood at the sink, singing along with a song on the radio. *Tie a mellow ribbon round pokey old me . . .*

She turned and looked at me. Smiled. Said, "Eggs for breakfast?"

"Sunny side up, please. Where are Dad and Linda?"

"They're showing Nonna's basement to some student who showed up at the door," said Mom, taking a carton of eggs from the fridge. "Dad says the guy sounded like he'd make a good tenant."

I sat down at the table and listened to the sizzle of the skillet and the humming of my mysteriously happy mother. My eyes slid to the crisp bow on the back of her harvest gold apron. The perfect curls in her steel grey hair. Her blindingly white tennis shoes. What planet had I been teleported to?

Mom placed a plate of eggs in front of me with a dollop of ketchup and buttered white toast points on the side. Just the way I used to like it, before I decided to purge away my weight the way Elizabeth Taylor did. I nibbled the crust as Mom sat down across from me at the table and folded her hands.

"So, what's this I hear about you and the paperboy?"

I stopped mid-nibble. "What?"

She scraped a splotch of dried tomato sauce off the edge of my placemat with her thumbnail, one of a set of four printed with famous paintings, a free gift with her annual subscription to *Canusa Homemaker*. I was eating off Van Gogh's *Sunflowers*.

"Bea Kendal called first thing," Mom continued. "Said you and her son had been together yesterday. That there was an accident and he was hurt. That she found the two of you on the couch in the house, alone," Mom paused for effect. "She thought Dad and I would want to know."

I shrugged. "Kendal and I met up at Cresswell's to sell comic books. What's wrong with that? Then we went for a bike ride and a car cut him off. I was just making sure he was all right. Besides, the ShipCo Guardian Angel was listening in the whole time I was at his house." I'd lost my appetite. The cooling eggs looked like big googly cartoon eyes staring up at me. "John Kendal is really nice."

"He *is* nice. And his mother is a lovely woman. But they're different from us." Mom glanced at my plate. "Eat your eggs, they're getting cold."

I dipped the sharp end of a toast point in one golden eye. For a moment I thought I could hear it screaming: *Augghhh.*

"I didn't think you and Dad were bigots," I said bluntly.

Mom sat back in her chair. "Your father and I are not prejudiced," she assured me. "How could we be? Look at what we put up with, growing up in this *mangiacake* town. They changed our names. Called us wops and garlic-eaters."

"Exactly. How would you feel if people didn't want you being friends with their kids, just because you're Italian?"

"But *cara*, what if you and John fell in love and got married? Think of the children."

The one remaining intact eye on my plate started dripping golden tears. I stabbed it with a toast point.

"*What* children?" I demanded. "We were talking. Just talking. Are you afraid his sperm's going to jump out of his body and into mine from across the couch? I'm not Linda, you know."

Mom looked away. I had brought up the Topic That Must Not Be Mentioned.

"We'll discuss this later. Go get dressed," she said curtly.

She was just taking away my half-eaten eggs when Dad and Linda walked in with the new tenant.

"And this sleepyhead is our younger daughter," said Dad. "Debbie, this is Benjamin Duffy, but he goes by Duff."

Oh no.

The Trespasser grinned at me, looking much younger than he had in the dentist's office when he'd botched my time hop. His long hair had been freshly clipped and he had changed into a clean but wrinkled white shirt and a pair of khakis so crisply pressed that they were no doubt picked up yesterday at Woolco with some of the money he'd gotten from Cressie. A gold crucifix glinted around his neck. He gave off a whiff of non-threatening religiosity, in an intellectual, folk-singerish sort of way. As if he'd known exactly how to present himself to make my folks trust him. The biggest change, though, was that the middle finger of his left hand didn't end at the knuckle. His hand was intact.

"Hey there, little sister," Duff said, and winked at me.

I stared at his peeling pink face, like the worst sunburn ever. I could smell cinnamon on his breath. He appeared younger than he was on Halloween night in 1969, picking 45s at the candy-store party.

There was no question now. The Trespasser had just hopped back into my life.

The Chronicles of Duff six

"What a coincidence. I just saw you yesterday, coming out of Cresswell's," I said, shaking Duff's hand. He was doing a great job of acting as if we'd never met before.

Duff winked at Dad, the way you do to the parent of a precocious child — trying to show that he had me all figured out.

"There are no coincidences. I saw your father's apartment rental sign at Cresswell's," he said.

"I hope you'll join us for breakfast," said Mom, and she set a place for Duff, right beside Linda. She smiled at him but showed no signs of recognizing him as the man who had argued with Billy at the Halloween party.

When Nonna Peppy toddled into the kitchen with Pepé the Seventh behind her, Dad formally introduced her to Duff as "Mrs. Pitalunga, your landlady." Nonna peered up at Duff through her bifocals, shook his hand and said, "Pleasure to meetcha," but didn't sound pleased at all, until he said, "You sound like you learned English in New York City. Lower East Side, if I'm not mistaken."

Nonna Peppy raised her eyebrows and smiled. "You're psychic. That's right, I'm a New York City girl, but I still like a quiet house."

"Don't worry, Mrs. Pitalunga, I'm the bookish type," said Duff.

161

Mom cleared her throat. "Why don't you tell us about yourself, Mr. Duffy?"

"Call me Duff. Not much to tell. I'm from Concord, Massachusetts. Did an undergraduate degree at Notre Dame."

"Good Catholic university," approved Dad.

Duff acknowledged this with a nod and continued, "I was doing research in graduate school at MIT when my birthdate came up in the draft lottery for the Domino Wars, so here I am in Canusa."

"What kind of research?" asked Linda. I was beginning to notice how intently she watched Duff. Like a beauty pageant contestant mentally undressing the host.

He hesitated. "A little hard to explain, Linda. I was working in a new field, an offshoot of biology and engineering. Robotics, essentially."

Dad waved a hand in the air. "Robots! Hell, St. Dismas Collegiate would snap you up, with or without teacher's training."

"Absolutely," agreed Linda, looking at Duff adoringly.

I sat back in my chair and observed my family. It was as if Duff had put a spell on them. My mom, usually suspicious of strangers until she knew them a decade or two, spooned another serving of fried potatoes and bacon onto his plate without even asking.

"Now we'll have to figure out what to do about those wine barrels in your living space," said Dad. "My father-in-law had about three years' worth of wine stored in them. Bottling it would take weeks, but I hate to just pour it down the drain."

Duff put down his fork and knife and made a little tent with his hands. "Simplest way would be to automate the process: pump the wine out of the barrels and across the yard into your basement for bottling. It's all physics, really. All we need are a few hoses and a pump. We'll need to fill and cork the bottles assembly-line style. It'll probably require at least five of us."

Dad nodded at this. "You, me, Debbie, Linda . . ."

"Don't look at me," said Mom. "The fumes alone would knock me for a loop."

I waved my hand in the air. "John Kendal's looking for work."

"How much would he want?" asked Dad.

"Carlo!" my mother protested. "Don't encourage her."

"Five bucks ought to do it."

"Okay, done. See how fast he can get here," Dad said and looked at Mom. "We need the help. And, frankly, I wouldn't mind having that boy where I can keep an eye on him."

* * *

Kendal borrowed a bike from a neighbour and rode over that afternoon. Even though Dad and Mom had met him at the door many times when he was collecting for his paper route, I made formal introductions.

Dad shook Kendal's hand, glancing at the mutilated one.

"Sure you're up to this? Not sure it'll be easy to bottle one-handed."

I winced at Dad's blunt reference to Kendal's handicap. Kendal just shrugged.

"Long as no one asks me to play the piano, I can use my hand just fine for most things."

Dad laughed. "I remember your father from the plant. I didn't agree with his rabble-rousing, but he was a good guy. Now let's get to work."

Duff got down to the business of emptying the wine barrels using a pump Dad had scavenged when a local machine shop had closed. Linda and I collected as many garden hoses as we could find and screwed them together to make a long rubber snake that would gulp down and regurgitate wine.

Linda and Duff stood at the pump end; Dad, Kendal and I waited at the workbench under the window in our basement with an army of empty wine bottles and Nonno's old corking machine.

"Kendal and I will fill. You cork, Debbie," ordered Dad.

When the wine started flowing, we quickly discovered the problem with Duff's plan — even with two of us bottling and one corking, we couldn't keep up. Within minutes, our clothes were soaked and the thick purple wine overflowed onto the floor, puddling around our shoes. The fumes were making me dizzy.

"Whoa, whoa, whoa," shouted Dad. "Debbie, run next door and tell Duff to shut it down."

"He should try closing off the flow every few minutes so we can catch up," suggested Kendal. "And maybe we should empty the hoses into cooking pots first, then into bottles — we can't work fast enough this way."

Dad nodded. "Just what I was thinking, son."

Son?

I ran next door to tell Duff the new plan. When I returned, it was obvious Dad and Kendal had kept up a stream of conversation, Dad pumping Kendal for information about what he wanted to do with his life. As I clattered down our basement stairs, I heard Kendal say, "I'm thinking of journalism, but my mom wants me to go to law school."

"Law is a good trade for a man," nodded Dad. "You could always write books on the side, like Earl Stanley Gardner."

"*Perry Mason?* I'd rather write stuff like *Fail-Safe*."

Dad nodded. "I'm not one much for fiction but *Fail-Safe* was a page-turner. Scared the hell out of me."

"Think it could really happen? I mean, some glitch causing an accidental nuclear war?" asked Kendal.

"Sure it could happen," says Dad. "More a question of *when* than *if*."

I stood on the stairway, listening. It was a conversation Dad had never had with me. We'd never discussed my career ambitions — never got further than him telling me to keep my marks up.

Once the last bottle of wine had been corked, and we were all sitting around the table in Nonna Peppy's kitchen, Dad poured out glasses for each of us, a bottle of ginger ale handy to cut the sour taste of the local Canusa grapes. The vines were a tough northern variety whose only quality for winemaking was hardiness.

"Saluté," said Dad, raising his glass. "It isn't up to Sparkling Sparrow standards, but not bad for backyard wine, eh?"

Dad took Duff's first- and last-month's rent and headed next door to give Nonna Peppy and Mom a taste of Nonno's final vintage. Meanwhile, Duff, Linda, Kendal and I went downstairs to Duff's new flat, walking from one dark, cramped, airless, earthy-smelling room to another while Linda told Duff about her program at the University of Toronto, where she had just completed her second year.

Duff tipped his head back and cracked his spine the way I'd seen him do at Cressie's. "I miss the academic life. Before my draft card arrived, I was doing a double PhD in genetics and bioengineering."

Linda wrinkled her forehead. "Wow. I'm not even sure what that is."

"I'm not surprised. It won't exist as a course of study 'til the 1980s," said Duff, running his hand through his hair. "You see, Linda, I've come from the future."

seven
Hotter Than Hell

Apparently, Duff's resemblance to Jesus made Linda believe anything he said.

Kendal seemed skeptical. "What *year* did you come from?"

"I was born in 1996," answered Duff. "The year of my hop, adjusted for tidal changes, is 2019. Or rather, *was*. Or maybe, *will be*. Verb tenses are tricky when you're jumping around in time."

Linda did the math. "You're twenty-three," she said, in a tone of voice that implied that this was the perfect age for any man to be.

"So, what's the future like, Duff?" interrupted Kendal, the sarcasm thick in his voice.

"Hotter than hell, man," said Duff, scratching his scalp. "That's how I got these burns. See, I lost my solar armour during a sandstorm in the Great Massachusetts Desert. I figured I'd be burned to death before search-and-rescue found me. No choice but to do an emergency hop. It was the only way for me to get out of the sun fast enough."

Linda stepped closer to him and touched one of his scorched cheeks, causing him to flinch. "I think there's some aloe vera in the medicine cabinet."

Upstairs, seated at the old vinyl-topped kitchen table, Linda dabbed paste from a jar onto Duff's face. The pale green colour made his face look mossy.

"Why's it so hot in 2019, Duff?" I asked. "Will Earth move closer to the sun?"

Duff shook his head. "Your atmosphere is thinning. You just don't know it yet. Five, six or so years from now, the scientists will finally start to catch on and warn people that Earth is warming."

"What's causing the atmosphere to thin out?" Linda asked.

Duff looked at her very sadly. "I don't know if I should tell you this, Linda. It might be too much for you to handle."

"You've got to tell us, Duff," she said.

His blue eyes seemed to be measuring her up. "Sometimes it's best not to know what's ahead of you."

Linda's hands went to her face. "Oh no. They're going to drop the Bomb, aren't they?"

Duff nodded. "Nuclear radiation is going to finish up what your parents' generation started with their so-called Atomic War of Deterrence. Turns out it didn't deter anything except your futures."

Linda put her head down in her arms.

"But wait a minute, wait a minute," protested Kendal. "You said that this was *already* happening. How's that possible if the Bomb isn't going to drop for years?"

"You guys don't get it, do you?" said Duff. "Eight years from now, World War Three will blast out a good chunk of our atmosphere and destroy the protective layer of ozone that keeps the sun from burning the Earth to a crisp. But the warming effect would be observable right now, if someone bothered looking for it. Look, the first atomic bombs were detonated in '45, and there've been megatons of nuclear tests since then. You don't think that has long-term consequences? Not to mention, Nixon's about to start underground testing near the Aleutians. That'll get the Soviets good and pissed off and start us on a road that'll end real badly when they push the button in '79."

"What'll happen then?" I whispered, thinking of how Duff had warned me about the 1979 nuclear war while I was in the dentist's chair.

Duff closed his eyes. "First, firestorms sweep the entire planet. After that, there's the Year of Atomic Rain. Nuclear fallout in the raindrops. Cities are turned into massive grave-yards. New York, Paris, Los Angeles — ghost towns full of the dead and dying. Let's see, what else. Animal extinction. Major crop failures. Anarchy. Birth defects." He opened his eyes and looked around the table at the three of us. "You really want me to go on? You're living in the end times, kids. Enjoy yourselves. By the time I was born — sorry, *will* be born — most of the big cities you know about exist only in the history books. Better see the Big Apple before it collapses into the Atlantic."

I thought of Nonna Peppy, back at our house with Mom, listening to the New York Metropolitan Opera live on the radio while she wiped the plates. She definitely couldn't handle this piece of news.

"I don't get it," persisted Kendal. "You said you were drafted. How does the government even know you exist if you haven't been born yet? Where'd they mail your draft card?"

Linda glanced at Kendal as she rubbed aloe into the backs of Duff's hands. I could tell she was annoyed by Kendal's persistent questions. But Duff stayed cool. "The government knows everything about us, man. Past, present and future. You can time hop but you can't hide. Lots of people do it, trying to skip out on their taxes. They blow all their money in their own time, then jump to a time with lower prices, like this one. That's where the Amazing Kreskin really comes from."

"I knew it!" I said. "Every time he shows up on Johnny

Carson, you can see in his eyes that he knows what's coming. Who else is here from the future, Duff?"

Duff thought about it. "Evel Knievel, Howard Hughes, Dr. Christiaan Barnard, Martin Luther King Jr., until he was assassinated, of course . . . and that guy who bends spoons."

"Uri Geller," supplied Linda.

"Don't girls ever time hop?" I interrupted, thinking of my own short jump forward in time.

"Some, but it's hard on the female reproductive system."

I crossed my arms over my breasts and glared at Duff. He hadn't mentioned this little detail before he'd sent me rocketing through puberty.

Kendal was sitting backwards in a kitchen chair, cowboy-style, staring at Duff.

"What are you going to do next? Go back to 2019?" he asked in a tone that implied he hoped Duff would do that very thing.

Duff shrugged. "Not sure I can. I didn't have time to leave a trail of crumbs. Kind of screwed the pooch on that one. Worse comes to worst, I might be stuck here."

Linda frowned at Kendal and me. "It's time to stop badgering Duff. He must be exhausted."

Duff yawned. "Yeah, I'm pretty wiped. Maybe I'll just roll out my sleeping bag in the back of my car 'til I can buy a cot and such."

"There are empty beds right here," said Linda. "Kendal will help you carry one downstairs, won't you, Kendal?"

And just like that, Duff, aka the Trespasser, ended up as our neighbour.

*　*　*

As night fell, after a light supper of sliced radishes with olive oil and crusty bread and a dandelion leaf salad, Duff, Linda, Kendal and I went out to the backyard with my telescope and a blanket. It was a warm, clear night, perfect for stargazing.

"Holy shit, the Milky Way," said Duff. "Too much atomic ash in the atmosphere in my day to see the sky so clearly. Mind if I have a look through your scope, little sister?"

"Be my guest."

Amazingly, Duff knew all the constellations and pointed them out like an astronomer — he'd learned from books, he told us, since few except the very brightest stars were visible in the polluted night sky of 2019.

I thought about what we'd always been told as kids. "If they blow up the Earth, can't we go live on the moon?" I asked.

Duff laughed sadly. "That was a fairy tale cooked up by NASA and Walt Disney, little sister. There's way more money in making war than peace. Despite what you're hearing, they're building missile silos on the moon, not geodesic domes and hydroponic gardens. Anyway, even in 2019, living on the moon is just a dream. Time travel turned out to be easier."

The air began to cool as night deepened. Stars crowded in, a shattered windshield against the blackness. Duff talked about the future, telling us how his parents had been in a hardened shelter that protected them from fallout. That's why Duff was born healthy and intelligent enough to go to MIT, or what was left of it in the ruins of Boston. Most of his generation was born to parents whose genes had been horribly altered by radiation, causing their children to mutate into not-quite-normal humans.

"I'm one of the Normals. A minority group," explained Duff. "Most people my age are Twisties."

"How come?" I asked.

"Their strands of DNA became twisted in unusual ways so they're exceptions, which is actually the politically correct term for them. 'Exceptionals.'"

"We've got plenty of Exceptionals living on Z Street right now. We call them Twisties, too," said Kendal. For the first time, it sounded as if he was actually weighing the possible truth of Duff's words. "What are Exceptionals like in your time? Do they have superpowers?"

Duff shook his head. "Not quite, although a subset of gene mutations did result in giftedness — psychics, shape-shifters, mind-readers. But most are underdeveloped or overdeveloped or just plain sick, Kendal. They die young, and painfully, usually of mitochondrial disorders. Some start off looking like Normals but as they age, they gradually get eaten by flesh-eating fungi or leprous moulds. Ninety percent of the world's population suffers from some type of inherited radiation sickness, so 'exceptional' is hardly accurate. Being genetically damaged is actually the norm."

Linda's voice broke the darkness. "The future sounds horrific. Isn't there something you can do to stop this?"

Duff cleared his throat. "We know every hop alters time in tiny ways, like wrinkles in a blanket. That's why sometimes you remember things from your past differently from someone else who was there with you. But we're concerned that an attempt to deliberately change history in a major way could have a sling-shot effect. Even if I could figure out a way to stop the Bomb, some other disaster of equal magnitude would have to rush in to take its place. Could turn out to be even worse. Hard to say."

"How could anything be worse than a nuclear war?" I asked, my throat dry. It was starting to dawn on me that I might have only eight years to live as a Normal. I wasn't sure I wanted to live at all as an Exceptional.

Duff shook his head. "To be honest, the impact of changing history is purely speculative. No one's actually done it. But we might be able to avoid future events, rather than change them, by collapsing the continuum we're living in now and merging with an alternate timeline that's similar to ours."

"Is that even possible?" asked Linda.

Duff nodded. "Theoretically yes, according to quantum mechanics. We've detected a low-bandwidth television transmission from outside our world. We believe what we're picking up to be alternate timelines, weakly coupled to ours, that were created by atomic blasts."

Kendal shrugged. "Big deal. I've been reading about alternate histories in comic books for years."

"I'm talking about science, not comic books," said Duff. "We've found an alternate timeline on the spectrum closest to us. Earth Standard Time. It appears to be marginally more enlightened; as in, not destined to start World War Three, although they manage to screw up the planet in all sorts of other ways. Theoretically, someone who exists in our timeline but not in theirs could be able to merge the two, but this person would have to be non-existent in their new timeline. We call such an individual an Ion Tagger."

"If the Ion Tagger didn't exist in the new timeline, what would happen to them?" I asked.

"Hard to say. The IT might simply disappear into nothingness, or survive, but in a very degraded, unstable state."

I shivered at Duff's clinical description of the fate he had been so eager to send me to.

"Sounds like a shitty deal for the Ion Tagger," I pointed out.

Duff shrugged. "What's one life when you consider the millions who would be saved? Yes, the Tagger might be sacrificed, but everyone else from Atomic Mean Time would carry their lives in Earth Standard Time, happily unaware of what had happened to them. Small price to pay, I'd say."

We lapsed into silence. Awed by the vast expanse of the sky, not to mention the mind-blowing magnitude of Duff's story, I played connect-the-dots with the stars, trying to knit together the Bull, the Crab, the Bear, the Seated Woman and my astrological sign, the Scales of Justice. Duff had told me back in the dentist's office that he'd established that I was the Ion Tagger, but this new, younger version of him seemed unaware of that discovery. Given the possibility of finding myself non-existent in the alternate timeline, I didn't particularly feel like enlightening him. Especially now that I had so much to live for.

I shifted my body closer to Kendal's, leaning against his shoulder. He turned to brush my ear with his lips.

Being in love didn't feel the way Linda had described it — like being eaten alive. Kendal was a friend, someone I could trust. The idea that we might have only eight years together made our love feel doomed and urgent — epic lovers struggling against a backdrop of world events. We were Zhivago and Lara in the Russian Revolution, Tony and Maria on the west side of New York, Bonnie and Clyde in the Dust Bowl.

There was no time to lose: I had to start living my life the way I'd been taught in duck-and-cover drills back at "St. Dismal's" — as if there was no tomorrow. From that day on, I decided no new experience would pass me by.

eight
Seduction by Comic Book

We called it Postapocalyptica, our bombed-out private planet with a population of two, if you didn't count the mice. Kendal pried away a loose board from the back corner of the abandoned candy store and led me into the dusty interior.

Although the wooden building was a burned-out wreck, the first floor stood. Piotr's father had made a half-hearted attempt to reopen but, by 1971, pornography and popsicles were available at every corner store and highway stop — the derelict building was eventually boarded up. The walls and counter were the texture of charcoal; the cash register, a scorched chunk of steel with the final purchase rusted in place up top: $6.66, like a prop in a horror movie. A few mysterious cans with the labels burned off sat on sagging shelves. Turned out we were right when we were kids and looked out into the darkness beyond the candy store and thought, *There be dragons.*

Old people on Tesla Road claimed the building was cursed. Kendal said its reputation made it the perfect make-out place. No one was inclined to trespass, outside of us. And unlike at Kendal's house, there was no ShipCo Guardian Angel eavesdropping on every word we said.

We lay side by side on top of a sleeping bag that Kendal had carried in and rolled out beneath a broken section of roof where the sun poured in. Kendal pulled off his shirt and I ran my hands over his chest and back and arms. I let him slide his under my shirt, inside my shorts, under my bra to brush my stiffened nipples. I couldn't bring myself to undress.

"Not yet, not yet," I said.

"Then when?" he'd groan, claiming the frustration was causing him extreme physical discomfort of a masculine nature unknown to me.

"Just — not yet," I'd answer.

When we'd gone as far as we could — as far as I would let Kendal go — we lay on our backs holding hands, waiting for his hard-on to subside, so we could start all over again. Sometimes we'd share a bottle of Nonno Zinio's wine I'd taken from the cellar or a bit of weed that he'd bought under the counter from one of the small-time Z Street milk stores.

"I wish you weren't so damn Catholic," Kendal mumbled into my neck.

"You're Catholic, too," I said.

"Only by default."

"What are you really, then?"

"Pagan," said Kendal. He rolled on top of me, kissing me, hard again through his cut-off shorts.

Despite the frustration, the non-sex with Kendal was more exciting than most of the sexual encounters I would go on to have in the years to come, not just because we were friends in love but because of the danger of discovery. Postapocalyptica wasn't much of a hiding place — my little chirps of pleasure might have easily been heard from the street, or Piotr's father might have returned to check on his property. Unlikely, but the thought of being discovered with Kendal excited me. I had learned something new about what would be called my personal sexuality: I wanted to be seen, to be caught in the act, to be in a position of danger with my lover. I did not want to feel safe.

One of the riskier topics we discussed in Postapocalyptica was the cause of Kendal's injury. Away from the ShipCo Guardian Angel, he felt safe to tell me that he remembered nothing of the so-called accident and little of the weeks leading up to it.

"Mom agreed to let me be hypnotized to make me forget," he told me. "They'd promised her I'd heal better if I wasn't having flashbacks."

Well, of course, I thought. Post-Traumatic Induced Amnesia by hypnosis: a psychological tool to help people who had been through physical trauma forget all about it. Used on torture and accident victims who wanted to put victimhood behind them and get on with their lives. Also, a handy way to make people forget inconvenient truths, like the possibility that living on the Z-Lands was making them sick. No wonder ShipCo had sent Kendal home with a ShipCo Guardian Angel to monitor his conversations for subversive content. He was no use to ShipCo as a rocket technician, but also no danger to them with his memory wiped clean of the secret I'd shared with him — that my dad had discovered that the Z-Lands was still dangerously contaminated by nuclear waste.

I wondered why ShipCo hadn't used the same brainwashing technique on me, or Linda or Dad. Then it occurred to me: *maybe they had*. Who knew what had happened during my lost year and a half? It would certainly explain why everyone in my family was so uncharacteristically upbeat.

Kendal sat up. "I brought something to show you."

I watched him pull a sheaf of comics out of his backpack. "Cressie smuggled more underground stuff out of the States. Crumb, mostly. *Zapruder!* and *Homegroan.*"

In *Zapruder!*, a crewcutted teenage boy stood before a girl with ribboned pigtails. His hardened penis bobbed out of his fly, the tip curved like a helmet; it reminded me of a cannoli. Wordlessly he pointed down at himself and the teenage girl got to her hands and knees and took the cannoli-penis in her mouth. *That's right, keep going, pretend it's candy,* said the boy, holding the girl's head to his crotch. Both boy and girl were thickly drawn, mountainous, grotesque — the girl in particular looked hideous to me.

I had the feeling Kendal was trying to tell me something.

"Has anyone ever done that to you?" I asked.

"Well, sure. After all, I'm sixteen."

The legacy of Angie Petrone, again.

"The drawings are so ugly," I said. "Especially the girl. I feel like whoever drew her hates girls."

Kendal shook his head. "Come on, Debbie, they're underground comix. No boundaries, no taboos."

"I guess so," I said, flipping pages. The stories were funny and sexy and shocking sometimes, aggressive and violent, especially to the women who were there to hold up their giant cartoony breasts, or to suck or seize the men's cocks, which had the look of weaponry. One had what looked like a bazooka hanging out of his pants. Another, a submarine. The exaggerated cocks made the men look powerful but the women's breasts and bums were just heavy and ugly, sexy only in the eyes of the bloated cartoony men who drooled rabidly over a protruding behind or erect nipples. I couldn't imagine ever wanting to see Kendal and me drawn this way. I'll bet Angie wouldn't have much liked it either.

We managed to spend an hour together in Postapocalyptica every day, going a little further each time. By the end of the week, I was letting Kendal slide an experimental finger between my legs, the spot I'd touch myself, but when he tried to enter me, I pushed his hand away.

"If I let you do that, you won't be able to stop," I told him.

"Yes, I will," he said.

"Stop anyway," I told him. "Not yet."

"When, then?" he said.

"I don't know," I said, thinking of what had happened to Linda. She never talked about the baby, and the one time I mentioned Billy's name, she told me that the nuns at the Toronto Home for Girls had helped her forget he ever existed. Perhaps Linda underwent the same hypnosis-induced amnesia as Kendal. If there was one thing at which the psychiatry of Atomic Mean Time excelled, it was making us forget unhappy memories and dangerous truths. That way, we could move forward with our lives, unsullied by knowledge or experience.

* * *

I didn't understand much about my own body, let alone birth control, having hopped out of middle school with a single sex-education class led by a heavily pregnant Mrs. DiPietro, who, on the last day of school, agreed to share her wealth of experience with the girls while Mr. Bonifaci the gym teacher talked, man-to-man, to the boys. All I got out of this talk was that losing one's virginity was quick, painful and bloody unless you had previously deflowered yourself on the pummel of a bike saddle or interfered with yourself with Tampax. As to the act of love, she was evasive about everything except hygiene and the excellence of a particular brand of douche. About birth control, not a word, until Judy-Garland bravely waved her arm in the air to ask, "What about the Pill?"

Mrs. D.P. folded her hands protectively over the gourd of her pregnancy. "The Pill is a Communist plot, girls. If the women behind the Iron Curtain are the only ones having babies, what do you think will happen to democracy?"

She went on to predict that the few women who did give birth after being on the Pill would produce disgusting creatures called hermaphrodites.

"Is that what you want?" demanded Mrs. D.P. "How are you going to decorate a nursery if you can't even tell if your baby is a boy or a girl?"

After sex ed, we were handed our Gestetnered middle school diplomas and went into the playground to pump the boys for everything they'd learned from the phys-ed teacher. They told us they had spent their class playing Capture the Flag, a game Mr. Bonifaci said would teach them everything they needed to know about sex. "Only the strong survive, gentlemen."

* * *

After our time together in Postapocalyptica, Kendal and I adjusted our clothes, crawled out of the wrecked store and went our separate ways with a kiss, Kendal to look for odd jobs in the half-assed businesses on Z Street, me to cover pages with monstrous half-men, half-animals and ravished, bosomy, wasp-waisted, bug-eyed women with laced corsets and wild tendrils of hair. I'd never stopped drawing, really, but the Famous Artists Correspondence School ad in the backs of my comic books had given me a new sense of urgency.

"We're looking for people who like to draw," the self-portrait of Norman Rockwell assured me, his penciled-in eyes looking kind. "Send away for our free no-obligation Talent Test Booklet and find out if you have hidden talent. Then get ready for a future in the lucrative and creative fields of cartooning, fashion illustration, graphic design, commercial art, still life, children's portraits . . ."

I filled out the coupon in neat block letters, shortening my first and middle name to initials so they wouldn't know I was a girl, found an envelope and stamp and walked to the mailbox, buoyed by twin senses of destiny and defeat. Maybe a famous artist was what I was meant to be. On the other hand, was there even a future to get ready for?

As I dropped my envelope into the mailbox, I noticed a sign on a telephone pole reading, PICKERS WANTED: 6 A.M. PICK-UP HERE.

Strawberry harvest had begun. It was time to close my sketchbooks and make some money. Sparkling Sparrow Wines wouldn't need farmhands until the late August harvest; it was strawberries or nothing.

nine
Tender Fruit

Kendal, Sandy and I arrived at the corner of Fermi and Lakeshore fifteen minutes early to make sure we got picked first. But the farmers weren't choosy: if you had one hand and two legs, you were in. Most of the fieldwork was done by migrant workers from Trinidad and Tobago, all black men. They lived on the farms through the summer and fall, boarding in bunkhouses, making money to send home, then moving on to the next harvest — tobacco in Tillsonburg or tomatoes in Leamington, whatever came up. Those guys were the ones who really knew what they were doing. We were just supplemental labour, the cheapest of the cheap.

All of us wore three layers of clothing. The top layer was to deal with the cool morning air. Once the sun burned off the dew, we could strip down to our second layer, and finally our third, around noon, when it was hot enough to work naked. But we wouldn't, because the strawberry bushes, the herbicide sprays, the scorching sun and the bugs, not to mention any patches of stinging nettles we might blunder into, would have set our exposed skin on fire.

We brought along paper sacks of sandwiches and as much liquid as we could carry. We knew the farmer would drive demijohns of well water into the middle of the field for us to drink, but it would be warm and metallic tasting. Sandy froze cans of Royal Crown Cola and carried them in a backpack. Kendal lugged a huge insulated jug of ice water.

"You're going to carry that thing around with you in the field?" said Sandy.

"You'll be begging me for water around one o'clock," answered Kendal.

To my surprise, the Donato twins were there, too, in terry cloth tracksuits and clean running shoes. They even carried matching purses.

"Picking strawberries is a great way to work on our tans," said Judy-Garland.

"Our bikinis are under our clothes," added Jayne-Mansfield and looked quickly at Kendal.

By the time the meaty-faced farmer arrived in his pickup, there were so many of us gathered at the corner of Fermi and Lakeshore, we had to stand up in the truck bed clinging to one another. The farmer drove fast — when he made a sharp turn onto the concession road out to the farm, Sandy almost fell out. Kendal caught her by both arms to steady her.

"I wonder if that asshole would stop if someone actually fell out of the truck," one of the other boys said.

"I doubt it," said Kendal. "We're expendable."

Once the truck had bumped its way into the field, we jumped out and the farmer drove off for more pickers. A field hand assigned us the rows we'd be picking and handed out wage cards. Twenty cents a basket. If you really wanted to make money, speed was essential; the faster you picked, the more you made. If you weakened, sat down on the job, passed out from the heat or started gobbling up the fruit you'd picked — as Sandy, in particular, had been known to do — you could come away at the end of the day with nothing to show for your work except a sunburn.

Acres of strawberries stretched before us toward the horizon of Lake Ontario. In distant fields, the migrant workers moved up and down the rows with astonishing speed. They had probably been at it since daybreak.

Sandy crouched at the start of the row in front of me, Kendal at the row behind me. Judy and Jayne stood a few rows away, awkwardly holding their baskets, trying to figure out what to do with their purses.

"Well, this certainly sucks," I heard Judy say.

*　　*　　*

By eight, Sandy, Kendal and I already had dropped our outer layers. The Donato twins were down to their bikini tops but kept their track pants on. They hadn't advanced very far down their row. I suspected this would be their first and last day of picking.

As we filled baskets, we placed them in the centre of the row, ganging them up, but from time to time, we had to stop picking and lug them back to where the field hand collected them in the back of a flat-bed truck. Going back and forth, laden with heavy baskets, took time, which, needless to say, we were not paid for.

By noon, I was in a tank top and cut-off denim shorts, Kendal in track shorts and a T-shirt. We had just about reached a line of trees that formed a windbreak.

"Let's stop for lunch," Kendal said.

"We're breaking, Sandy," I called to her. She was on her way down the row with two full baskets in her hands.

"I left my lunch at the top of the row," she yelled. "I'm going to bring these to the field hand first."

"Guess it's just you and me," Kendal said, and brushed my hand with his.

We found a spot in the shade, where the wind off the lake blew away the bugs. Sheltered in the trees of the windbreak, we were invisible to the other pickers. Kendal pulled off his T-shirt and spread it on the ground for me to sit on. I stared at the slick muscles of his chest and stomach. I never got tired of looking at him. Touching him.

We drank some of his water. He tugged at the edge of my tank top. "Why don't you lighten up a little? You must be hot." When I hesitated, he said, "No one will see you here."

"You will."

He shrugged and smiled. "That's okay. I'm your boyfriend, after all."

It was the first time he'd used that word, but he was, wasn't he? And I was a woman now, wasn't I? Maybe it was time to finally show myself to him.

I crouched in the shelter of the high grass, pulled off my tank top and unclipped my bra, dropping them on the ground in front of Kendal. I liked the way his eyes grew wide as he watched me undress; I don't think he really thought I would do it. I sat topless on Kendal's shirt, the sun and wind caressing me like two strangers; my breasts hadn't seen sunlight since I was four years old.

Kendal pressed against me, the skin of his chest warm and slippery against my breasts. I could taste strawberry juice on his lips. He nuzzled my neck, my breasts, my shoulders, even my underarms.

"Don't kiss me there! I'm all sweaty," I said, pulling away.

"I like tasting your sweat. Like Napoleon with Josephine."

I turned my head to look at him. He was actually *sniffing* me.

"That's weird." I laughed, pushing him. "Napoleon?"

Kendal lay back. "Yeah. It was something I read about when

I was doing research for a history essay I did last year. When old Boney had been off at a campaign for a long time, he would write sexy letters to Josephine. 'Don't wash,' he'd tell her."

"Ugh. Is that the kind of stuff you learn in high school history class?"

Kendal pulled himself overtop of me, his smooth chest resting against my breasts. "Oh, yeah, and we read all kinds of sexy stuff in English class, too."

With Kendal's hands on my hips, he went back to kissing me, his tongue deep in my mouth. I felt a pleasant ache between my legs. I could hear the distant grumble of a tractor.

He hooked a finger around the top of my shorts and tugged them down a little. I was just about to help him unzip my fly when Kendal levitated off me, shot back by an invisible force that turned out to be the farmer who had driven us to the field that morning. His meaty face was the colour of undercooked pork. He pressed his boot to Kendal's chest, pinning him to the ground.

"Get the hell away from her!" the farmer shouted at Kendal. "I told you coloured bastards to leave the town girls alone!"

I staggered to my feet, trying to cover my breasts with my tank top. "Sir, it's okay, he's my boyfriend."

The farmer looked back and forth between Kendal and me distastefully. "This ain't a whorehouse. You come back with me in the truck, girl. I'm calling your parents. As for you," he said, turning on Kendal, "if it were twenty years ago, I'd be getting out the horsewhip, but you're not worth the trouble that'd cause me. Get off my farm and stay off. Vamoose."

Kendal looked back and forth between the farmer and me. "I don't . . . have a way back to town."

"You think I give a damn?" the farmer shouted. "Get the hell out of here — now!"

I got back in my clothes as quickly as I could, sensing the farmer's eyes on my body. In the distance, Sandy and the Donato twins and some of the other pickers stood in a little knot, staring at us. The farmer's truck was at the edge of the field, so I had to walk the whole way back with him, hot with embarrassment. I turned to look at Kendal — he stood with hands hanging at his sides, not knowing what to do. When I started to walk away from the farmer and back to Kendal, he shook his head at me and motioned with his hand: *no, don't come back, keeping going.* Finally, Kendal started walking toward the concession road.

The farmer drove me back to his house, fury radiating off him like heat waves off a freshly tarred road. He said nothing until we reached his driveway; then he turned to me.

"That's what I get for hiring Z Street sluts. I'm going to give you a piece of advice that you should heed, girl. I've known a lot of coloureds over the years. That boy is not your people. Understand?"

I just stared at him. I wanted to spit in his face but I was frozen by my own embarrassment and an upbringing that made it almost impossible for me to be rude to an adult. When he demanded my phone number, I gave him the one for Nonna Peppy's house, a tiny act of rebellion. I would rather this news went first to my grandmother than to my mother.

He went into the farmhouse and returned a few minutes later, climbing back into the driver's seat of his truck. "Your father is on his way," he said.

"My father?" I was astonished. Nonna Peppy made Dad leave work to come get me? I was in even more trouble than I thought.

"I didn't have the stomach to tell the guy what happened, so I'll leave that up to you." The farmer reached toward me

— to open my door, I thought. Instead, he grabbed my breasts and kissed me so fast and hard that I barely had time to jam down the door handle. I almost fell out of the truck.

The farmer laughed as I hopped out and backed away toward the farmhouse. "You're too plug ugly for a Snugglegirl, anyways."

He threw the truck into gear and tore off toward the fields. I sat down on the stoop to wait. About twenty minutes later, a car turned in, kicking up dust at the end of the long driveway. It wasn't Dad's Country Squire, but Duff's Cutlass. He pulled up next to me and looked at me sternly.

"Fraternizing with the enemy, I hear? Get in, little sister. Your grandma wanted to send in the marines, but I convinced her to settle for me."

We didn't see the farmer as we drove back to the concession road, gravel crunching and popping under the wheels.

"I guess Nonna told you what happened," I said miserably. "Was she mad?"

Duff waggled his hand back and forth; he was starting to pick up Nonna Peppy's mannerisms. "Not mad enough to tell your folks. And what's she going to say to you? Don't kiss boys?"

I curled into the corner of the front seat, my arms crossed over my guilty breasts.

"Duff, in the future, is there still prejudice?"

He snorted. "That's eternal. What'll change is that a black guy and a white girl getting it on, or vice versa, will be no big deal."

"Everyone says it'd be hard on their kids because there'd be so much prejudice against them, they'd never have the chance to amount to anything."

Duff laughed. "Wait and see," he said, but wouldn't explain further.

I looked over at him, driving with one hand out the window, bobbing his head and singing along with the radio. I was beginning to understand why he looked so young and why his middle finger had reappeared. Duff wasn't really the Trespasser: at least, not yet. I wondered what would happen if his older and wiser self ever caught up with him, and me.

"Duff, do you remember me from . . ." I groped for words to describe the time before my hop. "From *before*?"

He glanced at me with an uncertain grin. "From before what?"

"*Before*, before. About a year and a half ago. I think I saw you on one of your earlier hops, like, around the time I was thirteen."

Duff shook his head. "In 1969, I was still a lowly postdoc, toiling on my thesis and riding herd on my idiotic graduate student. No hops for me, except to the local watering hole. Must be déjà vu."

I sat back and considered this. Was he right? Over time, everything that I remembered from before the hop had grown less and less real, the session in the dentist's office as uncertain as a dimly remembered dream. I discovered I even had memories of events that supposedly happened during the eighteen months I'd lost. Nonno Zin's funeral. The night I helped Nonna Peppy take Pepé the Seventh to the vet clinic after he ate rat poison. The math exam I missed because I was sick with my period. Had I actually lived through all those things or simply internalized my family's memories? I wasn't sure.

Duff interrupted my reverie, nodding at the windshield. "Look up the road."

Walking along the drainage ditch at the side of the concession road was Kendal, shirt off in the heat, head down, swinging his water jug. When Duff pulled over to pick him up, Kendal tried to wave him off. "I'll walk."

Duff reached past me to throw open the passenger side door. "No way, man, it's twenty miles into town. You're gonna pass out in this heat."

Kendal hesitated for a moment, until I said, "Please get in."

He slid in next to me in the front seat and stared out the windshield, his body as stiff as a block of wood. Duff peeled away from the stony verge of the road.

"Did you get paid?" I asked.

"What kind of stupid question is that?" said Kendal.

Those were the last words we exchanged until Duff pulled to the curb on Z Street. Kendal hopped out of the car and slammed the door, disappearing into his house without a backward glance or a see-you-later. He didn't thank Duff for the ride.

* * *

Back at Nonna Peppy's house, sitting at the vinyl-topped table, she poured me a cup of espresso. "He's a nice boy, but he ain't your kind, you know."

"But you of all people know about prejudice, Nonna," I pointed out.

She shook her head. "Listen: it's one thing to fit in with regular folks if you're Italian. Maybe you change your last name. You lose your accent. After a while, people don't even look at you different from anyone else. But your friend can't do nothing about the colour of his skin. And Shipman's Corners ain't Greenwich Village. You know what I'm saying? They might say, oh, that boy's as good as anyone else, but just wait 'til he tries to find a job or get a loan at the bank or even a rent a house that ain't on Z Street. *Cara*, that's just the way the world is."

She took a sip of espresso; I could see her struggling with what she wanted to say next. Unusual for her: she was usually pretty good at speaking her mind.

"The farmer said something about you being half-naked. Were you just kissing that boy or what?"

I felt myself growing warm. "Yes, just kissing. Pretty much."

"Pretty much," said Nonna Peppy, now looking me in the eyes. "Debbie, listen you to me: your sister wasn't much older than you when she got in trouble. You know what I'm saying?"

"It wasn't like that," I said.

"Okay, okay." She raised her hand. "This can stay between us girls. God forbid Madelena should have another daughter who keeps her up at night. Just be careful." She pushed a plate of freshly baked biscotti at me. "*Mangia*. You're getting so skinny lately, pretty soon you gonna disappear."

I nibbled on the biscotti, knowing I would need to find a quiet moment to rid myself of it before the digestive process took over.

* * *

I glanced at the kitchen clock: five o'clock. I slipped through the front door, wheeled my bike out of the garage and rode along Fermi Road until I found Sandy sitting on her front stoop, still in her work clothes. She gave a whoop when she saw me.

"I sweet-talked your wages out of the field hand." She pulled a few crumpled bills out of her jeans pocket. "You grounded?"

I shook my head. "Nonna Peppy ran interference. Guess you'll be picking strawberries without Kendal and me, though."

"What do you think he told his mother?"

"Nothing, I hope. It seems like every time he gets mixed up with me, there's trouble."

"You should call him," said Sandy. "Chances are, he'll answer the phone; I saw his mom drive by, making deliveries."

I made the call from Sandy's kitchen, where Mrs. Holub hummed along with *Dreams of the Everyday Housewife* on the radio while mixing a potato salad. It must be handy, having a mom who doesn't understand English. Kendal answered on the first ring.

"Are you okay?" I asked.

"What do you think?" His voice sounded thick.

"Meet me in Postapocalyptica?" I suggested.

"You're kidding, right?" said Kendal. "You almost get me killed, and now you want to tease me to death? No, thanks."

My heart sped up. Kendal had never sounded mad at me before.

"Can I come over to your place?" I asked.

A pause. "I guess so, but wait until it's dark."

*   *   *

Humid air hung over Z Street like a soggy beach towel. I cycled past the wreck of Bum Bum's house and saw Kendal sitting on the steps of his front stoop. The soundtrack of a television show seeped through the front window. *My Four Sons*.

Kendal stood up and walked toward the British Methodist Episcopal Church next door. I followed, pushing my bike. The whitewashed church glowed in the darkness, its high walls looking down at us as sternly as a tall pale judge. I became very aware of my heartbeat, Kendal's breathing, the night sounds and the rumblings of a skunk or raccoon nosing around in the garbage cans. When we were in the shadows of the alleyway, I got off my bike and put my arms around him. He didn't embrace me back.

"I love you," I said, apprehensively.

"Really? I'm not so sure about that," said Kendal. "You decided to wait 'til we were out in a field to come on to me. I try to make things safe and normal so we can be together without getting hassled, and you go out of your way to make sure it gets all fucked up. It's like you're radioactive."

My heart was pounding. "What happened wasn't my fault."

"We should cool it anyway," Kendal mumbled.

I hesitated. This was getting confusing. I said I loved him, and he said he wanted to break up with me? None of this made any sense. "Duff said it'll get easier."

I could feel his body tensing.

"Duff's a bullshitter of the first magnitude."

"But a lot of what he says sounds like it *could* be true," I pointed out.

"I'm not saying he's not a smart guy," said Kendal. "In fact, he seems amazingly inventive. That's the problem — it's like he's writing the script of a movie and trying it out on us as he goes along."

"I'd like Duff to be telling the truth," I said. "The future might be a mess but with all the other problems, no one would care about what the two of us look like."

Kendal rested his chin on the top of my head. The smell of him filled my nose. Maple syrup and sweat and deodorant. "Or we could just not care about what anybody thinks and agree to get married as soon as we're old enough."

"Married?" I said.

Through the open window next door, the familiar rhythm of a laugh track tried to remind everyone of how funny TV was supposed to be. I didn't know what to say. My mouth had turned to dust. I felt like running. I didn't want to settle down like my mom and have children and keep house, the Contessina to Kendal's Captain Crusher. It was always Crusher having the adventures, the Contessina stroking his fevered brow. True, she got to deck the bad guys once in a while, but I suspected the day was coming when I'd see her with a cocktail apron over her skimpy outfit, serving canapés to Crusher's buddies from V.E.N.G.E.A.N.C.E. while they smoked cigars and played poker, and occasionally sticking her head into the nursery to check on the baby. No thanks. I was determined not to turn into my mother.

"We're way too young to talk about marriage, Kendal," I said a bit primly.

"But you like the idea, right?"

I shrugged. We stared at one another. Something had shifted between us, as if he were standing on the edge of the canal with his hands in his pockets while I waved to him from the deck of a moving saltie.

Finally, he said, "I'd better walk you back to your house. It's pretty late."

I shook my head. "I can ride alone, Kendal."

Along Z Street and through downtown Shipman's Corners, every pedal stroke was a relief, taking me away from Kendal's anger, directed at me for reasons I didn't understand and at the world for reasons I stupidly imagined I did. At not quite fifteen, I actually thought I knew how a young black man growing up in an intolerant small town might feel in the face of raw hatred.

When I reached Cresswell's Collectibles, I braked and stood with my hands cupped on either side of my eyes, peering inside. I could just make out the shelves behind the cash. Whatever Duff had stashed there had helped him hop through time. Why not use it? The Contessina wouldn't shy away from time travel. Given the chance to travel forward in time, she might even willingly abandon her rough-edged lover, Crusher.

I tried the handle of Cressie's front door, but it was locked tight.

Back on my bike, I rode through the muggy streets. Even the lampposts seemed to be sagging in the heat.

I wheeled up the driveway of my house, the familiar closing theme of *My Four Sons* floating through the TV room window. Someone was humming along. I looked up. In the moonlight, I could see Dad sitting at the edge of the roof, something he did from time to time because it was as close as he could get to a mountaintop. His legs dangled over the eavestrough. He didn't realize I was there until I said, "Hi."

The shadow of his head tipped down at me. "You're home late. Hanging out with Sandy?"

"Yup," I said. At least it was a half-truth — I'd eaten dinner at the Holubs'.

Something hit the ground between my feet: a pair of weathered leather work gloves.

"Come on up," he said.

The gloves were about ten sizes too big, but they'd do the trick. I stepped into Mom's flowerbed — careful not to crush any of her beloved petunias — and gripped the white lattice-work clamped to the bricks.

When I got close enough, Dad extended a hand over the eavestrough and hauled me the rest of the way up.

"Come on, you monkey. Oop-a-la!"

I crawled onto the sloped roof. Lit by streetlights, the world below looked as well-ordered as a Monopoly board: rectangles of house lots marked by fences, a grid of streets and drainage ditches that seemed to have been ploughed with a sharp stick wielded by a giant.

Beside me, Dad lay flat on the shingles, hands behind his

head, gazing up at the sky. Ever since I'd hopped into 1971, he seemed to be getting younger by the day. Every morning he'd head off to the winery in his denim clothes, driving his bright yellow truck, whistling show tunes. Every evening, he came home with a new Sparkling Sparrow vintage for us to taste.

"Are you happy, Dad? I mean, with your business and stuff."

"Yes. Very happy," he said.

I paused for a moment, trying to decide how to push into delicate territory. "Did you know that Mr. Holub is trying to borrow enough money to open a restaurant?"

He turned to look at me. "What kind?"

"Ukrainian fast food. Like McDonald's, with perogies."

Dad snorted and looked back to the stars. "Igor's always been a dreamer. Good ideas. Bad follow-through."

"The anti-radiation suits in the cellar — did he make them for us?"

Dad turned his head to look at me again. "No, I had a craftsman do that. Igor sold the rights to the suit a long time ago, not that he made much off them. Problem is, no one really knows if they'll work. But I figured, what the hell? Cheaper than digging a bomb shelter."

"I guess he didn't get much capital out of the idea for the suits, huh?"

"Probably not."

"So — how did you get the capital to buy Sparkling Sparrow?"

"Why do you want to know that?"

"Just curious," I shrugged. "I mean, it is the family business, right?"

"Fair enough," said Dad. "ShipCo is my partner. They own half the winery, but I get a nice management fee."

"How come ShipCo wants to own a winery?"

"To keep people happy," said Dad. "See, we use a hybrid grape that has a calming effect."

Even to almost-fifteen-year-old me, this sounded suspicious. "You're drugging people, Dad?"

He lifted his hands in an expression of surrender. "Now, don't get all het up. ShipCo's doing it as a public service. I was angry for a long time about what they were doing in the Z-Lands, but the fact is, we can't do anything to change the world. Folks might as well be calm and happy instead of worrying themselves sick about World War Three."

"Maybe if they worried about it enough, they'd force the government to change things," I suggested.

"How, exactly, do you think they'd do that? Nothing will change, sweetheart. Until one or the other superpower pushes the button, we're deadlocked."

"And 'til then, we should all just chill out," I said.

"Something like that," murmured Dad. "All that activism of Dave Kendal's back in the '60s, and those people in the Z-Lands a couple of years back complaining about the radiation levels and getting themselves roughed up by Security — what was the point? It's not like any of them are going to be around long enough to feel the effects. The Bomb will put an end to them long before any mutations do. When you're older, you'll understand."

I lay back on my elbows against the slope of the roof. Dad's logic made sense, if you believed we were destined for nuclear Armageddon. Live, drink, work for ShipCo and be happy, for tomorrow we'll be bombed to shit.

I watched as the moon was eaten away by Earth's shadow, turning from a flat white plate into a round sphere the rusty colour of old blood. I could have reached up and grabbed it, bouncing it off the wall of the sky like a red rubber ball.

"The moon looks strange tonight," I said.

"It's eclipsing," said Dad. "The old folks used to call that a Blood Moon."

As I watched the moon turn deep red, it occurred to me that I was not in the wrong place, but the wrong time. If Duff's secret weapon could take him into the past, I might even be able to turn the clock back to the Z-Lands, to the very moment, perhaps, when Kendal's life was turned upside down, and mine along with his. Or back, back, back to when Kendal's activist father was eaten alive by a machine at ShipCo. We could also avoid the humiliation of the farm that very day. All mistakes could be corrected or prevented. Then Kendal and I could hop into an alternate continuum, untouched by bad karma, unembittered by hate and prejudice and dumb decisions. All I had to do was get Duff to show me how to use that secret weapon hidden in the Florsheim shoebox behind the cash at Cressie's.

ten
Shark Bite

Sandy stood in front of me holding a pair of silver tweezers. "This is going to hurt," she warned.

The pain brought immediate tears to my eyes. "Ow. What are you doing?"

"I'm plucking your brows thin, thin, thin. Like Mia Farrow."

"Mia Farrow is a blonde, for Christ's sake. And she was married to Frank Sinatra. Yuck."

"Check it out."

I opened my eyes. My eyebrows were gone. I looked like a different girl. One who was in a constant state of surprise.

"I didn't mean to pull them all out, but it's probably just as well. They were wrong for the shape of your face," said Sandy, pointing out the makeup chart from *Glamour* taped to her mirror. "I'll draw them back in the way they're supposed to look."

She picked up an eyebrow pencil, dark brown and sharply pointed, and pressed into the skin over my eyes — it hurt almost as much as having my eyebrows yanked out. In the mirror, my new brows hovered on my forehead like quotation marks. As if my eyes were trying to tell something.

"Now for the false eyelashes."

I watched Sandy apply a thin line of glue to the spidery lashes. "Where'd you get all this makeup from?"

"My dad made me buy it," she said. "When we went to the bank, he wanted me to make myself look older. Damn it all, now I got glue all over my fingers."

The feathery weight of the false eyelashes felt like a tarantula walking on my eyeball. I focused my one functioning eye on Sandy as she gripped the false eyelashes in a spring-loaded metal curler that looked like an implement of torture.

Despite the weight I'd already purged away, I felt like a cow when I was around slender Sandy. She did her best to boost my ego. As she sponged Cover Girl foundation in deep bisque all over my face, she said, "You have such great skin, Debbie. When I put this stuff on, it just makes my zits look bigger."

The Cover Girl turned my face into a blank canvas. I was now featureless, except for my sketched-in brows and large dark eyes staring back in the mirror. I had been erased. I could be anybody now.

Sandy went at me with eye shadow, liquid liner, blush and setting powder, then coated my lips with a tube of Cherries in the Snow, although she sighed and said that bright red lips were totally square for anyone but old ladies. My lips should either be bubble-gum pink or white as death.

The two of us stared at ourselves in the mirror, shoulders touching. We looked amazing — no longer high school girls from Nowheresville, we had been transformed into the cool, sophisticated girls in *Seventeen*.

Downstairs, Mr. Holub was waiting for us by the car. I'd never seen him so dressed up. He was wearing a suit, tie and shiny brown shoes. His black hair had been slicked down so that he seemed to be all forehead.

We were on our way to see Larry Kowalchuck, also known as The Shark. Sandy explained he was a rich guy who gave money to people who couldn't get it from the bank. That's what a loan shark was: someone who helped out people in a bind. And he was half Ukrainian, so Mr. Holub could trust him.

"If they both speak the same language, why does he need you? Or me, for that matter?" I asked.

Sandy dabbed bubble-gum pink gloss on her lips. "The Shark only does business in English. And he's a playboy, like James Bond. He likes having young chicks around. Keeps things relaxed while he's doing business."

Niagara Falls was always busy, but that day it was quieter than usual because of a cloudburst. Table Rock House, at the brink of the Falls, was empty except for a large Mennonite family around a table near the cash, the men in blue shirts and suspenders, the women in bonnets and long dresses. Outside, a group of Hare Krishnas in orange robes and yellow raincoats chanted a mantra: *Hare krishna hare krishna, krishna krishna hare hare . . .*

The Shark was smoking in a booth at the back, an ashtray in front of him overflowing onto a placemat printed with recipes for Fifty World-Famous Cocktails. He was younger than I had expected, his fair hair long to his shoulders and carefully blow-dried, his blond moustache shaggy. He was dressed in blue jeans and a denim shirt unbuttoned to expose a medallion in the shape of a circle with an arrow poking out of it — the "male" symbol — nestled in a mat of curling chest hair. When Mr. Holub shook hands with him, the Shark smiled and semi-respectfully half-stood. He looked at Sandy and me and gave a low whistle.

"You could be a fashion model, sweetheart," he told Sandy; then, to me, "As for you, you look like Snugglegirl material. I'd bet you show up in a *Playboy* centrefold one day."

His eyes really did look like a shark's, but instead of being dead black, they were an empty ice blue. He stared at me for so long that I had to drop my eyes.

"Sit here, sweetheart, I won't bite," he said, patting the seat beside him.

He stood to let me into the booth, then slid in next to me so that I was sitting between him and the wall. He immediately put his arm around my waist and pulled me so close that my hand had nowhere to go but the top of his leg. The Shark looked at me hungrily, as if I were a bologna sandwich.

"That's more like it," he mumbled.

The waitress was glancing over at us from the counter where she was gathering up cutlery and napkins to set our table. I tried to will her over to our table, but one of the Mennonite men signalled for his bill and she turned her back on us. I watched in despair as she disappeared through a set of swinging doors.

"We talk business now," said Mr. Holub.

"We talk business when I say we talk business," answered the Shark. He leaned back to take another drag on his cigarette. His knee rested against mine. Under the table, he took my hand and moved it from his leg into his lap. When the waitress showed up and said, "What can I get you?" he let go of my hand.

"Ice cream floats for the girls," he ordered.

"Vanilla, strawberry or chocolate? Neutron Coke, Mountain Dew or 7-Up?" asked the waitress, her eyes on her notepad.

"What you want, girls? It's on me," said the Shark.

Sandy ordered strawberry ice cream in 7-Up. When the Shark nudged me, I said, "Same for me." Mr. Holub ordered coffee.

"And for you, sir?" said the waitress to the Shark.

"Glass of water."

The side of my body pressed against him was damp with sweat.

"So, I've heard your idea," said the Shark to Mr. Holub. "Takeout Russian food, but it's really Ukrainian? Why don't you call it takeout Ukrainian food?"

"Is easy for people in this country understand," explained Mr. Holub patiently. "You say 'Ukrainian,' they not know how is different from 'Russian.' 'Russian,' they think Kosygin, Cosmonauts, Bay of Pigs, Sputnik."

"And that makes them buy your food?" asked the Shark skeptically, leaning back in the booth.

The waitress returned with the drinks on a tray; she set the ice cream floats in front of Sandy and me. They came in huge frosted glasses with long-handled spoons. I tried to push the ball of ice cream down into the 7-Up, but I couldn't eat because I was focused on the Shark's hand, which had worked its way under the back of my leg.

"Sputnik Burgers might not be a bad idea," mused the Shark.

As he carried on his side of the conversation, with Sandy busily translating back and forth, the Shark slid his hand under my bottom and rubbed his thumb against the crotch of my panties. I couldn't stand the sensation for another second without screaming; I also didn't want it to stop.

As if reading my mind, the Shark pushed aside the crotch of my panties and in one quick thrust, plunged a finger into me. Then, a second. In and out, push pull, touching me in places I'd never let Kendal go while his thumb worked lazily at the lump between my legs. I spread wider for him. Allowed myself to be impaled on him. All the while, the Shark continued to smoke casually with his free hand. I kept my eyes fixed on the place mat, staring at the pictures of all those cocktails. Sidecar. Gibson. Old-Fashioned. Rob Roy.

"Somethin' wrong with your ice cream, darlin'?" asked the

Shark, leaning in close. Tobacco on his breath. I shook my head.

Kitty-corner to me, Sandy's face had turned the colour of raw fish. The Shark was driving a hard bargain. Sandy was trying to explain to her father what the Shark meant by "compound interest." Sweat beaded on Mr. Holub's forehead despite the air conditioning in the restaurant.

Since the Shark wanted to bargain in English, Mr. Holub was going to try. "I think about America. A chain. Like McDonald's. You know McDonald's, Larry?"

The Shark leaned over the table, jabbing his finger at Mr. Holub and Sandy. "I've been to McDonald's in Buffalo about a hundred times. But they don't sell *varenyky*. They've got hamburgers, fries, soda, things Americans like to eat."

As the Shark made his point, he pushed a third finger inside me. Something snapped like an elastic band, followed by a sudden gush between my legs, a telltale cramping and shimmer of nausea.

Uh oh.

"Excuse me, I gotta go to the bathroom," I said weakly.

The Shark grinned at me, slid his hand out of my panties and squeezed my thigh. "You're excused. Wouldn't want you to wet yourself, sweetheart."

I walked quickly to the ladies' room. Outside, the chanting of the Hare Krishnas continued in the rain. Flashes of yellow and orange fabric rippled past the wet windows.

. . . hare rama hare rama, rama rama, hare hare . . .

The bathroom was empty. I went into a cubicle and pulled down my panties and sat for a few minutes, letting pee dribble out. I tried not to imagine the Shark's skin cells, his — what did they call it in science? — epithelia floating around inside me. When you became a woman, it seemed your body belonged to everybody.

My panties were bloodstained — the start of my period, unpredictable as usual. But the raggedy, stinging pain in my crotch told me that some of the blood had come from the Shark's sneak attack. He had clawed away my virginity, exactly the way Mrs. D.P. had described.

I slipped a tampon out of my purse and inserted it. Then I stuck my fingers down my throat. I didn't have much in my stomach, but it made me feel better to show my body who was boss.

I walked back to the table slowly, relieved to see money sitting in the little black tray for the waitress. Mr. Holub was saying something to the Shark, who nodded and shrugged. "Sure, they can go. For now."

For a second, the Shark's blue eyes caught mine and hung there. Then he looked away.

Sandy and I went outside. The drizzle and spray off the Falls soaked us in seconds. I wished I'd brought an umbrella. I thought about telling her what had happened under the table. But if I said it out loud, then it really *had* happened and wasn't just me imagining things. I'd be admitting I just sat there and let the Shark do dirty, sexy things to me. I had always been told to be polite to adults, to obey, but still, I could've pushed his hand away.

I reminded myself that we were all going to be dead soon anyway, when they dropped the Bomb. What did it matter who did what to whom.

Without talking about it, Sandy and I started walking. Soon we were standing at the brink of the Falls. It was always my favourite place to enjoy the view, but it was also everyone else's. In hot weather, the stone wall was blocked by tourists in shorts and golf shirts, holding ice cream cones in one hand and balancing little kids on the wall with the other. I'd heard that sometimes mothers accidentally-on-purpose let their kids fall in, but it never made the papers because if it did, everyone would be doing it. Such mothers usually ended up being strait-jacketed and shipped off to Toronto, never to be heard of again.

There were no children on the brink of death that day, only a clutch of people who looked like they might be from India, wearing plastic ponchos and posing for pictures in the mist — the kind of thing that caused my father to roll his eyes and point out that there wasn't enough light for a decent photo-graph. But they seemed to be having a good time, probably because they'd soon be going home to India with pictures of this grey, cold, drab place.

I stared down at the brink of the Falls. It was amazingly shallow, but the speed of the water meant that if you stuck just one finger in, the force of the water would sweep you over. This was all due to physics.

The only exception was a scow that had broken away from a tugboat upriver and had been swept toward the Falls. A historical marker told the story: in 1918, two men on board the scow opened the hatches, sinking it low in the water and grounding on rocks at the brink, where the water is deadly fast but shallow. The men were rescued with a line shot out from the hydro station — they had to scramble across it at night, because they didn't know how long the scow would stay on the rocks before it went over the Falls. One man went crazy and ended up in a lunatic asylum. The other spent the rest of his life telling the story to people in bars. The scow never did go over. One day, it still might.

"What do you want to be when you grow up?" Sandy asked.

"An astronaut," I said.

"That's a little kid answer. Girls can't be astronauts. Pick something real."

Usually, I would have given her an argument — by then we knew that the Soviets had trained a woman cosmonaut, even though she hadn't gone up — but I felt defeated.

"Dunno. What about you?"

"A stewardess," said Sandy.

I thought about that. "Good idea. It would be cool to be able to fly away from here any time you liked."

When Mr. Holub and the Shark came out the front door of Table Rock House, Mr. Holub had a big smile on his face. Sandy joined him and the two walked ahead, talking excitedly. The Shark put his hands in his pockets and fell in beside me.

"I've got to see you again," he said in a low voice.

"I can't," I said, keeping my eyes on the parking lot sign.

"Come on, you have to. Soon as I saw you, I knew you were something special. You know how?"

I shook my head and kept walking.

"Chemistry. Your body talking to my body. Telling me things about you."

"Oh, yeah, like what?" Despite everything, I really wanted to know.

"Like, you were itching to have your cherry broke. See, there are these things called pheromones that I can smell on some girls. Natural chemicals. You've got 'em in spades because you're naturally sexy."

"I don't believe you," I muttered, although I was starting to wonder if I hadn't heard something like this from the Donato twins.

I could hear him breathing faster over the staccato clip of his cowboy boots on the wet pavement. "You're very mature for your age."

"Really?" I said. I was sort of starting to believe him. "But I've already got a boyfriend."

The Shark gave a soft grunt. "He break your cherry yet?"

"No," I said.

"Know why? You were waiting for me to do it. In the olden days, special girls like you were given to the king first. In Shipman's Corners, I'm like a king."

"But I'm only fourteen. Well, almost fifteen."

He shrugged. "Who gives a shit about age? I'm twenty-eight. Nature doesn't care how young or old you are. You need sex like orange juice. It's good for you. Your pheromones say I've got to conquer you."

"But how are you going to find me?" I liked the idea of being naturally sexy, and even the part about being conquered, which sounded romantic, as if he was going to bring me chocolates and flowers. I just didn't want him showing up at our house during supper.

"You kidding? I got your scent on my fingers. I'll sniff you out like a bloodhound. See you around, little girl."

Before I could say anything more, he strode ahead, slapped Mr. Holub on the back and disappeared into the crowd of chanting Hare Krishnas and ice cream–eating Mennonites.

In the Charger, Mr. Holub switched on the radio. The comforting sound of Walter Cronkite's voice swelled up, telling us that President Nixon had approved the biggest underground nuclear test in history in the Aleutian Islands and that the Soviets were threatening retaliation. Blah blah blah — I'd heard all about it from Duff. According to him, the test would heighten the Cold War and lead to World War Three in eight years. Maybe that wasn't a big deal. I was starting to think the simplest way out of my problems was for the world to blow up.

"What were you and the Shark talking about on the way to the car?" asked Sandy.

I shrugged. "Chemistry."

Sandy laughed. "You're always boring people with that science stuff."

* * *

I asked Mr. Holub to drop me a block away from my house. When I got home, I ran upstairs and pulled off my dress and panties, sticking them between the mattress and box frame of my bed. Then I drew a hot, hot bath. Scalding hot. I got into the tub as it filled and put my face directly under the tap, letting it flow over my head. I pulled off the false eyelashes, taking most of my real lashes with them. Like everything else that day, it hurt, but this time the pain was a distraction. A punishment, like the Shark punishing me. There was something irresistibly dangerous about him. I wondered if the chemicals in my body were already calling out to him. Shame and excitement flared in me simultaneously.

When I got out of the tub, I caught sight of my wet pink face in the mirror. I looked like a shaved cat. I was going to have to cook up a lie to explain my lack of eyebrows and eyelashes. And it was going to have to be a doozy.

A rap at the door. "Debbie?" My mother's voice.

"Yeah?" I said.

"Your friend is on the phone."

"Tell Sandy I'll call her back."

"Not *that* friend," said Mom. "The paper boy."

I opened the door. When Mom saw my face, she crossed herself. "*Marone.*"

"Sandy and I were trying out a new look and she got a little carried away with the tweezers. It'll grow back," I said.

Mom shook her head and walked away.

I went to the hall phone by the Virgin's nook. As I picked

208

up the receiver, her downcast blue plaster eyes caught mine. *Watch yourself, kid.*

"Hello?"

The déjà vu was powerful and immediate. I mouthed Kendal's words along with him: "Meet me at Postapocalyptica?"

I glanced at the kitchen door where Mom was descaling the tea kettle. "I thought you wanted to cool it," I said to him.

A pause. "I'm sorry. I was mad. I didn't mean it."

Now it was my turn to hesitate. "I've got bad cramps. Let's wait a couple of days."

"I don't care if you're on the rag," said Kendal. "It's not like we're going to do anything. I've got some new comics."

I closed my eyes. "I'm not in the mood for more *Zapruder!* right now, Kendal."

"No more *Zapruder!*, I promise. I've got a new one called *Deviation* and an amazing *Silver Surfer*. Meet me tomorrow at noon."

I tried to imagine myself sitting in the derelict candy store, reading comics with Kendal like a little kid, after what had happened with the Shark that day. But there was no way to refuse him without more discussion; it was quiet enough in the kitchen that I suspected Mom was already eavesdropping. So I agreed.

"Great, see you then," said Kendal, adding, "I love you."

"Right. Yup. Me too," I answered, and put the phone in its cradle.

Back in my room, I lay down and hugged my pillow. The cramps were getting steadily worse, as if God was poking me in the tummy. I decided to put what happened with the Shark on a dusty shelf of my brain, like the cubbyholes behind the cash desk at Cressie's, where long-forgotten valuables gathered dust, their owners never bothering to come back for them.

I went into the bathroom to change my tampon. Even though I hadn't eaten anything, I managed to throw up some clear liquid. It left a bitter taste in my mouth but it was satisfying to get out every speck that had entered my body that day. I was purged now, inside and out. I was ready for the Bomb to fall and destroy me and every last man on Earth.

I didn't go back to Postapocalyptica the next day, or the next. To avoid questions, I asked Sandy to phone Kendal and tell him I was under the weather. Which I was: I took Midol and spent two days in bed with a hot water bottle and back issues of *Jasper the Friendly Ghost* and *Little Henry* — comforting, little kid comics. Even the ongoing love triangle between Velma, Betty and Artie felt too emotionally taxing. Menstrual cramps were one of the few things the U-shot couldn't fix, but they were working on it.

Finally, on day three, with the cramps subsiding and my period reduced to a trickle, a brown envelope arrived in the mail for me, printed with the words: IMPORTANT DOCUMENTS ENCLOSED: OPEN IMMEDIATELY!

It was my Free Talent Test Booklet from the Famous American Artists Correspondence School. The letter read:

Dear Mr. D.R. BIONDI,

Are you *ready* to take the first step toward an *exciting career* as a creative artist? CON-GRATULATIONS! The enclosed FREE Talent Test will open the door to the future of your dreams. Whether you're after a reward-

ing career, <u>good pay</u>, <u>travel</u>, <u>commissions</u> or
simply a *worthy creative outlet*, MR. D.R.
BIONDI, the teachers at the Famous American Artists Correspondence School can <u>get
you on your way!</u> Simply follow these three
steps:

1. <u>Complete</u> the Talent Test Booklet. Make
sure you have a sharpened HB pencil handy
and an eraser.

2. Place the completed booklet in the
postage-paid envelope provided and mail it
back to us. You don't even need a stamp. <u>We'll
pay the postage for you!</u>

3. Be sure to enclose your completed enrollment form so that if your test is satisfactory,
we can IMMEDIATELY issue you your
exclusive Famous American Art Student
Enrollment Code, assign you a teacher and
invoice you for your first 26 weeks of correspondence lessons at the <u>incredibly low
rate</u> of $11.55 per lesson, plus applicable state
or provincial taxes. That's right: for just
$300 (plus taxes), you could be on your way
to a <u>whole new career</u>. If your Test shows
<u>real promise</u>, or a UNIQUE CREATIVE
SPARK, our faculty of Famous American
Artists may recommend you for a <u>bursary</u>. If
you would like to be considered, please tick
the box on your form.

The letter was signed by Norman Rockwell himself. I stared at the $300 price tag. I'd thought the course was free. But no, that was just the talent test. Maybe I could get a bursary. After all, I had been learning from the Walter Foster *How to Draw* books for years.

I opened the Talent Test Booklet.

The first page asked me to draw the head of a deer. As in *How to Draw Horses*, I started with a rectangle. Too late, I remembered that a deer's head was a triangle. I drew and erased the deer again and again until the page was a mess of soft grey lead. Eventually, I wore a hole right through the page.

I threw the test booklet away. It was becoming clear that I didn't have the talent to be a famous artist any more than I did to be Kendal's wife or the Shark's lover. Three days and still no sign of Larry Kowalchuck, despite all those promises about tracking me down and conquering me.

I waited for Mom to leave the house and dialed the extension phone next to the Virgin Mary. Kendal sounded happy and relieved to hear my voice.

"I can meet you at Postapocalyptica after lunch," I said.

"I've missed you," he said.

"Me too," I answered.

He brought comics, but we didn't waste time on reading. Instead, we immediately got down to a frenzied make-out session. I encouraged Kendal to go further and further until he was doing what the Shark had done to me. At first I didn't think Kendal would know how to touch me, the under-the-table nature of the Shark's sneak attack making it seem unusually dangerous and exciting. I thought I'd never be able to feel that amazing tingling tension again. But Kendal knew exactly what was expected of him, no doubt from his relationship with

Angie Petrone. Afterwards, he grinned shyly at me, shook his head and said, "Wow."

"I felt something break inside. I don't think I'm a virgin anymore, technically," I confided — a lie of omission, not commission, as the priests liked to say. Kendal happily assumed that he was the one who had pierced that taut little membrane of purity between my legs.

And just like that, Kendal and I were a couple again. As easy as one, two, three. We agreed to meet every day in Postapocalyptica until fall term started.

* * *

With the Shark's high-interest loan, Mr. Holub's plans for fast food greatness were turning into reality. He bought a second-hand grill, deep fryer, cash register, splintery wooden counter and pop cooler and paid the first and last month's rent on an abandoned body shop. There was no room for tables and chairs and barely enough space for customers to wedge in and place their orders.

Mrs. Holub ran up some traditional Ukrainian blouses on her Singer — folkloric red and white with embroidery and rickrack. One for me, one for Sandy. Mr. Holub offered Kendal a part-time job stacking supplies and emptying trash — jobs Mr. Holub couldn't do every day because he still had his factory job. Better money than fruit picking, as long as we actually had paying customers.

The menu, hand lettered on a card above the counter, read:

Sputnik Burgers [as the Shark had suggested]
Laika Fries [named after the doomed dog
that rode Sputnik 2]

Perogi in a Box [Mr. H's original idea,
inspired by Kentucky Fried Chicken in a
bucket]
Borscht in a Bowl [I had my doubts about
this one]
Cabbage rolls
Coke [really, RC Cola]

Opening day was busy, with everyone in the neighbourhood coming in to check us out and shake Mr. Holub's hand. The biggest sellers were (as the Shark had predicted) not Ukrainian food, but burgers, fries and pop.

On the second day, the crowd thinned to a few shipyard workers from the other side of the canal. On the third day, Sandy and I stood waiting for someone — anyone — to walk through the door while Kendal tried to come up with advertising ideas. "Maybe we could put something on the radio," he suggested, but we were made to understand by Mr. Holub that one radio ad would eat up all his existing capital, including what little wages he was able to pay us.

Around noon, the door swung open and Mrs. Donato and the twins strolled in, wearing matching tennis outfits, and ordered Perogies in a Box, to go. As I made change, Mrs. Donato eyed me.

"You're looking quite svelte, Miss Biondi."

"Thank you," I said, dropping change in her hand and wondering if she'd tip us.

She didn't.

Thinking the Donatos would be our only customers that day, we opened a *NUTS* magazine on the splintered counter to kill time. While we were reading "Spy Versus Spy," the door opened and two handsome black-haired boys — one about my age, the other in his early twenties — walked in like they owned the place.

The younger boy was slender and tall; the older was a little shorter and as musclebound as a boxer. Muscle Boy fell immediately to examining the menu, furrowing his forehead as if he didn't understand what he was reading. The other boy broke into a wide, bright smile; although his face was peppered with pimples and a scruffy growth of beard, he was on his way to turning into a heartbreaker of the Latin-lover variety.

"Hi, Debbie! And Kendal, how you doin' man?" he said, and I realized the heartbreaker was Bum Bum.

He introduced the slow-reading bodybuilder as Rocco Andolini, his buddy and unofficial cousin. The two of them, predictably, ordered Sputnik Burgers and Laika Fries.

"So, what's it like on the farm, BB?" asked Kendal, kindly turning Bum Bum's awful nickname into a cool-sounding one.

Bum Bum shrugged. "Beats the hell out of any place Catholic Children's Aid would've sent me. Could be worse. Three squares a day. They make me pick fruit and go to church, but school out there ain't so bad. Pretty easy to just slack off and read science-fiction novels under your desk. No one really gives a shit. They just want another pair of hands to help out on the farm."

Rocco slowly chewed his Sputnik Burger, keeping his big cow eyes fixed on Bum Bum. He never glanced at Sandy or me. Whenever Bum Bum made a joke, he turned to look at Rocco, making sure he was not left out of the circle. I realized then what was between them: Rocco loved Bum Bum, and vice versa. Not just loved each other, were *in* love with each other. They could have been the Gemini, twin gods of the zodiac, but unexpectedly Bum Bum was the leader of the two. The smarter one.

When they left the store, waving goodbye and promising to return soon, we sadly watched them go.

"Wow, hasn't Bum Bum changed. He's a hunk now," said Sandy.

Kendal gave her a surprised look. "I thought he and Rocco seemed like a couple of fruits."

Sandy and I shook our heads at him. I said, "You're being prejudiced."

"That's impossible," said Kendal. "I didn't say I didn't like them. I just stated an obvious fact. They're queers."

Sandy flipped her ponytail over her shoulder. "He just hasn't met the right girl."

The afternoon dragged on. We closed down the deep fryer and started working our way through the cold pop, dropping money into the cash register. We were quickly drinking our way through a day's wages.

At the end of the day, Duff and Linda picked us up. The Cutlass coughed its way to the curb and idled while Sandy locked up. In the distance, we heard the sudden up-down wail of the town's air-raid siren. Sandy clamped her hands over her ears and shut her eyes; she had hated that sound ever since that day she'd wet herself during duck-and-cover drill. Within seconds, we heard the all-clear signal, letting us know it had been yet another false alarm.

"How often does that damn thing malfunction?" asked Duff through the car window.

Kendal shrugged. "It goes off a lot in hot weather."

"Where is the siren, anyway?" asked Duff.

"Roof of the high school," said Kendal. "The caretaker knows how to shut it down."

Duff nodded at this piece of information. "They should probably just decommission the damn thing."

"But what if there were an actual attack?" I said.

"Wouldn't matter. Intercontinental Ballistic Missiles travel too fast. All that siren gives you is about fifteen minutes of intense underwear-shitting fear before Armageddon."

"Gosh, thanks for letting us know, Duff," said Kendal. "Very comforting."

As we piled into the car, Linda asked, "How's business?"

"Seriously sucking," said Sandy miserably. "It better pick up soon. Today our biggest customer was the three of us."

Duff was in overalls, his long hair pulled up under a painter's cap. He was finding handyman jobs around town so that he could keep paying the rent until he started teaching physics and calculus at St. Dismas Collegiate. As Dad had predicted, they jumped at the chance of hiring a well-educated draft dodger, and a Catholic, to boot. Linda snuggled next to him to make room for me in the front seat. The two of them had become inseparable. I knew there was something going on between them, not only from the way Duff casually draped his arm around Linda's shoulder, his dangling hand playing with the ends of her hair, but because I'd woken in the night more than once to find myself alone, the pillows in Linda's empty bed rolled under the quilt just like when she got into trouble during the missile crisis. She was sneaking out regularly to go next door and slip through the unlocked back door, past the bedroom where Nonna Peppy lay sleeping and down into the basement to Duff's bed, then back up to our room before dawn. I watched her go in and out of our bedroom window through half-closed eyes, pretending to be asleep.

This must have been the sex thing the Shark had talked about: once you started, you couldn't stop. He'd compared it to Florida orange juice, but its addictive quality made it more like plonk.

That night I lay in bed, imagining Duff and Linda all over one another next door.

I turned onto my stomach and pushed my hand between my legs but couldn't work up enough enthusiasm. Even thinking about Kendal or the Shark didn't help. I hadn't seen the Shark since that day at the Falls and wondered whether he'd show up at Sputnik Burger to conquer me, as nature intended. In my imagination, I had turned him into a dashing David Niven or a rugged but articulate Sundance Kid, although he was more like an untutored Kyle Crusher. Even if the Contessina didn't mind bad grammar, the double negatives bugged me. I wondered whether he and Kendal would fight to the death over me.

Between the mugginess of the air in my bedroom and thinking about what was going on next door between Duff and Linda, I couldn't sleep. I got out of my bed and stood at the window, listening to the night sounds of Shipman's Corners. The chainsaw whine of cicadas, the unnerving scream of a cat in heat, the sound of hot rods drag racing on the long straight stretch of Fermi Road, running every red.

I took Linda's nail file and popped off the screen, just as I'd seen her do. The soft drop to the grass strip between our house and Nonna Peppy's was farther than I thought; standing below, staring up at the bedroom window, I wondered how I would climb back inside. Linda must have devised a method. I would, too.

The full moon blanketed everything in a bleached-out light the colour of French vanilla ice cream, as if I'd fallen into some type of ghost world. I walked quickly to the back door, which I knew would be unlocked; Nonna Peppy said turning a key was hard with her arthritis, and why bother locking up with a man in the house anyway? If robbers broke in, Pepé the Seventh would bark and she would scream and Duff would come running with a baseball bat she'd armed him with for this very purpose.

Inside the house, I stood in the living room, listening to soft snores coming from Nonna Peppy's room. Pepé the Seventh waddled out to greet me, tail wagging; I knew he wouldn't bother wasting his energy barking at me. A few scratches under his neck and he headed back to Nonna's room.

If I wanted to eavesdrop on Duff and Linda, I was out of luck; the long steep stairway into the basement was notoriously shaky and creaky. They'd hear me coming a mile away.

I took off my shoes and padded into the kitchen in bare feet. Might as well see if Nonna had something tasty in the fridge. I had been purging so religiously that I felt like it was time to binge a bit. As I stood at the fridge door, staring uncertainly at a bowl of leftover polenta and a half-eaten can of sardines, I heard someone say, "You're going to scare everyone to death."

It was Linda's voice, followed by Duff's: "No, I'm not. I'm going to shake them until they wake up."

Quietly, I closed the fridge, the rubber door-seal smacking like wet lips. Their voices were coming up through the hot air register; I'd forgotten that sound travelled from the basement this way. I lowered myself to the linoleum floor. Cigarette smoke drifted into the kitchen along with their voices.

"Let's take Debbie with us," said Linda.

Yes, do that, I thought.

Duff answered, "She's still just a kid."

Oh, well, thanks. The Shark sure didn't think I was "just a kid."

"I can't just leave her."

"She's got as good a chance here as anywhere else," said Duff. "It's not like it's going to be safe with us, honey."

Honey. Give me a break.

"Maybe we could come back for her later?" suggested Linda.

"I can't make promises," answered Duff.

Traitors. Hypocrites. Leaving me here to try to save the world, while they escaped to the future.

"It's dangerous for her in Shipman's Corners," Linda said, followed by a murmured statement I couldn't make out. ". . . so distracted. I'm the only one keeping an eye on her."

Linda was keeping an eye on me?

"I get it, I get it," said Duff with an edge of irritation in his voice. "Let me think about it. I've already messed up the space-time continuum enough to cause endless trouble. If I remove Debbie from the equation, it could be disastrous."

What? What did he mean by *that*? And what did Linda mean about me being in danger? So much in our family was left unsaid, I felt as if the walls would explode if they had to absorb one more secret.

When I stood up, the floor creaked loudly. I froze.

"What was that?" whispered Linda.

"Just your grandma taking a leak," said Duff.

As I moved stealthily through the living room to the door, I noticed an object on the sideboard: the black leather wallet I'd seen Duff pull out at Cressie's. I clicked the lowest switch on the Lady Liberty floor lamp and opened the wallet, pulling out a Massachusetts driver's licence in the name of Benjamin H. Duffy with a photo of him in a pair of black horn-rims and a pocket protector that made him look like one of the men at Mission Control. Date of birth: January 18, 1948. There was also a plastic ID card from a place called General Dynamics in Pomona, California, with Duff wearing a shockingly conservative crewcut and necktie; it gave his name and title as Ben Duffy, Electrical Engineer, Research and Development,

Military Aircraft Division. And sure enough, there was his draft card. I wondered why someone like Duff would be sent to Vietnam at all, when he could have been inventing novel ways to kill the enemy with robots and viruses and whatnot. According to Duff, history would show that Vietnam and the other Domino wars were an attempt to wipe out his entire generation and start all over again by mating old men, like Richard Nixon, with the last ten years of Miss Universe finalists, a conspiracy that sounded like the plot of the propaganda comic Kendal and I had read at Cressie's.

I slipped the cards back into Duff's wallet and returned it to the sideboard. Now I knew the truth. Just as Kendal had predicted, I was beginning to think that Duff was a class-A bullshit artist, his story about being from the future, a fantasy. I'd been brainwashed to believe him. Had I really lost two years of my life in a time hop, or was I turning into a plonkhead?

When the Famous American Artists Correspondence School called to speak to Mr. Biondi, Mom put Dad on the phone. After hanging up, he walked into the kitchen with the proud news that his youngest child had shown glimmerings of artistic genius — so much so, that they'd assumed I was a boy. A representative of the school was coming over to our house that very evening to discuss my future.

Mom snorted. "Coming over to hard-sell us, more like it. How did they hear about Debbie's doodles?"

"I sent away for a free talent test," I mumbled through a mouthful of toast.

"Congratulations," said Dad. "They said you have a unique creative spark."

He was so happy, I didn't have the heart to tell him that I had thrown away the test. I hoped that bit of information wouldn't come out while we were in the living room, awkwardly sitting through the Famous American Artists Correspondence School sales pitch.

*   *   *

The representative of the school looked nothing like an artist: he was a small man in a dandruff-dusted sports jacket, with nervous hands and a twitchy lip. He carried a vinyl briefcase bearing that self-portrait of Norman Rockwell I'd seen in the ad and the words: *We're looking for people who like to draw.*

Despite his twitchiness and the pungent odour of Old Spice and rye, the salesman said many things that my parents — particularly my father — were happy to hear. I had clearly demonstrated a high degree of artistic ability. There was absolutely no question of that; the school's adjudication process was strict and stringent and scientifically proven. This seemed odd, given that I didn't send in the test.

My mind drifted. I woke up again when he said that many alumni of the Famous American Artists School were themselves now famous: he rattled off the names of several well-known cartoonists whose strips appeared in the colour comics of the *Shipman's Corners Examiner*, including the one with the sexy hillbillies, Mom's favourite.

"She comes by her talent honestly," confided Dad. "I've always had a bit of an artistic streak myself."

I looked at Dad in surprise. "Since when?"

Dad lifted his chin. "I loved to draw when I was young. I wasn't bad. If I'd had some encouragement, who knows where I'd be now?"

The salesman swivelled his head toward Dad, lip twitching: it was the expression of a small cat preparing to corner a large slow-moving mouse.

"We have someone local available to act as Debbie's instructor right now, to provide marking, feedback, personalized lessons, even meet with her as often as once a week, and this individual is less than five miles from your beautiful home, can't beat that, but I can't guarantee that this opportunity will last: might be gone by tomorrow or even later tonight. You see, the good ones — and trust me, this instructor is a good one — get snapped up fast."

Giving a soft burp, he removed a fountain pen from his pocket and laid it on top of a form he'd quietly unfolded on the coffee table. Then he hung his hands between his knees and waited, eyes on Dad.

Mom scrutinized the small print. "Three hundred dollars seems steep."

The salesman sat back on the couch, folded his hands over his tiny paunch and gave a quiet sigh. "Spread over twenty-six weeks, that's only about ten dollars a week, breaking it down for you. Less than the price of a cup of coffee a day."

"I can break it down just fine for myself, thanks. That's over eleven dollars a week, which is about a dollar forty for a coffee," said Mom. "You can get a decent cup for a quarter in this town."

"Think of it as an investment in your daughter's future," suggested the salesman, changing tactics.

"The guy who sold us a set of encyclopedias told us the same thing," said Mom in a voice that sounded as if she suspected some type of international conspiracy of door-to-door salesmen.

The salesman looked over at Dad, who was reading one of the brochures.

"This sounds on the up-and-up. It would be good for Debbie to have a hobby," Dad said. Mom, the salesman and I watched him sign on the dotted line. And just like that, I became a student of the Famous American Artists Correspondence School.

After exchanging boring bits of adult blah blah blah about tax deductions and void cheques, the salesman shook my hand, presented me with my complimentary Famous American

Artist student portfolio and assured me that my instructor would be in touch with me within five business days. My course would be carried out by correspondence, with my finished assignments and the instructor's critiques passed back and forth by mail. Depending on what we could work out, we might meet even more often than once a week.

"It all depends on your level of ability, honey," the salesman told me, giving Dad a broad wink to show that he was in on the open secret of just how staggeringly talented I was.

When a postcard finally arrived on behalf of the Famous American Artists School with my instructor's name, address and phone number, I stood at the mailbox for five long minutes, staring at it. It read:

Mrs. Beatrice Kendal
105A Zurich Street

*   *   *

The first time I went out to Z Street for an art lesson, Dad drove me, even though I assured him I was more than capable of getting there myself.

"You've got to watch yourself in that neighbourhood," was his only explanation for the lift.

When we got to Kendal's house and Bea Kendal opened the door in her tie-dyed pantsuit and chic scarf, I could see Dad was taken aback — even more so when he came in and saw her paintings.

"I've always suspected Debbie had artistic ability," she said.

"She comes by it honestly," Dad said. "I've always had a leaning that way myself."

This seemed to impress Mrs. Kendal, who folded her arms and listened to a long description by Dad of the lost days of his youth, sketching dogs and farmhouses. Pretty soon Dad and Mrs. Kendal had completely forgotten me; when she offered him something cold to drink, he accepted, following her into the kitchen to continue the conversation. I had the uncomfortable feeling that they had, in the words of the older generation, hit it off.

Mrs. Kendal was an excellent instructor, far better than the business studies teacher who also taught grade nine visual art, my only arts elective at St. Dismas Collegiate — all he did was show us murky tinted slides of Renaissance sculpture and occasionally let us blow up a piece of pottery in the kiln. Despite the biography that was eventually cooked up for me by my publisher, which included an MFA from New York's prestigious Parsons School, my only art instruction came from Mrs. Kendal, who met with me every week to practise perspective, life drawing and colour theory. It turned out to be the best three hundred dollars my parents could have invested in me; years later, it would provide what would turn out to be my only marketable skill. Not to mention that, over those weeks of driving me back and forth, a friendship developed between Mrs. Kendal and Dad, making it easier for him to take a fatherly interest in John Kendal.

But I'm getting ahead of myself.

*　*　*

Fast forward to the first week of high school — not much of a change, even with those lost eighteen months, since my classes were full of kids I'd known since kindergarten. The biggest adjustment was seeing Duff roam the hallways in a short-sleeved shirt and clip-on tie, chased by kids in welding glasses, waving their chemistry homework and shouting, "Sir! Sir!" wanting him to look at their equations or answer a question about the periodic table. Enrollment in his classes skyrocketed when he announced that he would teach how to build a TV that could receive broadcasts from another dimension — a popular project in a town that could barely pick up stations from Buffalo.

Linda had weepily returned to university in Toronto with promises to come home every weekend. Duff had been spending a lot of time at our house ever since her departure, eating most of his meals with us, as if he were already some type of de facto son-in-law.

I eased into the routine of six hours of rotating classes every day, Kendal and I brushing fingertips or even stealing a kiss as we passed one another at the bell or meeting up after school at our lockers. We'd settled into the role of high school sweethearts; the younger, more progressive teachers looked at us with satisfaction. To underline the point, Kendal was elected student council president and captain of the basketball team, while I took up Linda's old position on the volleyball team and became the first girl to sit as student council treasurer. The first months of high school were a golden time for Kendal and me. It felt as if we had turned a corner into a bright, brave, colour-blind utopia.

On October fourth, I turned fifteen. Kendal took me to a movie. *Shaft*. He knew the guy selling tickets, so we were able to get in despite the movie's Restricted rating. As the trailer said: *If you wanna see* Shaft, *ask yo momma!*

We drove downtown in Duff's Cutlass, the battered chassis and U.S. plates giving the two of us an aura of grit and glamour. "Mixed-race couple sees *Shaft* at the Shipman's Corners Downtown Cinema — right on!" We were practically as urban as Buffalo now.

The plot was about how the "mob" wanted to "take back Harlem."

"I'm looking for a nigga named John Shaft," said a stereotypically Italian mobster.

"You just found him — *wop*," answered Shaft.

Kendal gave a snort of laughter.

I loved watching movies set in New York City. Dangerous. Dirty. Crowded. Unpredictable. One of two places I wanted to travel to with Kendal, the other being the Sea of Tranquility.

* * *

I had forced myself to stop worrying about the end of the world. Duff's wallet full of twentieth-century ID convinced me that he was nothing more than a con artist and that all my memories of hopping through time had sprung from my overactive imagination. Duff had never mentioned alternate timelines or me being the Ion Tagger. The whole idea of hopping into a parallel world, taking everyone on Earth with me, had begun to sound like the plot of a comic book.

And yet, every time I walked into the TV room while Dad was watching the Buffalo evening news, an ominous dark tension seemed to be tightly wound around every word that came out of Walter Cronkite's mouth.

The Strategic Arms Limitation Treaty talks in Helsinki — known as SALT — were not going well. Richard Nixon was about to press the issue of nuclear arms limitation with a no-holds-barred show of force on Amchitka Island, exploding the Cannikin bomb, the largest underground nuclear test ever carried out in America. A ragtag group of seafaring hobos predicted tsunamis and earthquakes. They said the blast would cause untold devastation to what people were starting to refer to as "Earth's ecology."

"Amchitka Island is on Russia's doorstep," said Duff. "What, exactly, is the point of a five-megaton underground nuclear test anyway?"

"They're trying to send the Ruskies a message," said Dad approvingly.

Duff cleared his throat, something he always did when he was about to disagree with Dad. "Not sure the Soviets give a damn. They have a considerable stockpile of nuclear weapons themselves."

My mother frowned and ladled out the lasagna. "*Ma che*," she said, sighing. "Politics at the supper table."

* * *

That year, October 31 fell on a Sunday, so the St. Dismas Halloween dance would be held on the thirtieth, a Saturday night. Everyone was excited by the news that Mr. Duffy was going to be "the man" for the Halloween dance, a cross between a bouncer and a chaperone. It was expected he would tolerate bad behaviour — drinking plonk in the bathrooms, pot smoking, fights.

Unexpectedly, Duff stood guard outside the gym door that evening dressed as a priest. With his hair cut short and a fake beard hiding his perpetually sunburned skin (I had decided he was suffering from eczema, not radiation burns), Duff was unrecognizable. Linda was at his side in a nun's habit.

"Except for the wimple, it's pretty comfortable," she told me, tucking a few stray hairs under her veil.

I had come to the dance dressed as the Contessina — flesh-coloured tights, high boots, ballet leotard, a purple-tinted beehive wig. Sandy wore layers of ragged petticoats that Mrs. Holub must have brought from the old country, and the tight red bodice and red boots of her traditional Ukrainian dance costume: she was supposed to be a gypsy fortune teller. She'd unbraided her hair and left it an uncombed mess, as if she'd just got out of bed, looking even more spectacularly beautiful than usual.

"Is that a Snugglegirl costume, Deb?" Sandy asked, shaking out her petticoats.

I frowned at her. "I'm a crime fighter. The Contessina Doloria di Largo, Captain Kyle Crusher's girlfriend from the *Agents of V.E.N.G.E.A.N.C.E.* comics. How does this look like a Snugglegirl?"

She shrugged. "Doesn't matter. You look really skinny dressed like that. Have you lost weight?"

"A little," I said, trying not to nibble on my bile-chapped lips. I seemed to be thinking about food all the time these days.

Kendal came as Shaft, wearing a turtleneck, sunglasses and leather jacket, with a water pistol tucked in his belt. He'd grown mutton-chop sideburns and wore a fake moustache that made me wish he'd grow a real one.

"You should dress like that all the time," I told him.

"Hotter than Bond. Cooler than Bullitt," he said, quoting the movie's trailer.

Judy and Jayne Donato dressed as the Pan Am stewardesses from *Coffee, Tea or Me?* and flirted with Bum Bum and Rocco, who had driven in from the farm. In old-fashioned three-piece suits, Borsalino hats and wingtip shoes, the guys were straight out of *The Godfather*. Bum Bum carried a violin case as a prop.

"Where'd you get the threads, man?" Kendal asked, adjusting Bum Bum's pinstriped lapels.

"Rocco's dad, Frank," said Bum Bum. "He's got a shitload of them stuck in mothballs. He's given them up for leisure suits, so he said they were all ours."

One of Shipman's Corners' many garage bands had been brought in to provide live music: with their combination of electric guitars, drums, mandolins and balalaikas, they were a Ukrainian-Italian fusion folk music group that had added some Led Zeppelin, Elton John and David Bowie to their repertoire. They had just kicked off the evening with "The Immigrant Song" — perfect for St. Dismas — when Linda fluttered up onto the stage in her nun's habit, shouting "Cut the music" and making a slashing motion across her throat. The lead guitarist handed her the microphone.

"I want you all to remain calm and stay where you are," said Linda. "We just received news from the States — Mr. Duffy will be making an announcement."

Duff's voice boomed out over the PA system, struggling to be calm, but slightly shaky — a nice touch. "Your attention please! The school board has just received an alert from the Emergency Broadcast System, which I have been instructed to read to you, as follows: a thermonuclear test was carried out on Amchitka Island earlier today at 12:01 a.m., Pacific Time. Dead radioactive birds have washed up on the coast of Siberia. The Soviet Union considers this an act of aggression. They have declared war on members of the North American Treaty Organization, including Canusa. NBC New York reports that NORAD is confirming that Soviet Intercontinental Ballistic Missiles have left their silos. In a short time, we will be under nuclear attack."

We looked at one another, a bunch of terrified teenagers dressed as superheroes and characters from gangster movies. This was the moment we had spent our entire childhoods preparing for. The drills, the duck-and-covers, the Emergency Broadcast System tests — it all came down to this. World War Three. And as our parents had always pointed out, Shipman's Corners would be the first to go.

Sandy put her hands over her face, silently weeping. I put my arm around her. Her body was trembling as if she were standing in a gale.

Duff's voice continued over the PA. "Please listen carefully to this emergency bus schedule: Welland Avenue to Niagara Street, bus 1A. Scott Street to Lakeshore Road, 1B. If you live outside those areas, catch bus 2C, that's 2C, and it will drop off any of you who live on the concession roads or on the other side of the Welland Canal. Please remain calm and line up quietly to dismiss. Buses will be in the parking lot momentarily. May God be with you all, and your families."

The rush for the doors knocked over some of the smaller kids who hadn't yet had their growth spurt. I felt a hand grab mine. Kendal's.

"It's bullshit!" he yelled over the screams. "It's got to be a prank."

"I know!" I shouted back. "If it was a real attack, we'd be hearing the —"

That's when the air-raid siren blasted down at us from the roof of the school, an up-down, up-down wailing like Planet Earth's collective death scream.

In the stampede out of the gym, I saw Linda's fluttering nun's habit disappear through the doors of the girls' change room. Strange, that she was running in the opposite direction from everyone else.

I started to consider who I wanted to die with, my family or Kendal. Duff had said that ICBMs could reach us in under fifteen minutes, barely enough time to go home and kiss Nonna Peppy and my parents goodbye. I had little faith in the anti-radiation suits in the basement, and even if we did survive, what would be the point of living in a world devoid of other people? Kendal's hand tightened around mine, settling the matter: if it was the end of the world, we were going out together. Caught in the current of the crowd, the two of us were pushed through the fire doors, with Sandy, Bum Bum, Rocco and the Donato twins close behind. The buses hadn't arrived and I doubted they ever would; the announcement was probably just a way to normalize the situation by making it seem like the authorities were in control. Judging by the crowd of milling, weeping teenagers outside the school, fighting over a single pay phone, that strategy wasn't working.

Kendal looked over our heads in all directions. "Where the hell is Duff? He should be out here, keeping people from freaking out."

"There's room for all of us in my car," shouted Rocco. "But where the fuck should we go?"

"Our new house has a fallout shelter," said Judy-Garland. "Mom keeps her canned tomatoes inside it."

Sandy hugged herself, shivering with fear. "I want to go home and be with my parents."

"I've got Duff's keys. I'll take you in his car while Rocco takes the rest of them to the Donatos," said Kendal, turning to look at me. "Debbie, go with Rocco. I'll check on my mom and your folks and be there as fast as I can."

I tried to protest but he kissed me, said "I love you," pushed me into Bum Bum's arms and got into the Cutlass, a few more kids from Sandy's block hopping into the back seat. Kendal peeled out of the parking lot just as Rocco popped the trunk of his car to carry more passengers.

The Donatos had moved into a sprawling split-level with a weeping willow on the front lawn. A jungle gym stood in the backyard, like the last cage in a zoo from which the animals had all escaped. Their subdivision was a tangle of dead-end streets and culs-de-sac, turning back on themselves like snakes eating their own tails. Piles of dirt and yawning pits, waiting to be filled by brand-new bungalows, made the neighbourhood look like a war zone.

As we ran up the front walk, Claudia Donato opened the door, a martini glass almost toppling out of one manicured hand, her hair backcombed into a brilliant dark dome, crowned by a rhinestone tiara. The sounds of party music and laughter spilled out of the house.

"You all look adorable!" she slurred, kissing me on both cheeks as she slopped her drink on the wall-to-wall. "You're so sweet — I could just gobble you right up. Come in!"

Inside the foyer, I noticed a goldfish bowl full of key chains — Mickey Mouse, Playboy bunny ears, War Amps of Canada, rabbits' feet, peace signs.

"Mom, didn't anyone tell you . . ." Judy-Garland started to say.

Claudia waved off the warning. "Honey, it's the usual malfunction. We turned on the TV and all we saw was *Hollywood Squares*. Daddy even called ShipCo Security. They said it was a Halloween prank; someone's jiggered the siren so they can't turn it off. Relax and have a drink, kids."

We trailed Claudia through a living room packed with middle-aged princesses, ballet dancers and movie stars. A few men were wrinkled hippies in bell-bottoms and silly wigs, or cowboys in Stetsons, their beer bellies flopping over the belts of toy holsters. Dusty Springfield's deep voice oozed suggestively out of the hi-fi.

Looking like they belonged in a gangster movie, Rocco and Bum Bum stood in the living room in their 1950s suits, sipping beer. The siren continued to rise and fall, rise and fall. Al Donato dealt with it by turning up the hi-fi. I drifted into the kitchen, where the twins had started arranging platters of

Ritz crackers topped with slimy canned oysters. The stench of hot Gruyère cheese floated out of a ceramic pot.

"Don't scald the fondue, honey," Claudia told Judy-Garland as she leaned down to sniff the pungent goo.

Claudia handed me a tray. "Manhattans, martinis and White Russians. Would you mind taking this around, love? There's a girl."

I weaved my way through the crowd, past Elizabeth Taylors and Bette Davises and *Rosemary's Baby*–era Mia Farrows sipping martinis and laughing loudly at the men's dirty jokes. Princess Graces plucked White Russians off the tray with dainty pink-lacquered nails and Claudia Cardinales spoke in breathy, fake French accents. Sailors and cowboys ogled the ballerinas and go-go dancers while sucking beer straight from the bottle.

On the other side of the room, smoking a pipe and nursing a Manhattan, stood the Shark, a Playboy medallion nestled in the thicket of chest hair bristling out of the top of his shiny black bathrobe. Next to him, an emaciated, balloon-breasted blonde, predictably costumed as a sexy Bunny, teetered on spike heels with one knobby knee cocked like a pony striking a pose. It took me a few seconds to recognize her. The blonde was Angie Petrone, or an inflated, sculpted and ruthlessly exfoliated version of her former self; she looked like a cross between an android from a pornographic sci-fi novel and some type of mad scientist's comic book chemistry experiment gone wrong. Her curly black hair had been bleached and straightened, her dark eyes turned acid green, her eyelashes curled and lengthened so that they brushed her forehead. Her waist was cinched tightly in a metal corset, from which hung a thin silver chain. The Shark had one end looped tightly around his wrist.

When the Shark noticed me, he whispered a word in

Angie's ear, then clipped her corset chain to a little hook on the wall, as if leashing up a very expensive dog. The type of animal valuable enough to steal, but too stupid to ever find its way home, like an Afghan hound. Angie looked at the Shark dully and sipped a cocktail the colour of congealed blood. She never shifted from that stilted cock-kneed pose.

Holding his highball glass over the heads of the crowd, the Shark pushed his way to me, his eyes eating me up, just like that day in the Falls.

"I know you from somewhere," he said.

I couldn't believe it. He'd torn away my virginity and left me with a summer's worth of ridiculous fantasies and he didn't even remember who I was?

"I met you at Table Rock House with the Holubs," I said, setting down my tray.

I could see recognition in his eyes. "Oh, yeah! You're so skinny, I didn't recognize you, is all. Those nice big boobs of yours are practically gone. Still cute as hell, though. And we can give you back the boobs easy enough. Let me pour you a drink."

He took me by the elbow and guided me to a shimmering castle of liquor bottles on the bar where a tipsy tramp leaned on a dimly lit lampstand, against a background of flecked gold wallpaper with a pattern of naked women in silhouette. The Shark's face and mine were reflected in a mirror that said CINZANO.

"Whaddya want? Tequila Sunrise? Rye and ginger? Sex on the Beach? Plonk?"

My eyes caught on a candy-coloured bottle that looked like the brandy cherries we drank in shot glasses at Christmas.

"That."

He picked up the bottle. "Dubonnet. French! You got taste. Rocks?"

"Uh — sure."

He grabbed a handful of ice cubes out of a bucket, dropped them into a highball glass and filled it to the brim with the thick red aperitif. Then he reached into the pocket of his robe and fished out a tiny white pill, holding it up between thumb and forefinger before plopping it into my drink.

"What's that?"

"Spoonful of sugar to make the medicine go down." He clicked my glass with his and said, "Here's to chemistry, little girl."

I tasted it. Sweet and sour at the same time, like my grandfather's wine cut with 7-Up. Blechh. I swallowed my first sip, then let the next one dribble back into the glass.

Across the room, Judy-Garland and Jayne-Mansfield were go-go dancing on the living room rug, surrounded by a gyrating posse of TV cowboys. The starlets and ballerinas looked on with crossed arms, their Virginia Slims smouldering angrily between sharpened fingernails. Meanwhile, Claudia pushed backwards through the swinging Dutch door, a roiling fondue pot balanced between pink piglet-shaped oven mitts. I had a vision of her tripping and spewing hot cheese all over the guests, but she staggered safely to the buffet table.

"I didn't know old people had Halloween parties," I tried to say, but it came out *I dunguhswun's dress luk Haween*, as if someone else's tongue had been stuffed between my teeth.

"You never heard of a key party?" The Shark slid his satiny arm around my waist, his fingers strumming my breast like a Spanish guitar.

I shook my head. That one little sip of candy-coloured booze was making me feel warm and loose and jangly, as if my shoulders and legs had been detached from my body. The Shark took the pipe out of his mouth and grinned at me.

"All the guys throw their keys in a bowl. At the end of the night, the chicks reach in and pick out a set. Whatever guy's keys they get, they gotta go home with him. No one knows who slept with who." He leaned in close to whisper in my ear, "You look so sexy dressed like that, you could be a Snugglegirl, know that? I can arrange an audition for you. ShipCo'd hire you in a flash. You'll love it. Parties, clothes, cruises. All the drugs and booze you want. And I get to show you the ropes so you know what the guys want. You'll love that, too."

Through the murk of my aperitif-and-unknown-drug-addled brain, light dawned. The Shark wasn't in love with me. He was a ShipCo recruiter.

"I'm not innerrested in being a Snug'girl. My boyfriend John Kendal will be here soon," I said, trying to be careful to pronounce every syllable.

The Shark burst out laughing. "You're dating a *Kendal*? That kid who looks like Meadowlark Lemon, used to date Angel? Oh lawdy, lawdy! If I knowed you liked that type, I'd've got myself a tan."

I threw the rest of my Dubonnet into his face. The red drink dripped from his nose as his leer turned into a snarl.

"You little fucking bitch, I'm gonna kill you." He tried to grab my arm, but I moved out of reach too fast.

"Go to hell," I said and pushed my way through the crowd.

Behind me, one of the Liz Taylors brayed a laugh. "A party isn't a party 'til Larry gets a drink thrown at him."

The Shark started to follow me down the hallway, but Rocco blocked his way. Bum Bum tried to catch me in a hug but I brushed past him in embarrassment. I searched for a bathroom where I could lock myself in, but the powder room off the front hall was occupied. I ran upstairs where I suspected I'd find a big master bathroom. Bingo: hot pink walls and a giant shower stall, the vanity covered in Claudia's makeup and shampoos and perfumes. I locked the door and lifted the fuzzy pink toilet seat, lowered my tights and plopped down to pee. Suddenly dizzy, I bent over, closed my eyes and rested my head between my knees. I wasn't sure whether the wooziness was because of the booze or the Shark's little white pill.

I still had my head between my knees when I felt a tap on my shoulder. I opened my eyes without lifting my head — had the Shark found me?

No. Worse than the Shark. Much worse: legs in white support hose ending in a pair of white crepe-soled Oxfords.

A familiar voice said, "I've had just about enough out of you, missy. Time to start coughing up what you know about a certain anarchist."

I lifted my head. Nurse Dotty was holding up a hypodermic needle in one latex-gloved hand and gripping my arm with the other. I tried to get up off the toilet seat but I seemed frozen in place.

As she reached down to angle the needle into my bicep, she said, "Larry's an asshole. He should've known better than to try to recruit a Normal like you. ShipCo prefers scraping the bottoms of barrels for their Snugglegirls. But his seduction pill was a useful coincidence. As you can no doubt already feel, it causes temporary paralysis. Very effective when you prefer your victim helpless."

I watched, horrified, as the tip of the needle pricked my skin. But something didn't make sense — *I felt pain*. If I were actually paralyzed, I wouldn't be feeling anything at all.

Taking a deep breath to summon all my strength, I slammed one knee straight up into the nurse's chest — a move I'd seen the Contessina do many times in *Agents of V.E.N.G.E.A.N.C.E.* while tied into a chair, to some beefy Russian henchman with an eye patch. Bringing down Florence Nightingale's evil twin sister was a piece of cake by comparison.

With a grunt of surprise — I could almost see the "OOF!" floating in a speech bubble over her head — the nurse collapsed like a broken bag of white PEI potatoes, the glass needle shattering into itsy bitsy shards on the marble floor. Whatever hellish serum she was trying to pump into me formed a nasty little puddle. As if some drunk party guest had mistaken a floor tile for the toilet.

I yanked up my tights and snapped up the crotch of my leotard while the nurse moaned and writhed among the splinters of glass. Blood trails were forming on her white support hose.

"I'd pre-treat those bloodstains, if I were you, Nurse," I said. "Didn't anyone tell you not to wear white after Labour Day?"

"You little bitch!" seethed the white witch, trying to stand. Putting my foot into what I judged to be the centre of her I Can't Believe It's a Girdle foundation garment, I thrust her back into the shower stall and turned the tap marked COLD on full blast. It was hard to distinguish her screams from the wailing of the air-raid siren. This was starting to feel like fun.

The doorknob of the bathroom rattled, followed by a sharp knock.

"Go away, it's occupied," I called out.

"Debbie?" It was Bum Bum's voice.

I opened the door and fell into him. Bum Bum wrapped his arms around me and kissed my forehead.

"Not sure Kendal would be happy to see us like this," said Bum Bum.

"Or Rocco," I said.

The rumble of Bum Bum's laugh reached my ear through his chest.

He led me down the hallway past a paunchy cowboy backing up a giggling starlet against the flocked gold wallpaper. As we descended the circular staircase to where Rocco waited for us, Bum Bum explained that Kendal had called with news that the air raid was a prank, but Duff and Linda had disappeared, along with Dad's truck. Now Mrs. Kendal was driving Dad all over Shipman's Corners looking for them.

Before we left, I glimpsed the Shark with one arm around Angie and the other around Judy-Garland, his voice booming over the party noises. "You look like you really could be a Pan Am stewardess, darlin'. Ever hear of the Mile High Club? I'm a member."

Bum Bum and Rocco shot their cuffs and adjusted their ties as I pulled on my crime-fighter boots.

"What now?" I asked, zipping up.

"We meet Kendal and track down that asshole, Duff," answered Rocco. "Looks like it's gonna be a long night, Contessina."

Gripping a crowbar, Bum Bum ran his hand along the edge of the crumbling wooden window frame above our heads.

"Broke in here once when I was ten. Wasn't too hard."

"Where's the window lead to?" Kendal asked.

"A shitter. And from there, Cressie's storeroom."

Bum Bum steadied himself on Rocco's shoulder, who knitted his fingers into a step for Bum Bum's foot. They counted together, one, two, three, and Rocco boosted Bum Bum high enough to lever the crowbar between the window frame and the ledge. One quick motion and the window groaned open, ancient paint chips flaying away like dead skin under a rasp. Bum Bum pumped the crowbar to widen the space, then slithered through headfirst. Next, Kendal jumped up, grabbed the sill with his good hand while Bum Bum caught the other, and scrambled in easily, his feet kicking the air behind him. My turn. One, two, three, and Rocco boosted me, but I didn't have the strength to pull myself over the sill and ended up dangling by my fingertips. Kendal and Bum Bum grabbed my hands and hauled me through the window, my arms shrieking with pain.

"You hardly weigh nothing," whispered Bum Bum, giving Rocco a thumbs-up. The deal was, Rocco would remain at his post in the alley and raise the alarm if Cressie — or anyone else — showed up at the back of the store.

"Ready?" asked Bum Bum. Kendal nodded yes for us both. I heard the squeak of hinges, and the space ahead of us yawned like a vast, windy black hole.

"I'm going to chance a light 'til we see where we're going," whispered Bum Bum. "Knowing Cressie, he could've set bear traps."

A wild, staring eye sprang up out of the darkness, startling me; Kendal grabbed my arm to steady me.

"Just a horse's head," he whispered. "From that broken-down old carousel in the park."

The flashlight raked the room, illuminating a stampede of horses, legs flexed, heads thrown back and nostrils flaring, some lying on the floor impaled on their poles, others slumped against the walls, flank to flank.

He angled the flashlight at the floor as we picked our way past upturned hooves and charging legs. Then he cut the light and gently pushed open the door leading into the store.

Streetlights illuminated Cresswell's Collectibles just enough for us to make our way to the wall of cubbyholes behind the cash. Kendal pointed up at the Florsheim shoebox on the top shelf, stepping on a footstool to slide it out.

"Let's get the hell out of here," he whispered, the box under his arm.

As we turned to retrace our steps, a supernova exploded inside Cresswell's, the light so intense that I was blinded for a few seconds. I spun in every direction until hands grabbed my shoulders and pushed me to the floor, a body — Bum Bum's — squashing mine. Grit on the floor ground into my face as voices shouted and glass shattered all around us. Someone or something was coming through the front window of Cressie's store. Eyes squeezed shut, arms over my head in duck-and-cover position, I heard the sound of boots hitting the floor planks.

I opened my eyes to bloody rose petals floating in the air, bouncing in the light of cherry tops rotating on the roofs of squad cars parked outside the front window. White circles, like the end of a reel of a Super 8 home movie, exploded in my field of vision, but I could still make out Bum Bum scrabbling at the floorboards with his fingers, yanking one up. A trap door. He swung his legs into the hole and dropped over the side, disappearing from view. Kendal pushed me after him. I fell onto soft, stinking earth, Kendal landing on top of me. We were inside a pit, maybe four feet below floor level. The odours of oil and mould and something I couldn't identify, and didn't want to, hung heavily in the air. Bum Bum pulled a chain to close the trapdoor and all was dark.

"Where are we?" I whispered. The smell was gagging me.

"Shhh," said Bum Bum.

Boot steps thundered over our heads. Fingers of light poked through gaps in the floorboards, feeling for us; Bum Bum's face was suddenly visible, his eyes staring upwards, one hand holding the trapdoor chain taut. He looked weirdly calm. As if he did this every day.

I could see now that we were in a crawlspace at the mouth of a larger tunnel. Light continued to stab at us but we were too deep to be seen. Still, I cowered into Bum Bum; he pulled me into his arms and whispered close to my ear, "Calm, now."

"Where the hell did he go?" a dead-sounding male voice demanded. I knew this voice: the policeman from the Pat Boone lie detector test.

"There was more'n one. They just disappeared," said another voice. "Try out back, they must have made a run for it."

"The Mounties should catch their own man," a third voice griped.

Then, the policeman's voice again. "No dicking around. Treat with extreme prejudice. Girls, boys, I don't give a shit. We'll pump them all until someone tells us where that Yammer went."

Bum Bum, Kendal and I could see each other's faces clearly now as the rosy pink lights of the cherry tops rippled through the crawlspace like a river of blood.

"Rocco," I whispered.

Bum Bum shook his head as if to say, *don't worry*. He began to move forward into the darkness, and Kendal and I followed. We wriggled on our bellies like three blind slugs. Pebbles ground into my hands and knees. Occasionally, I slid through something disgustingly wet and mushy, trying not to imagine what it might be.

Bum Bum whispered, "Stop." His flashlight clicked on, revealing a solid wall of greasy bricks. When bits of dry earth crumbled over us, I felt a rush of claustrophobic panic: What if the tunnel collapsed and we were buried alive? What if no one ever found us? Would it be a slow death, suffocating in the ground under Cressie's? Bum Bum's face loomed out of the darkness.

"You got the box?"

Kendal coughed. "Sure."

He pulled off the lid. Bum Bum's flashlight illuminated the contents: no solenoid. Instead, the box held a postcard of a bombed-out building, a shuffling ragged mass of humanity staring vacantly at the camera. On the back, in script lettering, were the words: "I love New York." But over the word love was a drawing of a heart with a slash through it.

"Duff left us a message," said Kendal.

We sat crushed together, until the last shout and boot step vanished. And then, we waited a little longer.

"Okay," said Bum Bum at last.

He pushed himself into a half-crouch and duck-walked into an alcove I hadn't realized was there. We were facing a wooden door sunken into the brick wall. Bum Bum knocked hard three times, paused, then twice again. The door shivered and reluctantly opened, letting in a blast of fresh air, and Rocco's head.

"What the fuck?" queried Rocco.

The three of us yanked at the door from our side and it gave way enough for us to squeeze through. Bum Bum turned to smile at me, his face covered in dirt.

"After you."

Legs trembling, I crawled through the opening into a deep window-well made of brick. I looked up. Rusty grillwork divided the night sky into a grid of stars.

"What was that place we crawled through?" I asked, after we'd each got out.

"One of Harriet Tubman's old tunnels for hiding escaped slaves. Shipman's Corners is honeycombed with them," said Kendal. "How did you know it was there, BB?"

"There isn't a hiding place in this town I don't know," said Bum Bum.

"Who were those guys?" I asked.

"Cops," said Bum Bum. "Canusa Mounties, most likely. Maybe some ShipCo MPs. They must have loved taking the boots to Cressie's window."

*　*　*

Bum Bum boosted Rocco, who pushed the grillwork aside, and lifted each of us single-handedly to the top of a brick wall that had once been part of a long-abandoned canal. One lonely ship's bollard, the concrete cap cracked in half, squatted in a patch of weeds like an iron toadstool.

None of us was old enough to remember the days when ships unloaded at the docks of stores in downtown Shipman's Corners, but we had all played beside the abandoned canal, with its rainbow of scum and dirty white foam. On warm days, the rotten egg smell drifted all over town. After a kid fell in and drowned under the thick froth, the town agreed to pump out the water and fill in the trench, but Cressie's back alley still had the look of a place where sailors had once swung barrels and crates off ships.

We slid down the embankment below the wall and picked our way through what would have been the bottom of the canal but was now a scrubland of weedy trees, junked stoves and wrecked cars. Rocco led us to where he and Kendal had hidden the Swinger and the Cutlass, in a thick patch of wild raspberry bushes.

The boys and I agreed that Duff's Cutlass had to go. Given what we'd just seen, there was probably an APB for it across Shipman's Corners and the Greater Canusa Region. I was pretty sure the evil Mustang-driving nurse would be part of the force. Headlights off, we took a fast, short drive to an abandoned canal hidden on a slice of scrubland between a private golf course and an engine train factory. The relentless shrieking of the siren continued as we drove the back roads and veered onto a rocky path.

We all put our shoulders to the back fender of Duff's car. It teetered on the broken concrete along the edge and finally tipped over the side into the frothy water below. Nose down, trunk in the air, the way you'd imagine the *Titanic* sinking, the Cutlass paused for a moment as it filled with water, then sank in a fizzy rush of tainted foam, like a giant Alka-Seltzer after a particularly nasty party.

Afterwards, as we walked toward Rocco's Swinger, a flash of light illuminated the horizon. In the distance glowed what looked like a raging fire.

"What the fuck," said Rocco. "Maybe it really is a nuclear war."

"No, the fields must be burning out in the township," said Kendal.

"It's all vineyards out there," said Bum Bum. "Those wood posts would burn like stink."

"Sparkling Sparrow," I whispered.

As we would later discover, someone had set all two hundred acres of grapevines alight.

* * *

Rocco pulled into the driveway at Nonna's house just as the siren stopped. We heard later that the school caretaker had finally figured out a way to disable Duff's solenoid: he took a blowtorch to it. It had been sounding for three continuous hours. Complaints of hearing loss and tinnitus would keep the Shipman's Corners audiologists busy for years to come.

When we wearily staggered into the house, Nonna Peppy was holding the phone, her face white. She held it out to me without a word.

"Hello?" I said.

"Debbie, it's Linda."

"Where are you?"

"On our way west. Hitchhiking. We're going to join those people going out in the boats to stop the Amchitka tests.

Debbie, Duff says there's a chance, an actual chance, that we could prevent World War Three. We could change the future and save all the people in those cities. Maybe even ourselves."

"Linda, Duff's crazy," I said. "The cops are after him."

The line crackled; I could hear the sound of truck horns and Duff's muffled voice urging Linda to hurry up, hurry up, their ride was leaving.

"Listen, sweetie, I have to go. Tell Dad we left the station wagon at the Husky truck stop outside Sudbury. Tell him I'm sorry about the vineyards, but Duff said it had to be done or no one will sober up and see what's going on. I love you all. I'll come back, I promise, soon as we get this done. Tell me you believe me."

"I believe you," I echoed.

"Tell Mom and Dad that I'll be fine."

The boys stood watching me. Pepé the Seventh was there, too, pressed against Nonna Peppy. Even though the siren had stopped, a residue of sound remained, a lingering noiseless echo of disturbed air, like thunder building up before a storm.

"I'll be back, I promise," Linda said again, and hung up.

*   *   *

Six days later, just before the real Cannikin thermonuclear underground detonation, we saw Linda and Duff on the news, part of a seafaring group going out into the Bering Sea to get close enough to Amchitka Island to stop the test. They said they were demanding a "green peace."

On camera, Duff pumped his fist in the air. Linda mouthed a chant along with the others. *Hell, no, we won't go.*

Mom, Dad and Nonna Peppy sat with their hands in their faces. Mom weeping, Nonna Peppy praying.

"Linda said they're coming back," I tried to reassure them. "She promised me twice."

I never saw Linda or the Trespasser in Shipman's Corners again.

I came to believe that all of it — the time hop, the lost eighteen months — had been part of my imaginary life. It was time to breathe the clean, fresh air of reality.

Every August, I pack up my old telescope and take the ferry out to Toronto Island to watch the Perseid meteor shower from the beach on Gibraltar Point. I'm astonished by how few people in the city are aware of the galactic grand opera whirling over their heads.

I've always wanted to watch it far from the light pollution of the city, somewhere the nights are so dark it's like being in outer space. That's why I agree to Darren's proposal of a week of stargazing on Lake Superior.

We discuss whether to use his all-weather tent or borrow his buddy's nineteen-foot RV. I vote for the RV. I want a comfortable bed.

"For a wannabe astronaut, you're not much for roughing it, are you?" says Darren.

"In space, you're weightless. Here on Earth, I've got to consider my back," I answer.

The RV is a minnow compared to the bloated whale motorhomes chugging along the highway. The cozy, cramped interior reminds me of a spacecraft. Darren's pots and pans and bottles of Campari, vermouth and red wine are neatly stowed in cunningly designed cubbies. It's kitted out with a tiny bathroom and kitchen and a bed that slides out from under the bench seat at the back when you press a button. It has hot and cold running water, a tiny pedal-operated flush toilet, sink, stove, fridge, microwave and speakers at the back where Darren plans to seduce me to the complete works of Vivaldi, AC/DC, the Allman Brothers and Holst's *The Planets*.

"I'll bet we have more space than they had on any of the Gemini missions. Impressive how they've made use of every scrap of space."

"We have a better on-board bar than the astronauts did," Darren tells me. "Did you not notice the split of champagne in the fridge? Tell me Neil Armstrong had anything like that to look forward to at the end of the lunar day."

To mark the occasion, he presents me with a set of silk sheets printed with pornographic images of the signs of the Zodiac.

"If this van's rockin', don't bother knockin'," he tells me with a grin.

The drive to Lake Superior is long, a full day and a half, but when we arrive, the view from our campsite alone is worth the trip: hard against a narrow rocky beach that lets out onto the endless expanse of the greatest of the Great Lakes, grey waves pound so close to us that I tell Darren to forget the AC/DC so we can listen to the sounds of the wind and water.

Darren drags a 30-amp electrical cord to an outdoor outlet that keeps our life-support systems functioning. We take our espresso out to the picnic table to enjoy the already-crisp air — "Summer ends a lot earlier up here than in Toronto," the other campers tell us — and build a fire to warm up for the meteor shower, which gets going around ten p.m.

Unlike in outer space, when you're stargazing from Earth, you have to contend with climate and weather. A storm front had trailed us north, socking in the night sky with cloud cover. A park ranger drops by our site and says, "You guys are here for the meteor shower, right? Conditions should be perfect by tomorrow night. It'll be a chilly one though, so dress warm."

We sleep in the next morning, preparing ourselves to stay up late and watch the sky. As we wait for darkness to fall, I go for a run. The slap, slap, slap of my trainers on the paved road between stands of trees out of a Group of Seven painting boosts my endorphins, helping me achieve the so-called runner's high. Three motorcycles roll up, revving their engines, as I approach the camp store. Predictably, two of the bikes are Harley-Davidsons, one black, one cherry red. I am surprised to see that the third is a white Kawasaki with Massachusetts plates.

Jogging in place, I watch the two Harley men dismount and pull off their helmets before going into the store, leaving the third rider to keep an eye on the bikes. Still astride his Kawasaki, he pulls off his helmet. He looks like a typical road warrior, likely in his sixties, his grey hair pulled into a ponytail. The skin on his face is pink and peeling, as if he has a skin disease. Eczema, probably.

No, not eczema. *Sunburn*.

I stop mid-stride. The shock of recognition takes my breath away. I stagger to a bench next to the camp store, sit down and put my head between my knees.

"Are you okay? Can I get you a drink?"

I nod without lifting my head. I already know it's the sun-burned biker talking to me. His breath smells like cinnamon chewing gum.

I hear coins being pushed into the drinks machine and look up to see him twisting the cap off a Gatorade as he walks back to me. Even the decisive, cocky strut is familiar. He hands me the bottle and I take a sip. He sits down beside me, looking at my face with concern.

I finally catch my breath. "I won't go with you."

He frowns. "Excuse me?"

I see nothing in his eyes that signals recognition. He doesn't know who I am.

"You're not diabetic, are you?" he asks.

"No, I just — sorry. Thought I knew you."

He makes a sound, halfway between a grunt and a laugh. "You thought you recognized me and felt faint? Should I take that as a compliment?"

"I mean, I thought I knew your face. It's all sunburned."

"That's windburn from riding in this weather. Look, are you here with someone? Maybe I should find them for you."

I shake my head. "I'm fine now. Really."

"Sure?"

I nod. "I'll walk back to my campsite. Thanks again for the help and have a good trip."

"You too. Take good care now," he says, and stands up, leathers creaking.

As he opens the screen door of the camp store, he smiles at me, his teeth white and straight in that red, ravaged face.

I lift my hand to wave my thanks. In return, he shoots me a peace sign and enters the store. His ring finger is missing above the knuckle.

It has to be Duff. Or, at least, the Earth Standard Time version of Duff. Which would explain why he doesn't remember me. Wouldn't be the first time I met someone from my non-existent past.

Despite what Sputnik Chick says, sometimes a coincidence is just a coincidence.

Slowly, I jog back to the campsite. In the distance, Darren swings an axe, splitting kindling for the fire, his wheat-coloured hair flopping into his eyes. When I run up to him, he sets the axe carefully on the picnic table and leans down for a kiss. I oblige him but he pulls back and frowns. "You okay? You look pale."

"A little dehydrated. I'm going to drink some juice and hit the showers."

That night, Darren and I join a crowd of campers on the beach to watch the meteor shower. The air is clear and cold and we lie on blankets on top of the gritty sand, staring straight up at the avalanche of shooting stars. I point out Orion the hunter and Cassiopeia the seated woman, Aries the Greek god of war and all the other familiar constellations. I connect the dots between stars to reveal images of gods and goddesses, real and mythological animals and ancient symbols like Libra's scales of justice. My sign. The Milky Way spills itself over the western half of the sky, cracking open the edge of our galaxy to let us peek into countless others.

Later, curled beside Darren in the back of the RV, I wake in the middle of the night. Despite the large body beside me, I'm freezing. I also have a killer headache.

Tylenol, I tell myself, but when I try to wiggle to the end of the bed that fills the back of the van, I find that I can't move. My head is strapped to a board.

Can't talk, either: my jaws are clamped shut. I suddenly become aware of metal screws that have been driven into my cheeks, Frankenstein-style. The only parts of me that can move are my eyes. Two faces in scrub masks look down at me. Mom and Dad. Mom's eyes are leaking. Dad pulls a sheet over my face. I try to scream but can't make a sound. The world goes white.

I wake to Darren shaking me. "You were having a nightmare."

This is the only good part of my recurring dream: waking up. Especially with someone there to comfort me.

"What was it about?"

I curl up into him. "I'm on an operating table. My parents are there. They think I'm dead. I keep telling them I'm alive, but they can't hear me."

Darren adjusts his position so that one arm drapes protectively over me. His face is warm and reassuring against the crook of my neck.

"I have a dream like that sometimes. I walk into a cave and meet this monster. Turns out he's my real father."

Coldness settles over me. As if I'm back in the dream. "What do you mean by your real father?"

Darren scoops me closer. He's good at comforting me. It's funny how so many things about him seem safe and familiar — even little mannerisms that on some level I realize remind me of Dad.

And a very little bit, I think with shame, of the Shark. His hands. The complexion. Something about the shape of his jaw. Sturdy handsomeness, absent the cruelty.

"I was adopted," he says.

Darren tells me what he knows. He was born somewhere in Southern Ontario. June 1970. Mom, an unmarried teenager. He says he's been trying to find her through an agency that helps adoptees find their birth parents. So far, she's refused contact.

"What about your father?"

Darren yawns. "His name was left off my birth records. Not a good sign. It means my mother either didn't want to identify him or didn't know who he was. I've never had a good feeling about who he might be. Only piece of information my adoptive parents got was that I might've inherited a weird blood anomaly," says Darren.

I sit up. In the world of Sputnik Chick — correction, in *my* world — there are no coincidences. "What kind of anomaly?"

He yawns and stretches. "Some kind of allergy to surgical drugs. I've never been under, so I've never had to dig into it. Anyway, it's rare."

"Pseudocholinesterase deficiency," I suggest.

He rubs his eyes. "Maybe. Only time it comes up is when I go to the dentist. He always knocks me out with gas instead of giving me a shot of novocaine."

When Darren finally falls asleep, I get up and dress in hiking gear, the warmest I can find, then step outside to watch the wheel of stars above me. Meteors are still falling. They must be laughing at me. I have fallen in love with my sister's lost son, and I have only myself to blame.

One tragedy averted, a thousand others rushing in to take its place.

The next morning at dawn, before Darren is awake, I slip into a sweatshirt and jeans, pack a bag, fold up my telescope and walk out of the campground to the highway. In the morning mist, a big rig approaches and I stick out my thumb.

The trucker takes me as far as the Little Finlandia Hotel, just north of Lake Superior Park. From the front desk, I phone the co-op store in Wawa and ask them to deliver a drafting table.

Time to pick up the dropped threads of Sputnik Chick's origin story.

I get back to work.

The Untold Origin Story of
THE GIRL WITH NO PAST

Volume 4
A NOOK IN TIME

featuring
OUR LADY OF THE ALGORITHM

one
Modern Bride
Shipman's Corners, 1979, A.M.T.

On the day of Richard Nixon's suicide, I saw a cardinal in our backyard, perched in a plum tree, the first time I'd seen one that wasn't on a Christmas card. It was as scarlet as fresh blood, smaller than I thought it would be, with the piercing cry of a train whistle.

"They're highly territorial," Dad said, passing me the binoculars he kept on his desk. He'd taken up birdwatching, having retired from Sparkling Sparrow and selling his shares back to ShipCo. "You should see his wife! She attacks her reflection in the window, thinking it's another female horning in on her mate."

I ignored my father's anthropomorphization. He just couldn't resist giving human emotions to other species.

"I've never seen one before," I said.

"It's because we don't use DDT on the vines anymore. The songbirds are coming back."

I took the bird's flashy presence as a sign of hope, even as the news of Nixon's suicide filled me with a mixture of sadness and dread. The gravity of the disgraced president's death was pulling everything toward the newscasts like a tractor beam. On the kitchen radio, the deep, respectful voice of a Canusa Broadcasting Corporation announcer described the tragedy for the hundredth time that day, as Mom washed dishes, the hot and cold taps going off and on, scrub and rinse, rinse and scrub. Housework had to be done whether ex-presidents were dead or alive.

Why did I care? It wasn't as if Nixon was a beloved figure, but I wondered whether the reason for taking his own life wasn't depression or shame over impeachment, but because he wanted to escape what he knew was coming. Say what you will about Nixon; he may have lacked insight into his own personal failings, but he had enough foresight to know that 1978 would be the year to cut and run — literally: first, he'd run a hot bath, then he'd opened the arteries in his wrists with a straight razor.

I was twenty-two and in my final year studying biosciences at the University of Toronto, perfect for a woman whose career plan was to go to the moon. Since the year Duff and Linda disappeared, I had lived what some might call a charmed life: good grades, good family, good looks and reasonably good health, despite occasional relapses into bulimia. I'd been helped by a psychiatrist who put me on a calming drug called Valium. Now, if I could only kick the Valium.

Best of all, I had the perfect boyfriend. Correction: fiancé. Kendal and I had set the date. Sadly, my beloved Nonna Peppy did not live to see me engaged. In my final year of university, she broke her hip climbing the cellar stairs with her arms full of washing, developed pneumonia and died in hospital. Her last dog, a schnauzer named Pepé the Eighth, passed away of a broken heart a few weeks later. To honour Nonna Peppy's memory, I promised myself that I would make a trip to New York City. It would be a journey I would make with the husband Nonna told me society would never accept.

No woman buys more than one issue of *MODERN BRIDE* in her lifetime. Same holds true of *Wedding Belles*, *ATOMIC BRIDES* and *Canusa Bride*. One weekend, Sandy brought a stack of the shiny bridal bibles to my house, along with a bottle of bootleg onion vodka. Mr. H had started selling his home-made hooch under the table at Sputnik Burger, now the most popular fast-food joint in Shipman's Corners.

I cast an eye over pages of blow-dried, moustached men and soft porn, hot-rollered blondes leering at one another across bubble baths in giant champagne glasses.

"Seriously? People do this on their honeymoon? No wonder Kendal thinks we should elope," I told her.

"What, and deprive your moms of their one and only chance to buy matching mother-of-the-bride and -groom outfits? How inconsiderate." Sandy raised her glass in a toast. *"Mnohaya lita!* Many years!"

We tossed back the vodka shots and got to work looking at pages of double-knit wedding gowns, feather-trimmed cape-lets, gloves, garters, veils, rings, lingerie and cakes shaped like the Taj Mahal as Bowie blasted on the stereo.

Still best friends, Sandy and I had spent almost four years in different cities — Sandy in Guelph studying nutrition and I in Toronto — but we had stayed tight, the kind of friends who not only finished each other's sentences but read each other's minds. By the end of the evening, just before we fell asleep side by side on the rec-room floor, we had started scribbling thought balloons over the heads of dewy-skinned brides, their doe eyes downcast before their ruffled-shirted, velvet-tuxed, page-boyed grooms. *Show me your dick, big boy! I'm only marry-ing you for your vintage beer-can collection. As God is my witness, I'll never be hungry again! You can lead a whore to culture but you can't make her think.*

Before the evening was out, we'd both picked the male model we'd most like to sleep with: a strawberry-blond, bearded Viking in a tartan tux for Sandy (we agreed he'd definitely look better out of the tux than in it) and a bulky body-builder type with curly black hair and a sweet smile for me. He was wearing that year's most popular colour for tuxes: powder blue.

"Looks like a nice Italian boy," pronounced Sandy.

"Not that nice, I hope," I said.

Our sarcasm not only helped us undermine the saccharine silliness of the magazines, it distracted us from world events that were getting scarier by the day. After Amchitka, the Cold War had gone down for a nap, waking up with a start in 1977 when NATO discovered that the Soviets had been brazenly building up missile silos on their border with Finland, shiveringly close to the edge of the Iron Curtain.

Meanwhile, Western science marched on, synthesizing music and cheese and aerosolizing underarm deodorant. The Amchitka activists organized themselves into a group called Greenpeace and warned that pollution and pesticides would kill us as surely as the atomic bomb, just a lot more slowly. They spoke of the Earth in spiritual terms, as if the planet was being stripped, flayed and burned alive, like a medieval saint. The government tolerated them. ShipCo ignored them. The company's new approach was to pretend to be in favour of arms limitation and environmentalism. By then, they knew how dozily complacent we'd all become.

As Duff had predicted, scientists had discovered that the planet was heating up: they blamed chlorofluorocarbons, or CFCs, for gnawing a hole in the ozone layer that protected the Earth from the sun's radiation. Predicting an epidemic of skin cancer, Greenpeace issued a manifesto demanding that we immediately give up our CFC-laden aerosol hairsprays. The Donato twins responded by stockpiling cans of Final Net in their basement. ShipCo launched an ad campaign that promoted green living while gently pointing out how many

Canusians fed their families and paid their mortgages by working for the good folks in the CFC industry.

In the busy year leading up to our wedding, the Cold War plunged even further into the deep freeze, relations between the Eastern and Western Blocs getting icier than ever. Nixon's suicide caused so much soul-searching in the States that the sympathy vote unexpectedly swung the election in favour of Gerald Ford. Meanwhile, the world's longest undefended border got a lot less friendly after Pierre Trudeau finally won an election and married a Cuban socialite. *Who wants to do business with Castro's brother-in-law* was the way Vice-President Reagan put it.

Most worrisome of all, NASA's space station, Skylab, was lazily losing orbit like an old man falling out of bed; everyone knew that a ton of space junk was going to crash somewhere on Earth in mid-1979. The Soviets claimed the falling station was a ploy to disguise an attack from space on the USSR. I thought it sounded like a simple case of technical incompetence. Skylab seemed to have been doomed from the start, losing a heat shield when it was first sent into orbit. Ever since, it was one damn thing going wrong after another. Not surprisingly, NASA decided to let the station fall to earth — burning up on re-entry, they hoped — rather than pour more money into what was already obsolete technology. Some scientists urged the space agency to send the station deeper into space to float with other dead satellites like Vanguard and Telstars I and II. But that cost money, something NASA suddenly seemed to be short of. Instead, they paid for a public relations campaign to reassure the citizens of Earth that the chances of any one human being being hit by Skylab were six hundred billion to one.

In large cities, an unnerving low-level buzz that no one could identify became the background noise of day-to-day life; the newspapers dubbed it the Hotwire Hum. In New York, Con Edison claimed the hum wasn't electrical in nature. Finally, a Jungian psychotherapist wrote a book theorizing that the Hotwire Hum was the sound of suppressed anxiety leaking out of the collective unconscious, and someone had T-shirts printed up with the words: *I survived the Hotwire Hum.* Doctors began to notice an uptick in heart attacks during the nightly news. No wonder the discos were packed.

All through those tense months, as missile silos sprang up like brush bristles and Skylab moved closer and closer to Earth, Sandy, Judy, Jayne and I conducted high-level negotiations with caterers and weighed the merits of traditional vows versus the poetry of Rod McKuen.

Then there was the question of the first dance. Should Kendal and I start our lives together to "Reunited" by Peaches and Herb or the Bee Gees' "How Deep Is Your Love"? The day we finally settled on Barry White and the Love Unlimited Orchestra doing "Love's Theme," a news flash on CBC Radio informed us that U.S. negotiator Kissinger had abandoned the Strategic Arms Limitation Talks after getting into a fistfight with his Soviet counterpart. No one was negotiating in good faith, not even on his side, said Kissinger, nursing a broken nose and two cracked ribs. The SALT talks were dead. Détente, an elegant word used to describe the process of getting both sides to relax and take a stress pill, became a bitter punchline on late-night talk shows.

As I placed an order for five hundred monogrammed white matchbooks, the Doomsday Clock of the Atomic Scientists ticked thirty seconds closer to midnight. But Kendal refused to give credit to Duff for anything more than a lucky guess.

"I never said the guy was stupid. He may even have been prescient. But at the end of the day, are we headed for World

War Three? Don't think so, Deb. You're not going to get rid of me that easily."

∗ ∗ ∗

The day of my shower at St. Dismas Church Hall, Kendal and my father stayed home and watched the Stanley Cup play-offs. Dad liked the Toronto Maple Leafs; Kendal, the Buffalo Flames. They sat in the basement rec room, drinking beer and arguing over stats. *Bonding.*

The ink hadn't dried on Kendal's master's degree when he'd started working for a community newspaper out in Louth Township while freelancing for big dailies outside Canusa, in cities like Hamilton and Toronto. But journalism just didn't seem like man's work to Dad, who thought Kendal had more of a future as a criminal lawyer.

I'd watched Kendal flirt with Dad, leading him on. "Yes, I suppose I have the marks for law school. I'll give it serious thought, Mr. Biondi."

"Call me Dad," my father said, his hand on Kendal's shoulder.

And then there was Kendal's mother. Whenever we were at her house on Z Street, there was a script the three of us would follow:

> MRS. KENDAL: Debbie, how wonderful to
> be in a profession where you could find the
> cure for cancer! You should think about that,
> John.
> KENDAL: Journalism *is* a profession, Ma.
> MRS. KENDAL: Still, I think you should
> listen to Mr. Biondi. If only your father were

alive to see you go to law school! He'd never
believe it.

Once Mrs. Kendal had played the dead father card, neither
Kendal nor I knew what to say. But I could tell that Kendal
sort of liked the idea of law school. And once he was a lawyer,
it was just one small step into politics. Which Kendal would
have been great at: he was good-looking, articulate, popular
and sociable. And funny. And *smart*. My university friends
loved him — "Oh, Deb, you are so lucky, Kendal is so wonderful," et cetera, et cetera.

In my mind's eye, I could see us at our ranch house in some
upscale Toronto suburb, Kendal watering the lawn while I took
our adorable mixed-race children off to Montessori school.

Problem was, I wanted to go to the stars.

It *could* happen. NASA had started recruiting women scientists as mission specialists, a Canadian neurologist among
them. It was only a matter of time before some lucky girl
found herself sitting on a highly flammable hydrogen-oxygen
fuel mixture, hurtling into the region of maximum dynamic
pressure. Why not me? I had the science education required of
astronauts. Now I just needed to get into peak physical condition. I'd started running laps at Varsity Stadium, and when I
was back home in Shipman's Corners, I ran beside the canal,
from Lock 2 to Lock 4 and back. Sometimes, the sailors on the
lakers and salties cheered me on. In an effort to turn myself into
a bundle of taut, high-twitch-fibre muscles, I had even started
going to the testosterone-laden weight training room at Hart
House. Always the only woman working out on the machines,
I felt every pair of eyes in the room crawling up and down my
little black ballet leotard. At least the younger guys pretended
they were indifferent to my bench presses and chin-ups, even

if the conspicuous bulges in their gym shorts proved otherwise. I got less respect from the fifty-year-old coach of the university boxing team — "I don't want to fight," I explained, not entirely truthfully. "I just want your help to condition myself the way boxers do." Instead, he gave me a condescending leer and dismissed me with, "You women's libbers think you can do anything, but you're still just girls," then sent me on my way with a pat on my bum.

Rather than sparring and skipping with the boxers, I took up marathon training with the track team, running in the smallest men's running shoes I could find. I jogged up Spadina Road to the steps of Casa Loma, then sprinted uphill toward the St. Clair Reservoir. I was getting faster, fitter and stronger. When I crooked my arm like Popeye, a hard knot of muscle popped out of my skinny upper arm. I was sure I had a future in space as long as I didn't get myself caught in a subdivision, with kids and a mortgage, parent-teacher interviews, a busy husband to keep house for and an aging parent to look after, like Mom did. Until Nonna Peppy died, my parents could barely go away for an afternoon, let alone to outer space.

Despite my ambitions, when Kendal proposed, I said yes. And yes to the big traditional church wedding my family wanted.

By that time, Linda had been gone for seven years. At first, Dad had tried to involve the police, who shrugged and said Linda was an adult. They suggested we try searching the hang-outs in Toronto's Yorkville district or the Yonge Street strip where desperate girls went on the stroll. To the cops, Linda was just another runaway. Nonna Peppy had hired a private investigator from Buffalo who took her money but said the trail had gone cold. In his opinion, Linda was probably living somewhere under an assumed name with Duff and his radical friends — *Yammer tree-huggers*, in the detective's words.

I was, for all intents and purposes, an only child, dragging my family's future around with me. If I didn't marry and have kids, what had been the point of my parents and grandparents immigrating to Canusa? To keep the family line going, that's why. Now it was all up to me. Otherwise, as Mom pointed out, Nonno Zinio and Nonna Peppy might just as well have stayed in Italy and been murdered by the fascists.

No pressure.

*　*　*

That June, I wore a floral print Gloria Vanderbilt wrap dress on the stage of St. Dismas Church Hall, unwrapping shower gifts as Mom and Mrs. Kendal looked on proudly. This was no cozy cucumber-sandwiched function where you could get away with wrapping up a set of measuring cups and a couple of tea towels. Mine was a full-on orgy of decadent consumerism, a celebration of crystal stemware and place settings and his 'n' hers anti-radiation suits, each lavish gift breathlessly described by Jayne-Mansfield at the microphone while a heavily pregnant Judy-Garland taped gift bows to a paper plate hat that I would wear for photographs. Sandy logged each gift in a journal so that she could help me write two hundred and fifty thank-you notes. I felt as if we were in an alternate reality where women's liberation had never happened, not that the movement had picked up much traction in Atomic Mean Time. In 1979, I didn't even have the right to keep my own name. Once married, I'd officially become Mrs. John Kendal, and Debbie Biondi would cease to exist.

Fortunately, there was plenty of booze. The St. Dismas Catholic Ladies' League had mixed up a spiked punch, heavy on the rum, grenadine and ginger ale. Bridal Veil Punch, they called it. After my sixth cup, feeling an urgent need to empty my bladder, I teetered down a set of stairs and along a hallway until I found a door.

You'd think I would have noticed the lack of a LADIES sign or a universal female figure in a triangle skirt — maybe it was all that grenadine-sweetened rum. Instead of a bathroom, I found myself in the room being used to store piles of my new brand-name kitchen appliances and home decor products. All two hundred and fifty of them, each one a lead ball shackled to my legs. Hard for a girl to hurtle to the stars with six avocado-green fondue pots clanking along behind her.

Surrounded by my new toaster oven, Cuisinart food processor, KitchenAid mixer, Hamilton Beach blender, reclining lounge chair, quadraphonic stereo system, colour console TV and assorted crockpots, I screamed. One long, loud scream. Followed by another. And another.

I waited for Mom to rush through the door, demanding to know what was wrong. All I heard was women's laughter and the click, click, click of high heels on the linoleum floor outside.

I wiped my eyes as I walked out of the room, still needing to pee. Urgently.

Down the hall, I finally found the bathroom. Pushing open the door, I was hit by a shower of chatter and synthetic fragrance, the sounds and smells of tipsy women putting their faces back on. I slipped into a stall, hiked up my dress and released a stream of Bridal Veil Punch into the toilet bowl as tears wrecked my makeup. I wasn't just crying over the fact that I now owned three industrial-size slow cookers, but because I had cheated on Kendal with a guy I'd met in the weight-training room. Bob O'Something. There were so many Bobs at U of T. This one was a varsity wrestler. He couldn't figure out how to retract the spring-loaded bar on the leg extension machine; there was a trick to it. It was all physics, really. No matter how strong you were, if you didn't pull it back just the right way, it was immovable. Seeing him grunting and straining, I waltzed up in my ballet leotard, grabbed the bar with one hand and pulled it down, *thunk*, as though it were nothing. The football players working out on the weight machines started laughing. So did Bob after I explained the trick to him.

I could tell he was a little embarrassed and kind of shy, by the way he stood running his hand through his curly dark hair. From the weight room, we went to a coffee shop, then a pub, then his room — mercifully, a single — in Tartu College.

I slept with him only once. I'm not even sure why, although he did bear a strong resemblance to the *Modern Bride* "groom I would fuck" whom Sandy and I had picked out that night we got hammered on homemade vodka. I was up and out of his bed before dawn, walking home through the empty streets of Toronto.

The very next day, Bob and I bumped into one another at the cafeteria and he asked me out.

"I'm afraid I can't," I told him, glancing around to see if anyone was watching us.

"You're not, you know, mad at me, are you? I'm sorry, I know I got a little carried away last night . . ."

As if I had nothing to do with it.

"I'm engaged," I told him.

Bob shook his head. "You're marrying the wrong guy. He doesn't even know you."

I almost laughed. "He's known me since we were kids."

"That's my point. He still thinks of you as a little girl."

"How can you say that? You don't even know him."

"I know more than you think." His bulky shoulders tensed up. He looked hurt, angry, confused. "Well, fine, then! Go marry the guy. I hope you have a swell life together," he said, and walked off with his tray.

Yes, I felt guilty. Yes, I knew it was a warning sign that I wasn't ready for marriage. Kendal was the only man I'd ever slept with, before I met Bob. I lay awake nights, asking myself why I had let it happen. I knew I wasn't happy, but it wasn't for lack of trying.

I loved Kendal. Who wouldn't? Eight years earlier, he had been a devoted friend in the months it took me to pull myself together after my sister's disappearance. He had been dumbfounded but loyal as I tearfully ruminated about my broken body image and the way my family equated food with love as I went through treatment for bulimia. When I turned sixteen, we finally had sex: *real* sex, not the half-assed kind that leaves you a technical virgin. We did it in his bed while Mrs. Kendal was away for a landscape painting weekend and I was supposed to be sleeping over at Sandy's. He'd even borrowed a copy of *Your Body, My Body* from one of the feminists at the Z Street Youth Drop-in Centre and read the bits about female pleasure. How could I *not* love a man that considerate?

I was still sitting on the toilet, my snot-streaked face in my hands, when someone banged on the stall door.

"Deb? You okay?" Sandy's voice. She must have recognized my gold velvet platform shoes.

I hesitated. "No."

"Open up."

"I'd rather be alone."

"Open up or I'm crawling under the door."

I opened up. When Sandy saw my face, she shooed away the women crowding in to see the weeping bride-to-be and walked me back to the storeroom I'd just left. She found a box of Kleenex and poured me a glass of water, and we both agreed that the Bridal Veil Punch had quite a kick, considering it had been concocted by a bunch of sixty-year-old Italian ladies. Sandy chalked up my tears to that quintessential woman's problem: a case of nerves. I told her that my nerves were just fine but that I had doubts. And guilt.

"Why guilt?" asked Sandy, frowning at me. Her face was so close to mine, I could have kissed her. Even thought about doing it. Instead, I fished a crumpled Kleenex out of my pocket and blew my nose.

"I cheated on Kendal."

Even as the words were leaving my mouth, I knew that telling Sandy was a mistake. I felt a subtle change in the pressure of her arm around my shoulders. Her eyes narrowed to sharp blue checkmarks.

She didn't say, *You really must be unsure of this wedding, Deb. Maybe you should call it off.* Or even that old standby: *What's your hurry? Maybe you're just not ready yet.*

Instead, she said, "How could you fool around on a great guy like Kendal? Are you fucking crazy? He's, like, the perfect man."

Looking back, I can see now that I tripped over that moment as if it were a bunched-up section of carpet. I switched tactics and agreed with Sandy that I was indeed suffering from nerves; why else would I commit such a disloyal act? What sane woman would betray a fine man like Kendal? I tried to explain to Sandy that I wasn't sure myself why it had happened: the man meant nothing to me. It was as if my brain and my heart had gone into suspended animation for a night.

"Just pretend it never happened. Let's not talk about it anymore," Sandy suggested. "This is too fucked up."

And so, I began a hesitant march toward our wedding day.

* * *

With my hair coiled into snoods on the sides of my head, I looked like a medieval princess in an ivory Qiana double-knit gown while Kendal stood straight and tall and handsome beside me in a three-piece dark blue tuxedo — to his credit, he had turned down Tuxedo Royale's efforts to put him, Bum Bum, Rocco and the other groomsmen into trendy powder blue and ruffles. My attendants, Sandy, Jayne-Mansfield and Judy-Garland, were in unapologetic burnt orange with bell sleeves and high waists, the mound of Judy-Garland's pregnancy sticking out like the prow of a ship. A week after the wedding, she would give birth to fraternal twins, whom she would name after those prewar style icons, Clark Gable and Katharine Hepburn.

After kissing me passionately to the tinkling of five hundred glasses filled with pink champagne, Kendal stood and made a funny yet moving speech that had both my mom and his wiping their eyes. Bum Bum — or as most people now called him, BB — made the toast to the bride and joked about how one of the perks of being our best man was that he got to go with us on our honeymoon. To save money, he had agreed to chauffeur us to our romantic hideaway — not to a champagne glass bubble bath in the Pocono Mountains, but a place that had become synonymous with grit and crime and urban break-down: New York, New York. I owed Nonna Peppy that much.

two

Out-of-This-World Honeymoon

Ten hours on the New York State Thruway. That's all it takes to travel from Shipman's Corners to the dystopia of New York City. All the way down the Hudson, we passed through one small town after another, stopping to pump gas and eat at greasy diners where Kendal, Bum Bum and I sometimes drew stares. White girl, black man, and a gay Italian guy in gold satin gym shorts, muscle shirt and earring — let's just say we stood out. Those towns felt a lot like Shipman's Corners, except for the American flags everywhere, snapping in the wind in front of schools and fire stations and on bumper stickers reading *America, love it or shove it*. Somewhere near the New Jersey border, we started to hear the low, steady thrum of the Hotwire Hum, as the small towns turned into the suburbs of a broken-down megalopolis. Through the windshield we stared down the esophagus of a giant gorging itself on car-choked malls, junkyards, chemical silos and empty billboards. When we emerged from the exhaust-fumed gloom of the Holland Tunnel, my first glimpse of Manhattan was a garbage can on fire in the middle of a vacant lot that gaped incongruously between two rows of buildings, like a mouth with its front teeth punched out.

* * *

Check-in time at the Hotel Excelsior in Greenwich Village was three p.m. Bum Bum dropped us out front at noon.

"Where you staying, BB?" Kendal asked.

"At a friend's place. I'll leave you his number. Call me when you get sick of all that tourist shit and I'll get you into the best disco in the city." He drove off, waving at us in the side-view mirror.

A double amputee perched on a barstool at the hotel entrance held open the door for us. He was wearing a bandanna over his long hair and a ragged denim jacket embroidered with the American flag. When all he got from us was a polite thank you, I heard him mutter, "I left my legs in New Zealand for you cheap assholes."

The lobby reeked of old tobacco and fresh fumigants: the acrid smell of cockroach killer reminded me of Sputnik Burger on a Monday morning. From a giant polished wood radio in the corner, a horse race ran itself out while a morbidly obese man in a size four hundred sports shirt nodded over the *Daily News*, his flesh spilling over the sides of a cracked red leather recliner. A girl about the size of one of the man's legs rocked back and forth behind the barricade of a steamer trunk, eyes fixed and mouth open. Her head had been shaved at the sides, a strip of hair down the centre of her skull moulded into an alert mohawk, tinted parrot blue.

The front desk clerk stared at us. His eyes strayed off in different directions on the sides of his narrow head. Like a fish.

"We run a clean house here," said the clerk. "You 'n' your bimbo kin get thuh hell out!"

Kendal said, "We have a reservation. Mr. and Mrs. John Kendal." I placed my left hand, with its Grantham Plaza Discount Jewellers wedding ring, on the counter.

The man tipped his flat head to focus on the ring and made a jerky little bow. "No offense. Gotta be careful these days is all. Stay alert, like the guv'ment says." He riffled through a box of index cards. "We putch youse on the sixth floor. Honeymoon suite. Not ready yet. Still cleaning up from the previous party."

I didn't want to think about what the previous party had been doing.

From a cubby behind the desk that reminded me of the cash at Cressie's, the clerk took out an envelope and a heavy iron key that looked as though it would open the door to Frankenstein's castle. "Letter for choo."

The envelope was addressed *To the Newlyweds*. Inside, a note from my second cousin in Brooklyn:

Hi there, Mr. and Mrs. Kendal. Hope married life's treating you well. If you get tired of that shithole you're booked into, we'd be happy to put you up. In the meantime, here are tickets to Evita, *the best musical in town, and an invite to treat you to dinner at Patsy's Restaurant this Friday. (Sinatra eats there.) Talk soon, Donnie*

I folded the letter and slipped it into my purse. "If we can leave our bags here, we'll go for a walk for a couple of hours. How do we get to the Lower East Side?"

The fish-eyed clerk pulled out a badly Xeroxed map of Manhattan, much-handled and rendered in a tiny scale that turned the city blocks into hamster droppings. He rattled out rapid-fire directions. I nodded, lost in all the numbered streets and avenues, but Kendal followed the whole thing.

"Oh, and by the way, air-raid drill, three times a week. We geddit oudda da way before cocktail hour."

"This hotel's actually got a shelter?" asked Kendal, an edge of disbelief in his voice.

The clerk turned his flat head to fix Kendal with one rolling eye. "Sure. A *hardened* shelter, down in da basement."

I knew that anywhere in the States we went, we'd be facing this. New nuclear attack preparedness drills. They were talking about reactivating them in Canusa, too. Even the Emergency Broadcast System test signal had reappeared to interrupt television shows.

"Youse two gotta funny accent. Where ya from?" asked the clerk.

"Canusa," Kendal and I said together.

The clerk muttered, "Land of milk 'n' honey."

I couldn't tell whether or not he was trying to be funny.

*　　*　　*

On Bleecker Street, the smoggy Manhattan sun leered at us. A yellow cab cruised by and slowed to a crawl, the driver angling his mirrored aviators in our direction. "Special price today for out-of-towners," he shouted. Kendal and I kept walking.

Heat radiated off sidewalks full of little girls in hot pants and tube socks flying along on four-wheeled roller skates, guys rolling racks of polyester shirts out of sweat shops, old men hitching up their pants in doorways, looking up and down the street with paunchy arrogance. Hustlers in leisure suits and sunglasses sold watches from cardboard suitcases, keeping an eye out for cops. And then there were the Conspiracy Freaks with their The End is Nigh sandwich boards, selling access to hardened shelters in midtown and anti-radiation suits in every style and colour. Back home, even Cressie's was starting to stock second-hand "rad suits," as they were known. The ad campaign claimed, "Now you can take your bomb shelter with you!" but everyone knew that all the suits offered was a day or two of protection while you watched everyone around you die.

Over the traffic noises and the blare of transistor radios, we could hear the Hotwire Hum everywhere we went, a steady, low drone like a sustained bass note on an organ. The thrumming sound even reached inside buildings and down into the subways. Unnerving, at first, but like the native New Yorkers, we were getting used to it.

It took us an hour to reach the Lower East Side, the Brooklyn Bridge looming on a skyline dominated by a jumble of grim warehouses that would have been at home on Z Street. Apartment blocks in dingy brown-grey brick, cross-hatched by iron fire escapes, turned the streets into shadowy canyons.

"This is the place. Twenty-seven Orchard Street," said Kendal in front of a boarded-up tenement. On the front stoop, a weathered man of no particular age — he could have been anywhere from twenty-five to sixty-five — pulled a ring of keys almost the size of a hubcap out of the pocket of his baggy overalls. "You looking to get inside?"

"Are we allowed to?" I asked.

The man shrugged. "I'm the caretaker. If I allow you, you're allowed." He made a show of looking up and down the street. "Who's gonna stop you, the FBI? They got bigger fish to fry, sweetheart."

"My grandmother used to live here," I said. "We're from Canusa."

I was discovering that being from Canusa was like a get-out-of-jail-free card; in New York, no one thought we were capable of doing anything interesting enough to be bad.

The caretaker unlocked the door. "Watch your step. No one's lived here for better'n forty years, except cats and rats and pigeons."

"Rats?" I said as the caretaker unlocked the peeling wood door.

He handed Kendal a flashlight. "Yous'll need this."

An arch of metal grillwork framed the inner foyer, as if inviting us into a grand entranceway, instead of a steep set of broken stairs clinging to the interior wall. We climbed, carefully, breathing in dust and the sharp tang of urine.

"Cat pee?" I asked the caretaker.

"Yeah, 'n' people's, too. They sneak in here sometimes to squat in the flats. That's most of my job, keeping trespassers out."

Kendal pushed open a door into a tight little room with a window giving out onto another tight little room, which gave out onto a boarded-up window. A weak ray of sunlight pushed through, picking out a rumpled carpet so thick with dust that all trace of a definable colour had vanished.

"I guess we're trespassers, too," I said.

"Nah, youse are just tourists. Don't see many. Hardly no one wants to visit New York no more."

"We're on our honeymoon," said Kendal.

The caretaker coughed. "Interestin' choice."

"So why are you guarding this abandoned building?" I asked.

"Some rich bitch is raisin' funds to renoovate this place, turn it into a moozeum. A moozeum to what, I got no idea. Like those fruitcakes who want to fix up Ellis Island. You been out there? Jesus, it's just about fallen down and sunk in the ocean."

Peppy had said she lived at this address in a railroad flat, by which I thought she meant she could see the elevated trains pass by. She had explained to me that it meant an apartment without a hallway: to get from one room to the next you had to walk through each room, one after the other, like the boxcars on a train. "You couldn't have no privacy in a house like that. You wouldn't believe what you'd catch people doing while you were just trying to get to the shitter at night, excuse my French."

I tried to imagine Nonna Peppy as a teenager, living in a place like this with her brother, sister-in-law and four nieces and nephews before returning to Italy to marry Nonno Zinio. It was only two rooms, a sink in one of them signalling its purpose. "Was this room the bathroom?"

The caretaker coughed. "Whadya think this is, the Ritz? This is the kitchen. The john's in the hall. One for every two flats. Hell, I remember my pop saying in the old days, before the city made the landlords put in indoor terlets, you had to go down them stairs and out the back to the privies to do your business. Day or night, winter or summer. Same thing to get water. Up, down, up, down. Stank like hell out there, too. Not that it was much better inside."

"You remember when there were people living here?" asked Kendal.

The caretaker coughed again; I was starting to realize that was the sound of his laughter.

"You kiddin', I grew up here," said the caretaker. "That's how come I know my way 'round the place."

By the time we got back to the Excelsior, exhausted and starving, the honeymoon suite was ready for us.

The elevator clunked and groaned its way to the top floor, operated by a dwarf in what looked like a Girl Scout uniform. I had a hard time not staring at her; she was a heavily made-up platinum blonde, hair scraped into a long ponytail, gilded shadow on her eyelids. For a moment I could have sworn I saw a third eye in the middle of her forehead winking at me. Must have been the heat.

"You two look normal. Sweet enough ta eat," she observed, her tiny catlike tongue darting out to lick her lips. "Where ya from?"

"Canusa," we answered together.

"Explains it. Sixth floor. Watch yer step."

We tried to politely refuse the help of an elderly bellhop but he squeezed into the tiny creaking elevator with us anyway and grabbed our bags. Up on six, he unlocked the door and marched around the honeymoon suite, waving his hand at the amenities: a rusty tub in the dimly lit bathroom, a TV with a broken dial shoved onto the armoire and the red light that signalled an air-raid siren was a test, not "da real deal." Finally, he shoved up the window to let in a blast of heat and smog. "Great voo of da Village, f'you like that type thing," he wheezed. He stood, breathing hard, hands behind his back, until Kendal dug fifty cents out of his pocket.

After the bellhop left, Kendal said, "Alone at last."

We pulled back the thin coverlet on the bed and I lay back on the pale yellow sheets, scratchy with bleach, and watched Kendal go down on me. I clearly remember coming that particular time, the racket of the city floating in through the open window like exotic music, the smell of an animal being barbecued drifting up from the street below.

Kendal scooped me into his arms. "Are you happy, Debbie?"

I put my arms around him. "Yes, of course."

"I love you," he said.

"I love you, too."

I wanted to be happy. I really did. I *was* happy with Kendal.

And yet, a nameless worry chafed at me, as if something important had slipped my mind in the midst of all the monogrammed matchbook ordering and wedding planning. I felt as if I had lost my prime directive. As if I'd missed a boat on which I hadn't even booked passage.

Kendal got up and looked out the window, unselfconsciously naked. He was still lean and muscular and beautiful, his narrow sensitive face approaching pretty. The perfect man, as Sandy liked to remind me.

Afterwards we got into the tub and let the showerhead intermittently spit cold water at us. I was just about to suggest that we reconsider my cousin's offer to put us up in Brooklyn when the air-raid siren went off. I crouched down in the tub and covered my head, Kendal trying to reassure me. "Look, the red light's on, it's only a test."

Ever since that night eight years earlier, the sounds of sirens — ambulances, fire alarms — sent me into a panic, my heart racing like a sprinter's crossing the finish line. Kendal coaxed me to my feet and into my clothes. Poured me a glass of water and handed me a Valium from my purse.

Down the stairwell, we descended to the hardened shelter of the Excelsior, the other guests ahead of and behind us. From the look of their slow hand-in-hand descent, it appeared that the morbidly fat man and the skeletal girl with the parrot blue hair were together. The other guests grumbled and burped their way down with weary acceptance; they did drills three times a week, someone said, and I began to realize that they weren't so much guests as long-term residents of the Excelsior.

The so-called hardened shelter looked like the basement kitchen of St. Dismas Community Hall: blue-tiled walls, pebble-grey linoleum floor, rows of cupboards and shelves where the hotel stored canned food. Instead of doing duck-and-cover, like the old days, the guests milled apathetically around the room, bickering quietly with the fish-eyed clerk, until the all-clear sounded.

We climbed the stairs to our room while the rest of them stood in the basement smoking and waiting for the dwarf to summon the ancient elevator. I felt my knees jelly under me as I walked the six flights. My panic at the sound of sirens did not dissipate quickly. Our family doctor had prescribed the Valium to take the edge off, but the dosage needed to be higher and higher to have any effect.

We dressed and went out onto Bleecker Street. Kendal looked so handsome. He told me I was beautiful. I searched my heart for happiness and when I didn't find it, I decided to act happy until I felt happy.

Next to the Excelsior, a café unconvincingly advertised cheap, good food. Dixie's Diner. We stepped inside and took seats at a stained linoleum table for two in the flyspecked bay window. A waitress appeared and dropped shiny menus in front of us, then stood with her pencil poised over her notepad, waiting to take our order.

As I weighed whether to order French onion soup or chicken pot pie, I heard the pad fall to the floor, followed by the pencil pinging off the table.

"My God. My God. He said you'd be here today."

For the first time, I looked at the waitress' face. Dark eyes and a curtain of long dark hair. Difficult to guess her age: young, I thought at first, although the lines around her eyes, the darkness and haggard thinness, suggested a hard-knock life. Otherwise, her face was strangely like my own.

"Debbie," she said, wiping tears.

I recognized the waitress now: Linda.

three
Our Lady of the Algorithm

Duff and Linda's apartment in Alphabet City was carpeted with junk: valves, bolts, tools, copper piping, batteries. A welder's helmet and torch sat on a titanium workbench. There was little else about the contents of their living room I could recognize beyond a battered love seat, one leg held up by the *Encyclopedia Britannica*, H to M, which Duff had stolen from the New York Public Library for its thickness. On what looked like a squat portable TV set — but I now realize was a hand-built PC — a strange scene was playing itself out: a headless, four-legged robot pranced like a horse, its multi-jointed legs leaping up and down tirelessly. After a few seconds, the horse was replaced by another giant metal animal, running in snow on canine legs.

"Military robots. Duff says armies can't march on mutated DNA," explained Linda, sitting wearily at a battered table to remove a pack of cigarettes from her purse. She lit up with a shaking hand. "How're Mom and Dad, Debbie? And Nonna Peppy?"

"She died last year."

Linda looked grief-stricken. "Oh, I'm so sorry."

Yeah, you're sorry. Right, I thought bitterly.

I said, "Mom and Dad basically spent their lives worrying themselves sick about you. Nonna Peppy even hired a detective.

When that didn't work out, she tried a psychic. Mom's been hoping for divine intervention."

Linda put her face in her hands. "I couldn't come back after Amchitka. They were looking for us."

I sat down across from her in a broken plastic chair. "They who?"

"They everyone. CIA. Interpol. Those ShipCo goons. Probably the fucking KGB, for all I know. They may act all lovey-dovey with Greenpeace, but anyone actively involved with the movement is on a watch list." Her eyes finally managed to meet mine. "It hasn't been easy for me, either, Debbie. Duff's been dropping in and out of my life for years. When I go to bed at night, I never know whether he'll be there in the morning. Half the time, he's on a time hop — either forward to the MIT lab in 2019 to do more research or backwards to Shipman's Corners in the '60s. Trying to help someone save the world, apparently." She gave me a resentful glance through a pall of cigarette smoke.

"When did you start smoking?" I asked.

She exhaled and pushed the pack of Merits in my direction; I shook my head. "Everyone smokes in Alaska. I quit a couple of years ago when I started singing in bars, but a few weeks ago I started up again. Stress." She left the explanation at that. "What does it matter? The world is coming to an end."

"Who says?" demanded Kendal. "You still buying Duff's bullshit, Linda?"

Ash dropped off the end of her cigarette onto a huge stack of magazines: *The New Yorker*, *Swingin' Bachelor Pad*, *Paranoid Mechanics*, *TIME*, *LIFE*, *LOOK*, *Rolling Rock*, *The Economist*, *Citizens of Science*.

"Open your eyes, Kendal. The press keeps writing about how we're on the brink of all-out war. Mutual assured destruction.

Or haven't you had the pleasure of a full anti-radiation suit drill in New York yet?"

"We were in a drill at the Excelsior," I said. "No anti-radiation suits, though."

"The Excelsior? That's freak central. A hotel for Twisties. What're you doing there?" said Linda.

Kendal wandered restlessly around the apartment, picking his way over bits of machinery. From the bathroom, he called, "Debbie, you've got to see this."

I left Linda smoking at the table to join Kendal. The bathtub was piled full of solenoids, copper pigtails just like the one I remembered Duff pawning in Cressie's.

"Duff's stash of secret weapons," murmured Kendal.

"They're not weapons. They're tools," said a voice behind us.

We turned to see Duff in the doorway. He looked like he'd been hit by a train, his skin a patchwork of pits, scabs and sores. Gaunt and emaciated, he seemed to have aged twenty years in the last eight. He leaned heavily on a wooden cane.

There was no hello, no exclamations of surprise, no hugs of greeting. I knew why, too. We had been expected.

"Solenoids aren't a weapon, kids, just the interface between the mechanical devices of your time and the digital systems of mine. Handy, when you're trying to make do with archaic technology. That's how I kept the air-raid siren going so long. Programmed it."

"Why all the secrecy, then?" asked Kendal.

Duff grunted as he dropped heavily onto a rolling desk chair, resting his cane on his knees. His skin was so degraded, it looked like it was sliding off his face.

"Because solenoids are only allowed in the hands of the military and the industrial complex that works for them. I was under the radar in Shipman's Corners until some bright bulb connected me with a missing solenoid from Bell Labs. Early use of a cross-border license plate matching database. They were trying to catch cigarette and booze smugglers and came up with me. Gotta be one for the history books. Hope you thought to ditch my car."

"Don't worry, we figured out that much," said Kendal.

Linda was standing behind Duff now, hands on his shoulders. The two of them were ground down, sick, exhausted. Linda looked as if she'd been stretched on a rack, her arms stick thin. The prettiness of her face had sunken into the hollow-cheeked gauntness of a woman who smokes and drinks too much.

"So much for saving the planet," I said bitterly. "I guess scaring the shit out of everyone and breaking our parents' hearts was all for nothing."

"It's not over yet," said Duff. "The solenoids aren't the key to stopping World War Three. You are, Debbie."

He pressed a button on the PC and the robot animal warriors faded to grey. "MIT wanted me to design military robots. Boots on the ground that never wear out. Believe it or not, they're still fighting land wars in the future. But I wanted to focus on reversing the negative effects of nuclear fallout. Environmental degradation. Starvation. All the disgusting mutations replicating themselves in the general population like fungi. How'd you like to have a baby who starts out looking healthy and normal, then turns into a yeast culture one night in its crib? It's no picnic living in a nuked world, kids. Only solution seemed to be: leave this fucked-up time behind and hop into one marginally safer. But first, we had to find an Ion Tagger."

"What the hell's that mean?" demanded Kendal. "And what makes you think my wife is one?"

I glanced at Kendal. His habit of referring to me as "my wife" was getting on my nerves.

"Apparently, you've forgotten what I told you back when we first met. An Ion Tagger is someone who has the ability to bring history to an end game and drag everyone in it to another continuum. Like a global game of tag, with the Tagger as It. Think of it as tagging every human being on Earth at once. Taking them out of the game, so to speak. Their timeline collapses and everyone in it merges with their alternate selves in a parallel world. They barely realize anything has happened to them. Then the game starts again in another continuum, with everyone carrying on as if they'd been living their lives there all along."

"But how do you know I'm 'it'?" I asked.

"We worked out an algorithm, modelling for certain mutations at the cellular level that I found on your cheek swab back at Plutonium Park. And there's something else." Duff hesitated, as if he didn't want to go on.

"Tell her, Duff," urged Linda.

I shivered at the touch of the cold shawl of destiny draping over my shoulders.

Duff sighed. "The Tagger can't exist in the target timeline. Because if she did, her very presence would disrupt the flow of time in the new continuum. Who knows where that could lead. While others achieve a singularity with their alternate selves, the Tagger remains as she was in her original timeline."

"Are you saying I won't exist anymore because I was never born in the other continuum?"

Duff and Linda exchanged looks; I had the feeling that there was more she wanted him to tell me.

"Something like that," mumbled Duff. "Tell you the truth, I'm not really sure what tagging would do to you."

"But what exactly do you expect me to *do*?"

Kendal looked alarmed that his wife was taking Duff seriously. "Deb . . ."

Duff said, "Come with me to 254 West 54th Street. Midnight. We'll meet up with my colleague, Gabriel. If Debbie follows his instructions, we'll all wake up tomorrow in a better world."

Kendal laughed sarcastically. "Let's get this over with now. I want Debbie to see what a crap artist you are, so we can go back to our honeymoon."

Duff shook his head. "We can't get in 'til midnight. And we'll never get in looking like this."

"What do we do 'til then?" I asked.

Duff said gravely, "We go shopping."

We suited up at an open-air storefront on Canal Street. I found a skin-tight gold lamé jumpsuit, feather boa and pair of thigh-high gold boots. Linda picked out a shiny pink plastic dress and purple platform shoes. She told Kendal he needed to choose from two extremes: a three-piece suit — preferably white — or glitter-spangled gym shorts, tube socks, running shoes and nothing else. Kendal opted for the suit. We found Duff's outfit at a Salvation Army Thrift Store: checkerboard flares and a shiny silver shirt. He'd lost so much weight over the past eight years, the wet-look fabric stuck ghoulishly to his protruding ribs. Linda told me it was a symptom of a disease of the immune system called timesickness, caused by staying in the past too long.

We disposed of our original clothes in a Salvation Army bin and killed a couple of hours at a diner, nibbling on pie and drinking coffee while Linda chain-smoked and gently urged Duff to eat. Kendal picked unhappily at a club sandwich.

At a quarter to twelve, we headed for the rendezvous with the mysterious Gabriel. The Hotwire Hum was louder than I'd heard it before. The farther we walked, the more intense the sound became, as if we were moving toward its source point.

As Duff and Linda walked ahead of us, hand in hand, Kendal whispered to me, "This is how it's going to be, Deb? Letting this asshole hijack our honeymoon?"

"God, Kendal — my sister is a basket case. I can't abandon her now. I have to convince her to leave Duff and go back to Shipman's Corners."

Kendal said nothing, just looked straight ahead at the glittering dung heap of midtown Manhattan on a Saturday night.

At 254 West 54th Street, the line-up wrapped around the block. As we joined the end of the queue, a bare-chested man dressed in satin jogging shorts, tube socks and silver basketball shoes walked toward us. Bum Bum.

"Hey, why didn't you guys tell me you were coming to 54? I work here when I'm in the city. Under the table. You don't have to wait in line if you're with me."

The four of us followed Bum Bum as he pushed his way to the front of the line, curses and a few smashed bottles following in our wake. At the entrance, a bouncer in a tux stood sentinel in front of a purple velvet rope. When he saw Bum Bum, he shook his head.

"You're just a busboy, BB. Two guests, tops. You know the rules."

"Have a heart, Jimmy. They're out-of-towners."

"Big fucking deal. We gotta mix up a different salad every night." The bouncer eyeballed us. "I like the chicks. Killer ass on the one in gold. The older one's a bit skanky. What the hell, she's in. The old guy with the cane — who are you kidding, pal, check yourself into a hospital. Black guy with a lobster claw for a hand, wearing a white suit — dunno." Jimmy waggled his hand, Nonna Peppy–style. "I got a few Oreos in there already, not sure I want more."

"What did you call me?" said Kendal, stepping forward, flexing his good hand.

Behind us, a group in hard hats and bullseye T-shirts that said *Hit Me Skylab* were shuffling impatiently. "Stay or go, but make your minds up, assholes," one of them griped.

"Girls go in with BB. Everybody else, sayonara," said the bouncer.

Duff put his hand on Kendal's shoulder. "Got any dough?"

Shrugging Duff off, Kendal dug for his wallet. He handed the bouncer a wad of bills. I was pretty sure it was all the money we had left.

"That enough for all four?"

The bouncer stuffed Kendal's bills in his pocket and lowered the velvet rope. Bum Bum opened the door. A pulse of strobe light and the electro beat of *Arsonist of Love* spilled out onto the sidewalk.

"Okay, beautiful nobodies, get your asses in there," grunted the bouncer.

We stepped into an entranceway lined with the marble torsos of generic Greco-Roman gods, their oversized testicles dangling at eye level. Overhead, crystal chandeliers dripped like stalactites. A plush carpet ran up the sloping floor like a long wet tongue. I felt like Dorothy entering a decadent version of Oz with Kendal the Lion, Linda the Scarecrow and Duff the Tin Man at my side.

We followed the red carpet into the beating heart of the club, a humid barn-sized room stuffed with feathers and leather and spandex and flesh. Lots of flesh. Strobe lights dismembered the crowd into a jumble of body parts — fists and arms, chests and legs, crotches and thighs — moving to the four-to-the-floor disco beat.

We pushed our way through the sweaty crowd, our feet kicking up clouds of glitter. It was like wading through stardust.

Duff took Bum Bum by the arm. "Where's the rubber room?" he shouted.

Bum Bum pointed to a catwalk high over the dance floor.

"Top floor. VIPs only."

"We're expected," said Duff. "Take us up, brother."

No one stopped us from climbing a spiral staircase to cross the catwalk to a dungeon-like door at one end. A heavy iron ring was bolted to the centre of the black leather door. I looked down on the heads of the crowd, bobbing like waves below the grillwork floor of the catwalk.

Duff gripped my arm. He was holding me too tightly, too possessively, but I didn't shake him off. Something inevitable was unfolding. I wanted to see what would happen next.

"This is where Debbie parts company with us," said Duff. "Gabriel is waiting for her inside this room."

He grasped the iron ring and started to pull open the door for me. Kendal slammed it shut again.

"Debbie doesn't go anywhere without me."

"You can't be part of this, Kendal," said Duff.

I wanted to tell Kendal that I would be fine on my own. That I'd come right back to him when I was finished saving the world. But before I could say anything, Kendal pushed Duff in the chest, sending him staggering toward the edge of the catwalk. Duff windmilled his arms, trying to regain his balance. Before any of us could grab him, he collided heavily with the railing, snapping it under his weight with a gunshot-like crack. Duff fell backwards toward the dance floor.

The crowd screamed. Duff's cane clattered at Linda's feet. She stood frozen, hands on her face.

Duff never reached the dance floor. I watched him plunge down, down, his surprised face looking up at us. Before I could shout a warning to the crowd below, Duff vanished, as if an invisible hand had plucked him out of mid-air, like Michael the Archangel catching the Beautiful Alda.

I was overwhelmed by déjà vu. I had already been with Duff at this moment of time, at the culmination of his fall, in the Z-Lands, 1969. He would land on top of a junked banana bus, where I would see him melt away from timesickness.

Bum Bum yanked open the black leather door. "Get the hell in there before they call the cops. They'll kill you, Kendal!"

Kendal grabbed my hand and we ran into the room, the black leather door shutting behind us with a muffled thud, followed by a hiss, as if an airlock was sealing.

The quiet was unnatural. The music and voices from downstairs could no longer be heard. Even the Hotwire Hum had stopped dead. Whatever happened in this room was meant to take place in private and utter silence.

The walls were upholstered in black rubber. In one corner, a wet bar was forested with liquor bottles. In another, a potted green Ficus benjamina plant fingered its way up a wall. A round red velour bed luxuriated in the centre of the room. Before it, a TV sat blank-screened but glowing.

"Gabriel?" I asked, tentatively.

The TV screen suddenly came to life. A test pattern. The NBC peacock.

Please sit down, said a voice.

Kendal and I looked at one another. We sat on the velour bed and faced the TV.

Watch, said the voice. *This is what is going to happen tomorrow.*

five
A Nook in Time

It started the way we'd always been told it would — with the whine of the Emergency Broadcast System signalling the beginning of the end of the world.

A news announcer in the NBC studio sat at a woodgrain desk, a sheet of paper in his clenched hands.

"Today, July 11, 1979, at three a.m. Atomic Mean Time, the disintegrating NASA space station, Skylab, fell to Earth in the USSR, with large sections of fuselage smashing into the Kremlin, causing significant loss of life. The Soviets consider this an unprovoked act of war conducted from space. Intercontinental ballistic missiles have been launched at NATO countries including the United States of America, the Dominion of Canada and the Industrial Region of Canusa."

The newsman stopped and rubbed his eyes, before reading out the addresses of the hardened shelters in all five boroughs. All subway trains had been stopped with the passengers inside, he explained, and any New Yorkers on the streets or at work in a place without a shelter were to immediately enter the tunnels. Those with anti-radiation suits should don them now while keeping in mind that their actual efficacy in a nuclear attack was untested.

The announcer's hands trembled and a sheen formed on his forehead. A loud boom startled him. The bulletin fluttered from the news desk to the floor. The TV picture swayed.

Without anything to read, the announcer seemed to look out at us, probably at the lone cameraman in front of him.

"Is that it, then? Is that all we can do?" asked the announcer, and the cameraman's voice could be heard answering that he had no further instructions but they'd better get their anti-rad suits on.

"Oh Jeezu —"

The screen went white.

Kendal's fingers tightened around mine.

"Is that it, then?" said Kendal, echoing the announcer's words. "Tomorrow is the end of the world?"

As you know it, said the voice. *Watch.*

A shaky visual filled the screen. A woman was holding a mic in both hands, hunched over as if expecting something to pounce on her from above. What was left of her sunny blonde hair hung in her face like strings, patches of bloody scalp visible. A charcoal starburst stained her dress from shoulder to waist. The cloth over one breast had collapsed like a deflated soufflé. Her breast was crushed, also part of her shoulder. How was she able to stand? What I could see of her face was blistered and scorched, like Duff's. Someone was talking to her. A cameraman, videotaping her.

"Talk to me Sally," said the man's voice. "Just keep talking, it's what you do so well. You don't have much time left."

The woman opened and closed her mouth a few times, before rasping out, "I saw them all die, down in the subways. The sea breached the pumps. I got out with the crew. I saw my producer floating over the subway tracks, his anti-rad suit half torn off."

"The anti-rad suits aren't worth shit," said the cameraman.

Sally's face fell in on itself. She lifted her hand to wipe her eyes. Sinews hung from the back of her arm, her skin peeling away. She was disintegrating.

"I can't."

The man's voice now, pleading, "You're a pro, Sally. Keep talking. The batteries are dying."

Sally giggled suddenly. She was losing it.

"We're *all* dying! Who gives a fuck about batteries?"

"We have to document this," he answered. "Get a grip. Remember who you are."

The woman took a slow, shaky breath and pulled herself straighter, her wounds now grotesquely visible.

"We're in New York. July 11, 1979. Central Park. For the record. In case anyone finds this. Look at it. Please."

She stepped out of camera range. Where the park had been was now a smoking gully. Body parts were scattered over the ground. Amputated arms and legs. Headless torsos. Twisted and broken anti-rad suits, melted into the bodies they were supposed to protect. So much for efficacy. A black-orange glow bruised the sky. In the distance, searchlights raked the horizon. Like the waking nightmare of my childhood after having my tonsils out.

"Why the lights? What are they searching for?" I asked.

Signs of life. Signs of further attacks. Who knows? They aren't sure themselves. A waste of a generator, if you ask me. It was a very confused time. Correction, it will *be a confused time.*

"What happens to Sally?" I asked.

I really don't know. Sally isn't special, just a dying reporter. She's one of millions of walking wounded. Maybe her friend will do her a kindness and finish her off. Radiation sickness is an extremely nasty death. No gently-into-that-good-night, I can assure you.

"Do we have to watch more of this?" I asked.

I just want you to understand why you have to change history, said the voice.

"But changing history would cause all sorts of unexpected disruptions to the time-space continuum," Kendal pointed out.

How do you know that? The voice sounded amused.

"*Everyone* knows that," I broke in. "In time-travel stories, that's the rule: don't change anything or you'll unleash something even worse."

There are exceptions, said the voice. *No matter what might come in to fill the void in time, it will not be as bad as nuclear war.*

I looked back to the TV, to Sally's image frozen on the screen just before it pinholed to nothing. The blank screen mirrored Kendal and me in our stupid disco outfits, on the edge of the bed. We both looked dazed.

One of you is unexpected, said the voice. *This is* her *mission. And* mine. Ours alone.

I looked at Kendal and wondered whether Duff was right. Maybe he had fucked things up by barging in with me.

"I'm staying with the woman I love," said Kendal.

You're dealing with something much more powerful than love, pointed out the voice.

"'There is only one who is all-powerful and his greatest weapon is love,'" said Kendal. I recognized the quote from an issue of *The Silver Surfer* we'd found at Cressie's when we were kids.

There was a sound of rustling in the room, as if a breeze had started blowing. The leaves of the Ficus benjamina shivered furiously as its tendrils thickened and poured out of the pot and toward the floor. The plant was growing at high speed, like a Disney stop-action nature film. Its central stalk yanked itself out of its dirt bed and moved toward us; it was turning into something that looked almost human: a man, his body covered in moss. Crawling with it. No, not moss: mould.

Kendal and I watched the floor plant transform into a body seething with green spores, shifting and rearranging themselves, and finally into something almost normal.

A man holding a briefcase.

He looked familiar. Curly black hair, broad shoulders, dark eyes, dressed elegantly in a suit, shirt collar open to reveal a gold chain — understated, by the standards of 1979. He did not look like the freaks downstairs in their feathers and leather and latex, but the type of young man you might expect to meet in a backgammon bar, sipping Manhattans and reading *The Wall Street Journal*.

It was Bob the Varsity Wrestler. My one-night stand.

"Are you Gabriel?" asked Kendal.

He smiled and shrugged. "Call me whatever you like. Gabriel is a code name. Those MIT fellows love aliases. Makes them feel all mysterious and secret agency. I'm the one who does all the heavy lifting." He shot his cuffs and straightened his collar.

"Are you a Twistie?" I asked, remembering what Duff had said about mutants.

Gabriel grimaced. "I prefer 'Exceptional.' 'Twistie' is quite offensive."

"Oh," I said. "No offence meant."

Gabriel waved his hand. "I make allowances, given that you're from a less enlightened time, Debbie. Best we let bygones be bygones and get started."

Kendal wasn't buying it. "Anyone can throw a B-grade horror movie on a TV monitor. We're being hosed. Let's go back to the hotel, Debbie," he said, grabbing my hand and pulling me off the bed.

"I can think for myself, Kendal," I said, sitting back down.

I was starting to feel as if we had actually turned into Kyle Crusher and the Contessina — and, as always, Crusher was making all the decisions.

Before Kendal could start to argue with me, Gabriel settled matters. Standing at the bar, pouring himself a Scotch and adding a liberal amount of water, he said, "It's too late to leave now."

"Don't try to stop us," Kendal warned.

Gabriel shook his head. "I don't have to. The room won't let Debbie leave."

Glancing around, I saw that the padded leather door had been replaced by an unbroken stretch of black rubber. We were in a sealed cube.

"Are you kidnapping us?" I asked.

Gabriel frowned and shook his head again. "I can't leave here any more than you can. The hands of the atomic clock ticked down to midnight and stopped. We're sitting in a nook in time. Every clock on Earth stopped the moment you stepped into this room. Time can't see us. We're going to change history so dramatically that we'll rip a hole in the time-space continuum. The timeline we're living in will collapse and the Tagger — that's you, Debbie — will deliver us into Earth Standard Time where all of us will merge with our alternate selves to live in that more peaceful continuum. When you leave this room, you'll feel as if you were gone for a nanosecond. Meanwhile, you might have been in here for hours or days. Maybe even a lifetime."

"Why would a lifetime be necessary?" I asked.

"Because you need training. Everything you do must become muscle memory. Atomic Mean Time sits on the knife-edge of the end of Normal life and the beginning of a level of suffering beyond the scope of anything you can imagine. Ergo, we leave nothing to chance. Once we're on Skylab, we're going to have to work fast."

"What's Skylab got to do with anything?" I asked.

* * *

Gabriel picked up the remote controller. "Ah, I see my friend Duff played his cards rather close to his chest. Let's watch some television, shall we?"

The TV came to life to an upbeat "march of progress" theme, like NASA's world of tomorrow films of my childhood. The title screen read, *Skylab: Technical Specifications for America's First Manned Space Station.* A deep voice said, "Hello, kids! Today, let's learn about the flight and navigation systems of the McDonnell Douglas Orbital Lab, otherwise known as SL-1, or Skylab."

Cartoon astronauts waved at us from outside the space station, the familiar solar sail painted with a Sparkling Sparrow "Have a Nice Day" smiley face.

I'm not sure how long we sat in the room. I felt as if we had fallen back to childhood, watching ourselves on TV in an animated show called *L'il Debbie and the Kendal Kid*. Gabriel admitted that this all-encompassing childhood nostalgia was part of the plan by the MIT boys. A brilliant way to get us up to speed on Skylab's engineering and navigation systems in record time. A child's brain is so much more malleable than an adult's, better able to quickly absorb information, especially when presented in the form of a cartoon. Just like the ones Kendal and I used to watch every Saturday morning in Shipman's Corners.

The cartoon broke down the mission into a series of steps. Basic mechanical repairs. Reprogramming of navigational systems. And trickiest of all, repositioning the solar sail Skylab needed to gain power, a task that necessitated a spacewalk, much to my excitement. Finally, after hours or days or, for all I know, a lifetime, the cartoon's end credits began to roll. Gabriel stood and stretched.

"You two have learned as much as you can, short of a cerebral implant, and I don't have the skills for that. Time to hop."

From inside the leather padded bar, Gabriel took out two flight suits and helmets. Then he took two syringes out of his briefcase.

"What is this, the *Fantastic Voyage*?" I asked as Kendal and I donned the flight suits. "Are you shooting a tiny inner space craft into us?"

"Not far off," said Gabriel, swabbing the inside of my arm. "I'm injecting you with Quantum Nanothrusters — nanobots that temporarily transform your body into an organic rocket. Hopping through time and space is as much an inner journey as an outer one. The MIT boys call this 'swinging Schrödinger's cat.' You're about to be in two places at once — here and on Skylab. I'll do both of you, then shoot myself up. If you find yourself alone in the Skylab workshop, don't worry, I'm on my way."

Kendal and I lay back on the round bed and held hands. I watched as the needle slid smoothly under my skin and found my vein. A tiny prick of fear, then I slid my arm inside my flight suit and zipped myself up.

Kendal turned his face toward me and smiled as Gabriel shot him up.

"Love you," he said.

We didn't even have time for a kiss.

* * *

303

I woke up tethered to a chair, staring through the dome of my helmet at the corona of the sun just starting to rise over the curvature of the Earth. Like dying and opening your eyes on God's face. Skylab's workshop was empty, bits and pieces of lab equipment floating around me. A caliper here, a scalpel there, petri dishes suspended in the air like tiny glass saucers. Alone in a space station in a dying orbit around the Earth, I was trembling with terror, excitement or both.

A few seconds later, as promised, Gabriel was beside me.

"Where's Kendal?" My words echoed in my ears through the radio set inside my helmet. I could see half of Gabriel's face reclining in the chair, one brown eye fixed on mine.

"He's not coming. I kind of lied to you."

I tried to throw myself at Gabriel, forgetting that I was tethered in place. My arms waved in slow-mo as I tried to throttle him.

"You fucking fucker, what have you done with Kendal?"

"Relax! He's safe and sound on Earth, where he belongs, sleeping off the sedative I gave him so I could get him out of my flight suit. Only you and I were injected with the Quantum Nanothrusters." He unclipped his tether, then mine, so that both of us floated in the weightlessness of the workshop.

I lifted my hand to try to wipe angry tears from my eyes, absent-mindedly smacking the front of my helmet. I wanted nothing more than to punch straight through Gabriel's helmet into his Twistie face. He pulled me into his arms in a clumsy bear hug, the two of us floating together as I railed at him.

"Is this because of the one-night stand?" I shouted into my headset, my helmet clattering against his.

Gabriel winced as my voice bounced around his helmet. "The MIT boys strictly provisioned this trip for two people — you and me. It's nothing personal, Debbie."

"Nothing personal?" I took a swing at him but couldn't connect. I grabbed one of the calipers floating around the workshop and tried flinging it at his head. Cocooned in my flight suit, I couldn't throw with enough force. Gabriel nimbly pushed himself out of the trajectory of the lazily moving projectile.

"Calm yourself. We've got a job to do. Saving Earth. Remember?"

I looked at where Gabriel was pointing, toward the blue and white marble of Earth suspended in dark space. Kendal was down there, along with everyone else I loved.

"It was Kendal's own fault. He was just so doggedly devoted to you," Gabriel pointed out.

I kept crying and hurling myself at Gabriel. Finally, he caught me by my wrists. "Heads up. I'd love to continue discussing your love life, but we're in a dying space station hurtling toward Earth. And we don't have much time."

I tried to wipe away the snot dripping from my nose and hit myself in the helmet again. I ran my tongue over my upper lip and said, "Okay, let's do it. I'll kill you later."

Skylab, if you look at old NASA photographs taken by the astronauts who manned it — and they were all men, every one of them, until I turned up — looked a bit like a ship under sail. A windmill shape on top of the station was actually a massively powerful telescope.

The solar sail on Skylab had always been a problem. I remembered hearing about how it had been damaged when the space station was first sent into orbit on a Saturn V rocket originally built for the scrubbed Apollo 18 mission. Astronauts had been sent on an unplanned spacewalk to make their workshop habitable. With the heat shield broken, NASA had jerry-rigged a parasol; the astronauts had deployed it to lower the interior temperature of the workshop to a livable hundred degrees Fahrenheit. And now, Gabriel and I would do the same in order to reprogram the station for one last blast to push it further into space where it would float in permanent orbit with other dead satellites, including ones I had watched through my telescope from my own backyard. Vanguard. Sputnik. Telstar I and II. So many others. An armada of space junk floating high above Earth.

Life-support systems weren't operational on the disabled space station. Not that it mattered. Most of our job would be done outside rather than in.

A spacewalk. Kendal had been so excited when he heard about that. I tried not to cry in my helmet as I prepared to enter the airlock. To work on the solar array and send Skylab deeper into space, away from Earth, Gabriel and I hand-railed our way to the solar sail.

We hung in nothingness two hundred and seventy nautical miles above the Earth, as if we were truly sailing in space. I clung to the handrail and looked, and looked, and looked at the continents of Earth, the hanging rubber ball of the moon, the precise pinpoints of light from the stars. Out here, they didn't twinkle the way they did on Earth, but shone with a brilliant intensity.

"I made it, Kendal," I whispered.

"We have a job to do, Debbie," Gabriel reminded me. "I know it's amazing but we don't have time for sightseeing." And with that, he opened the toolkit and took out a solenoid.

"Handy things when you've got a system to override," said Gabriel. "Duff's been working on souping up archaic twentieth-century technology for years. Now you know why."

The work was easier than I expected, like fixing the sail on a boat while floating underwater. Or maybe it just seemed easy because I had spent a lifetime preparing in the rubber room, practising the procedure until it had become embedded in me. Muscle memory. Gabriel and I re-entered the airlock, then the main workshop to reprogram Skylab's orbit. While we worked, he gave me an important safety tip: because I hadn't previously existed in Earth Standard Time, I'd need to be careful to maintain the same body mass at all times, give or take a few ounces.

"Other people are just integrating with their bodies in the other continuum, but you have no vacuum to fill. So once you hop into E.S.T., better make sure you don't gain or lose weight, or it could be bad for you."

"Bad how?" I wanted to know.

"Bad as in parts of your body could start melting away."

Gabriel also explained that we would return to the room in New York where we'd started. I expected to find Kendal there, asleep on the round velour bed, or groggy and mad as hell at missing the adventure of a lifetime, or maybe just sitting at the bar in Studio 54 nursing a Scotch. But he'd get over it. We would finish our honeymoon, go back to Canusa and live out the rest of our lives.

Getting shot back to my own time and place was tricky in zero G's. Gabriel had to get creative with the sleeve of my flight suit. As we waited for it to take effect, I said, "Kendal's going to be pissed when he hears I went on a spacewalk without him."

Through the visor of his helmet, Gabriel's eyes were lowered. Avoiding contact with mine. I didn't like what I read there.

"What's wrong?" I asked.

Gabriel looked up. "I bullshitted you about Kendal," he said.

My heart began to sprint. "What did you do? Tell me he's still alive down there!"

"Oh, yes, yes, of course, what do you think I am?" Gabriel reassured me hastily. "It's just that when I heard Kendal quoting the Silver Surfer, I knew he'd never give up on you. He's the messianic type. A one-woman man. Full of his own importance. Wants to save the world. And he's going to, once he's safely in Earth Standard Time. Problem is, you're the one who has to get him there. All he'd do is get in the way, trying to protect you. Not to mention, he's too important in the world of tomorrow to be in on this caper. Kendal's like a KerPlunk piece: pull him out of the game and everything around him collapses."

My agitation was increasing; I had a feeling this was all heading somewhere very, very bad. "Just get to the point."

Gabriel stared at me through his visor. "After your time hop, he'll have no idea you ever existed."

I tried to seize him by the shoulders but my hands slid off his suit. "When we get back, you're going to make him remember me again!"

I couldn't see his face now, but I could hear his voice through my headset, telling me evenly, "Sorry, Debbie, but I won't be going back. This was strictly a one-time deal, like the night we spent together."

I swung myself around in the weightless cabin so I was looking directly into the visor of his helmet. "What?"

He grimaced. "Suicide mission. I'm an Exceptional, sweetheart. With no water to hydrate myself, I can't hang onto this shape any longer. What's one Exceptional, more or less, right? I won't exist in a few seconds. By the way, I love you."

And with that, I watched his smile collapse along with the rest of his head into a shower of spores inside his helmet.

I was alone, floating inside the dying space station. A tiny, frightened fish, trapped in the belly of a larger fish, about to be swallowed by the universe.

Through the flight deck window, an object loomed: a dull white sphere the size of a beach ball. I wept with wonder and terror when I recognized Telstar I, the communications satellite I'd followed by telescope from my backyard in Shipman's Corners. Space junk now, the satellite was in perpetual deep orbit. As it silently collided with Skylab, the Plexiglas window before me shattered, floating like Mylar confetti in zero gravity.

Despite my helmet, I instinctively closed my eyes. When I opened them, I found myself tumbling blindly. I sensed that I was no longer inside the confines of the space station. But if I'd drifted through the broken window into the vastness of space, where was the debris of the collision, not to mention the stars and the Earth? I was in a black void so complete that I thought I had been buried alive. That was the moment I realized I was in a wormhole, burrowing through the dark matter that separated one continuum from another. I was no longer afraid. My mind had stretched far beyond feeling anything but awe.

Time bulged around me, rubbery and thick, thrumming with the tension my actions had created — I had deflected time's arrow and sent it hurtling at the taut surface of history. Over my headset came a low groan like the sustained bass note of a million pipe organs as Atomic Mean Time ruptured and flatlined. Perhaps that sound was the collective screams of a billion-odd humans as they were sucked through the wormhole with me to unite with their alternate selves in Earth Standard Time. I don't know if anyone experienced what I did on my first hop to 1971, when I woke up naked and shivering in the vineyard before I joined with my older self. I suspect some people might have noticed a brief bout of dizziness, perhaps a touch of motion sickness, as I tagged them into Earth Standard Time: too much sun, they'd tell themselves later. For the briefest possible time, all life on Earth was both dead and alive, until time started up again and history flowed smoothly on, catching all of us in its current.

Atomic Mean Time was no more.

* * *

I came to in the middle of the rubber room, still in my flight suit. The first thing I did was puke in my helmet: it was not unlike waking up from anaesthesia. My gold catsuit was neatly laid out on the velour bed, waiting for my return. Cleaning myself up at the bar sink, I became aware of something in my clenched hand: I opened it to see my Lady of Lourdes medal on its fine gold chain. All that was left of my life in Atomic Mean Time. Now I had to find out what had happened to my husband, my sister and my friend. Despite what Gabriel had told me, I was sure they would all be waiting for me in the nuke-free world of Earth Standard Time.

I didn't believe that Kendal would not know me. Maybe he'd suffer from short-term amnesia, but certainly he would not forget me forever. How could he? There would be all the shreds of our life together. All those other friends and family, wondering where I was. Not to mention a joint bank account. Wedding gifts. Half-written thank you notes. As much as marriage wasn't easy for me, I couldn't cope with the idea of Kendal simply dropping out of my life. I leaned on him in the same way as my monthly prescription for Valium: to steady me, soothe my panic attacks and keep me from lapsing into anxiety and bulimia.

Narnia-like, the door had reappeared in the rubber wall. I stepped back into my catsuit, turned the knob and left the room.

A gale was blowing through the empty hallway, as if a large invisible window had opened. For a microsecond, the world went to greyscale. I reached out to steady myself against the wall but my hand touched only air. I was suspended in a void but should have been in free fall: nothing solid was holding up my feet. I was slipping out of the nook in time.

Time skipped like a scratched record. Repeat, repeat, repeat, jump ahead. I lost a few seconds, or maybe minutes, until the world snapped back into place, like an electrical grid coming back on after a power failure. I found myself once again in the heat of the dance floor of Studio 54 in the summer of 1979, the crowd surging against me as I pushed my way toward the entranceway. The catwalk was full of dancers — no sign of a man having fallen from it that evening. The railing had been repaired, if it had been broken at all. The red carpet had turned to purple. Modern chandeliers glittered overhead — had they looked like that when we came in? I didn't think so.

Out on the street, the bouncer was not named Jimmy, but Marc, judging by the shouts of the women on the wrong side of the velvet rope — *Marc, let me in and I'll give you head in the bathroom!*

I checked my watch. Two minutes to midnight — about the time we'd gone into the club. Despite what Gabriel promised, I had fallen back an hour. I suddenly became aware of an unfamiliar feeling: I felt unwell. My throat was sore. I was achy and a little nauseated, as if I was coming down with something. Thanks to the U-shot, I hadn't felt this sick since my bout of tonsillitis when I was thirteen. I ached to be in bed, back in our hotel room.

I waited and waited. One a.m. turned to two, then three; no Kendal, no Bum Bum, no Linda. I hailed a cab to take me to the Excelsior, but the few dollars I had in my purse had disappeared, along with my ID and credit cards. When I told the cab driver that I had no money, he pulled over and abandoned me on the curb of Fifth Avenue, just outside Tiffany's.

I felt like Audrey Hepburn, without the tiara.

By the time dawn broke in Earth Standard Time, I was curled up against the storefront with a fever of 104 Fahrenheit, according to the doctor who saw me that morning at Saint Clare's Hospital in Hell's Kitchen. The nice New York cops took me there. All of them talked just like Nonna Peppy.

six

Timesickness
July 12, 1979, E.S.T.

I burned up on a gurney in a noisy hallway while an intake nurse jotted my particulars on a clipboard.

"Please call my husband," I croaked. "We're from Canusa."

She looked at me as if I was quite mad. "Where is Canusa?"

"North of the border," I said.

"You mean Canada." She didn't even look up. "What's your husband's telephone number here in New York?"

"I don't know. A hotel in the Village. The Excelsior." A coughing fit stopped me from talking further. I could barely draw a breath. My chest felt as if it were being crushed by an elephant. "Please, give me something," I managed to beg.

"The doctor has to see you first," said the nurse, staring at her clipboard as she walked away. I was nothing special in this hall of suffering: two gurneys over from me, a woman in restraints was screaming that cockroaches were eating her face off.

Two hours later, my cough was competing with her terrified screams for the doctor's attention. After a cursory examination, I was diagnosed with pneumonia and pleurisy in both lungs, complications of a type of viral infection that had been eradicated in Atomic Mean Time thanks to the U-shot: influenza.

The intake nurse returned. "I looked up Hotel Excelsior. Number's out of service. One of the orderlies said it's been torn down for a condo development."

313

Head lolling, I tried to focus on her indifferent face. Fighting to form coherent words, I managed, "Wha' — 's gone overnight?"

The nurse finally made eye contact with me: "They razed it six months ago. Your hubby isn't there, honey." Then she bustled away, her crepe-soled shoes kissing the linoleum.

* * *

I was in the charity ward at Saint Clare's for six weeks. By the day of my discharge, I was still barely able to stand on my own. When I kept insisting that I had had the Universal Vaccine and was therefore immune to all known infections, I did a stint in the psych ward at a notorious hospital ironically named Bellevue, where a psychiatrist diagnosed me as possibly psychotic and suffering from shock — what we'd now call post-traumatic stress disorder. They administered electroshock therapy. I'd rather not talk about that.

Finally, a kind social worker made it her mission to find someone who knew me, who would look after me. She patiently took down the names I could remember of family and friends in New York and Shipman's Corners. She called directory assistance, presenting me with a list of unfamiliar numbers that I dialled from a payphone in the hall, asking the operator to reverse the charges. None of them would accept my collect calls: not my cousins in Brooklyn, not Sandy Holub or Beatrice Kendal. No one knew who I was.

The social worker tried tracking down John Kendal in Shipman's Corners and Toronto but the number of men with that name defeated her. I also tried every Linda Biondi and Pasquale Pesce in New York City. Nurse, construction worker, accountant, anthropology professor at Columbia. None of them was my sister or my friend.

Worst of all was when I tried calling my parents in Shipman's Corners. I had a moment of hope when I heard my mother's voice agreeing to accept the charges.

"Debbie? How can this be true?" Her voice was shaking.

"It's really me, Mom. I'm down in New York. I want to come home."

She gave a sob, followed by the sound of muffled voices. I thought I could make out, *Give me the goddamn phone.*

Dad was on the line now. "Who the hell is this?" He sounded furious.

"It's Debbie, Daddy." I started to cry. Duff had said I never existed in Earth Standard Time, yet clearly they knew who I was.

"Is this some type of sick joke? What are trying to do to my poor wife?" shouted Dad just before he hung up the phone.

Discharged from Bellevue with a bag full of Medicaid antipsychotics, I was still weak and confused, not to mention flat broke. No credit cards. No identity of any kind. Even my university education had disappeared. Any records showing that BIONDI, D.R. had graduated summa cum laude from the University of Toronto with a bachelor of science had vanished, as if the hand of God had dabbed celestial Wite-Out on my official transcript.

I was a girl with no identity. No past. No family or friends. No husband. And no immunity to a long list of miserable diseases that I caught in succession over the space of six awful months — chicken pox, measles, mumps, whooping cough and repeated bouts of the flu. Shivering with fever for weeks on end, I began to wonder whether the flu was actually worse than radiation sickness.

I discovered that a lot of other things had changed, too. In Earth Standard Time, everything was a little out of sync with the timeline I had left behind. I was surprised to learn that Nixon was alive and well, writing his memoir in California, while two of the Kennedys had been assassinated back in the '60s. Our longest-serving prime minister, Robert Stanfield, hadn't won a single election, and that one-term leader, Pierre Trudeau, had been PM for twenty years. He hadn't married Castro's sister, but someone named Maggie, who'd left him to party at Studio 54, of all places. Protest songs by the likes of Bob Dylan and Marvin Gaye — marginal singers at best in Atomic Mean Time — were revered in Earth Standard Time. Instead of the annual Cuban Missile Crises of my childhood, Earth Standard Time had seen only one. And instead of flattening the Kremlin, or hurtling deeper into space, Skylab had crashed in Australia (the day after I'd met Gabriel the Twistie — sorry, *Exceptional*), killing a single cow. So much for the falling space junk starting World War Three.

Four months later, I was living at a women's shelter in the Bronx. Viral infections had broken my body; being diagnosed as psychotic and delusional almost made me finish the job myself.

One evening, standing on the front stoop sharing a cigarette with another no-hoper, watching the nightly parade of hustlers and hookers, I saw a beautiful young man in a pair of gold boxing shorts and a tight T-shirt, obviously waiting for a trick. Bum Bum.

Staggering over to him, tears running down my cheeks, I put my arms around him. He embraced me back. "Do I know you?"

"Yes," I sobbed. "We knew each other in another world. You were my friend."

Bum Bum stood with me at arm's-length, his dark eyes searching my face. "I remember you from my hometown. Shipman's Corners, up in Canada," he said slowly. "We were in middle school together."

I almost shouted with joy. "Yes. St. Dismas, yes, you and I were both there."

"Your name's Debbie, right? I could swear the teachers told us you were . . ." He hesitated.

"I was what?"

He paused, then said: "That you were dead."

Bum Bum's hands tightened on my shoulders. Holding me up.

He could have left me there on the sidewalk or gently guided me back to the shelter. But he didn't. Maybe it was the residual memory of our friendship in Atomic Mean Time. Or maybe it was something simpler: compassion. Bum Bum understood what it was like to hit rock bottom.

I clung to him so tightly that it was hard to get me into a taxi. He told me he'd left Shipman's Corners for New York after dropping out of high school. When I mentioned Kendal, he shook his head and said the Kendals had moved away from his neighbourhood back in the '6os.

"I lost contact with the guy after that. We hung out with different people. Kendal was always one of the smart ones."

Bum Bum took me home to a tidy little bachelor pad where he had been living for years. He made soup, built me up, nursed me back to health, listened to my crazy stories about stopping a nuclear war. Most importantly, he believed me.

"I feel like I dreamed all the stuff you're telling me," he said. "It seems so familiar. When I saw you on the street, I felt like I knew you, as if everything that happened that day, happened before. What do they call that?"

"Déjà vu," I told him.

But there was more to it than that. One night, when the two of us were companionably slumped on his couch sharing a doobie, eating popcorn and watching a movie on the *Late Late Show*, Bum Bum looked at me and said, "I kinda remember being at a party like this one with you."

On a snowy black and white set that Bum Bum had liberated from someone's trash can, Russian dancers, blonde starlets, a black woman in a French maid outfit and a baby elephant were dancing by a pool with Peter Sellers. Psychedelic sitar music played in the background. Nothing made sense. I didn't know this version of the swinging '60s. If anything, it looked more like the 1970s in Atomic Mean Time.

"It was a Halloween party," I mumbled, my mouth full of popcorn. "Remember anything else?"

Bum Bum thought about it, his eyes on the movie. Now Peter Sellers and a starlet were romping in soapsuds. A woman in an evening gown fell headfirst over a balcony into the pool. The French maid did the Watusi.

"Some asshole dressed like the *Playboy* guy was coming on to you. You threw a drink in his face," said Bum Bum.

"You and Rocco saved me."

"Who?"

"Your boyfriend in Atomic Mean Time."

Bum Bum laughed without meaning it. "I *know* who Rocco is, Debbie. We were together in Real Time, too."

"Atomic Mean Time was also real," I reminded him.

"I know, I know, but it's not 'real' anymore, is it. Anyway, Rocco broke up with me and got married because his family couldn't stand the idea of their oldest son being a fag. I'd rather erase the jerk from my memory."

I reached over and took his hand. Sometimes I was so

focused on my own problems, I forgot that Bum Bum had had heartbreaks, too. But knowing that he could remember something of the old past gave me hope. If he remembered me, maybe others would, too. By which I really meant Kendal.

* * *

Eventually, when I was strong enough, we went searching for Linda. Locating her turned out to be easier than I thought. I saw her face on a poster stuck to a telephone pole.

She lived in a lower Manhattan loft, paid for with royalties from a record she'd made with Dylan's producer, same guy who discovered Springsteen. Under her stage name, Lindy Bond, she packed them in at CBGB's every night. Thanks to my hop into Earth Standard Time, her personal history had changed for the better.

When she opened the door and saw Bum Bum and me standing there, I could tell by her shocked expression that she recognized me right away. Her dead sister, Debbie. I showed her the Lady of Lourdes medal.

"I thought Mom and Dad buried you with this," she said, holding it in her hand. "How can it be possible that you're alive?"

I tried to explain my time hop to her, as I had to Bum Bum, but the look in her eyes made me stop. She turned to Bum Bum and asked him to come into the kitchen to help her make tea.

I could hear them in there, whispering about me.

"What's the matter with her? Is she psychotic? Schizophrenic?"

A short silence. "She's been through some major shit," mumbled Bum Bum. "I figured she was a runaway."

"My parents must have sent her away. They did that to me once, but they let me come back. No wonder they kept the casket closed. My God."

"Why'd they want to get rid of her?"

"Let's just say she was a handful."

"You should tell them."

"No way. Mom's health isn't great. Heart trouble. I'd rather just let Debbie live here quietly, but I'm leaving on tour soon. I've already sublet the place."

"I don't mind if Debbie goes on living with me," said Bum Bum.

A short silence as this good news sunk in; I could just imagine Linda's relief at Bum Bum volunteering to take responsibility for me.

"Do you need money?" she asked.

"Wouldn't hurt," said Bum Bum.

In Earth Standard Time, Linda was the doting daughter, while I was the long-lost one. Why rock the boat? In the end, Mom died never knowing Linda and I had been reunited. Dad started losing his memory a few years later — dementia symptoms, the doctors said. I cried for days when Linda told me. Not only for Dad, but also for me: now there was no chance he'd remember me, in either time continuum.

With Linda's money, Bum Bum paid the first and last months' rent on a little railroad flat not far from Orchard Street, where Nonna Peppy had lived. He continued to bus at Studio 54, among other places, but he was tired of sleeping with rich clients for tips. It was getting too risky because of a new retrovirus emerging in New York. Back in our apartment, I spent most of my time sleeping, reading, watching soap operas, familiarizing myself with the twisted history of Earth Standard Time, trying to let my mind and body heal, wondering what the hell I would do without an identity.

Bum Bum did well in New York. He turned out to be a smart guy with cool ideas and the instincts of an entrepreneur; within a couple of years, he'd started running a bookstore and print shop in the Village. One day, he brought home a copy of an underground comic that he'd printed called *Raw*.

"We're selling it at the front cash. You'll like it," Bum Bum told me, handing me an issue called the "Graphix Coffee Table Book for your Bomb Shelter." I sat and read one visceral story after another, including one about a family of mice during the Holocaust. In a radio interview, I heard the creator say it was a way to work out painful family stories, to deal with a horrific legacy in a way that he could manage.

I can do that too, I thought. Then: I *must* do that. For my own sanity.

Comic books are one of the places where you can turn what a psychiatrist at Saint Clare's Hospital called "delusions" into alternate realities that readers desperately want to live in. A medically acceptable way to turn fantasy into truth. I've met hundreds of people eager to do just that at comic book fan festivals.

Bum Bum saw a want ad in the *Village Voice* for a graphic designer/art director for a pulp magazine called *Psychics of Fortune* based out of Fort Lee, New Jersey. He convinced me to let him take me out there, even borrowed a car for the trip across the George Washington Bridge to a tumbledown industrial park to meet my future boss, Madame Gina. She asked me if I had a portfolio, and of course the answer was no, so I demonstrated my drawing skills on the spot. She was impressed by the realism of my horses, but she still wasn't sure I had the right stuff for a fast-paced career with the number one psychics' magazine in America.

"Let's consult the experts," Madame Gina said, and took out her tarot cards.

When Death, the Devil, the Tower, the Ten of Swords and the Hanged Man turned up in succession, Madame Gina's face went grey.

"Destiny brought you here. The cards don't lie. You are from the old doomed time. You are the Tagger, destroyer of an evil world, saviour of humanity."

"Does that mean I'm hired?"

By way of answer, Madame Gina shook my hand so hard that her heavy rings left deep purple bruises on my fingers that I have to this day.

Turns out, she was part of a group of Exceptionals who were living in Atomic Mean Time 1979.

"We were looking for respite from our mutations by hopping into the past. Of course, it didn't work," said Madame Gina, sighing over shots of a clear, pungent liquor that reminded me of Mr. Capitalismo's homemade onion vodka. "When you collapsed Atomic Mean Time, we couldn't believe our luck. We all tagged along with you into this time. Our physical mutations vanished, leaving only our psychic abilities." She leaned toward me and touched the side of her nose conspiratorially. "That's how we get by in this timeline without identities. Craps tables, lotteries, playing the ponies. That gave us the do-re-mi to start the magazine. We can enjoy life as long as we observe the rules: no big weight changes, no children, no formal property ownership. Cash on the barrelhead."

"How come you remember being tagged when no one else does?" I asked.

Madame Gina waved one ringed hand dismissively. "More do than you think. Remembering the old time requires spiritual insight. Most Normals are too distracted to notice anything except the boob tube," she told me, then patted Bum Bum's hand. "Present company excepted, of course."

Bum Bum stood up, suddenly uncomfortable. "I'm going to buy some smokes."

As he slid through the beaded curtain of Madame Gina's office, she nodded at his disappearing back. "Your friend could remember everything about the old time, if he let himself. For a Normal, he is an exceptional man in many ways."

"He's very kind, if that's what you mean," I said.

"He saved you," said Madame Gina. "And you saved everyone else. He is an exception even among Exceptionals. Accept him as your guardian and advisor. He may know more about your past and future than you do."

* * *

Working for *Psychics of Fortune* helped rekindle some long-dead creative spark, the one the Famous American Artists Correspondence School had talked about in their ads. Madame Gina showed me how to capitalize on the limited psychic ability I had acquired during my time hop to make a nice nest egg at craps and roulette in Jersey City. An unintended pleasant consequence of being the Ion Tagger, and one I feel that I richly deserve.

A couple of years later, inspired by *Raw* comics and the crash of *Challenger*, I had the confidence to draw the first issue of *Sputnik Chick: Girl With No Past*. At first I churned out my little underground comic on Bum Bum's Xerox machine and sold it in his bookstore, but after the obscenity charge, the series turned into a worldwide phenomenon and Grey Wizard became my publisher. I've even sold the film rights, although I'm still waiting to see the project greenlit by a studio. They're such unreliable fuckers in the movies. They either let the concept wallow until it dies a natural death or suck all the juice out of it in an attempt to reach the broadest possible market.

Despite my successes, a question continued to eat at me every day: what had happened to Kendal? I wouldn't know for sure until the dawn of the internet age. In 1995, sitting in front of my PC, I learned that he was in Toronto. I was able to follow the trajectory of his career as he went from lawyer, to head of an environmental organization, to deputy mayor of the city, to leader of a federal political party. So, he had been destined for law school, all along.

In 1986, Kendal had married a woman identified in the archives of the *Star*'s Society pages as Alexandra "Alex" Holub, Sandy's name in Earth Standard Time. Inspired by her father's mission to popularize ethnic food, she went on to launch a chain of Eastern European–themed fast food restaurants, Mr. Yumchuck's.

I cried when I learned about Kendal and Sandy. I tried to deal with my anger and sorrow by developing a storyline in which Sputnik Chick stalks her ex-lover Johnny the K, shadowing him to the house of his fiancée, CC the waitress. Sputnik Chick spies on the two of them through a window as they make love. Then she goes home, gets drunk and finds some Twisties to beat up.

At least I was living in New York City, far, far away from the CBC national news. In Canada, Kendal was everywhere — on TV, radio, in the newspapers. Living in the States, I could pretend he didn't exist. That all changed six years later when my spidey sense sent me to the window of our condo in lower Manhattan and I saw the first plane hit the tower — a disaster rushing in to fill the void. I leaned my head against the superheating glass of the window and prayed to no one in particular.

As borders closed and identity requirements tightened, it became obvious that Bum Bum's lack of a green card — and my lack of an identity — would be a problem. Even my cleverly forged passport wouldn't cut it much longer. And so, in 2002, we returned together to Canada — Toronto, to be exact. A place big enough to lose ourselves in.

I never really settled down in one neighbourhood, just went from hotel to hotel, a lifestyle I liked well enough. Bum Bum set himself up in a nice loft apartment where I crash whenever I need someone to split a bottle of pinot noir, watch TV and experience normal life. If you can call Bum Bum's life normal.

When I felt ready, Bum Bum drove me to Shipman's Corners. I wanted to see for myself whether every shred of my past had truly vanished without a trace.

My childhood home on Fermi Road was covered in aluminum siding. The grapevines had been ripped out for a swimming pool.

The wreck of the candy store had been torn down to make room for a Valvoline oil-change shop. As we drove past the Holub house, I noticed two young girls in hijabs in the tiny front yard, kicking a soccer ball back and forth. Like everywhere else, newcomers to the neighbourhood were replacing the older postwar immigrant communities.

In King George Park — what I had known as Plutonium Park — the Atomic Bomb memorial engraved with the names of the Radiant Dead had vanished; only the statue of the soldier fainting into the arms of an angel remained, chiselled with a list of all the conflicts where Shipman's Cornersians had laid down their lives: World Wars One and Two, Korea, Afghanistan. The Atomic War of Deterrence had never taken place, apparently, although I read in a history book that a similar idea had been floated by Churchill. Cresswell's Collectibles had been replaced by a tattoo parlour and the old Royal Bank building had been subdivided into the offices of mortgage brokers and collection agencies. Déjà vu tingling, I asked Bum Bum to park out front.

He frowned. "Why do you want to stop here?"

"I don't know. Just wait for me."

On the sidewalk, I scanned the list of businesses in the old bank building. One caught my eye: White Fin Financial.

At the reception desk, a sixty-something blonde in a crisp white blouse was working at a computer. She looked up at me with a coral-lipped smile, and I saw that she was wearing a necklace with DOTTY spelled out in script. It was her, all right: evil Nurse Dotty from Atomic Mean Time was a grand-motherly secretary in Earth Standard Time.

"May I help you?" she asked in a sweet voice that implied she had no memory of me kneeing her in the chest and push-ing her into a freezing cold shower.

"I'm interested in buying a commercial property. Do you handle business mortgages?"

Dotty nodded. "Absolutely. Larry's got a client with him, but if you can wait a few minutes, I'm sure he'll be delighted to speak with you."

"Larry . . . ?" I said, raising my eyebrows.

"Kowalchuck," supplied Dotty.

A familiar instrumental played softly on the sound system; it took me a second to recognize Barry White and the Love Unlimited Orchestra playing "Love's Theme" — the first dance at my wedding to Kendal back in Atomic Mean Time. I took a seat and flipped through the *Shipman's Corners Examiner*. "More layoffs announced at ShipCo Automotive," read the front page. The local economy was shifting to service sector jobs, some idiotic alderman said reassuringly, as if mopping the floors of fast food restaurants was a reasonable way to fill the void left by the vanishing factory jobs. No wonder the whole town seemed down in the dumps.

As I closed the paper, I felt a presence in front of me and looked up at the Shark, his thinning blond hair plastered into an unconvincing comb-over. He'd kept his aging body trim, but the explosion of red blood vessels on his nose advertised his taste for cocktails. He peered down at me through unfashionable aviator glasses.

"Larry Kowalchuck, pleased to meetcha," he said, and offered his hand.

I shook it, introducing myself by my real name, but he gave no sign of recognizing me. We went into his office, where he lowered himself into a high-backed Naugahyde chair behind an oak veneer desk.

"Now, what kind of business property would a beautiful lady like you be after?" he asked with a grin. I suddenly felt myself back in the Donato living room, fending off his come-ons. I couldn't hate him anymore: he'd turned into a cliché of a dirty old man, unaware of how repellant he was.

I smiled. "I'm opening a spa in Shipman's Corners. Something high-end."

He leaned across the desk and smiled at me lasciviously. "Spa, eh? How much you looking to borrow?"

Thinking fast, I said, "Five hundred thousand, give or take. Depending on location, of course."

The Shark gave a low whistle and leaned back in his chair, the vinyl squeaking under him. "Half a mil? You Martha Stewart or something? You could buy and sell most of the businesses on this street for a quarter of that. You'd have to cut and curl a hell of a lot of hair to turn a profit."

"I wasn't thinking of just hairstyling. Manicures, pedicures, facials, all that."

"Uh-huh uh-huh uh-huh," said the Shark, regarding me with open amusement. "Look, up in Toronto you might get women paying top dollar to keep their faces on straight, but here in Shipman's Corners most of 'em are the do-it-yourselfer types, know what I'm saying?"

I crossed my legs. "Should I take my business elsewhere?"

The Shark raised his hands in mock surrender. "Whoa there, Oprah, don't get touchy. I'm just trying to tell you how it is. Look, why don't I close up early and take you out to dinner at Soaring Starling Wine Bar? Or Yumchuck's Ukrainian Eats, if you like ethnic food? I'd love to discuss your business plan."

I stood up. "I'll have to take a rain check, Larry. Duty calls in Toronto. But if you give me your business card, I'll shoot you an email next time I'm in town and we can do lunch." I offered my hand for him to shake.

Larry let his eyes walk all over me. To my surprise, he kissed my hand.

"I'll count the days," he said, smirking.

When I found Bum Bum watching his coffee cool in a Tim Hortons down the street, he said, "How did it go? Discover anything important?"

I shook my head. "Nothing at all. Let's go."

On the way out of town, as we approached the on-ramp to the Queen Elizabeth Way, a sign caught my eye. VICTORIA LAWN CEMETERY.

"Let's see if we can find the family grave," I told Bum Bum. "Turn right here."

He shook his head and left-turned to the on-ramp.

"No matter what we find, you're going to fall to pieces and it'll be my job to put you back together again. I'm tired of that, Deb. Just go home and live your life."

As we passed a sign reading TORONTO 100 KM, I wondered if that's where home was now.

*　*　*

In 2004, I decided to find out how Kendal and Sandy — excuse me, "Alex" — were getting along without me. Google told me they were living in Toronto's Riverdale neighbourhood, an affluent but not filthy rich area on the other side of town from Bum Bum's west-end condo in hipsterland. One weekend morning, I hung around Withrow Park, a few doors away from the Kendal family's renovated Victorian. Eventually, John Kendal came out the front door with his twelve-year-old twins, Nelson and Marushka. I already knew their faces and names from a steady stream of media coverage about their lives, given Kendal's public profile as an environmental lawyer and newly minted Member of Parliament. Some hoped he'd skip over politics altogether and become a diplomat. I suspected Duff knew what he was doing when he told me that if I saved Kendal, I'd save the world.

In faded jeans and a leather bomber jacket, Kendal looked as handsome as ever. My eyes fell to his left hand: normal. The grotesque disfigurement by blowtorch had never happened in E.S.T. The kids were beautiful, of course: leggy and slim, with Kendal's curly black hair and his wife's blue eyes. Half black, half Ukrainian — what else would you expect?

Kendal laughed as Nelson and Marushka told him a story about their homeroom teacher, every step of their perfect feet breaking my heart. I followed the three of them to a painfully trendy coffee shop where Kendal ordered an espresso and hot chocolates for the twins. I sat two tables away, trying to look absorbed in my MacBook while I eavesdropped. I learned that Marushka liked mini marshmallows in her hot chocolate and Nelson was late handing in a history project on Louis Riel because he hadn't done the required research. *Read the graphic novel, kid,* I felt like telling him.

Once, while the kids were squabbling over Pokémon cards, I noticed Kendal's attention wandering. His eyes skipped around the inside of the coffee shop until they met mine. He offered me that half-smile I knew well. Thinking he'd recognized me, my heart picked up speed: I wondered if he'd come over to my table and look down at me with a *Do we know each other?* Or better yet, *I've been looking for you all my life.*

Then I saw his eyes climb over me to the pretty young woman sitting at the table behind me, her notebook open — a CBC reporter who had interviewed him numerous times, I learned from the conversation that ensued between them. He hadn't offered me a smile of recognition, just the look famous men give middle-aged women who recognize them in coffee shops.

Sitting in the cozy café with its piped-in jazz and fair trade coffee, observing Kendal's perfect life and healthy kids, felt like tearing the scab off a not-quite-healed wound. I couldn't stop picking away at it, almost enjoying the hurt of scratching at tender spots. This could have been my life, I thought. I resented the kids for being normal. I hated Kendal for being happy. Because neither word could describe me.

What a monster I am.

I went back only once more to the Kendals' neighbourhood, hoping to catch sight of the woman I'd known as Sandy. I knocked on the front door, not knowing what I would say to her if she answered.

When it opened, I found myself face to face with a tall black man in his seventies wearing a Maple Leafs sweatshirt. Grey-haired, bearded and fit-looking, like someone you'd see on a sailboat in a retirement planning ad, he was the kind of guy you'd invite over for a beer. The lopsided smile, the angular nose, the almond shape of his eyes — he was an older version of Kendal.

But not my Kendal. I was facing Dave Kendal, who in E.S.T. obviously had not died in an industrial accident at ShipCo when his son was a kid.

Dave was smiling when he opened the door but when our eyes met, his expression changed from welcoming to puzzled.

"Can I help you?" he asked.

I stared at him, this aged man who did not live to see his thirtieth birthday in Atomic Mean Time standing before me in the glow of good health. That's when it occurred to me that the whole Tagger thing might actually have been bullshit. That I'd simply been sacrificed to give Dave Kendal a lifetime to play a role he didn't get to play in Atomic Mean Time: raising a future world leader. Did he know that I'd given up my identity for him? That I'd been forced to give up his son? That his grandkids should have come from me, not that backstabbing bitch, Sandy?

"Help me? Only if you can give me back my life," I said.

Inside the house, a familiar woman's voice called, "Dave, who's at the door?"

It was Bea Kendal. She and Dave must have been babysitting the grandkids for the weekend while Kendal and Sandy enjoyed some alone time. Sweet.

Dave called to his wife, "It's no one, hon."

"Then why are you still talking to them?"

From the depths of the hallway, she walked briskly to the door. She'd aged well. Grey hair, stylishly cut. A strong, trim figure — lots of yoga and boot camp, no doubt. None of the worry lines I remembered: this was a woman with a comfortable life, a devoted husband, and a loving son who was expected to become Canada's first black prime minister. None of the tragedies of the old time had touched her. No young widowhood. No door-to-door job in a hateful little town. No child whisked off by the authorities to an industrial school — which, let's face it, was just another name for slavery.

She stood at the door beside her handsome, undead husband and looked steadily at me. She knew me. More precisely, she *remembered* me. I opened my mouth to say something that would make her call me by name, but before I could think of anything, she gently moved in front of her husband. Shielding him.

I could see her struggling to choose the right words to push me out of the life I'd been robbed of. Although, in fairness, it was the Trespasser who'd set me up. Presumably for some higher purpose, saving-the-world-wise.

"Please don't trouble us again. Goodbye," she said.

Her eyes never left mine as she closed the heavy wood door in my face.

I arrive by seaplane carrying Dad's belated birthday present in a hockey bag — my old telescope. Waiting for me with Linda by the dock, Dad politely introduces himself, as if we are business colleagues meeting at a conference for the first time. He's a little stooped, but still tall. A handsome guy, considering his age. The old ladies in long-term care must be all over him. Unusual for a man to outlive his wife by so many years; poor Mom died suddenly of cardiac arrest, listening to the CBC Radio News in her kitchen. She was not quite seventy.

"Carlo Biondi. And you are?" he says, giving my hand a firm shake as the pilot hoists my luggage out of the plane. At least his grip is strong, even if his mind isn't.

"Her name is Debbie," Linda explains before I have a chance to answer.

"Oh, of course, of course. One of Maddy's cousins from the old country," he says to Linda, before turning to me again. "And you are?"

Linda has aged into a fleshier version of Mom: thick hair the colour of steel, her face a worried road map, but her underlying prettiness lingers. We sit together at the wooden table in her big kitchen, watching Dad meticulously unwrap the gift I've brought for him.

"Wonderful," he says, pulling out the telescope. "Orion. Big Dipper."

"That's right, Dad," I say. "You and I used to look at the stars together. Remember?"

Dad smiles and shakes his head, no. "Sure, sure," he answers.

When I comment on Dad's condition to Linda, she slides her eyes toward him as if telling me, *talk to him, not about him* — but then goes on to speak on his behalf. She tells me Dad is in a program to help stimulate his brain cells. Not a cure, of course, but exercise and music therapy have been proven to preserve cognitive function, even in people with advanced forms of dementia. The point is stimulation is good for Dad's quality of life. For — as Linda puts it — his soul.

"I hope Crazy Lady Island is good for my soul, too," I comment, pouring another cup of rooibos tea — they sure drink a lot of it in Linda's house. I miss my chai but it's too mainstream for her. Vodka martinis — forget it.

Linda sighs. "I really wish you'd stop using that stupid name. 'Crazy Lady Island.' What's wrong with plain old Gabriola?"

"Crazy Lady is more fun," I tell her. And more accurate: Bum Bum coined the name when I told him about Linda's health regime and dietary habits.

"An Italian-Canadian woman who's given up coffee, bread, wine, cheese, pasta, gelato, chocolate, salt, olive oil, leather and sex. Her entire birthright, going back to the days of Marco Polo. Your sister is one crazy lady," he observed.

Hence, Crazy Lady Island.

Mind you, I'm not sure about the sex. I'm making assumptions, based on the absence of anyone I can positively identify as Linda's partner, male or female. Of course, Linda would have said the same of me, until I told her about running out on Darren. I needed some type of explanation for suddenly turning up on her doorstep; it was less exhausting to tell the truth than to concoct a believable lie. I told her about the trip in the RV, without explaining that Darren was her own lost child: that would have been too weird. I just said that we'd had a falling out — my fault, not his, of course — and after a few days at the Finlandia Hotel near Wawa, I'd headed for Thunder Bay; from there, I took a plane to Vancouver, then a seaplane to Gabriola.

"Sounds like a lot of jumping around just to get out of someone's bed," observed Linda.

*　*　*

My sister's house is like a sensory deprivation tank. I have spent three gluten-free, caffeine-free, meat-free, alcohol-free, sex-free months in her spare room.

We go for hikes and kayaking together. Visit Dad three times a week in Nanaimo. I start taking yoga classes at Linda's friend Jasmine's house, the only one I've met on the island who seems like a possible partner for my sister.

One evening, Jasmine comes over with a bouquet from her wildflower garden, a platter of homemade California rolls and a couple of joints. Linda and her friends don't indulge in alcohol or tobacco, but smoking pot is perfectly okay. I find that strange but remind myself that it's not my house. As we lounge around the kitchen table with the inevitable tea and a smouldering doobie, Jasmine casts our astrological charts. I give her my date and time of birth, and she says, "Sun in Libra. Moon in Gemini. Sagittarius rising. Whoa."

I frown at her. "What do you mean, 'whoa'?"

"As in, interesting, imaginative, creative," she says. "But whoa, I sure wouldn't want to be in love with you. You're a little inconstant, perhaps? Restless? Unpredictable?"

Linda snorts. "That's putting it mildly. She was a trouble-maker from the get-go. Boys, booze, drugs, sex, you name it. She ran away from home when she was thirteen. My parents pretended she was dead. Even put up a headstone in the cemetery so our grandparents would accept that she was gone. Debbie and I didn't meet up again until she tracked me down in New York, just before she turned the train wreck of her life into material for her comic book."

I'm stunned. "Is *that* the story you concocted to make sense of my existence? That Mom and Dad faked my death? Come on. Even when you got sent away after you got knocked up, they didn't concoct some story to hide the truth."

Linda gives me a lethal look as she sucks on the doobie.

"Fuck you," she suggests sweetly.

Jasmine is starting to look uncomfortable. I'm grateful when she tries to change the subject. "What were you doing in New York, Linda?"

"I was honing my craft. Finding my musical voice. Of course, all that ended when Mom died and someone had to step up to the plate to look after Dad. Whom Debbie never bothers to visit, unless it suits her." After a long toke, she adds, "Good thing one of us decided to act like a grown-up."

Linda pretends not to notice that I've started to cry. Jasmine reaches out, trying to take my hand as I stumble out of my chair.

"Excuse me," I mumble, and return to the spare room where I shake out my bedclothes, turn jacket pockets inside out and scrape the bottoms of purses and backpacks with my fingers, searching for stray lorazepam. No luck. A Joni Mitchell song drifts out of the kitchen. Oh fuck me, these aging hippies don't know when to give it a fucking rest.

Quivering with anger and lorazepam withdrawal, I lie down on the bed and grip my Lady of Lourdes medal in my fist.

I wake the next morning, fully dressed, with a raging hunger. All that second-hand pot smoke. When I go into the kitchen, Linda is there, improbably brewing coffee and scrambling eggs. Making something that I like, for a change. An apology, of sorts. Unbefuckinglievable.

"You're up," she says, and gives me a hug. "I'm sorry for going on the way I did. Jasmine reminded me that we all cope with trauma in our own ways. Mom and Dad banishing you is unforgiveable — I get that. Given everything that's happened to you, it's no wonder you fell into your own little fantasy world. Forgive me."

In her world, I'm the fantasist; she's the steely realist. Yet, her eyes keep sliding away from me. I see something unfamiliar in her face. Guilt.

I stare at her. "Linda. Look at me. Do you remember Duff?"

She ignores me. Looks down at her coffee cup. Then, "Yes," she mumbles.

"What about Billy? And the baby they took away from you?"

I watch her spoon brown sugar into her coffee. Since when did she sweeten anything?

"Why do I think I'm so pissed?" she asks the tablecloth. "Look at what you took away from me."

My hands turn into fists on either side of my placemat. I struggle to remind myself that my sister is a typical Normal of Earth Standard Time. Smug. Blind. Closed-minded. Her comfortable existence depends on denying truths that unsettle her.

"Because of me, you have your musical career. Your house. Crazy Lady Island," I remind her. "You're better off in this timeline, no matter who you lost. Look at what *I* lost."

Her hand is shaking. The spoon clatters against the rim of her cup.

"Fuck you. Fuck you. Fuck you. Fuck you," she says to the tablecloth. "I wish you'd stop making me remember things that couldn't possibly have happened."

"Like what?" I ask quietly.

Still not looking up at me, she answers: "Growing up in that other . . . *place*. Billy. The baby. Duff. The Z-Lands."

I open my mouth to say something like, *You may not like thinking about that other world, but at least you are fully part of* this *one. Unlike me, you* have *a home and you* have *a past, even if you remember it unfolding in two different ways.*

But there is no point in badgering Linda. Like so many people, she simply chooses to forget memories that do not make sense. And why should she? Earth Standard Time is full of curators of the past: teachers, filmmakers, TV producers, novelists, content providers, speechmakers and Tweeters. Even if Linda hadn't existed in an alternate timeline, others would be constantly snipping and spinning the tattered threads of her memories into the fabric of accepted history. It's amazing anyone trusts their own memories about anything, really.

"At least you've still got Dad," I remind her.

"I lost Dad a long time ago. I'm as lonely as you are," she answers.

Sensing that she'll say nothing further on the matter, I finish my coffee and leave the kitchen.

＊　＊　＊

One Saturday, Dad and I sit down together at Linda's kitchen table with pencils and sketchpads. I show him how to draw horses, the Walter Foster way. He's not bad.

I tell Linda that I'll find an art therapist to work with him, one on one, after I go. "I'll pay," I volunteer.

She nods, washing the dishes. "That's quite nice of you," she says very, very stiffly. Which is when I realize that Linda is angry with me.

"I'm sorry, what did I do this time?"

She slams down a pot in the draining rack. "Nothing. Absolutely nothing. That's the problem. You have nothing to do with Dad ninety-nine percent of the time and then show up and be Miss Congeniality." I'm caught in the headlights of her ten-thousand-foot stare, so much like my mother's disapproving look that I feel as if I've time hopped back to our kitchen in Shipman's Corners.

I have no idea what to do now, so I say, "Do you want me to leave?"

She goes back to washing dishes. Again, just like Mom — faced with conflict, she cleans something.

"No. That would upset Dad."

There's really nothing I can say to that. Linda's feelings about me don't factor in. Nor do my feelings about her. There is only one priority in her life: Dad.

＊　＊　＊

One good thing is that while I'm sitting at the drawing table in my bedroom, the origin story practically writes itself. For the first time, it feels safe to own up to where the Girl With No Past actually came from; it's just a version of my past, after all. Not that anyone would believe it.

Just before my birthday, I call my editor at Grey Wizard Comics back in Toronto. The relief in her voice travels down the line, all the way to the Gulf Islands.

"Scan and email me the pages," she says. "I'll book you for the next ComicFanFest."

I almost say that I'm not coming back. That I'm hanging up my inks and retiring to Crazy Lady Island. At the same time, I realize that would be like a living death. So I decide to do nothing at all except sleep in most mornings, draw with Dad and do yoga.

The second very good thing is that I kick lorazepam. Not by myself, mind you. Linda finds me a therapist specializing in prescription drug addiction. Retired, of course. Someone who used to work on the mainland and decided to do something artistic, like everyone else who lives here. Her name is Cynthia: a tiny, wrinkled, Yoda-like woman. Although she has the face of a boomer who has spent too much time in the sun, there's something childlike about her. Something unfinished. When I mention this to Linda, she explains that Cynthia suffers from Turner syndrome. "She's had medical issues all her life, poor thing. She's wonderful with Dad."

She comes to Linda's house every day, helping me get clean after over thirty years on this drug — my replacement for the Valium I was hooked on in the late '70s. With Cynthia's professional help, meditation exercises with Jasmine, large doses of health food–store melatonin and many sleepless, sweaty nights, I'm finally ready to face life as it really is, unfiltered by emotional cheesecloth.

❋　❋　❋

November. Just when I'm starting to think it's time to return to my own version of real life in Toronto, a surprise visitor arrives on Crazy Lady Island. Linda waves him into my bedroom, as if he wanders into her house every day at six a.m. I open my eyes at the sound of the doorknob turning, and there he is. Bum Bum.

"Hey, Sunshine," he says, and sits down beside me on the bed.

I smile at him from my pillow. "What are you doing here, Bum?"

He pushes my bangs out of my eyes. "Why can't you call me BB, like everybody else?"

"Because I know you better than everybody else." I reach up and touch his face. "Your scruff is going grey. How is that possible?"

He grins at me. That beautiful, kind face. "I've decided to start aging gracefully."

We sit for a few minutes, quietly, holding hands in the morning light. That's one of the things I've always loved most about Bum Bum. He isn't afraid of silences, to just be with me, enjoying one another's company. I sometimes think of all the people I've loved in my life, I've loved him best of all.

"I've brought someone who wants to see you. The Maytag man."

I sit up. "Darren? Why?"

He laughs as he shakes his head. "The Miele went on the fritz. I called the number on the sticker on the door and Romeo showed up. While he was fixing the machine, he told me quite the tale of woe, you running out on him without explanation in the wilds of Northern Ontario. I gave him a drink, then dinner. Seems like a nice guy. Bit of a philosopher. Not an asshole. Sense of humour. Well educated. Comic book fan. A little young, perhaps, but perfect for you, actually."

"Kendal was perfect for me, too. Look what happened."

Bum Bum snorts. "Do you really want to be First Lady of Canada? Not much chance to do that and be a comic book creator with street cred."

I shake my head. "Okay, I get your point. But Darren and I shouldn't meet again, Bum. Some complicated genetic connections there that I really don't want to have to explain to him."

"Why don't you explain them to me?" he suggests.

"He's Linda's lost baby boy from Atomic Mean Time. Which means he's my nephew. There are some pretty strict taboos about that kind of thing."

Bum Bum crosses his legs. "My spidey sense tells me that you may actually be slightly off-base here. As you yourself have told me umpteen times, just because something happened in one timeline, doesn't mean it happened in the other."

I stare at him, sensing something. Déjà vu. I don't get it as often as I used to. And I've learned to listen to Bum Bum's hunches. He's an exceptional Exceptional, after all, one who can actually own money and property. He's like the king of the Exceptionals.

"Okay," I tell Bum Bum. "You get to play matchmaker, just this once."

Darren and I meet on neutral territory, a local bar-restaurant called Grizzly's. After a polite kiss, we sit looking out the window, watching the seaplanes come in. The atmosphere between us is a little tense.

Finally, I jump in: he is the wronged party, after all. I apologize for the Lake Superior vanishing act. I explain my concerns about his rare genetic blood anomaly and mine, the lost nephew, his date of birth, even his appearance and technical skills.

Darren sits back in his chair and shakes his head. "Coincidence."

I sip my vodka martini, dirty and wet, just the way I like it. What a relief to taste alcohol again.

"There are no coincidences. You and I are closely related. Simple as that."

There's a moment of silence between us as this sinks in.

Darren takes a gulp of wine and frowns. "Anyway, who says I want to get back together with you? I just thought you owed me an explanation. Thank you for that, at least."

I feel sudden embarrassment and disappointment. And here I thought he came to Crazy Lady Island to get me back. How stupid can you get?

"How's your origin story going?" says Darren, mercifully changing topics.

"Finished, finally. Turned out to be a revenge tragedy, just like you said. Jealousy, betrayal, conflicted emotions, all that. Just like life here on Crazy Lady Island."

"Congratulations," he says, topping up his glass. "Mine's finished, too."

From his jacket pocket, he takes a folded printout and hands it to me. It's an email from Adoption Services Ontario. As I read it, he tells me what it says.

"My biological mom died five years ago. Her background: Greek-Canadian. Dad: still unknown. I was born in Sarnia, Ontario. The genetic anomaly is something called malignant hyperthermia — and I don't have it. What's the one you've got?"

"Pseudocholinesterase deficiency," I murmur, examining the report. Doesn't appear to be a forgery. I look hard at Darren and realize: he doesn't look like anyone in my family. That Nordic face. That blond, blond hair. His dark, dark eye colour is really the only thing that suggests an Italian, and how many people have that? A lot of Greeks, apparently.

He smiles and picks up my hand. "Look. You and I both know we have a connection. Let's give this another try. Take a trip to Vancouver. Check into a bed and breakfast or rent an RV and head south. See where the road takes us."

I lean across the table for a kiss. "Forget B and Bs and RVs. I prefer hotels."

As our lips meet, I think maybe, just maybe, Linda's right and I imagined our lives in Atomic Mean Time. Maybe it was the lorazepam, and before that, Valium. The trauma of New York. Electroshock. My own restlessness and frustrated desire for adventure. An overactive imagination. Time to breathe the clean, fresh air of truth. Linda's truth. Everyone else's truth. I can forgive myself and move on with my life. And not be a crazy lady anymore.

As I turn over these thoughts, sheepish but also relieved to finally find myself living in the same reality as everyone else, a small, blonde head appears in the window. My therapist Cynthia is coming into the Grizzly with a determined look on her face. Almost bossy. A look I've seen before.

When she spots our table, she rushes over. "There you are, dear. I need you. Or rather your friend here." She turns to Darren and extends a hand. "Cynthia McClintock. I understand from Linda that you're a repair whiz?"

"Did your washing machine break down, Cynthia? Dishwasher?" I ask.

She laughs and shakes her head sadly. "Oh, no, no, sweetheart. Something much more challenging than that."

I've never been to Cynthia's house before. It's a tiny bungalow with a spectacular view and a slumbering garden out front that I'll bet is a showpiece in the summertime.

"Anne-Marie didn't tell me 'til this morning," she says, as

if I already know who Anne-Marie is or what she might have revealed.

"I'm sorry, Cynthia, but who is Anne-Marie?"

Cynthia laughs. "Oh, what am I thinking? She's my partner. And she's an artist like you, dear. Whenever I was working with you at your sister's house, Anne-Marie's students were always here with her."

She leads us into a solarium, full of plants, where Anne-Marie is painting. She has a head of grey hair, wound into a stylish updo. She's lying with her head on a pillow, a paintbrush between her lips as she dabs at a seascape on a small canvas bolted above her face.

Cynthia removes the brush from Anne-Marie's mouth to make introductions. I try to act as if there is nothing odd about meeting a mouth painter in an iron lung more than fifty years after the last polio epidemic. As we chat about the weather, and the sea, and Anne-Marie's latest work, I find myself wondering how two people could have any type of life together when one of them is encased in a steel box.

Finally, we get to the point of the visit. "The respirator is breaking down again. I can feel it," says Anne-Marie. "Sorry to be such a bother."

Cynthia puts a hand on the metal body of her partner. "No trouble at all, dear." She looks at Darren. "They keep wanting her to switch to a tracheotomy tube, but what's the point? They can cause their own complications. Infections and such. We've had other repair persons tune up Lisette but it's become almost impossible to get parts for her."

"Lisette is the respirator," clarifies Anne-Marie. "Our pet name for it. Nicer than iron lung."

"I give names to machines all the time," laughs Darren. "I'll need to do a little research about parts availability. Do you have Wi-Fi?"

I watch this scene unfold before me with a combination of detachment and astonishment. How could I not have recognized Cynthia before? The blonde Doris Day pageboy. The odd body shape. Most of all, the bossy attitude. I don't bear her any ill will for the stolen *Wonder Woman* comics, but as Duff always said, there are no coincidences.

While Darren googles "replacement parts for iron lung" on his smartphone, I tell her, "I just realized that you and I were in the hospital together when we were kids. You were called Cindy in those days. We played fallout shelter under the cribs and one of the nursing sisters let you keep my comic books when I went home. Remember?"

Cynthia laughs and shakes her head. "I'm afraid that's a false memory, dear. I did meet a little girl named Debbie in the hospital who loved comic books, but it was a very popular name in those days. That Debbie died having her tonsils out, poor thing. Something to do with the anaesthesia. You must be thinking of another Cindy — there were millions of us, too."

I stare at her, not sure what to say. She turns her attention back to Anne-Marie.

Linda is wrong after all: I'm no crazy lady. I'm the Girl With No Past, alive and dead at the same time.

I go out to the deck. Watching the waves, I feel myself sinking into an unfamiliar feeling. Contentment. Perhaps even happiness. I could stop checking in to hotels and live in an actual house, with high-end appliances that Darren would keep in working order despite the manufacturers' warranties and a guest room for Linda. Maybe she could bring Dad for visits.

I could grow old with Darren. Retire to a farm or a little island like this one. And when we are very old, and one of us gets sick, we could move to a retirement home with a view of the sea and sit quietly together, holding hands, waiting for the sunset.

As I spin out this narrative in my head, I hear the distant sound of a motorcycle downshifting gears. I turn and sure enough, there it is, tearing along the road at the end of Cynthia's property.

A white blur. White as cocaine. White as an angel.

I think about running into the house or jumping into the sea, but what's the point? You can't escape your destiny. No matter where I go, he'll find me. I wonder what it will be this time? Climate change, no doubt.

I didn't recognize you at Superior, he'll say. When I told my buddies about you, they said, you idiot, she must have been your Tagger. That's why she almost fainted when she saw you. Go find her.

I wish you hadn't bothered, I'll say. I've met someone. I'm not going anywhere.

Ten years from now, this island will be under water, he'll tell me gravely.

I guess all the crazy ladies will have to move to the mainland, I'll shoot back.

It's no joke, Debbie. We're facing an environmental disaster on a global scale. So you've found some guy to hold hands with in the retirement home while the two of you starve to death due to massive crop failure. Big deal. We've located a clean, safe time spectrum, just one short hop over from this one. Earth Savings Time. Now it's all up to you.

You're a hallucination, I'll tell him.

He'll look hurt. Or amused, perhaps. Why do you say that?

Because you died. You melted away of timesickness.

He'll shrug. What's *dead* anymore? If you want the details, they uploaded my consciousness into a neural network, then a

347

biomechanical body. MIT's been doing that on the quiet for a while now.

You're a cyborg?

He'll shrug. Grin. Call it what you will. I could arrange the same for you. Gets around the whole timesickness-and-death thing. Let's discuss it after the hop. Shake a leg, we've got a planet to save.

I'll turn to look back at the house. Through the studio window, I'll see Darren talking to Cynthia. Our eyes will meet as I put the helmet on, adjust the chinstrap and climb on the back of the Kawasaki, catching a whiff of cinnamon on the rider's leathers.

I'll notice a flash of copper metal by my leg. A solenoid, welded to the drive train. I'm sitting on an electromagnetic transducer on wheels. This is even better than the Silver Surfer's intergalactic surfboard.

Through the window, Darren will look at me, his mouth an O of surprise. Our eyes will meet. I'll lift one hand. He'll shake his head. I'll make a V with my fingers.

Peace. Live long and prosper. Goodbye.

The rider will upshift into fourth gear. Then fifth. Crazy Lady Island will turn into a blur.

* * *

Or none of this will happen. Maybe the rider will pass me by.

* * *

I stand, looking out at the road, at the sky, at the white blur of the bike, at my lover on his smartphone in the window of the house, and wait to see what happens next.

My thanks to Bruce J. Friedman of the Humber School for Writers, who mentored this novel before I realized I was writing one. Thanks, too, to my agents Kris Rothstein and Carolyn Swayze, who embraced this book in its earliest form, and my editor Jennifer Hale, creative director Crissy Calhoun, publisher Jack David and the true believers at ECW Press. The Toronto Arts Council, Ontario Arts Council Writers' Reserve and Canada Council for the Arts through the CBC Literary Prizes all ponied up funding that bought me precious writing time. Thanks also to *ROOM*, *Accenti*, *Riddle Fence* and *Untethered* for publishing stories based on early versions of several chapters.

Thanks to everyone who read drafts and offered suggestions or provided expert advice on things medical, technical or art directorial: Diane Bracuk, Chris Caswell, Lisa de Nikolits, Jake Edding, Joey Edding, Eufemia Fantetti, Rick Favro, Izzy Ferguson, Koom Kankesan, Dr. Laurence Lee, Lesley Kenny, Heather McCulloch, Maria Meindl and Susan Rynasko. Licia Canton and Jaime Rubin, thank you for your encouragement at critical moments. A shout-out to my friends from Laura Secord Secondary School, especially Debbie Luhowy, the late Kathy Hryb and Shelley Smith Passfield for sharing memories of the day her father made us think the world was about to end.

Finally, thank-you to my husband and creative partner in comic books, Ron Edding, for the love, fun and inspiration.